HONEY

Agía Sahnta Book 2

Mariel Pomeroy

ebook Amazon IBSN: 9798985544688

Paperback Amazon ISBN: 979-8-9855446-7-1

IngramSpark Paperback ISBN: 979-8-9855446-6-4

Cover Design by: William Hatch

Glyph Design by: Sarah Crisp

Edited by: Taylor Robinson at Taylored Text LLC

Published by Mariel Pomeroy at Book Daddy LLC

Also in this series:

Helfyre

Honey

Book 3 (TBD)

Content Warnings

Mention of harm toward animals/ dead animals
Mention of child SA (Chapter 28 only)
Physical violence
Blood play
Knife play
Breath Play
Public shenans
Drinking and drugs are bad for you, kiddos
CNC
Disordered eating
Individual gets misgendered
Excessive language
Suicidal ideation
Torture
General shithead behavior
Cliffhanger

This book/story is not written to be taken as guidance on the sexual dynamics of a healthy relationship. This book is meant for people 18+ ONLY—it's an adult fantasy romance that contains graphic violence, general dark themes, swearing, and sex scenes—and should in no way be misconstrued as a depiction of a healthy relationship.

To those who can't remember their childhood because blacking out memories of it was the only way they survived.

-M

Meet My Monsters

Calmani Deities

Old Brite Gods

Aether (Ay-ther)

Theia (They-ah)

Old Dark Gods

Manāt (Man-aht)

'Amm (Ahm)

Children of the Gods

Children of ' Amm

The Nephilim race

Avarice

Leviathan

Sirens

Varcolac

Shadow Heretics

Syraphem

Shifters

Wraiths

Shayṭān

Fae

Variety of dark creatures that populate *Aljira* and parts of *Lyria*

Children of Aether + Theia

The Mithra race

Dioscuri

Malek

Fae

Brite Heretics

Nymphs

Shifters

Moyrai

Variety of light creatures that populate *Keloseros* and parts of *Lyria*

Children of Manāt

Kaymaat

Children of the Kaymaat

Helren

Djynn

Other creatures that live in *Lyria*

SKRIPT + WORLD

Lujha

Nephilim Language

Natye (Naht-yay) - No

Yadha (Yah-dah) - Pull

Jah alay (Jah ah-lay) - I'm leaving

Traveske (Trah-vesh-keh) - Kitten (term of endearment)

Ant aljah (Ahnt al-hah) - What the fuck

Alya minth bajal mien (Al-yah min-th bahal mi-jen) - Tastes like fucking mine

Arrê (Ah-reh) - Stop

Ahid (Ahid) - Calm

Jia (Yah) - Don't

Aysah elyah (Ai-sah elle-yah) - Get her

Yah (Yah) - You

Aljah (Al-hah) - Fuck

Inah ya shae (Eeh-nah yah sheh) - It's nothing

Gefah khatya (Ge-fah kah-teea) - Wrong room

Ya lijah (Yah Li-shah) - Oh shit

Ha takal bisnaha? (Hah tak-ahl bis-naha) - Do you speak her tongue?

Aistrah (Ai-strah) - She needs rest

Shah lahry (Shah lah-ree) - Good morning

Kajha (Kah-ha) - Liar

Brujal (Brew-hall) - Funeral

Mashkah (Mah-shkah) - Pet

Algah qymat Mashkah (All-gah kee-maht Mah-shkah) - Worthless little Pet

Zyra (Shee-raw) – Husband

Gjóssa

Mithra Language

Dey peynjao (They pain-how) - I'm not hungry

Skotá (Sh-ko-ah) - Derogatory term for the Nephilim

Ylea gia mé (Ee-leh-ah hee-ah may) - Come for me

Kanys ajos den borej na sas kanyja na to niosta-ha afto ejktos elenchyo (Kahn-ees ah-hos den boh-reh nah sahs khan-yah nah toe neeoh-staaha ahf-toh ehk-toes ehlen-cheeoh) - No one else can make you feel this out of control.

Kanys ajos den borej na sas kanyja na to niostaha afto ejktos elenchyo eít (Kahn-ees ah-hos den boh-reh nah sahs khan-yah nah toe neeoh-staaha ahf-toh ehk-toes ehlen-cheeoh ay-eet) - No one else can make you feel this out of control either

Gamisyeno maljka (Gahm-ee-senyo mahl-shikah) - Fuck-ing asshole

Sýz (Sh-ee-j) – Husband

World

Vortex - A way to travel between realms as well as within the realm

Eyrid - Coin

Epísmos - Seat of power in Keloseros

Alshaytan - Seat of power in Aljira
Siada - The lords in charge of different Aljiran territories
Rasmí - Nephilim who've sworn their loyalty to the Siada
Nahr Alnufus - The River of Souls
Solas - The energy that powers Aljira
Magyck - Both magic used by Brite + Shadow Heretics, as well as the word used to describe different creature's abilities or powers

The world in which our stories take place was born after Earth was torn to pieces by its inhabitants. Mortals survived, but it was a bare existence before the new Gods claimed it for themselves. Theia, Aether, Manāt, and 'Amm created new realms and stood them onto different energetic planes across Lyria, which was what they called the remnants of the mortal realm. Then, they filled them with their offspring, abandoning the new creatures to their own devices after the fact.

The Gods left their younglings with little knowledge, delighting in watching them stumble through the realms that were forced upon them. Both the Nephilim and the Mithra were speechless before they met the mortals, each race breaching their border walls to find answers within the world that had existed before them. The Gods had always spoken Calmani, a language never before heard on this planet, but one that echoed across the different existences they'd held in the past. They did not share their tongue with their offspring. So, the Nephilim and the Mithra learned from the mortals in broken fragments. Lujha, the Nephilim's tongue, was born of the surviving mortal language Arabic, the spoken word that populated small towns near the Aljira border. The Mithra spoke Gjóssa, which was born of the surviving mortal language Greek that populated towns in the north, near Keloseros. In both instances, the language started as almost perfect translations. But through the years, when the immortals took to their realms exclusively, it became more of a derivative. Some phrasing remains nearly similar to the language of origin, while other words and structures have been lost in translation and dialect, re-melded by the Nephilim and Mithra.

The bridge language was one of a myriad of others that survived Earth's apocalypse and carried through the realms by necessity— a way for the Nephilim and Mithra to communicate.

As with all history, the narrative is dictated by who is telling the story. Keep that in mind as you venture into this world.

PRONUNCITION GUIDE

Names

Aheia - *Ah-hey-uh*
Arioch - *Ari-ock*
Ophion - *Oph-ee-on*
Lúc - *Luke*
Tariq - *Tarr-eek*
Shiron - *Shy-ron*
Emryn - *Em-rin*
Aylee - *Ay-lee*
Karyme - *Car-ee-may*
Aljira - *Ahl- hee-raw*
Kal - *Call*
Siraj - *See-raj*
Mazikeen - *Maz-eh-keen*
Safiyah - *Sah-fee-yah*
Nyco - *Nee-co*
Sahren - *Saw-ren*
Kamaria - *Kah-mah-ria*
Hashem - *Hah-sh-ehm*
Hani - *Hah-nee*
Tei - *Tay*
Syn - *Sin*
Nyra - *Nee-raw*

Farah – *Fay-raw*
Keosha – *Key-osha*

Intention

I wrote this book with a very particular aim.

Not only did I want to make you understand my characters and tell their story, but I wanted each chapter to feel a specific way. I wanted you to not only feel the characters' emotions, but to feel what it might be like in their shoes. So, some chapters might give you the ick, some might confuse, and some might be uncomfy.

My goal with this book was to make it an experience in all sense of the word.

XM

Chapter 1

Aheia

Fear was fickle because it was misunderstood.

It hid in the dark place next to the tragedy that made beauty shine, and the worry that anchored excitement, steeping it in trepidation.

A necessary evil.

Or maybe not evil at all.

Maybe happiness wouldn't taste as sweet without the feeling of impending doom that crawled after it. And maybe fear, like all the other seemingly unbidden emotions, was simply a warning; a warning that historically, caused raised hackles and sharpened blades clenched in trembling and unsure hands.

Aheia was no different.

Because fear had always drawn out the contempt for herself. She'd viewed the emotion as a weakness that had her balancing across frail eggshells on her tiptoes. But for the first time since she could remember, fear didn't matter.

"They nourish you," a soft voice said, an echo across the impossibly large span of nothing that surrounded her.

The dulcet tone conjured colors that weren't there before, strips of reality that fluttered on little wings, tethering themselves together in front of Aheia's eyes, and plastering across the aching darkness until the expanse of a landscape filled her vision.

She'd been but a smattering of consciousness for longer than she could remember, floating in nothing but black ink, but now that her eyes filled with color, a new awareness weighed Aheia down—the feel of her body. Her back pressed into something pillowy and her fingertips explored the new surface below her carefully with each deliberate inhale. The air was soft, filled with moisture, and it carried the smell of a forest with it—the pools of stagnant water, the earthy underbrush, the flowering night plants, and the fog around her. She let the petrichor expand her lungs as her gaze traveled over the underside of thick, domed mushrooms with wide, brown gills that stretched from the stalks and shot up toward the dark blue sky above. Heavy vines were strung between the different fungi, symmetrical, green leaves as big as her hand sprouting off of them and catching water in their bowl-like centers.

When she looked down, Aheia realized she was lying on her very own mushroom. A *huge,* silky mushroom wider than the tree trunks she'd seen within the *Callay Forest* of *Keloseros.*

Her chest was calm and peaceful, until her eyes snagged on another body laying next to her. A female that looked a lot like Aheia; white, long hair bunched at her neck, and navy-blue leathers underneath a long, burnt-orange tunic wrapping around her torso. It curved along her breasts and stopped just above her belly, where Aheia spotted dark ink that crept down the side of her hip.

Fear was fickle, and it had evaded Aheia until now.

Until she saw the female's face—or lack thereof.

"But you need to be careful." The words came from the mouthless body—the same sweet voice that had pulled her into existence. The frayed edges of her chin and her forehead danced like smoke, as if the light rays had bent and the female's likeness was just out of reach. "The ones that nourish you and the ones that poison you can look the same. That's why we are careful in the forest, right? You need to pay attention to the things you can't see. Do you remember what I taught you?"

"Yes." The answer came from Aheia's lips, from her heart, before her mind could even dissect the question asked. It gave her pause, and it wasn't the intrinsic knowledge and the speed at which she knew for certain, but it was the sound of her own voice. It sounded young, much too young to be hers. "The roots."

The faceless female shifted, and it looked like she readjusted to stare up at the sky.

Can she see without eyes?

Aheia followed her action and traced the outline of the impossibly tall fungi, considering how odd it was that they themselves had cream shelves growing off the sides of their stalks. She held out her hand and reached for the little spores that rained down around them, while white specks danced across the air.

"Can you feel them?" the faceless female asked next to her, spreading her long, tapered fingers across the red spotted cap they were lying on.

Aheia mimicked the movement, fanning out her limbs and feeling a low thrum beating against her palm. She inhaled sharply, eyes wide, letting this new sensation creep up her arm, warm and sticky. Syrup in her veins.

"Yes," Aheia said breathlessly.

The pulsing inside of her grew, heavy air filling her lungs as thin strings started emerging on the plants surrounding her like blood vessels. The vines that had been so dark before sprouted with color, thick, corded veins running through them, a bright rainbow that danced and shifted in front of Aheia's eyes. They fed into every leaf and jumped to the small insects and moths that were flying around the glow of iridescent nightshades. It was an energy that seemed to connect it all, and it reverberated in her chest, like an ancient heartbeat that echoed across each life form.

Everything around her was alive.

Everything was connected—strung together.

"One day you'll be a part of it."

"When?" she asked.

"When the Gods will it." There was a smile in the discombobulated voice. It was wistful, hopeful even.

"I'm hungry," Aheia exhaled the words, feeling her stomach compress, a pull tugging at her from somewhere behind her navel.

"I know, but too much might kill you. Too much might kill me just as well, dearling," the female said. "Because fate is just as hungry as you are."

Aheia looked over at her in question, but she was already up, moving to the edge of the giant mushroom, and in the process of lowering herself to the ground. She scrambled after her, peering over the side.

"Jump," the female said, flexing her fingers, and Aheia complied, even though the height scared her. When she was on the ground, she realized it wasn't just her hands that were small and her voice that sounded young, but her eyeline barely reached halfway up the mushroom's stalk. She dug her naked feet into the soft, warm earth and her eyes closed instinctively, as she let herself feel the cold water that hung in the air, too small to see.

"You don't want to miss the snakes, do you?"

Aheia's gaze snapped up towards the female, something itching at her mind, a recognition that wouldn't quite bare itself to her. She brushed the odd feeling aside as the warm breeze tousled her white hair, tangling it around her face and arms, a slow smile on her lips. Her heart was happy here. It ached at the hiraeth she felt for this place.

A place that felt like home.

A place long forgotten.

Bright citrus, verbena, and bergamot tinged the leathers against Aheia's cheek as she nestled into the female's side and the scent brought tears to her eyes. Her chest tightened, her little fingers squeezing, worried that if she didn't hold on, this moment would slip through her fingers like sand. They held each other like any measure of space might tear them apart as they fell into a steady pace, and Aheia watched the horizon above change to a deep orange—the color painted in one clean brushstroke behind dark purple mountains.

Home.

It echoed inside of her just as the heartbeat of nature had, and she knew it was true.

If she just held on, she could stay.

"Look." The female reached out her hand, and let her fingers brush against Aheia's shoulder, bringing back a small luna moth perched on top of her knuckles. Velvety, white wings gleamed in the soft fireflies that lit around them and the insect's proximity would have been unnerving if the female wasn't treating it as such a treasure—with such reverence.

"Blessed day, sacred night. We thank you for the life around us, for our survival," the female said, reaching her hand down to Aheia, who turned her gaze up in question.

"Go on, kiss its wings."

Her stomach roiled at the thought, but it was accompanied by guilt. Because deep down, she knew being disgusted was some sort of sin.

So, she leaned towards the moth, loosening a breath and when her lips touched the velvet, the ground shook. She jumped, the small stones under her feet digging into her soles as the dirt and moss covered earth cracked apart. The gashes ran deep, splitting from below her body like she'd been the reason for the disruption. The faceless female's limbs were still outstretched, her hair curling up into the air as if the wind had stopped mid-gust and pinned the thick strands to the sky. Aheia watched in horror as black sludge bled from the cracked earth, curling up her legs in a tight coil that covered her skin in its entirety. It was oozing and shiny, and everything around her was frozen, save for her. She screamed, and when she did, the blackness forced itself into her mouth. The taste was iron, was warm, and sick against her tongue, clawing its way down her throat until she couldn't breathe, couldn't see, couldn't hear anything but her own heart. The sludgy arms devoured her, yanking her down through the world. The weightless feeling turned her stomach, and she opened her mouth again, only for silence to burst from it while her chest weighed heavy with a scream that she couldn't let go. The wind whipped through her hair, and landscapes she'd never seen before rushed past her. She was falling, and fast, breaking through layers of iridescence. Cities and far-off skylines rushed past her, wolves with snarling mouths eating their dead prey, and waterfalls that cascaded from the edges of floating islands. Her tears bubbled up and away from her as her limbs flailed, and she careened toward a bright, shimmering border of light. Her body crested the retina-burning light, and the air exploded from her lungs as she slammed into a hard surface.

Aheia gasped, cold air filling her lungs. It bit and tore at her body, and swept the black ooze from her like a storm cloud. She blinked, bright light blinding her now as she spit out the taste in her mouth. Red blood splattered the icy ground under her fingers. Her complexion blended with her surroundings and her hands were bigger than they'd been a moment ago.

White trees stood tall around her in a perfect pattern, spanning so far she couldn't see where they ended.

Keloseros.

A lancing pain speared her back, forcing her onto her knees in hopes of finding relief, but the movement only made it worse. It intensified, and blood started to pool, dripping from her chest.

White spots bordered her vision as she gripped the drenched, black fabric over her heart, feeling the burning of a probed wound. A ragged sob worked its way up her throat, the noise bouncing off the unnervingly perfect trunks over and over again.

"Watch the shadows." They're lying to you. A tattered voice scraped against the back of her mind.

"There aren't any." Aheia choked just as her world changed—rearranged while she bled out on its ground, staring at the dark spaces that bared themselves behind her reality. Like all of it had been a facade in a play. But now the curtain was rising and she could see between—the place where the sinister things lived.

As her surroundings fractured, so did the air, split by a careening object that whizzed past Aheia's head and landed in the snow with a deafening thud. She yelped, staring at the pearly handle of a dagger sticking from frozen ground. Another fell to her left and yet another just in front of her, fast, fast, faster, until it was raining weapons. She screamed, trying to press herself against the trunk of a tree, the pain in her back growing until she couldn't move. It felt like she'd been impaled against the bark behind her, and all she could do was sob silently while the knives kept falling and hitting closer and closer. Tears rolled down her cheeks, her fingers twitching with defeat as familiar beady eyes invaded her field of vision.

The moth.

Nausea burned Aheia's stomach as the insect's wings fluttered, fluffy antennas twitching slightly, jutting out from a furry body as it stared at her with that uncomfortable gaze. It held her attention until the pain in her hand tore it away, and she screamed, eyes forced down to the knife that had impaled her. The agony of it *burned* and her blood welled quickly, pooling on the snow and ice below.

Gods, please, she begged as another knife razed the air in front of her like an answer, slashing through the side of her calf. Aheia convulsed in pain, finding the moth again with pleading eyes. It had brought her here, hadn't it?

Please help me. She couldn't speak it, not when her voice died the moment she parted her lips. *Please.*

But it only watched as a third blade sheared through the air and buried itself in her shoulder, slicing into her flesh.

Aheia's lips were wrenched apart in a silent scream, her vision obstructed by her tears when the moth jutted forward, and vaulted towards her, forcing its body into her mouth.

Chapter 2

Arioch

Blood ate the ice below Aheia's body just like death had consumed her. It soaked into the fabric of her shirt and stained her pale skin as if it wanted to cover up what had happened to her with broad strokes. It was thick and messy, and it tainted the white blanket of snow around her until she was laying at the center of a dark red halo.

Arioch couldn't grasp onto anything in that infinitely poisonous moment, nothing past the heat that poured from the soulless void in his chest and ate at his insides like acid. It burned and twisted itself into his shadows as his knees dug into the brittle Keloseros ground next to Aheia and the *magyck* under his skin screamed.

His darkness screamed because he couldn't—because the air strangled and expanded until it throttled him and ate his voice.

No.

Moments were often stretched thin, barely remembered in an immortal's life. But here, the blink of an eye had changed everything.

A moment ago, she'd been alive.

A moment ago, she'd promised him that she'd return to *Aljira* with him.

He forced his gaze from Aheia's form to find his knife on the ground and without a thought behind the action, he grabbed it, vision fraying around his periphery.

Hers would not be the only death in this Gods' fucking forsaken forest.

Arioch grit his teeth and latched onto his own shoulder, the one that Ophion had wounded in their fight, digging his fingers into the flesh until a sharp pain lit up his nerves. His chest shook with a roar but he kept pushing—deeper and deeper, until all he could think of was his blood and the tissue being pulled apart.

The pain was sobering.

It cut through the haze that wrapped itself around him, coaxing his reality back in a rush. The sounds of his surroundings hammered into his sides, pressing against his eardrums in a deafening way as he locked onto a new fixation.

Ophion.

The *Malek* was grappling to his feet a few paces away; Lúc's jaguar biting into his calf, bright red blood splattering across the white snow in thick, glossy drips.

Arioch lunged for the *Mithra*, grabbing ahold of the lame wing that Ophion was dragging across the snow behind him, and tore him back. The *Ćist's* pale skin split around his blade and Arioch cut until the dark red color filled his vision, until his eyes pulsed with shadows. They were trying to find their way from his skin while the Brite realm kept him bound to the most mortal version of himself he'd ever be. Mortal, like Aheia had been mortal in his realm. Fucking powerless.

Ophion's screams of pain dampened when blood and fire filled the air.

"Mazikeen!" The shout came from behind him, and he wasn't sure who'd called the *Ifrit's* name. The familiar voices felt distorted, just like his vision, like looking through glass that held water and it took him two more heartbeats to realize it was Emryn who was sprinting toward him, her dark wings tucked. He looked from her to Ophion and then overhead with enough time to catch Mazikeen falling from the sky above him. The air around her body crackled and the fire that had enveloped her form began to flicker as she raced to the forest ground.

Maz cratered the snow and dirt below her, embers scattering into the air like she'd fallen into a pile of burning ashes, and the realm shook with the impact. The snow around her melted down as Arioch and Emryn crashed back against a tree trunk, narrowly missing the Ifrit.

White. White. White.

Paint them red. Paint them all fucking red.

Arioch's head hit against the wood, his eyes burning while the fire inside of him ate the oxygen in his lungs like it demanded his life now, too.

He vaguely registered Maz—her large outline shrinking down until she was in the body he recognized, far from the force of nature he'd seen moments before, her light fading.

Fading. Fading. Fading.

He felt like he was fading just as well.

"Arioch." Emryn's voice was a hushed groan as she heaved him from her and rose to her knees, her taut wings bleeding with scrapes and cuts. "We need you," she said, her fingers digging into his temples, forcing his gaze. Her eyes were stern and frantic, if the duality of it was possible, her dark skin slick with sweat, curls coming loose from their leather ties.

Fuck. Get your shit together and get them out of here.

Urgency laced through him when he looked at the *Nephilim* that had followed him into the bowels of Keloseros—would follow him anywhere, even when death loomed.

Mazikeen was trying to stand.

Kazim was straining against Aylee and Shiron.

Kar was picking up Aheia's corpse, her eyes glazed and unfocused, her shoulders shaking. He knew it was his fault. That she was forced to feel the pain of this day with him. The empath felt it all.

"Sedate him," he growled at Emryn, his voice hoarse and he didn't have to tell the *Syraphem* who. She nodded, crossing the snow, reaching her blood-streaked arms toward Kazim. They were lucky that the *Shadow Heretic's* genetics allowed for lower level magyck, because without it they'd have to drag Kazim home kicking and screaming.

"Maz," he groaned, getting to his feet, while Lúc shifted in front of him. Those purple eyes, however, remained when the claws of his jaguar didn't, when his skin replaced fur, when he spit in his hands and ran them across his messy black hair. He was covered in red blood; his teeth bared, but not in a smile, no, in an expression that demanded more.

The Ifrit's attention was weak, her eyes drooping slightly, the embers flickering with exhaustion. Even her hair was almost extinguished, the deep, orange cracks in her skin suffocating slowly.

"I can feel it," she said, her words as static as her gaze. "We're near a *vortex*."

He'd counted on the *Calmani* in her veins, the recognition of the old magyck that ancient beings like her felt, and that ran within the vortexes around their world, to aid her. It wasn't explainable as such, just as the stars weren't explainable, just as the tides held their secrets. But he'd known the chances, had known of different gates' existences in Keloseros, and had staked everything on them finding one here. He didn't possess the *margaritári* needed to return, not enough for all of them, and his Nephilim had known and followed him anyway.

He'd tried to deter them the night before, had wanted to take Aheia here alone.

They'd all but laughed at the thought.

He didn't deserve their loyalty.

"This way," Maz gasped, her steps faltering, her body crumbling under its own weight. But before she could hit the ground, Arioch caught her side, crying out in pain when her embers cooked his skin where they connected, his already fucked up shoulder cauterizing. He clenched his teeth and swallowed the noises that threatened to crawl up his chest as she took his strength and he gave her his flesh.

"Bring him," Arioch grit out in an unrecognizable voice, eyes finding Lúc. The Shifter went and seized onto Ophion without hesitation, while Shiron steadied Kaz, who was slumping where he stood.

Footsteps started to break the silence around them, and it was that sound setting them all into motion. The Mithra were coming, and he focused on that—on the image of those Brite fucks surrounding them—killing his friends, killing his *family*. He hung onto that thought because that horror would spur him on. He needed to imagine the worst, to handle his reality, to listen to the vicious whispers of his shadows that outlined exactly what they'd do to their enemies once he was out of this poisonous fucking realm.

They made their way through white trees, the uniformity of them unsettling. He hadn't noticed it before, but the spacing was odd, like they had been planted by hand with a ruler. The pattern of them started to become dizzying while Maz became heavier and heavier, fusing with his skin as if they were merging into one form. He choked out a groan, the fire punishing. He'd feel this wound even after Emryn healed him. Because her fire was laced with Calmani too, and it would burn into him, past his skin, and flare every time he thought about this day.

Kar was on his left, carrying Aheia, and he let himself look, just for a moment.

He'd wanted to keep her when those blue eyes begged him to, back in Aljira.

He'd wanted so badly to keep her.

And it was selfish. Even if she'd refused him in that church, he'd have dragged her back.

"There!" Lúc barked, his voice still a low timber, the kind he didn't shake for a long while after shifting.

Arioch refocused, his shadows searing alongside the *Djynn* as his eyes rose to the magyck in front of them. The vortex shot straight out of the cold ground, a clean rectangle of color amongst the white. Its corners looked sharp enough to pierce skin, a blue hum roiling inside like a maelstrom.

He could feel it too now, the pull, the heat, the conflicting way his magyck recognized the Calmani but couldn't understand it. It was two entities trying to communicate in a language unbeknownst to the other. But Maz knew. Maz's magyck spoke the same dialect even.

She reached her hand forward and steadied herself, the cracked skin of her fingers sinking deep into its depths and causing ripples across its surface. Nephilim couldn't pass through a portal if the magyck had been fortified by the Mithra, but Calmani spoke to Calmani and bypassed the lesser laws of nature. The Ifrit closed her eyes, lips parted while Arioch watched, his body starting to shake under the strain. Sweat dripped down Mazikeen's temples, the bleeding, blue swirls refracting from the little pearls of exhaustion as the vortex in front of them gave a low, ominous sound.

The ground vibrated with it, and Arioch felt it in his very bones, the shift that was taking place. The blue magyck twisted its wisps into a red that leached from its dark center until the entirety of the gate was filled, casting a sinister, maroon glow over the snow.

Instead of repelling them, the vortex now invited them near.

"Come on, it won't hold for long," Mazikeen grunted.

They made their way through as the shouts grew louder. The anger was building now that Arioch's body was going numb, and his shadows could feel the nearness of *Lyria,* the mortal realm. He didn't know where they'd land, but he did know what would happen when they did.

Chapter 3

Arioch

His shadows tore away as soon as the air around him turned warm and invasive. It clung to his wounds and felt heavy on his shoulders, but the relief at the realm shift was greater than the discomfort.

When they emerged from the portal magyck, they were bathed in the sun of yet another desert. The sand was not red here like it was in his *Borderlands*, but beige instead, and the heat made the air flicker.

The vortex they'd bled from was tucked between the sandstone columns of a long-forgotten structure, pillars rising in jagged lengths towards the sky like flowers looking for nourishment. Vines were climbing around the ridges of the rock, breaking through the sand that seemed so completely suffocating and consuming beneath.

Time was slow, drawing past him as he stared at the ivy. It survived in this desolate landscape—bloomed, even.

The venom inside him spread as he turned toward the one face of the ruin that was still intact. The tall, tapering stone wall of what used to be the front of the structure still held stained glass. It was colorful except for the white figures depicted with wings, hands outstretched like they were gifting the people below with something.

Of fucking course this is where they'd put a gate.

An old place of fucking worship for the Mithra.

He spun the shadows that curled around the far pillar into a large dome that encircled them all until the only light within was the Mithra vortex. He would trap the Ćist like ants under a glass while he sent the others back home.

"Get out," Arioch snapped at the Nephilim standing with him. "You know what to do."

He readied himself for when Maz pushed off his side, charred, and burned parts of his skin peeling from his muscles when they separated. He fell to his knee, gripping his shoulder just at the edge of the wound, and massaged the unaffected skin like it might offer him some relief.

He shifted his shadows as the other demons ran through the darkness, stretching his magyck and funneling them toward one of their own vortexes across Lyria. It would take them all back to Aljira in mere steps—it would take them back to Tariq, who was waiting with the *Falkri*, ready to fight when the time came. Today would end in bloodshed far beyond what the Mithra had planned for. Arioch owed them retribution, and he had for a long time now. He should have done this the moment he found Kazim's corpse on the red sands—burnt beyond recognition. If he had, maybe he'd have found out it wasn't true, that the body had been a fucking decoy and not his brother. He'd never forgive himself for that.

A new volatile thing wormed its way into his middle, one that felt permanent, an etched curse written across his insides. It was guilt. The kind of guilt that was useless because there was no way to change the past.

He cleared his eyes as best he could, facing the vortex, whose whir filled the cocoon of shadows he'd formed, and his fingers pinpricked as the fire swept through him. He would swallow everything whole if he couldn't redirect this—fucking implode. And just as his shadows stretched almost unbearably, the red whirlpool at the center of the vortex bled back into the blue. Slowly at first and then all together.

Arioch waited by himself. It was how it had to be in the end.

He bared his teeth, letting his darkness seep into his chest, and into the parts of him he usually pushed it away from.

Here, the magyck was on his side.

The magyck that had picked him.

It demanded blood and death.

And it felt like relief when the first of the Mithra broke through the vortex. They looked disoriented, faltering as they stumbled into his playground, a cloud of shadows so dense the sun couldn't pierce it.

Arioch's teeth clenched and his magyck darted, slinging itself around the first of the Ćist, his body in motion before his mind could catch up. He fought with his hands, with his nails, with his teeth, until he disarmed the first Malek and tore into his wings. The Dioscuri next to him tried to summon his light, but Arioch's shadows suffocated him before much more than a spark burst from his fingertips. Their need for vengeance and retribution felt like his own, but different—two warriors who shared the same enemy.

They were sentient, and he didn't control them any longer as they went after the death, the pain, and the blood they desired. Cold shivers wracked his body as the slickness of it coated his tendrils, numbing the burning pain in his shoulder. It was a feeding and an offering, somehow pushing him further and faster, his eyes straining from the pressure in his head.

The Mithra were swarming from the vortex now, none of them living long enough to alert the ones still in Keloseros as Arioch tore and cut and ate at their lives to satiate whatever hunger inside of him felt he deserved it. It was an afterthought, noticing the Nephilim now at his side. He saw dark wings, he saw black fur, and he saw Tariq tearing into someone just to his left. The demons were pouring from the shadows behind him, but it all barely registered.

Arioch met Tariq's black eyes, the *Leviathan's* dark hair tangled around the curls of his horns just as he let his shadows fall.

That fucking sun. It was blinding for a creature that wasn't used to its presence and Arioch saw red in the shadows of his past that suffocated him.

Red and Kazim's burned body. Red and Aheia's lifeless form.

Red.

The blood had turned the sand into chunky mud underneath the stacked bodies when the vortex finally spluttered and died. It remained as just an archway now, locked to anyone who had come through to defend their realm.

Lives had been lost on both sides, but Arioch's Nephilim were savagely dwindling the remaining Mithra as he walked through the corpses, his shadows languid at his sides. He imagined Ophion hadn't expected this response.

It's not what his father would have done. Sahren would have brokered a deal. But Sahren would have never given their kind asylum to begin with, not for all the souls in the world.

A body stumbled out in front of him, a scared young *Fae* male, and Arioch kept his features neutral as he snatched the short Mithra up by the neck and squeezed hard enough to crack apart his spine.

It was quick.

It was him showing the last bit of mercy he possessed.

He blinked the sweat from his eyes, shadows pulsing as he surveyed the tableau in front of them. Where the sun had shone high on the horizon when they'd started, it was now painting the sky a deep purple, darkness looming as the exhaustion set in. There were few Mithra left, and to their credit, they looked ready to die with their weapons raised. Kar and Aylee were tearing at the limbs of a Dioscuri who had gone after them with his light, while Shiron and a few of the trainees looked to the dead bodies. The ruins had devolved into more of a crater, columns splattered with sickly beautiful ribbons of scarlet and black, the stained glass depiction of the Mithra near the front of the church shattered in colorful shards.

It was odd with battles and war. There always came a moment, it seemed, where both sides collectively took a breath and licked their wounds. The Mithra's hourglass had run empty, and their own kind had forsaken them, doomed their lives when they closed their vortex.

Sent to slaughter. Leaderless.

The sweat-soaked warriors were breathing hard, kernels of sand whirling through the air with the commotion. Arioch had never eaten so much dirt in his entire life, hadn't been covered in so much blood. He'd never be able to rid himself of it completely, and he didn't care to.

He lived in reminders and this was simply one more.

Lúc's growl filled the air, tangled up in the last fight that was yet to die out, as both sides watched. Two dozen Mithra were standing near their vortex, hands shaking; some with fear, some with resolve, and others with exhaustion. His own were waiting, palming their weapons, or caressing their magyck. But Lúc was still going, straddling another Shifter that looked like he'd tried to turn, a bushy white tail pushed between his body and the sand, sickly yellow eyes, and the beginnings of a snout forming. He'd been killed somewhere in the process, but that didn't deter Lúc, who was still tearing into his chest, ribs cracked apart in a gaping wound.

The sounds of flesh and organs, of Lúc's growls, permeated the air. He looked feral, his gaze a dark purple and detached, his mouth smeared with blood, and his hair slick with it, too. He was rummaging around like an animal, intestines spilling between the bones that were sticking out from the chest cavity, and sliding to the floor. The Shifter was entranced when he fought, and insatiable, like no measure of blood would ever be enough, akin to the *Avarice's* shadows.

Arioch watched Tariq wipe the back of his hand across his sweaty forehead, intensity boiling in his black eyes as he approached Lúc. He sank to his haunches and narrowed his gaze, blood from Lúc's attack splashing across his cheek. The Shifter hadn't broken away from his fixation with the dead body below him and he didn't let up his ministrations until Tariq reached out his hand and cupped his chin.

Murder was etched into every inch of Lúc's until the Leviathan caressed the Shifter's jaw, and spoke hushed words in his ear. That's when the purple gaze started to clear.

"Which one of you fucks matters?" Arioch aimed his question at the last of the Mithra.

No one moved and for a moment it seemed they stopped breathing altogether.

"Your *Epísmos* is dead. His life was taken as payment for another," he said, moving his shadows back, seeping across his Nephilim and swallowing them one by one, sending them back to their vortex across Lyria.

"There will be an answer to the bloodshed you've caused," a limping Mithra spat, his nostrils flaring with indignation. The short male clenched his broadsword tighter, his stance coiled like an animal ready to pounce. But Arioch bared his teeth, stepping closer, close enough to smell the bite of clean soap mixed with dirty sweat.

"This bloodshed *was* an answer." The words filled the space long after *Alshaytan* stepped away. He didn't wait for a response, following the carefully laid path toward Aljira, and tapering his magyck as he went, leaving the last of the live Mithra behind on the desert floor.

CHAPTER 4

ARIOCH

Arioch awoke with a start.

His muscles hurt, a hollow pain shooting up his arms that fed into his temples. He was laying in a pool of his shadows, the pressure at the base of his spine spreading between his thighs.

He scrubbed his face, letting himself live in that split second of confusion that came with waking from a dream. But it came and went, replacing the warmth of sleep with cold awareness.

It had only been a few hours since Shiron came to give him the message that the Mithra abandoned the Aljiran border. Their surrender had been anticipated because they'd fought for the last thirteen days, the obligatory time period in their belief system when an Epísmos was killed by an enemy. It was quiet now, the white flags they'd littered the red sand with, just beyond his border, blowing away in the wind.

Cause abandoned.

Arioch would join the rest of his demons to help with the dead, but it had been three days since he last slept and his mind felt bruised.

The few hours he'd managed this evening weren't enough, nor remotely restful.

He was used to it.

His fingers worked over the needles in his shoulder, the one that Mazikeen had wounded and Emryn had healed, the one that ached worse than the rest of him, even though it looked normal. He lay there, on the couch in the common room, and let his shadows breathe until all he felt was the burning. The burning that hadn't left him alone since Keloseros.

She wouldn't leave him alone.

Aheia.

She walked through his dreams and twisted him into knots.

Sometimes they fought. Sometimes they fucked. Sometimes she just smiled. That's how he knew it was a lie. She'd never smiled for him before.

It's why he tried not to sleep when he could help it.

He didn't want to see her anymore.

But tonight he'd needed it. And his dreams had been especially cruel.

Her skin was cold. So fucking cold—the frigid kind that wanted to attack and leave patches of him frozen, stuck, and burning. Always cold. Cold until he ran his hands between her legs. When he did that, she lit up with something like starlight. Ethereal. She was warm then.

A growl vibrated through him at the unwanted, leftover feeling of lust that had been brought on by his dream. Another thing that felt like torture. Fucking unwanted.

He leaned forward, readjusting his cock, and reached for the glass he'd left on the gold table in front of him. The liquor burned his dehydrated throat, while parts of his dream forced their way into his hazy mind. His eyes became unfocused as they watched the flames across the room dance and diffuse. Hushed whispers flitted through the air—the magyck in his veins coming alive under his thoughts. It was the other reason he couldn't let her go. Because his shadows refused, forced him to remember, forced him to feel things he didn't want. Too fucking sentient for his own liking.

Murder had fed them, so had the adrenaline, but it wasn't enough. They wanted more. They wanted everything.

Arioch leaned back on the couch, tendrils of his magyck grazing across his neck, over his stomach, and down his legs like they were coaxing him, trying a soft approach for once when he didn't want any of it. But the friction they offered made his breath shallow, and his thighs flex anyway. He glared down at his laces, like all of this shit was their fault for feeling so gods damned tight across his groin.

Fuck's sake.

He clenched and unclenched his hand for a moment, and then cursed under his breath, pulling the leather apart and sliding the heel of his palm against his cock. He growled, relief already starting to loosen his shadows as the pleasure twisted into his stomach. This is what *they* wanted even though he didn't.

"Shit." He inhaled a sharp breath, feeling the reprieve, as he stroked himself roughly, bringing up his hand and spitting in his palm. He leaned his head back against the couch, the blood rushing through him while the Solas orbs above him died and were reborn over and over again. The energy ate his vision until it was her again, just the fuzzy memory of something he'd held in his hands for seven days.

He'd never gotten to fuck her little mouth the way he'd wanted to. But he could see it in the darkest parts of his depraved brain—those pink lips stretched taut around him, her hands grasping his thighs as he forced himself deeper. She choked in his fantasies. She cried there, too. She spasmed, and he'd fuck her like that until she got close to passing out, and she liked that.

In his mind.

But his little goddess had liked his hands around her throat in real life too and had come in a pink flush that threatened to turn her pale skin purple. And it was her face that was his undoing. He let himself remember something real for just a moment, let himself imagine her expression when they'd fucked in the caves, surrounded by his shadows. How her eyes had rolled into the back of her head, how her body had arched and clenched, how it had felt ... How it had felt significant in a way he didn't understand.

His release was dull, but the disgust and anger that curled themselves into his middle when the thick ropes of come painted his shirt were anything but.

He exhaled roughly, shoving his still-hard cock back in his leathers. Then he pulled the black fabric over his head and balled it up, walking over to the fireplace just as Lúc entered the common room.

The Shifter's dark eyes watched him closely, his thumb playing with the leather clasp around his dagger. He leaned against the marble wall while Arioch threw his shame into the fire.

"Really hated that shirt, huh?" Lúc asked, an ever-present smirk tugging at his mouth. He bit his lip ring and pulled it between his teeth, watching the thick plumes of smoke drifting up the chimney.

"It was your shirt," Arioch said humorlessly.

Lúc blinked. "Was that a joke?"

Arioch sent him an unamused look. "What do you want?"

"Ophion's awake—well, as awake as the fucker can get." His grin widened and his tongue swiped across his teeth like he was excited to revisit their new favorite torture toy.

Feathers.

Fucking. Feathers.

So delicate, so soft, so breakable.

Ophion took a labored breath, blood drip drip dripping from his mouth, his eyes puffy with bruises, and skin paler than usual, if that was at all possible.

The near-silent little splashes of liquid on marble sounded loud against Arioch's eardrums, feeding the headache at his temples. A headache that seemed pretty ever fucking present since they'd returned from Keloseros.

"You haven't answered my question," Arioch drawled, shadows threading his vision as he watched the Malek fight against his manacles. Every tug at the restraints that kept him strapped to the black slab of rock underneath him, pulled at his wings that were stretched out and secured by two iron hooks against the dark walls on opposite sides. Ophion cried out in pain, trying to recover his breath while Shiron crossed his arms, leaning nonchalantly against the cell wall, his fingers sliding across the *achlary*, the devotional beads, around his throat. His amber eyes watched carefully, dark threads of hair hanging into his face.

"You haven't given me a reason to," Ophion choked out, his shoulders shaking.

Arioch sank to his haunches so he was eye level with the Malek and notched his knife right behind the fucker's ear. Fear glinted in those red-rimmed, blue irises.

Aheia's eyes.

No.

"You'll kill me either way," Ophion said, but his voice wavered.

"If you're lucky," Arioch tilted his chin. "And if you're not, I'll just continue to take the parts of you that interest me." His nose twitched and his muscles tightened. Heat shot down his spine, and he could feel everything inside of him humming at the prospect of whittling away at Ophion. "Until there's nothing left."

Skin him.

Arioch could keep him alive for that, could cut through those fine little ligaments that kept the skin married to the meat and pull slabs of it off him. One by one.

Animal hide.

"I don't think he heard you, brother." Lúc danced his fingertips across the chain that held one of those long wings secure, a vicious grin spreading his lips. Then he yanked down hard, and Ophion's body bent at an unnatural angle, a guttural yell breaking from his chest. "Are you listening, Ćist?"

Ophion's breaths were quick and ragged as he tried to move, to lean away from the Avarice's blade. But when the Malek stayed quiet still, Arioch cut into the skin behind his ear, just to watch him cry out in pain again. The sounds those vocal cords made under torture had his shadows shuddering.

Red blood stained his hand and he moved enough to see his knife buried in a thin layer of flesh—deep enough to bleed obscenely, but not enough to kill him anytime soon. He kept the blade there and watched his toy shake and choke with the strain to keep perfectly still.

"What did you do to Kazim?" Arioch's voice dropped to a low growl.

Ophion's breath rattled like his lungs were filled with rocks.

"Helped show him the light," he spluttered.

Fucker.

Arioch stood and discarded the knife, wiping his dirty hands on dirtier leathers, while Ophion loosened a breath. It almost sounded like relief, and that fucking sound was almost as pleasurable as his screams. Because any time the Malek experienced relief, Arioch twisted it into pain, and he'd continue to do so until it was all the Malek would expect from those short moments of comfort. He'd take the meaning of the word and eat it.

"Playtime isn't over," Lúc said, spitting a smattering of blood and saliva onto the marble, before he turned to Arioch. "He still thinks that, doesn't he? That it'll end."

"This doesn't stop just because you can't keep your eyes open." Arioch chuckled humorlessly in Ophion's general direction while the Shifter ran his fingers across the black blade in his hand, eyes trained on the colors that the Solas orbs bounced off the curved side. He'd traded his usual dagger for one that was hooked and looped around one of his fingers. It matched the smirk he wore on his lips.

Arioch leaned down. "You forget that while the light is yours, the darkness is all mine, and you won't find anything soothing there. Only nightmares, I'll make sure of it." The words felt hot and raspy against his tongue. He had an assortment of fun injectables he could play with to make Ophion's sleep just as restless as his waking hours.

"Deep breath, Epísmos," Lúc said, a taunting edge caressing his words as he gripped onto Ophion's gray hair and wrenched his face up. He traced the flat edge of his blade up the Malek's throat, crimping the beard hairs there and pressing into his windpipe. "Don't worry, we'll make it painful."

Shiron pushed away from the wall, heaving Ophion's left wing off the hook from the far side of the room with a sick squelch. The feathers fell, and the Malek's body jolted, a sharp cry on his lips.

"Steel yourself," Arioch said, sliding his fingers across the ridge of Ophion's wing. "We're just getting started."

This was the beginning.

His hands would be next—the dirty fucking hands that had touched Aheia, that had touched Kazim. But Arioch wanted his pride first. He wanted his fucking identity.

The Malek groaned in agony, his body spasming as Arioch straddled his back, knees pressing into the side of his bruised ribs.

"You c-can't," Ophion choked, while Arioch gripped the white appendage tighter, looking down at his back in disgust. His skin had been perfect, completely untouched before the black dagger split it. No calluses on his hands or feet. No reflections of a hard life, because he'd never known hardship.

"It seems that I can." He ran his fingers down those feathers, giving it a beat past anticipation because he wanted to see that small spark of hope flash in Ophion's blue eyes before he took it away. When it bared itself, he fucking ate that too, biting into the junction where the wing connected with Ophion's back.

Fucking feathers.

Arioch locked his jaw until he felt the ligaments tear while the Malek fought against iron, fought against the Avarice, fought against Lúc's knife that he was gleefully holding to his throat. But none of it deterred it, no, it only spurred him on.

He gnashed his teeth like it would give him the respite he needed, as if the pain he inflicted on the Mithra might bring Aheia back; as if it would erase what had happened to Kazim.

But that was not how it worked.

Pain.

Rage.

Numb.

Repeat.

A broken, manic roar tore from his chest as he clamped his jaw together, feeling the hot meat underneath the fuzz of Ophion's wings. But not even the crunch of the bones nor the sickening sound of skin tearing apart let him find anything but the searing flames that charred his edges.

"*Yadha*," he pulled back, his voice thick like he was sliding it across a rough grate as he met Shiron's eyes. The Nephilim tipped his chin without hesitation, wrenching the wing in unison with Arioch, until the bones cracked and the skin tore apart. Blood splattered across Lúc's smile, and Ophion cried out, his body falling against the slate underneath.

Arioch spat out remnants of skin, before he surveyed the fucker's lopsided anatomy. He'd done a nasty job pulling off the large appendage, and every fucking part of him wanted to repeat the treatment on the other side, but not now. No, Ophion was barely hanging on to his coherency.

That won't. Fucking. Do.

"We'll leave it at one for now," he deadpanned, wiping his mouth on his shirt, while Lúc reached for a long log that rested beside Ophion's stone slab. Then he pulled a lighter from his leathers and held the flame to the end that had a soaked cloth wrapped around it. They could have used Emryn to keep him from bleeding out. But instead, Lúc pressed the flames against the wound on Ophion's back, burning it enough to cauterize it while Arioch hauled the bloody wing over, dropping it in front of the Malek to make sure he had a good view of what he'd lost today.

Then, he collected his shadows in a vortex against the wall so that Shiron and Lúc could head back to the surface.

He was alone in that cave with Ophion now, and it should have felt different.

It should have felt *more*, seeing his enemy bleeding and broken in front of him, but it didn't.

He was numb.

Chapter 5

Arioch

He walked along the cracked floor of *Gehenna*, Koutávi trailing him with two other *Varcolacs*.

Arioch's thumb slid across the rock in his hand, the last part of Aheia that had remained in Aljira after her death. It bothered him because it shouldn't have bothered him. It was just a *lápis*—a crystal, one that she'd had in her leather pouch when she tried to barter for asylum in his realm. So why was it lingering in his dreams? Why was it cradled in her small hands in so many of them?

He turned it over under the low, iridescent light of the *Nahr Anulfus.* The souls seemed to watch him with those dead eyes as he crossed the river and stepped through the jagged rock gates in front of him. He ducked into the dark spiral staircase that wound its way past the intricate levels, finely tuned to stroke the genetic intricacies of whatever rested there to keep it contained. With every barrier he passed, the energies shifted around him, each one pushing against his skin in a different way. They were meant to keep anything that wasn't allowed into the abandoned realm out and anything already imprisoned behind its walls.

The souls in the Nahr Anulfus, for instance, could never leave because the water and air around them were charged in such a way that kept them pulled in that never-ending loop. It's also why his steps were repelled when crossing it, as if there was a thin glass-like barrier between him and the glowing water.

Everything had its place down here, and every level dealt in different restrictions.

His fist clenched at his side, wedging the small stone in his palm as he cleared the last step. He'd been here to see the oracle about questions he couldn't himself answer. But they'd denied his visit, and kept the stone gates closed in front of him. Which meant he had to smear his blood on the wall and wait for *them* to approach *him* for an audience when it suited them.

It was why he had the stone with him now. He wanted to see if they could tell him anything about its significance. But when they refused him, he'd redirected his route.

And now he was feeling the dread that blistered inside of him every time he came to see Aheia.

She was gone. But he couldn't seem to stop himself from needing her proximity, even now.

You have to stop. It had become a new mantra for him. He needed to stop because she was his past and he was living there with her instead of fixing the fucked up future that he now faced.

Regardless of what the stories said of him, regardless of what the mortals and Mithra made him out to be by calling him *Mithrek Morta,* he did not command death; no one did. He only watched it drag lives past him.

Death did not discriminate and didn't live in anyone's hands, just as poison wouldn't stop its effects for its handler.

In its nature, it was a gentle thing, no matter how much it was despised, no matter how much *he* despised it. It happened to any creature just as life did—the only sure thing, even amongst immortals in one way or another. Death's hands were not on the blade that had pushed between Aheia's vertebrae. Nor were its lips on hers when she took her last breath. Death wasn't the violence, it was what came after. After the blood, after the screams, after the fucking pain. It was tranquility—the eye of the storm that surrounded him. Though, he felt anything but calm when the darkness split for him and the rock shifted, the wall opening up into an adjacent cave. A blue glow seeped across the black ground, coming from the frozen lake at the center. Stalactites hung from the ceiling like long icicles, circling the stone slab at the far wall, where Aheia's corpse lay, separate from all of those other rotting bodies.

It was cold here; the ice frosting the walls keeping her chilled. She looked the same as she had when she'd been alive.

Why couldn't she defy him one last time? Drop the veil and just—

Death is imprinted on your shadows. You'll never tear yourself from it.

The thought permeated him as he stepped closer, and leaned his hands against the stone that supported Aheia.

She was wearing the same oversized clothing that she'd walked out of his realm with, blood still coating her. It stuck together strands of her white hair and streaked the hollow of her neck, crusting over the frozen wound at her chest. Her soul, an iridescent shade of gray, lay on the ground beside her. The river had held her for however long it took him to call on a *Wraith*—the collectors of the dead—to retrieve it from the sludgy water.

Wraiths walked the cities, towns, and landscapes across all realms, and they were seen all the time—it was simply that no one could remember them after they looked away. Gehenna was the only place that enabled them to stay in one's memory. Their race held no allegiance, no Gods, no creatures, and no realms. A Wraith's only master was the ending of time, and they walked hand in hand with it where Arioch seemed to shadow them both, to pick up the mess it left behind.

He let his eyes drift across Aheia's pale skin. There were no signs of decay or rot, like she was merely sleeping. Her soul just as vacant as her body.

The mortals believed that there was some sort of a life after death, many Nephilim did too. He knew better. Bodies and souls alike, hundreds a day populated under his eyes, juiced of anything that made them spark. Nothing lived on down here, and to think otherwise was fucking delusional.

He snarled, staring at Aheia's small form like maybe if he hated her enough for leaving, she might jolt back.

His shadows dripped down his back, uncoordinated as he smoothed the hair away from her face. Touching her felt horrible, fucking horrible, and that uncomfortable echo she'd left behind hummed with the remnants of the bond they'd shared when he held her soul.

It made no fucking sense. He hadn't known her long enough for this type of recognition and yet, he felt her like she'd been in his world for years not seven days.

She'd lived and died an enigma.

According to Kal, the Ćist that had come to collect Aheia on Ophion's behalf, she'd been part Nephilim.

But that didn't make any sense either. Ophion would have never wasted his time the way he did, fucking hunting her down because her mother had fucked some demon. And not because she'd defied him either, not even with his pride being the size of the *Badlands*. He'd spent too much eyrid, put in too much effort for that to be the answer.

Besides, he knew in his bones that neither Nephilim nor Mithra would feel how she did when he'd taken her inside of himself. *Bullshit.*

It was intrinsic knowledge that ran in the threads of fate that constricted his chest. The kind of answer that didn't come from his own mind but from the ancient power that lived inside of him. She was something else entirely. But what she was or wasn't didn't matter now, hadn't mattered then, not once he'd decided he'd keep her. It had only been a tool—something to bargain.

So, he'd live with the cold, hollow thing she left and let her keep whatever small part of himself she'd stolen in the process.

This was the last time he'd see her.

"Will you keep her here, or put her with the others?" Arioch's healed arm itched when Mazikeen's voice slithered around him, her tone deep and sultry.

Put her with the others. His skin crawled at the prospect of throwing her body with the rest.

"Here," he said, his throat scratching with the word.

The Ifrit looked recovered, though it had taken almost ten days for her to gather her strength. She hadn't broken into her unbridled form in centuries, and it had drained her completely. Her bonds were broken, and she'd repaid her debt to Arioch, but she'd asked to stay anyway and he was glad for it.

Maz seemed to prefer the dead, the silence, and the stillness they offered. And he liked meeting her down here. It made Gehenna a little less desolate.

"To meet an immortal so fearful of life ... Maybe death was a welcome reprieve from that suffering," Maz said, walking around him, her eyes trained on Aheia. Her fingers hovered just over the crown of her head, her pupils fiery. "I will continue to keep watch."

"She doesn't need to be watched anymore," Arioch snapped.

Mazikeen's eyes glowed in the dark, conviction bright. "You hold on so tightly to the perpetuity of death," she said, the embers in her skin flaring. "When you have no less proof of that finality than you do of life thereafter."

"Proof lives around us," he said coldly. "There is nothing here to suggest anything but a dark end. Dead bodies, dead souls. That's all there is down here, nothing alive but the monsters we're supposed to keep locked away. No Gods that meet the dead and shepherd them into some beautiful existence, either."

That thought had its hand around the throat of so many when all it was was a distraction. A justification.

Religion, a fucking circle jerk of oppression.

Maz stared at him. Through him.

"Some of us *monsters* have seen beyond time, Alshaytan. Don't forget that." Her eyes narrowed, and she focused back on Aheia. "Besides, it's not real, you know, time. It's a measurement that mortal beings require to keep track of their little, unimportant lives. It doesn't mean much to us, does it? And if time doesn't matter, and lives could span forever, how do we know when death has claimed us? Many living beings have been dead longer than the bodies kept in these caves."

"Words that perpetuate hope for the hopeless," Arioch growled, feeling unprecedented anger build and build.

"Or maybe words that singe the ignorant," Mazikeen said with an edge to her voice.

"Watch it," he snarled.

"If you take offense to something I did not attach your name to, maybe you should evaluate why for yourself," Maz said simply before stepping to the side, her flames warming his body.

He cut her a glare but locked down his response. This wouldn't end anywhere amicable, and he didn't have the wherewithal to train his words the way he needed to. He hadn't wanted to fight, but somehow it was all he felt capable of.

"The Mithra have been quiet?" Mazikeen asked, and Arioch was thankful for the change of subject, even if it was only adjacent.

"For ten days," he said, giving Aheia one last look. It had been twenty-three days since her death.

"You think they'll simply stay that way?"

"For the next forty at least," he said, and then he parted with the stone in his hand, laying it on Aheia's chest.

Mazikeen nodded thoughtfully.

"I didn't think about the *pénthrum*," she said slowly as they turned and Arioch's shadows scraped across the floor behind him. "Since Ophion isn't dead." Her eyes flashed and her lip pulled into a dark smirk.

Mithra did everything with a reason behind it, a calculation. After the death—or presumed death—of an Epísmos, they allowed thirteen days for all of those who swore personal fealty to him to exact their attempt at revenge. It was the length they believed Aether took to eat Theia in her entirety. After came the fifty days of *yrenía*. Stillness.

"What will happen next?" Mazikeen asked as they walked towards the mouth of the cave and the staircase just beyond it. His chest felt tighter with each step he took.

"They'll figure out their next move, the next appointed sovereign, grieve if they're so inclined."

"How do Ophion's people swear fealty?" Mazikeen ran her dark fingers through her fiery hair, the thick, glossy dress that was ever present on her body swimming along her curves.

"Blood oaths. It forces their hand like magyck, depending on what they swear."

"Even if he's not dead?"

Arioch met her eyes. "When enough people believe something, it doesn't matter if it's real. The energy that is lent through faith will make it true. That's how that frivolous book the mortals plastered a religion around and follow so blindly holds magyck. It's all just energy exchange."

"Calmani doesn't operate on whims," Maz said, flicking invisible dirt from her skin.

"Our magyck isn't nearly as strong as yours," he said, looking towards the steps that led deeper into Gehenna. "So much of it is belief-driven. Like those little *faerie tales* the mortals have come up with, the kind that would put a fae's life in clapping hands." It would be simpler if their life was truly like the books it inspired. In those stories, Aheia might have awoken with a plea, or a kiss.

“Faeries,” Maz scoffed, a languid eye roll making her look more bored than usual. “If only the mortals knew how many walked amongst them.”

“It would crumble some of those precious beliefs. Maybe one day we’ll enlighten them.” Arioch almost smirked, but the muscles in his face felt heavy.

“Perhaps.” Mazikeen smiled and then looked up at the steps overhead. “The dead have not stirred since.”

Since Aheia had last visited Gehenna alive.

“The cut in the seam has not changed.”

The crack that formed along the desolate ground, the one Arioch had sent his shadows into to find out how deep it went. Unending.

“It seems everything is back to normal.”

An open and closed story.

Chapter 6

Aheia

Aheia gasped and retched at the reminder of the moth in her throat. She clawed at her neck in horrified shock, until she realized that what she felt stretching her esophagus wasn't real, and she had no trouble breathing. She sealed her lips shut tight, her stomach squeezing at the phantom reminder of what it felt like to have the creature's thick body and velvety wings inside of her and her stomach shuddered. But eventually her fingers relaxed and with the waning of panic, an odd amnesic calm washed across her. It was akin to walking for miles but forgetting the landscape as it passed by. It was thinking so much her brain hurt, but not being able to recollect a single thought. It was seasons changing with ease, even though hours felt arduous and the days never ceased.

The muscles inside of her seized and released, while her eyes met nothing but unending darkness above her and it was that odd stillness over her head that made her realize that her own shivers were the only movement inside of her body.

Her heart had stopped beating.

The pain she'd felt just moments before, the knives that had rained down on her in a different world entirely, had abdicated. But now she wished for them back, because what took its place was a numb beast, the kind that demanded so much more penance than pain did. Because the word numb itself was a fallacy. It was never that. It was heavy. It was suffocating. It was a vacuum. And she found herself within it here as her fingers sifted through granules beneath her.

When she looked to her left, she saw the large expanse of a black lake stretching as far as the eye could see, its glassy surface placid like an eerie mirror. Except there was nothing to reflect but the empty sky above her. No stars, no moon, no color. The only thing in this world was the thin stretch of sand Aheia was lying on and the water that seemed to border it on either side.

The sand wasn't cold or warm. It wasn't coarse or soft. It just was. She didn't question her place or how she'd gotten here. In fact, for the first time ever, she felt like she'd never meant to be anywhere more. And the lack of color in the landscape was ok because Aheia was glistening. She was colorful.

She'd pulled all the stars from the sky and collected them as dewdrops on her skin; the brightness refracting from her into the void above. She was bleeding it, watching her essence melt into the sand, melt into the sky, vibrating like an alive thing. As alive as something heartless could be.

There was no ice in her veins now, no darkness there either.

But it seemed she wasn't the only disruption in the expanse of this impossible dream of hers. She pushed herself up, going rigid as she was faced with the same moth from her memory.

A different dream.

A different lifetime, it felt like.

The same moth.

It just stared, and the faceless female's words echoed in her mind, the words she'd spoken to the moth before she brought it close.

Blessed day, sacred night. We thank you for the life around us, for our survival.

Aheia reached her glistening hand towards it then.

"Why are you important?" she whispered into the unnatural silence, soft echoes bouncing all around them. "You've taken me places," she said, inching her starlike fingers forward. "Where are you guiding me?"

And just as she was about to touch the little insect, it turned from her and flew towards the lake. Aheia watched it glide over the water, a perfect reflection against the liquid that made her question which one was real. Then, when it was far enough from shore that Aheia couldn't see the little gold details of its wings, it turned to look at her, like it was expecting her to follow.

Aheia exhaled slowly.

Even the deadly things don't last.

Permanence doesn't exist in dreams.

You have no heart.

So, she followed the moth, letting the tepid water eat her feet as she walked over smooth rocks, the colors in her skin reflecting underneath the surface. Little waves rippled from her and ruined that perfect mirror as she waded further. She had almost reached the moth when it moved again, this time dipping below the surface, and shooting past her into the water.

Ok.

She looked overhead once more at the black nothingness vortexing above her, and resigned herself, letting the water encase her as she dove in after the insect.

She kicked her feet, straining to keep her eyes open and on the moth, while venturing deeper into the dark blue abyss.

The stillness was loud against her eardrums, now that not even her heartbeat or the rushing of blood kept her company. Her strokes through the water felt arduous, and the white flicker hard to follow in the murkiness, even as she glowed. The pressure around her body held her just as the sand had, and something within that knowledge was calming. It made her realize that just as her chest had been hollow and her heart had stopped beating, her lungs didn't seem to need air any longer. So, she opened her mouth, letting the water seep between her lips and wash down her throat, as the moth in front of her rounded the top of a large rock that cut up from the landscape.

It was odd, inhaling water like it was oxygen, but maybe starlight didn't need oxygen, or maybe anything could be oxygen in turn. Did the moth need air?

She lit her own way across the coarse boulder and when she crested it, her lips parted in shock. The moth was a small dot in the distance now, and it was swimming toward a town that was swallowed entirely by water. It was so big she couldn't tell where it ended, foggy blue eating the far off edges. She made her way closer, letting her eyes drift over the roads that carved through mismatched buildings. Each one was peeling with a different color, some exteriors adorned with wood, some different types of rock, and others just clean sheets. There were statues and wrought iron lamp posts that rose from the dirt in jagged lines, and willow-like trees whose leaves danced in the soft streams of water. It felt whimsical ... forgotten.

The moth had dove into one of the houses on the outskirts whose exoskeleton was bare. There was no roof, only walls and broken pieces of wood that lay against the sand-brushed stone underneath her. Aheia let herself float closer, noticing a small glint from inside, like a sparkle. She paddled deeper, following the soft glow through a dining room with mismatched chairs and a heavy wood table, through a hallway that held empty ornate picture frames on papered walls and further yet into an open room.

Aheia realized the origin of the light when she saw the gold chandelier floating in front of her, curved metal dripping in refracting diamonds. It hung above pink couches with intricately carved wood backs and arms, that sat around a navy blue, almost shimmer-coated table. The living room was set up to face a haphazardly bricked fireplace and only two walls erected around the entirety of the room. A few empty canvases propped against one of three massive bookcases that were sunk in the ground at uneven angles.

Where am I?

Her fingers drifted across the smooth spines of leather-bound books as she walked the length of the case, letting herself look at the little draping plants that Aheia didn't know the names of hanging across the tops. A soft piece of fabric was secured on one of the shelves and she reached for it, pinching it between her fingers. There was a *'K'* etched onto it in ornate gold thread, the edges of it torn apart.

She grit her teeth, feeling a sharp pain hit her mind just as she touched the delicate embroidery, and a silent groan bubbled from her lips. Lashes of bright lights cut across her mind and she held the fabric tighter.

There's something in the corner of your eye.

Panic built in her gut for the first time since she'd been here.

She stilled, hand dropping the cloth she'd been clinging to, letting it float towards the surface above slowly and her skin pebbled in fear, fear that existed because she still had a mind. Something was looming, something dark and cloudy. And when she shifted to find it, it moved along with her, hiding in that one spot that everyone was scared to look.

The corner of their eye.

It's where the darkness lingered. Just out of sight. Deniable.

Aheia felt something rush past her, moving the liquid near her face and she yelped, swallowing an ungodly amount of water in the process.

Something was with her.

But it wasn't the moth. Whatever this was had to have been at least her size.

And then she saw it.

No longer from the corner of her eye, but right in front of her.

The creature crawled from behind one of the bookcases on gangly limbs. It was pale white, its body translucent enough for Aheia to see the books through its chest as it passed by them. It reminded her of the dead souls she'd seen in Gehenna, except it possessed no features, only long tapered limbs, and a round head. Smooth. Faceless.

"The shadows are lying to you."

Aheia's awareness prickled as she noticed another off in the distance, through the asymmetrical bay window in front of her.

"You don't belong here."

More and more of them drifted from the houses, making their way close with odd, slow movements.

Move!

She started to kick her feet, grabbing onto the floating chandelier and heaving herself up faster, just short of the piece of cloth with the *'K'* stitched onto it that she'd let go.

The flimsy fabric flurried at the disruption she was making, her muscles screaming with the effort it took to swim like this.

But the creatures didn't seem to have the same problem as her, coming out of the deep like a formation that wanted nothing more than to wrap its vine-like limbs around her and pull her under.

She jerked her chin, trying to see how far she was from the surface, and recoiled at what she saw above her.

A body.

A body surrounded by long, white hair. Blue eyes stared back, lips parted, floating like a corpse in an expanse of dark water.

Her body.

Her twin was wearing black, oversized clothing, and the only color on her came from a small crystal that sat against her sternum, an eclipse of moths crawling across it.

Her mother's stone.

She looked below her again, seeing the creatures getting closer. What would happen if they got ahold of her? Her eyes drew back to the body above just as that Aheia opened her mouth.

Too much might kill her. The body's lips mouthed it and she heard it in her mind, said in her voice. *Choose.*

Choose. The word echoed. One simple word, one little syllable.

Chose what?

Aheia felt the familiar indecision when faced with options she didn't know how to pick, but she didn't know what it meant.

Her insides were barren. Not cold. Not constricted. Not anything ...

Her chest was a void.

Her heart still.

Her soul ... *her soul.*

She didn't feel anything. Not until she looked back at her mother's stone. That's when her chest ached, and the familiarity of it held her in its cradle. She needed to touch it, needed to hone that emotion because down here in these waters she was alone. The crystal might make that ok.

She reached out a soft, colorful finger and trailed it down the hard surface of the gem, watching the moths flurry.

The contact sent a heated current up her arm, but she couldn't move, her eyes widening at the sensation that was spreading through her. The twin twitched, and when she did, Aheia felt a pull from just behind her navel. She was ripped forward, colliding with herself in a mind-numbing strike. Her mouth opened to gasp for air, but was forced to swallow water instead. She choked in surprise, the water rushing against her from all sides and slamming into her mercilessly, no longer her ally.

CHAPTER 7

LÚC

Lúc was panting, tears streaming down his face. The anger he'd felt was trickling from his chest and pooling in his stomach, turning into something heavy and hot. He'd pulled the liquor from her bony grasp, but she'd fought and the bottle slipped from his little fingers, shattering on the floor.

"Pick it up," she slurred, the shards of glass cutting into Lúc's skin as he cowered. "Pick it the fuck up."

He whimpered, backing away on his knees, the jaguar in his chest rattling the cage around it. "I'm sorry, I didn't mean to."

Ow. His skin stretched with the effort to contain the beast.

"You made me waste the last of our juice," his mother groaned with such desperation that his insides twisted tight, her red eyes drooping slightly, loose curls falling around her face. "The least you could do is fucking fix your mess,"

He hissed, his knuckles splitting apart with the sharp tips of his claws.

No, no, no, no.

"Don't you dare." His mother hissed, surveying the room as if she was expecting someone to burst in through the wall. "Don't you dare dirty yourself like that."

Lúc winced at the insult. He knew she hated him for what he was, for what his father was, but that didn't keep her from using it to her advantage—to use him and his strength to feed her needless addiction.

He couldn't help the shift his jaguar tried to force when his little chest was so full of fear and anxiety, tonight's impending fight looming. The wolf he'd be facing was twenty, near twice his age and had an advantage in size as well. Just the thought made the cuts from the panther Lúc faced last night burn all across his still recovering body.

"*Maman,* I'm sorry, I didn't mean to," he squeaked, his claws scratching the wood underneath.

"No!" His mother fell to her knees into the puddle of dark brown liquid, her eyes wild. "Stop. Doing that. Just stop." Her words were running into each other as she shuffled towards him on all fours, the smell of her sweat imprinting itself in his nose. The blue flower print on her dress turned brown as it sloshed through the wetness, and dark black blood swirled into the mixture as the glass cracked under her palms.

She didn't notice.

She never noticed.

And Lúc knew she wouldn't remember any of it tomorrow.

But he would remember.

He'd never forget.

"Look at what you did, worthless *dreske.*" She was crying now, bending down towards the splintered wood floor. The ridges of her spine were pronounced under the stretched material of her dress because where she could have spent the money he made for them on food, she'd spent it on liquor.

An investment. She'd called it.

"Please don't," he whispered, his eyes flickering with the jaguar's presence as he watched her tip her head and lap at the dark liquid. More of an animal than him, even though she was just a Leviathan.

"I have to do this because of you," she mewled.

Lúc crawled back, his fingers pulsing around bloody claws, leaving his mother hunched over, lips pressed to the dirty floor, hands bleeding with new cuts.

Panic surged in his veins as he fought the urge to wretch. He'd never touch liquor. He'd never touch drugs. He promised himself that. Never.

It ruined her.

It ruined him.

"You know why you're here, right?" Lúc asked, playing with the cherries in the shot glass that the *Siren* had brought over with his drink.

Dáinn looked like a little doe, wide-eyed, with a streak of fear in those brown irises. He opened his mouth and closed it, looking from Lúc to Tariq, who was sitting across the couch with one of his latest pets, Nyra. The music was loud, the Solas rotating through dark colors with the sound as it caressed the dancing Nephilim at the center of the room only a thin curtain away.

"You've been preaching those radical ideals of yours all while scamming poor families out of *eyrid* with promises of salvation," Lúc said, as the demon leaning casually against the edge of their booth took a step forward. With his arms crossed and that skull mask covering his mouth, Illion looked every inch the enforcer he was.

Lúc leaned closer, baring his teeth. "What could a gutter rat like you offer, in ways of salvation anyway?"

Dáinn looked over his shoulder hurriedly like he was searching for a way out, but Lúc kicked up his boot, keeping him in his spot. The Fae gripped the edge of the table, his breath shortening.

"No, I—" He fumbled as Lúc stood. "I was just—"

Yea, alright.

Lúc picked a cherry from the glass and pried Dáinn's lips open with it. The juice stained him red as he forced the sweet fruit inside before plucking up two more and repeating the treatment. "You know what they say about Fae that open their mouths when they should just fucking keep them shut,"

Dáinn bit down on them with almost no hesitation, mouth full of their flesh as he shook his head like it wasn't a fucking rhetorical question. "What's the old saying, Tariq?" Lúc mused, as the male's gaze shot to the horned Leviathan who offered nothing but cold amusement in way of help.

"They lose their tongues," Tariq answered from his spot on the couch and Dáinn choked on the cherries, gripping onto his chest as he coughed.

"That's right," Lúc purred slowly, licking the juice off his fingers before leaning into his victim's ear. "If you ever feel the need to revive your old business practices, you make sure to remember how full of my cherries your mouth was—how you almost choked on them. Then take notes and keep those pretty lips shut."

He trailed his hands up the outside of Dáinn's thighs, and when he looked down at him, his body was shaking, pupils so big, the brown was almost eaten entirely.

"You understand?" he asked.

"Y-yes," Dáinn gasped, finally managing to swallow the cherries. "I'm s-sorry,"

"I'm sure you are. Fear famously brings out truth in others, doesn't it?" Lúc let a manic grin split his lips, sliding his hand onto the Fae's neck. "You know me, Dáinn, you know what I like—what I like to do to our enemies. Consider this the nicest warning I've ever given." Then his eyes caught Tariq's, and he felt the heat ignite at the base of his spine under the attention. "Next time I'll break out my knives and see how talkative you are when I take your favorite body parts from you,"

The male trembled, nodding feverishly.

"Tell Arioch I'll take it from here," Illion said gruffly, gripping the back of the Nephilim's shirt and tugging him to the side.

"W-wait," Dáinn stammered. "I thought this was a warning,"

"It is. You're still alive, aren't you?"

Dáinn's eyes widened. They were pleading—at least the dumb fuck was smart enough to know his life would be pain going forward. The demons Illion employed—a loose term for a position they couldn't willingly accept nor leave—picked up the shit jobs, the painful jobs, the jobs no one else wanted. Illion would brand Dáinn as one of his, in service of the *Rau*, and it would be his life until Dáinn decided it wasn't liveable anymore.

"I'd rather die," he said hoarsely.

"You still have that option. Now, get the fuck out of here," Lúc said coldly, nodding his thanks to Illion, who clamped a heavy hand on the Fae's shoulder and ushered him away. They disappeared into the crowd and Lúc sat back down against the leather couch, picking up his drink and shooting it back. His skin was itching with anticipation, his jaguar purring and squirming, rattling the cage bars inside of him. It felt like being fucking edged in the worst way—*talking* instead of cutting. He grit his teeth, letting the liquor burn, eyes returning to his company.

Nyra was leaning into Tariq, sliding her hand up his thigh seductively, while Lúc spread his own a little wider, resting the back of his neck against the leather couch behind him. He propped up his boot again and slid another cherry between his teeth.

Tariq hadn't stopped watching him and that didn't change when Nyra tried desperately to capture his attention. This wasn't about her, it was never about anyone else.

Silly thing.

A silver glint captured Lúc's attention, and he followed it to the collar clasped tightly around the Fae's neck—a collar Tariq had slipped around her throat last time they played.

"Does your *zyra* know who gave this to you?" Tariq asked, sliding two fingers into the little space between the leather and her skin provided as Nyra's breath hitched.

Lúc's cock thickened in his leathers, seeing the way Tariq was affecting her, seeing how desperate she was. She'd do fucking anything for them, and that was a dangerous game.

"No," she said with a slight waver in her voice.

Tariq slid his tongue across his canines, finally looking at her. "Do you wear it around him?" His voice was hard, those black eyes of his a dark, desolate wasteland.

"Yes," she breathed, trying to close the space between them.

Lúc raised an eyebrow.

Fucking fae. *Little liars.* All of them. But it was amusing seeing her try.

Tariq's eyes snapped to hers, and his fingers closed around her slender neck. Lúc wet his bottom lip, feeling his breathing shallow, and the blood pumping through him fast. He liked watching. He liked it most in public. But it was Tariq's intensity that got him so Gods damned hard.

"Don't fucking lie to me," Tariq growled against her mouth, his nose twitching.

"You think her zyra suspects she rides more than that sleek *caravan* out front when he's not around?" Lúc sucked his piercing between his teeth, watching her eyes move to him cautiously, as her little tits heaved.

"Well?" Tariq's tongue grazed across her bottom lip, and Nyra shuddered visibly, her shoulders caving slightly.

"N-no, he doesn't know," she confessed, blushing a sinful shade of red.

Tariq's eyes grew darker, and Lúc's awareness sharpened when they did. "Or maybe he does, maybe he's happy to have someone take you off his hands ... Maybe he'd rather bury his dick elsewhere."

Nyra gasped, shock imprinted on her face, like she didn't know if Tariq was telling the truth, and hoped he wasn't.

Self-righteous thing—fucking other people without her other half knowing, and acting hurt at the idea of him doing the same.

Tariq only tightened his grip and repeated his question. "Do you wear my pretty collar around him?"

She tried to free herself again, but when he wouldn't let up, she crumbled. "No."

"Then I'm not interested," he deadpanned, his expression cold as he let go of her collar. She stumbled back, falling against the far side of the couch, her skirt riding just high enough for Lúc to catch a glimpse of her pretty red silk and thigh garters.

"Aw, she got all dressed up for you," he cooed, as she snatched her bag.

"Fuck you," she hissed, clawing at the collar while she tried to squeeze around the table. But Lúc moved his boot to keep her from leaving.

"W-what are you doing?" She fumbled her words, her eyes shining with lust.

He leaned forward, wrapping his hand against the outside of her leg. "You wanted to be our whore, *begged* for it even if I remember right. On your knees and everything." He smirked. "Don't act like we're doing anything you don't want us to when"—he slid his fingers across her soft skin and up between her thighs, cupping her pussy—"it gets you so fucking wet."

"No, that's not w—" Her chin tipped and a soft moan tumbled from her lips.

"Not what you want?" Lúc removed his hand, yanking her down onto his lap instead. She mewled, pressing her chest against his, her nipples hard behind the flimsy fabric of her shirt. He squeezed the swell of her ass and ground his cock against her cunt, feeling the heat of her lies against his laces.

"Not what you want, hmm?" he rasped, breath hot and sticky. "Tell me."

"I don't want it," she squeaked, her hips rolling against him, chasing her pleasure.

Lúc's gaze shifted to Tariq, who pulled out one of his inhalants and lit it, dragging the drug into his lungs slowly. It felt so fucking good to hold his attention when nothing else did.

The two of them liked pleasure just as much as they liked pain. It didn't matter who or what gave it to them and there was no jealousy lost between them. That wasn't what this was. This was what it looked like for them to be a constant while everyone else changed around them.

His demon looked fucking sinful—black curls hanging down around his horns and into his eyes, his shirt tight across his corded muscles. They flexed when he dropped the inhalant in his drink and stood, making Lúc's first heart beat faster, eerily aware of the second dormant organ next to it.

"Leave now or don't. Up to you," he told Nyra sternly, his face all hard lines as he rounded the table and sat next to him.

"Stay. I want to stay," she whispered quickly.

Tariq's lip curled, but it wasn't a happy expression. It was what it looked like when he cornered his prey. "Then take out his cock and ride him."

"Be nice," Lúc drawled, watching Nyra's eyes dart around them, completely unsure of herself.

Tariq gripped the nape of Lúc's neck tightly, dragging him close, while Nyra squirmed. "I don't give a shit about her—why would I be nice." He said it loud enough for her to hear, and she winced, her fingers shaking against Lúc's abdomen. "Just another body that helps me fuck you in more imaginative combinations." His black eyes sparkled.

Asshole. But Lúc's heart fluttered anyway.

"Here?" Nyra hissed timidly. "I know somewhere we can go—"

"No." Tariq's gaze shot to hers. "Here or you leave."

Nyra looked behind her again, at the crowds of people that populated the dance floor just beyond their booth, a thin film of a curtain the only separation between them and the other demons. They'd see. Easily. And that shit made Lúc's dick ache harder. That and Nyra's hesitation. He loved how uncomfortable this was for her— lived to push others; to see what would bend them, what would break them, and what they would risk for just a little bit of pleasure.

Nyra wanted to risk everything.

She pulled at his laces, the action hurried and sloppy, like now that she'd made up her mind, she couldn't wait another moment. Her hands crept below the leather, her warm skin sliding against Lúc's cock, and his nerves lit up. He groaned, holding Tariq's eyes as she got onto her knees, shifting her focus to the crowd one more time before wrenching up her skirt and leaning forward against Lúc's chest so she could slide herself onto the head of his cock. He hissed, his hand kneading her ass as she rocked her hips back slowly, swallowing his length one inch at a time with no fucking preamble.

"How does she feel?" Tariq asked, the low timber of his voice making Lúc's jaguar run its claws down his insides.

"So fucking tight," he growled, as she moaned, her hands digging into his shoulders for support.

"Don't stop until he comes," Tariq directed harshly, waiting for Nyra to nod, her eyes already glazed and unfocused. And when she started to ride his lap, grinding Lúc's cock so deep inside of her that he could fucking feel resistance, Tariq shifted his focus. "And you"—His breath made Lúc's skin break out in gooseflesh—"Don't you fucking dare come."

Lúc's lungs failed him as Nyra coaxed out his pleasure and Tariq stole it, holding it in his fist tightly.

No. Fuck.

Sick amusement lit Tariq's eyes, like he was daring Lúc to say something.

Try me. It passed between them silently.

"Oh *Gods,*" Nyra panted, her wet cunt already starting to pulse as she ground her clit down against Lúc abdomen.

"Don't fucking do this to me," he pushed between his teeth, sweat pearling at his hairline as his muscles flexed and the pleasure sparked down his spine.

"Shit, *shit,*" Nyra cried, her hips jerking against him faster and faster until she tipped over the edge, her nails leaving marks underneath the fabric of his shirt. She'd been so ready for him that it took no time at all for her to come. The degradation and the idea of being shared between them had gotten her little body close before he even touched her. It had gone down the same way last time they met up.

Her orgasm gripped him tight, her walls milking his cock like she wanted to suck out his come as she collapsed on top of him. Lúc respired air, gripping her waist, thankful for the reprieve. Until Tariq spoke again.

"I didn't tell you to stop. I told you to make him come,"

She made a pathetic little noise, looking up at Lúc with pleading eyes before she adjusted, and exhaled slowly, gathering her strength. Nyra started moving again, still on the high from her release, and it was fucking torture.

Lúc bared his teeth, watching Tariq slip his fingers between them, massaging Nyra's clit roughly.

"Oh fuck," she shook her head. "I need a moment."

"Do you?" Tariq asked, keeping his hand in place, working her harder.

"It's too much," she stuttered, her hips bucking wildly.

"That's not for you to decide."

She whimpered and turned desperate eyes to Lúc. "Please come for me. I can't—"

"Shit," he groaned, feeling her tease his orgasm closer as Tariq lifted his fingers, glistening with her arousal. *Too much.* She had no fucking idea.

"Does she taste as good as she looks, *Lúci*?" he asked, dipping them into Lúc's mouth.

Gods fucking damn it ... *Lúci* ... That fucking nickname.

He sucked off Nyra's juices, fighting the way Tariq's little term of endearment tugged at his heart. *Lúci* would be the death of him, and Tariq would smile while his life ran through his fingers.

"Good boy," Tariq growled, and the praise slithered through him, his pleasure hitting like lightning. His hand shot to Nyra's hips, trying to slow her down, but she did the opposite. Her eyes shifted to Tariq, picking up her pace, her arousal dripping messily against the base of his cock.

"F—" Lúc's fingers flexed on her skin as he tried to work himself back from his orgasm.

"Hands on the couch," Tariq commanded, gripping Lúc's chin. "Now."

His muscles were twitching, but he did what he was told, white-knuckling the fabric.

"You want to come?" he asked as Lúc's hips jerked.

"Y— fuck." He lost his train of thought when Nyra's second orgasm crested and she cried out, falling forward, her back bowing. Her body spasmed around his cock and Lúc let out a shuttering groan, his hips jerking when she didn't stop.

Fucking mercy.

"You better not," Tariq warned, almost softly.

Lúc's vision flickered, purple streaks bleeding into the colors around them, and he could feel the animal inside of him pacing

It got worse when he met the crowds eyes past the curtain—so many fucking eyes, all of them watching.

"I can't— I can't hold on much longer," his voice was hoarse as his cock leaked inside of Nyra.

"What did I say? No. Fucking. Coming," Tariq said in his ear, pulling one of his chest-holstered knives free and sliding it against Lúc's trachea.

"No, don't please," he begged, because the blade got him close, the blade made his balls tighten, the blade forced him to let go even when he tried to deny himself.

And Tariq knew that.

Good for breeding and not much else.

Those words forced their way into his mind just like Tariq forced the blade and it wrenched the control from him. He let go of the couch, and gripped Nyra's hips, fucking her so hard she stopped moving and braced instead. The knife cut into his throat when he pushed closer, his teeth bared, his jaguar roaring inside of his chest. "There's my vicious boy," Tariq said, dragging his teeth across the shell of Lúc's ear.

"Make her stop," Lúc gasped against the heat of split skin.

"Lúci, this is my favorite part," Tariq hummed against his temple. "Seeing you sweat and whimper, seeing just how hard you try for me." It was fucking derogatory. "Why the fuck would I stop her?" He spit the last words, gripping the couch just behind Lúc's head, growling filthy fucking things into his ear.

"Fuck, please don't do that," Lúc ground out, hot blood trickling down his neck, eyes glued to Tariq's. "You'll make me—"

"*Dirty dreske,*" Tariq hissed, and the insult knocked his pleasure through him like a caravan in the street.

You don't have a choice.

"Fuck," he gasped, gripping Nyra's ass and hauling her off of him, his cock pumping hot come across his shirt and against her legs. The wetness soaked into his clothing, his vision flickering with the aftershocks of his orgasm.

Fuck me. So much for the fucking shirt.

"Good," Tariq said to Nyra, stroking down her wild hair as she looked up at him with tired eyes. Her lips were parted, spit dripping from the corner of her mouth. "Now, leave."

"What?" she stammered, blinking away the haze.

Tariq didn't repeat himself.

"When can I see you again?" she whispered, shame lacing her question.

"If we want to see you again, we know where to find you," he said, hard eyes drifting over her face one last time before returning to Lúc.

She swallowed, lifting herself off of Lúc's lap with a wince. His come strung between their bodies as she gathered herself on shaky legs, pulling her skirt into place. The Shifter watched, but he didn't dare say anything when the Fae wobbled through the curtain and left them alone in the booth.

"You're having a hard time following directions today." Tariq wrenched Lúc's chin back only to thumb apart his lips and spit in his mouth. "Did I give you permission to come?"

Lúc shook his head, the warm saliva sliding to the back of his throat, keeping his mouth open for the Leviathan as he drew out his tongue as far as it would go.

"Next time, I'll make you take my cock while she fucks you," Tariq rasped, dragging his own tongue across Lúc's from the tip all the way to the root inside of his mouth. "Then we'll see how well you'll listen."

Lúc whimpered; he couldn't help it. His breathing was still shallow and uneven as he watched Tariq unlace himself and fist his cock, pulling it from his leathers. The black rune tattoos that Lúc knew printed the top of his thighs poked out just behind his laces and bled onto his length, turning into geometric shapes that decorated his demon from base to tip. The Shifter had drawn the pattern himself, inking the tall, horned Nephilim above him with his needles. The memory alone made his tired dick twitch in his leathers.

Gods.

He was so fucking perfect.

"Go on, make it up to me," Tariq growled, pumping his hand slowly.

Lúc glared at him in defiance, his jaguar raging inside his chest as he slid to his knees in front of him, and replaced Tariq's hand with his own.

"Tap my thigh if you can't take it," he said, his face devoid of any amusement as Lúc flicked his tongue across the head of his cock. The salty precome replaced Nyra's taste and Lúc moaned, sucking Tariq into his mouth. He couldn't breathe, and his mind stuttered. It was exactly what he fucking needed.

He kept his eyes on the demon above him, because he knew he'd get reprimanded if he didn't. He hollowed his cheeks and watched with elation as Tariq tipped his chin, the veins in his neck popping.

"You want me to use you, Lúci?"

Lúc nodded eagerly. *Fuck yes.*

Tariq's eyes sparked, and he moved his hand into Lúc's hair, shoving him down hard. The Shifter gagged, his tongue pushing against his bottom lip as he worked his hands to stroke the part of Tariq's cock he couldn't reach.

"Fuck." Tariq's hold tensed in his hair, while his free hand brushed down the column of his throat. "I can feel my cock in your fucking throat, Lúci."

Holy fucking Gods.

"I want you sore and bruised tomorrow. Fuck, I want to hear it in your voice when you speak."

Lúc flexed his legs, muscles straining to keep himself in place under the violent thrusts.

"You're going to remember this every time you open that slutty fucking mouth, aren't you?" He groaned, bucking harder. "How you got on your knees for me in front of all of those demons who are watching us now, and let me use you."

Lúc couldn't do anything but hold on, his eyes dripping in tears, his heart pounding in his ears as the Leviathan took his pleasure.

"Keep it open, Lúci, relax your jaw," Tariq coaxed, his hold so tight that Lúc felt strands of hair come loose. He moaned, looking up with eager eyes as his lungs screamed for the oxygen he was being denied. Tariq's cock thickened and pulse on his tongue and Lúc held on to his leathers for dear fucking life as he slammed into him hard until his release splattered down the back of his throat.

The Shifter sucked down every bit of Tariq's come, his nostrils flaring when he finally managed a ragged inhale.

"Don't swallow," the Leviathan grunted, pulling his length free slowly before leaning over Lúc, and sliding two fingers across his lips, a dark smile on his face.

"I'm going to head out first," Tariq said, taking his sweet fucking time to lace up his pants, all the while watching Lúc sit there with come in his mouth. "Don't swallow till I leave."

Lúc's skin prickled with awareness, but he kept his features calm, letting himself smirk slightly. Tariq stood, forcing Lúc to shuffle back and leaned down to bite the Shifter's jaw before he headed towards the door.

When he was out of sight, Lúc got up from the floor, his knees aching as he swallowed Tariq's release, and tried as best he could to fix his appearance. His leathers were full of Nyra and him, the laces soaked, and his shirt didn't look any fucking better.

Fuck's sake.

Knowing Tariq, he'd make Lúc wear this the rest of the day. Heat bloomed at the back of his neck at the thought.

What a fucking mess.

His hands were sticky, but he ran them through his hair anyway, trying to breathe through the energy coursing in his blood. His jaguar was fighting, and the need to shift was stretching his skin. Tonight had taken the edge off, but every time he managed to dull the creature inside of him, it just came back stronger once the haze wore off.

He rolled his shoulders, trying to find some sort of relief, but the tightness wouldn't let him lean into it. He tipped his chin and scrubbed his face when something caught his attention. He saw it in the corner of his eye—a flicker. It had come from the Solas orb above him.

"What the fuck?" Lúc tilted his head, keeping his gaze on the small light source as it pulsed and frayed, losing its brightness.

He wrenched apart the curtain and saw the same was happening in the other room.

"Lúc!"

His attention snapped over to the backdoor, where Shiron stood with Tariq. He shouldered his way through the crowd toward them.

"What's going on?" he asked, the orbs flaring again.

"Shykoya sighting," Shiron said, his eyes drawing down Lúc's appearance.

"What?" Lúc's brows furrowed.

Those leathery fucks hadn't crawled from the Sephy Forest in months.

"They plowed through Keosha, a Gods damned hoard. There's a caravan outside. Come on."

Arioch

The *Siada* in charge of Keosha, Kamaria, had sent word early in the morning about the outlier town torn apart by the Shykoya—monsters that had plagued his realm for near a decade. Their bodies were getting stacked at the outer border of the town, long limbs outfitted with black tipped claws on both their feet and hands. They had no eyes, but in place their mouths spanned almost the entirety of their faces. Weathered skin stretched across bones, each one thinner and more dilapidated than the next, but regardless of how frail they seemed, they were deadly and strong. White venom seeped from the pile of dead monsters, the kind they carried both in their teeth and talons. If bitten or scratched, it would enter the bloodstream and burn the afflicted from the inside out. It was near unstoppable and even when the Heretics managed to halt it in its tracks, the affected areas never ceased their burning.

The broken shards of the protective border that had been put in place ten years ago to keep Aljira safe against the Shykoya glowed faintly in front of him. It was ripped at the seams, but the light remained, fading in the weak parts, the parts that the Shykoya had shredded with their claws. The partitional magyck was laced with the very poison they carried in their bodies, repelling them like oil to water. But the magyck had weakened over the years, and the monsters had found a way in.

Arioch hadn't considered them a true problem, not when the border held steady and their sightings were sparse. The Sephy Forest housed a myriad of deadly creatures and it wasn't his place to murder a species that could be easily wrangled to one part of their world. But that didn't make *this* any less fucking horrifying.

The streets ran with black blood now, dead bodies littering the trash-filled alleyways as he walked back toward the broken border from the town square.

Nephilim he couldn't help were bent over their loved ones, trying to revive their poisoned corpses—lifeless bodies spiderwebbed by raised, white veins that still carried the

Shykoya's death sentence. They'd need to be collected and burned, too, to avoid contamination.

Shiron and Tariq were wiping the cobblestone of body parts, helping collect the monsters that the Falkri had been able to kill before they reached the outskirts of the forest in their mindless retreat.

The Heretics that worked with him at the compound were trying to help, but most everyone who had been bitten or clawed—infected with the thick, milky venom—had died quickly and that was a mercy. Because the ones that the healers had been able to save were screaming in pain until their throats bled. Those Nephilim had one foot in Gehenna and begged to have their lives taken instead of saved because the pain was unbearable and didn't wean off.

Large pyres had been created at the edge of the town, so they could break down the gray bodies with fire. Aylee was in charge of overseeing those.

Arioch passed the flames, stepping toward the trees, the darkness of the forest in front of him swirling and beckoning him closer. It was like a compulsion—staring down the dingy cracks between the branches, a void collecting against his eardrums until the crackling and the crying behind him melted away.

It was soft at first, a languid stroke against his spine, a brush of feathers over his skin. He thought he'd imagined it—the pull.

But then his body jerked, his shadows flaring under his skin. His magyck was reaching, pulling him away from the chaos behind him, away from his dying people, away from the crumbling town, and deep into the underbrush. It took over his fucking mind.

It tried to control him.

His muscles were aching from how tight he twisted them, but it was no fucking use. The shadows shot from him like tentacles, pulling him through the trees like a rag doll. He gripped at the bark, at the ground, raking his fingernails across blades of grass, trying to regain his control, to no avail.

He fell prey to the magyck until he saw what his shadows did, felt what they felt, and when he did, he ran with them instead of fighting them.

Chapter 8

Aheia

The water wanted to kill Aheia.

It wanted to consume and fill her.

Waves knocked into her head as she tumbled in circles, her lungs suddenly screaming again. They strained when she gulped down what little oxygen she could above the surface before being pulled into the depths again, her eyes stinging with the violence of the water.

The current swept her under, and it felt like the liquid was sentient, holding her in its palm, drowning Aheia its sole aim.

She pried her lids apart, seeing blurry dots of light above her. They looked like stars, and they were the only way she could orient herself in this mess of turquoise. She kicked hard, doing her best to trail the bubbles she created. But every time she got close, her fingers grazing the surface, she was yanked back under.

When her lungs fought back, and forced her lips apart in desperation for air, water poured down her throat instead. This time it felt nothing like oxygen.

Blackness started creeping in around the corners of her vision and her legs failed, as she stared overhead, seeing distorted shapes looming close.

This is it. This is how I die.

The darkness moved in quickly, reaching for her like those luminescent creatures had, and Aheia let herself go still.

But what she had taken for an obstruction in her eyesight suddenly grabbed a very real hold of her, yanking her upward so fast, that the water rushing past almost felt like a solid. The pressure around her arm ached, and her limb felt like it was going to pop out of its socket as she crested the surface.

"Tei, *aysah elyah*!" an unfamiliar voice sounded on her right and shortly after, she felt another set of hands hoisting her from the cold grips of the waves.

She coughed and spluttered at the dirt digging into her knees as she collapsed onto wet earth. A riverbank.

"Fuck. Water," Aheia choked out, trying desperately to blink the film from her eyes.

The air stretching her battered lungs, and it felt like she hadn't inhaled in years, the action new and unlearned as the taste of peppermint stung her nostrils. Her eyes burned, but she forced them open anyway, taking in her surroundings.

The sky above her was blue and purple with bright stars, their light bleeding through dark leaves around her like the sun might. The trees were tall and the thick old bark looked almost black in the glow of the moon. There were smatterings of lichen growing on the surface, turquoise, green, and shades of purple. Flowers sprouted sporadically on the small branches full of misshapen leaves. Droopy flora cascaded from them like some of the white willows she remembered from Keloseros.

Yet another landscape.

Her heart sank, and her lip quivered as sadness poured into her chest. She was so tired. She didn't want to do this anymore.

"*Yah*!"

She startled at the voice, and her movements froze when she met the brown eyes of a tall male with dark skin. *Eyes.* He had eyes. Not only that, he had a face, and hair, and she could even see the little gold studs in his ears.

A face.

"What?" she choked out.

"*Aljah—*" He shook his head. "And that's why we get briefed about not swimming in the river."

What the fuck is going on?

"Might have helped if you'd used your left hand instead of keeping it balled up the way you did." The male scoffed, stare flickering to her fist.

Aheia looked down bewildered and he was right. She hadn't paid attention to how tight she was clutching it until now. Her fingers shook as she peeled them back, looking down at the stone that was tucked into her palm—her mother's gem. She stared at it, mesmerized, drawing her wet legs up tight. Every part of her ached, muscles she didn't know she had, screaming at the smallest of movements.

"What's your name?" the brunette asked.

"Aheia," she said quietly, not a thought of lying about it in her mind.

"I'm Tei," he said gruffly, and then nodded to her other side. "They go by Nyco."

Her head swiveled to her right and she all but jumped, seeing a second person crouching near her, their gold-flecked hazel eyes watching Aheia carefully. Their hair was a mess of dark brown and white curls, strands bleeding down against their brow. Deep brown hues married patches of pale skin on their face, their neck and their arms, in a delicate pattern.

"And what are you doing this far south?" Nyco asked, cocking their head.

"I-I went for a walk in the forest." She shrugged, unsure of where 'this far south' was but becoming increasingly aware that she was wet, and alone, and without a weapon.

They let their gaze fall down her body, eyebrows shooting up. "You were walking, barefoot, in oversized leathers, covered in blood through a forest that most are taught to avoid? Interesting choice."

Aheia looked at herself for the first time since she'd come to. Her arms were smeared with crusted blood, the black fabric of a large shirt clinging to her.

"And then you what—decided you'd jump in the river?" Tei sounded annoyed.

"I clearly needed to wash up," she said, keeping her voice measured but sharp. "It got away from me."

Tei scoffed, "That, the *Asara*"—he pointed behind her—"looked like a good idea?"

She shot a look over her shoulder, seeing the violent waves ripping past the landscape.

It looked anything but inviting.

"Fucking *strangelings*." Tei rolled his eyes. "Nyco, we'll get our asses chewed if we don't get back. Your theory is bullshit. Come on."

"Simmer," Nyco drawled lazily, reaching for Aheia. She flinched, feeling their fingers on her chin.

"You look pale," they murmured, turning her head back and forth like they were inspecting her. "Do I know you from somewhere?"

"No."

Their eyes narrowed and she let herself truly look at them for a moment. Their thick, cotton wrappings draped across black leather pants and were tucked into heavy boots. They also wore multiple necklaces, and one long earring dangled from their right ear, which held a myriad of stones and ended with a gold crescent moon.

"What are you doing this far south, if you're taught to steer clear?" She used the information they'd given her, even though she didn't know what any of it meant, or why there was anything wrong with this part of the forest.

"I'm not like most." They grinned, a flash of white teeth. The smile reached their charcoal-rimmed eyes, and the gold flecks in the hazel glowed around their dark pupil.

"Get on with it," Tei harped, making a dramatic show of waving his arms in a nondescript direction towards the forest.

"Go," Nyco snapped. "Get out of here if you're going to be a problem."

"You know you really—" Tei started, but before he could finish, a flutter of wings dove right in front of his face. "That fucking bird." He was flustered, taking a step back as Aheia watched a large, white owl land on Nyco's shoulder. It had starlike eyes, slick white feathers tipped in a dark navy, and small flecks of blue splattered across its wings in a random pattern.

She reared back at its size.

"Noctua, be nice to the little warrior," Nyco cooed, running their knuckles against the side of the Strigiform's face. She leaned into them, snapping her beak twice just as Tei opened his mouth, his face screwed up in anger. Before he could get out another word, though, he stopped, his eyes narrowing. His ears twitched, and he turned slowly, training his attention to the forest behind him. Aheia felt Nyco shift from their spot on the ground, following Tei's gaze.

"Ah shit," Tei growled. "Get up, *Aleah*, get behind us."

"What?" she asked.

"*Shhh*." Nyco held up their hand, and the underbrush prickled around them as the air shifted. It was silent. Troublingly silent.

Then suddenly, out of the dead air, a loud scream rocked them, the owl on Nyco's shoulder bristling her feathers and snapping her beak in response.

"What the *fuck* was that?" Aheia hissed, pressing her palms against her ears, the impossibly shrill notes still rattling through her.

"Something that scared an animal that doesn't scare easily," Nyco said, leaning into Noctua just as she pushed off their shoulder and took flight.

"What?"

"I told you." They flashed their gaze to Tei. "I told you those Syka were acting out of the ordinary."

"What are Syka?" Aheia asked, trying to understand what was going on.

"Stags," Nyco told her quickly. "Nimble, carnivorous little fucks, we followed them here, right before we found you."

"But—" She couldn't get out her question because Tei held up his hand.

It was silent, but Aheia's heart was beating out of her chest as she watched the darkness shift.

Her heart.

The heart she'd lost.

Her chest wasn't hollow anymore.

Oh my Gods.

Her eyes widened at the realization, her gaze still trained on the grove ahead. The longer she stared, the more little outlines formed, whispers of trees and shapes that magnified as her eyes became dryer. All of the sounds that had disrupted the night before were gone, as if all the animals were holding their breath alongside them.

"We need to go," Tei said, the moonlight shadowing his features menacingly.

"Wait." Nyco held up their hand.

"For what?" Tei hissed, his footing unsteady against the ground, muscles flexing like he was holding back the sprint building inside of him.

Noctua flew up above the treetops as if in answer to Tei's question and scree'd loudly.

"This way," Nyco hissed under their breath, nodding toward the direction of the vicious sound that had rattled them moments before.

"Are you fucking crazy? You'll run us right to our death," Tei growled.

Nyco turned, features hard, but decided. "You're not *listening*."

"Listening?! The Syka ran the other way, we should follow them," Tei threw back, and Aheia watched his feet slide in the dirt, aiming in the opposite direction like he thought he'd surely won the argument.

"You are blind to this forest. The trees know and you're not listening."

"Yea, I don't fucking speak tree," Tei growled.

Something familiar scratched at Aheia's mind. Something that felt a lot like déjà vu.

"And you do?" She asked. "Understand?"

"*She* does." Nyco nodded toward Noctua.

Tei's eyes lingered for a split second too long, that conviction Aheia had seen shifting.

"Fucking *fine*. Come on," he barked in frustration.

And at that, all four of them took off into the forest, the stars following them in a splattered pattern where their light broke through the trees. Thick, dark roots slithered across their path, and even darker vines hung in their way. The further they ran, the more their path was obstructed, and it felt like they were disrupting something old and untouched. Even the air smelled different here, heavy and thick. It was mossy and deep, curled with fog that blew around their bodies in wisps. It became difficult to see, and Aheia focused on Nyco, on the white in their hair, and the occasional squawks from somewhere atop the tree line.

Her lungs burned, the wetness clinging to her cold skin, and she held onto her small stone with a tight grip because she had the overwhelming sense that it was all she had left. With each lout from Noctua, Nyco calibrated their path.

She's guiding them.

Aheia's side stitched, and her fingers curled into her waist, each step becoming clumsier than the last. Her lungs were wringing so tight they refused to use the air they were given. Too full, yet suffocating. And just as the dark spots started to form in front of her eyes, the three of them broke into a clearing. Aheia stumbled, spilling from the webbed vines that tore at her limbs, and fell forward into short, green grass.

"Fuck," she hissed, the gem she'd been clutching rolling across the dirt. She scrambled toward it and scooped it up as a hand hoisted her up by her bicep. Nyco pulled on her arm in a sour sting, urging her forward across the clearing and Aheia fell over herself trying to keep up. She had been so focused on the ground and not hitting it a second time that she hadn't noticed where she was being dragged. Not until she heard another squawk, and Nyco tugged her to the left, did she finally look up.

Her jaw dropped.

An atrium.

It stood tall and imposing, tucked against the far side of the clearing. Overgrown paths cobbled with old rock led toward it, every inch of the structure covered in nature. Green flora hung down the tall cut glass walls, and a raised texture dusted the windows—the kind Aheia imagined she could collect on the tips of her fingers if she dragged them through.

Where am I?

Noctua dove by them once more before flitting up toward the tallest of three domes atop the atrium, where another two owls circulated amongst the stars.

"*Come on*!" Tei shouted, already waiting at the entrance.

Aheia picked up her pace, and Nyco helped keep her steady as they made it to the path that led inside. They let go of her, pushing her past the broken doors as Tei shucked the heavy, unhinged pane of glass back into place. Nyco assisted, while Aheia's eyes darted across the space in front of her. It looked forgotten.

Dark, creeping plants climbed up the inside just as they did on the outside. It was desolate and quiet and it smelled of stagnant water and the perfume of flowers that had grown on the backs of dead animals.

There were beehive-patterned holes cut into the top of the domes, and nests were suspended down at different lengths from above. Branches and straw hung from the small platforms, and when Aheia squinted, she could see more of them.

Owls.

The small dirt path she was on was bordered by stones, and led her to a small fountain that was situated in the middle of the room. The fatigue was setting in, and she was so thirsty, her throat dry, as she crouched down and dipped her finger in the filmy water. It was cold and stale, lily pads sprouting across the surface and sparse reeds bordering it.

The reflection in the water rippled, as she watched the mirror image of the owls above.

"Where am I?" she murmured out loud, walking past the fountain and looking at her reflection. Her skin looked almost gray ... dead.

What an odd dream.

She stepped forward, touching the cold glass just underneath the mirror image of her eyes, fighting the urge to look away because all she ever saw in herself was her mother. Andromeda stared back, and every time she did, Aheia felt herself crack a little further. The cold in her veins slithered and pebbled the flesh down her arms as she fixated on the blue so intently that the rest of the world blurred. She could pretend it really was her mother then, just for a few moments. Because her fair features melted into the background and were slowly replaced by Andromeda's thick black hair and her sharp cheekbones.

What do I do?

Her eyes burned with the effort not to blink because if she blinked, this would be over. If she blinked, she may well wake up somewhere new, and she didn't know if she could bear it. Not again.

Tears trailed down her cheeks, the image of her mother flickering in front of her as she tried her best to hold on.

But her best was rarely good enough, and eventually, her eyelids pressed shut against the dry sting. She rubbed the back of her hand over them, massaging in the pain for a moment before peeling them back to look at herself in the glass pane one more time.

Except when she met her reflection, it wasn't her anymore.

Chapter 9

Aheia

A choked gasp worked itself from her throat, and her feet slipped against the ground when she met the gray, eyeless face of a monster. It was gangly with leathery skin stretching across thin limbs, white slimy globs dripped off of long, pointed teeth. Talons swung out and hit the glass, making it vibrate so hard that some of the thick, green residue tumbled to the floor. Aheia squeezed Andromeda's crystal in her hand, hearing the slight crack run through the glass—the only thing separating her from this beast.

"Get back!" Nyco yelled as her eyes widened, watching the creature abrade the iron where the glass panes met. It scurried across the atrium wall like gravity was only a suggestion, and Aheia followed it with her gaze as another shriek sounded, louder this time, the burst of energy knocking her back against the cobblestone. Her arm flew to her head, narrowly saving her from the impact as shattered glass rained down on her, shards of it slicing open her skin. Owls were flurrying around, wings brushing against her cheek, her shoulders, and her back, like they were urging Aheia to get off the ground, flying around the dome of the atrium, undercutting each other in a mess of feathers and cries. She looked around, finding several of the animals lying on the ground, blood matting their feathers, some of them still twitching.

The patchwork ceiling above splintered as dark bodies crawled along the outside of the building.

Click, click, click.

The nauseating sound of claws against glass.

Click, clack, snarl.

"What are they?" Aheia choked, scrambling towards Nyco and Tei.

"Shykoya." Nyco swiped one of their knives from its holster. "On your guard." They threw out their arm, pushing her back, while the three of them watched the cragged hole, teeming with bodies. She saw the monsters breach the barrier, screeching as they cut themselves on the jagged, broken parts of the ceiling, leaving black, oozing blood behind. The first creature impaled itself, but the others followed closely, scurrying over its back and climbing down the walls.

Aheia watched in horror, her throat constricted as the Shykoya made their way inside, dripping down into the room like a viscous liquid, smooth and effortless. Their movements were quick, and when they landed on the floor, they hurled themselves in the direction they were facing, the first few smashing into the glass walls, like they didn't know where they were going.

Nyco jostled Aheia, holding up their knife, fingers clenching the blade. "Don't let them touch you," they said, eyes blazing.

Aheia squeezed her gem and took the dagger by the hilt, grasping it so tightly her knuckles turned a lighter shade of white.

"What happens if they touch you?"

"Their claws are poisonous." They pulled another knife from their back.

"But their skin is thin—aim for the heart or the head," Tei said, right before he took off toward the Shykoya closest, latching himself onto its back and slicing a blade across its gray throat.

Another came straight for Aheia, its limbs flailing. She jumped out of its way, brandishing Nyco's dagger clumsily as they took on two of the monsters at the same time. She was uncoordinated, and her slashes were haphazard, but she managed to impale one of the knives in a Shykoya's shoulder nonetheless.

"Behind you!" Tei yelled and Aheia whirled around, narrowly escaping another monster. It ran past her and smashed into the wall with such force that its skin split and the Shykoya's blood splattered across her face. She tasted it on her tongue. It was rotten and acidic.

Tei ran up to her, just in time to vault into another straggler, its defeated cry stinging Aheia's eardrum.

The shockwave propelled her back and her body flew against the glass wall with a heavy thud, her skull cracking against it. Every part of her felt like a pulse point—like she was her heart, and it was exposed to the cold air around her. Her fingers were shaking, blood dripping from between them, and when she opened her clenched fist, her eyes found the gemstone. A crack ran down its center, a crack that had cut into her palm, dark, pulpy blood coating its craggy edges.

Her chest caved.

This thing, however insignificant to anyone else, was the only thing she recognized here. It felt familiar when everything else felt borrowed. It was as if the crack that splintered it ran through her at the same time—hot and cold and pure agony. Her breath came in short bursts as panic twisted around her throat, and she choked on the air that didn't stretch her lungs right. The pain of it fractured her like a tangible thing and she cried out, her fingers digging into her own ribs for relief.

She could barely prop herself up, and saw Nyco in the distance, grappling with two monsters. They were fighting like their dagger was an extension of themself, fluid and concise, but the monsters were quick, and they were strong. A scream tore her attention away.

"*No*," she managed, still supporting her side, as she watched thick, black claws sink into Tei's chest across the atrium. He fought back, but another Shykoya descended on top of him before he could kill it and muffling his cries.

White feathers dashed past her, and blood exploded onto her face. But Aheia didn't have time to focus as another monster hurtled forward and she was forced to crawl to the side, dodging the black claws of another, while a third clamped its teeth an inch from her throat. A gurgled noise left her mouth as pain shot through her, talons tearing at her arm. Her fingers flexed, and she dropped her stone when long teeth dug into her wrist, blood welling and pooling hot against her flesh. A searing pain fissured through her, as she fell forward a wheezing, gurgling noise spilling past her lips.

She met Tei's dead eyes as the caustic white venom ate into her cells. *No.* She sobbed, willing the useless hand that still held a dagger into movement.

Please, please, please. She begged, managing to snatch up the knife with her other hand just as the monster bit into her harder. She croaked out a gravelly noise, whipping the weapon back with as much force as she could muster, before sinking it into the Shykoya's neck. It yowled in pain, but she didn't let up, pushing until she felt bones crack between the squelching flesh that pushed against her fingers.

Her vision started to fail as more leathery bodies descended on her. She smelled them and had the taste of them on her tongue. The salty desperation of a monster. Her fingernails bunched up the rotting skin in her last efforts to find a way out, but she could barely breathe now.

It felt different than the past times she'd been near death—the times in her other dreams.

This felt final.

She lost her fight, reality slipping quickly, everything pressing in closer, closer, closer. Until suddenly the monsters on top of her went flying, ripped from her in one fell motion. It was an out-of-body experience, watching the nearest one flailing, its white-tipped claws scrambling to meet anything as it flew through the air.

The wind licked at Aheia's wounds, the sky shining above her through broken glass as she tried to move, tipping her chin to the side with the last of the effort she possessed.

She blinked her heavy lids, trying to clear the shadows that were drawing across her eyes, seeing blurred floor and white feathers in her line of sight. Fire was consuming her, spreading through her bloodstream quickly, and it was that, she told herself, that made her see the impossible, delusional things playing out in front of her.

Because they couldn't be here.

This wasn't real.

She choked on a breath, tears running down her face as she watched Lúc race across the atrium with his knives drawn.

The Shifter launched himself onto the back of a Shykoya that was toying with Nyco, just as two large, dark wings stroked into view, covering what was happening behind them. Emryn dropped to her knees at Aheia's side, cracking the leather-skinned skulls of two monsters that were grappling to push upright off of each other. Her wings were sleek in the moonlight and sharp, and one of them held the impaled head of a Shykoya.

Lúc and Emryn.

But it wasn't just them.

No, please.

Her chest stuttered when she saw him and something inside of her broke a little further. This was cruel, this was too much. Because she could see his face now too—his unruly black curls as he fought, the shadows that moved across his skin like they were just as alive as him, the gray, steel-hulled eyes with bright embers buried between the threads. And she realized then the shadows in her vision weren't there because she was fading. They were his.

She whimpered, watching Arioch tearing through the remaining creatures. His magyck caged two of the monsters, swallowing them in darkness as he gripped the torso of another with his bare hands and pulled it apart.

He was lethal.

Aheia's body convulsed against the cold stone, and Emryn's hands pushed her back down as the gashes etched across her bubbled with venom. She sobbed, feeling the foam gather on her tongue, the glacial cold spreading through her blood.

"Ar—" She gasped it out, barely audible.

But he heard.

His eyes landed on her and the world seemed to cease its rotation. He made his way through the blood and gore, those eyes focused, and tired, his shadows stuttering off his back and she knew ... She knew this wasn't real. It couldn't be. But for a moment, she pretended this was it—this was true, and she was dying here on this cold floor. Because death felt welcome, it felt like a friendly embrace when the alternative was waking up in yet another place, falling through yet another sky, a lake, a world.

So, she pretended like she was greeting an old friend, and held that feeling close.

The warm sorrow ate her up and her mind shut down, lullabied into delusion by rushed words and dull shuffling noises around her. Everything became muffled and she could see his lips moving, but it was just noise as she was pulled to the edge of consciousness. She teetered there, watching a moth landing on Arioch's shoulder, its big, beady eyes staring at her while the darkness wrapped around her so tightly, that there was no way for any light to break through.

Chapter 10

Arioch

Arioch held the wound at Aheia's neck while his magyck compressed the gashes on the rest of her body.

Not again.

Fuck. Not again.

His shadows bulged, demanding to touch, demanding to fucking *feel* her. They'd been the reason that he found her. It was his magyck that pulled him from Keosha when he felt her echo like a curse in his veins.

You were dead. He hadn't fucking accidentally missed a heartbeat.

Dead. Cold. Lying in Gehenna.

She'd been gone.

His fingers went numb and his shirt was cold, soaked in her blood as Emryn worked magyck across Aheia's form. The Shykoya's stench—the decay and rot—clogged his nose. It smelled like he was standing amongst the dead in Gehenna, and it gripped his stomach tightly when it mingled with her fragrance, the unmistakable notes of *achlys.*

His impossible creature, still, cold, corpse-like.

Bleeding and broken.

But he felt it alive now—her heart.

"I don't understand." Emryn was packing Aheia's wounds, disbelief in her brown eyes. "She's not—" Her eyes darted across Aheia's body. "The poison isn't affecting her like the others. She should be dead."

"She should be dead regardless of the Shykoya," Lúc said, dropping onto the ground, helping Emryn re-pack the sites she'd filled with gauze.

She should be dead.

She'd been dead.

Her body. Her soul.

Every bit of her.

But Emryn was right, the poison wasn't affecting her like the victims they'd seen in the past. Those cuts the Shykoya inflicted should have infected quickly and carried the poison to her heart. She should have white veins tattooed on her skin where her blood vessels were located, but none of that was happening. Instead, the venom leached from her like a pen held against wet paper, like it was escaping her. The white was stark against her blood and it looked like her hair, like her realm, and it reminded him of that moment on the frozen ground. The first time she'd left him.

He'd kneeled like this for her then, too.

Not fucking again.

His fingers shook as he compressed her with his magyck while Emryn pulled at the edges of her torn skin and ripped the connective tissue over her muscle to force crushed blue flowers underneath. They used the same ones to stop the spread of the venom in Kamaria's territory that night, and the few attacks that had preceded this sudden fucking madness. They were infused with Dark magyck, and red-tipped, only found growing on the underside of bay tree roots, suffocated with soil.

It felt like a fucking dream, but that couldn't be, because those never felt like this—he never *felt* her like he did now. The remnants of whatever bond they'd shared all those weeks ago were jumping at each pump of her heart, pulses of lightning that charged his blood. Each one strummed fate's golden strings, steady against the pads of his fingers.

Fucking impossible. A word that was losing meaning with every moment he knelt with her. It was almost foreign to him by the time he noticed the blue lápis laying behind Emryn's left wing. The crystal was broken down the center, nestled in the overgrown cracks of the cobblestone.

"This will strangle the poison, but it's thin magyck. I don't have what I need to heal wounds like this." The Syraphem wrung her hands of excess blood, splattering the cold floor.

"The healing wax in Keosha will help." Arioch's attention was drawn to the warrior across the room. Nyco. He recognized their multi-colored hair. They were crouching over a dead body. "Their salts are the best in the realm." They didn't look up, fingers drawing a black-stoned bracelet from the dead Falkri on the floor.

Emryn nodded, pulling over the bag that held her tinctures, the leather pushing aside one of the dead owls while the others flurried and cried. The sorrow was loud on the wind, dark vines curling on the breeze where the atrium glass had been shattered. And he could taste it. Death. He saw it in the wings all around him, like it was watching.

The next two days were spent evacuating the crumbling parts of Keosha so that they could start their rebuild. Two days of his people spread thin between salting the earth and leading *brujals* with the families of the deceased. Two days of Aheia encased in a thin layer of wax that was closing the gashes on her body. She was safe at the heart of the territory, under Kamaria's watchful eye, but that didn't change the fact that Arioch felt like he was strung over a bow as he sat in one of the circular, underground rooms in the council house. The ceiling was made of packed dirt, and the air smelled like rain and flowers. Soft blue hues traveled through the fog around them in tight wisps, the light provided here by little turquoise pools of water that refracted the stars through tunnels that led to the outside.

Arioch leaned back in his leather chair, between Lúc and Aylee, letting his Nephilim speak for him because he had to focus on keeping his thoughts where they belonged when all his shadows let him focus on was Aheia.

He saw now how foolish he'd been with his worry for her echo when she was dead. An echo would have been bearable compared to this—this deafening fucking hum that was stuck in his head.

It plagued him, bouncing off the walls and making such a fucking racket that he couldn't sleep. It was the stroke of a tuning fork and not even when he held her soul had it been so loud. But at least when he had her essence in his body, he'd been the one controlling things. Whatever was happening between them now ... it was not in his hands.

The connection didn't make sense. It might have, if he'd known her longer, because the whole point of taking souls in the first place was to assimilate them into magyck. It took *weeks,* not fucking days. But that didn't change the thought in his mind—that a part of her had been merged with his shadows. She wasn't just in his head; she was in his bloodstream, in the darkness of his veins.

Dangerous.

Salamander, the black snake coiled around Aylee's neck, hissed, while Embyr, the white one, squirmed around in a soft circle in front of her, its pink tongue jutting out and tickling Arioch's forearm. He looked over at the Nephilim, her short blonde hair tipped dark red, matching her lips and nails, while her blue eyes watched him carefully. Aylee shared the color of her eyes with the lápis that was safely tucked in Arioch's palm.

He'd found no insight in Kamaria's books about it. Nothing helpful, anyway. He could read about the chemical makeup of the crystal until his eyes burned, about how common it was, how it was found in all three realms and held virtually no significance.

Insignificant. Except for the fact that it had appeared with her—his little mystery. His headache.

He scratched his fingernails across his scalp.

Both of them should be in Gehenna. But instead, she was submerged in wax and soil in the infirmary. She was healing when others afflicted by the same poison didn't heal, begged for death instead. Not Aheia.

That's why he'd asked Emryn to collect some of her blood. If she wasn't affected by the poison, there was a slight chance that the Syraphem could try to make an antidote. It was a long shot, but fuck if his life hadn't been a fucking series of them one after another.

"Why did this happen?" Hani asked, their eyes fixed on Emryn. They had been discussing the border, and its failure for the better part of an hour now, the room devolving quickly. The Siada were all talking over each other, and the air in the unventilated space became thick with breath and panic. "*How* did this happen?"

Arioch's eyes flicked to Emryn, whose expression was trained, but he saw the twitch in her wings, the small tick that she'd never quite unlearned. It bared her frustration to no one but him. Him and Kar.

The empath who sat across from him raised her eyebrows in his direction, like she was checking in with him. She twirled her now teal-colored hair around her fingertips, green eyes piercing as he dipped his chin, and ran his fingers across the seam of his lips. "It has been a decade since the border was first crafted. It's expected to weaken if the Heretics who wove it are afflicted," Emryn continued.

One of the original weavers had fallen ill, sat on death's door biding their time. Emryn thought it was the reason for the border's failing—why the Shykoya had been able to break through the weak points.

"Partitional magyck takes a piece of the practicing Heretic." Impatience strained her voice. "No matter what moral compass it serves. Nature isn't meant to be split off and when we force it, it takes a piece from us in turn."

"Those ... *things* aren't natural," Hashem spit through gritted teeth and Emryn's wings twitched again. Arioch avoided forcing her into situations with her father when he could, but tonight was unavoidable.

"By definition they are. They live in the forest, most likely created by 'Amm just like the rest of us. It's not a stretch—ancient magyck has been sleeping in the underbrush for longer than any of us have been alive. There could be hundreds of different creatures we've yet to meet out between those trees."

A murmur peppered the thirteen Siada.

Arioch caught Emryn's eye. She was right. As far as he was concerned, the Nephilim were simply the ones who held the realm now. If something more dangerous, something with bigger teeth, decided it was time to rid the land of them, there was only so much to be done. Nature, just like fate, couldn't be fought once she made up her mind. But he didn't need that idea spreading any more panic.

"We'll restring the parts of the border that show signs of weakness," she continued, "It will take a few weeks—"

"*Weeks*?" Hashem asked.

Emryn cleared her throat. *Twitch*. "It's complicated magyck."

Kar rolled her shoulders.

"Maybe someone more experienced should be in charge of it then."

Arioch flexed his hand under the table, and cleared his throat, leaning back in his chair. The room's attention redirected toward him, and the commotion that had been bouncing off the walls ceased. Even the blue wisps in the air seemed to stop moving.

"Are you questioning my orders?" he asked Hashem.

The Syraphem's eyes were sharp, and his tick mirrored his daughter's.

Emryn didn't need protecting. Arioch wouldn't defend her. He'd defend himself instead, and take the brunt of the accusation in his insinuation.

"I am allowed to question choices that are made when they affect my realm, am I not?" Hashem tipped his chin.

"Territory."

"What?"

"Your *territory*. *My* realm." Arioch brushed his fingers across the tabletop, Embyr slithering between them. "And to answer your question. Yes. But do it in a productive manner next time. Heckling a timeline won't change how long it takes." He readjusted. "It does, however, affect the time you're wasting in this meeting." That kind of bullshit could have been summed up in a letter after the fact—one that Arioch could have burned in his fireplace. "If you have an idea on how to aid the process, I am more than happy to listen, but if your insight is simply 'get better Heretics', then I don't see the point."

Hashem clicked his tongue, but Arioch didn't give the air time to settle.

"Kamaria," he got the Syraphem's attention. "Whatever your city needs." The statement didn't need clarification.

She nodded, her dark skin creased below her eyes in exhaustion. Twenty Nephilim murdered by the Shykoya and ten mercy killings, many of them at Kamaria's hands. It had been a long few days.

"Emryn." He stood, fixing his shirt, the one that was still covered in dried blood. "Finish this." Then he nodded at Lúc, who had gotten out of his chair when he did. "She'll be able to handle any other concerns you might have." He let his stare linger on Hashem before heading toward the door with the Shifter.

“Still trying to big dick his way through.” Lúc grinned as they entered an identical room across the hall.

“Doesn’t work when you don’t have the equipment.”

Tariq was sitting in front of Nyco, whose eyes were red and glassy. They stood in silence, and an owl whose name Arioch couldn’t be bothered with perched on their shoulder.

They watched as him and Lúc walked in, and their shoulders straightened slightly.

Nyco had helped with the brujal arrangements for Tei, handling his sister and his rites. They’d only just gotten back to Keosha after spending the last few days with the grieving Falkri.

“Repeat what you just said,” Tariq snapped, crossing his arms.

“I was—” Nyco swallowed. “I was explaining what happened.”

“He knows,” Tariq said coldly as Arioch passed him, clapping him on the shoulder. Nyco had debriefed them the day Aheia came back—just the important parts, but they hadn’t had a chance to go over the details.

“Right.” The owl squawked, like she was arguing, but Nyco ran their fingers over her beak. “Well, the Syka were acting strange.”

Arioch raised his eyebrows, sitting next to Tariq who pinched the bridge of his nose in frustration.

“Fuck's sake. What they're *saying* is that"—the Leviathan looked back to Arioch—"They left the other Falkri because a few glorified bucks wandered onto the outskirts of Keosha.”

“Yes,” Nyco said quickly and without prompting, eyes snagging on Lúc, who was leaning against the wall nonchalantly. A pink tinge worked its way across their neck, their eyes stuttering back toward Arioch. "They don't venture towards the city—ever. Not if they can help it. Sure, occasionally one wanders off, but never a whole herd. Their migration keeps to the northern part of the Sephy Forest near *Álfheimr*," they continued, as if that alone would explain everything.

Tariq looked ready to jump out of his seat, his fists balled like all he wanted was to bash them into the Nephilim's throat. But Arioch shook his head, discreetly enough for no one else to catch it. The horned Leviathan's jaw ticked and his stare blistered as it returned to Nyco, who was doing a good enough job at holding their ground. It was the little ticks at the side of their neck, the occasional shake of their fingers, that gave away their nerves.

"Check in with Shiron," Arioch said to Tariq.

"What?" Tariq looked angry on a good day, but right now he looked like fucking death. He didn't like being dismissed, but Arioch didn't have time for this. Didn't want to deal with his interjections.

"He's finishing off the border patrol," he said simply, keeping his arrogant and cold exterior in place.

"Anything else?" Tariq asked in a low growl.

"No."

Fine.

It floated between them without the word being spoken and Tariq stood, rolling his shoulders. The muscles in his arms rippled as he stretched and took his sweet time adjusting before finally heading for the door. When he passed Nyco, the Nephilim shrugged to the side slightly, avoiding his tall frame. Their eyes darted after him, and the owl ruffled her feathers like she was offended just as well.

Once Tariq had left, Lúc sat in the now empty chair, pouring himself a drink.

"Ok," Arioch drawled slowly, leaning forward and resting his elbows on his thighs. "Then what?"

"They pulled towards the river—the Syka. They seemed so disoriented," Nyco said, and their voice sounded steadier then. "It's when I saw *her* in the Asara. She was barely breaking the surface of the river."

Her. Arioch's shadows stirred.

"I jumped in after her, and Tei helped me pull her out." Their eyebrows drew together and their voice faltered slightly at the demon's mention. "For a moment I thought she was a *Banshee*, all pale and white—but her eyes were pleading, not vengeful. She seemed so lost, just holding onto her little blue gem, turning it over and over again. It was like she didn't really care about any of it—about the drenched clothes, about the fact that the night was freezing—none of it," they continued.

The crystal in Arioch's pocket became heavier at its mention, and he fought the urge to reach for it. *How the fuck did she end up in the Asara River*?

"Then all hel broke loose, and we heard the screaming—the same screaming from Keosha. We ran, but Aheia was having a hard time keeping up, and it was clear that we weren't going to get away with her in tow so we hid instead." Nyco said, eyes moving to the Shifter again.

Lúc was pushing on his lip ring with his tongue, paying more attention to his drink than the Nephilim in front of him, and Arioch inhaled slowly, snapping his fingers to draw back their attention.

Fuck's sake.

"And—" He started, but as he did, the door to the room burst open.

"Alshaytan." One of the blue-robed healers popped in their head looking flustered. "Your—The Mithra—she's awake."

Chapter 11

Aheia

I can't breathe.

Her lips were rigid—covered.

Her eyes couldn't open either.

The only air she managed came from her nose, and it wasn't accommodating the amount she needed now that her blood was moving too quickly. The rushing of it was the only sound in her ears. *A vacuum.* She couldn't see. Couldn't hear.

Is this death?

The air was heavy with spice, and when it was all she could focus on, it made gooseflesh break out across the back of her neck. Claustrophobia was making her heart beat out of her chest as she twitched, trying her hardest to push against the sheet covering her. There was a slight give somewhere on top when she moved her knee, and she groaned, the noise muffled as flashes of crashing waves filled the black expanse behind her eyelids. The trepidation struck through her in a hot line. *Water.* She jerked again, with all the strength she could muster, and this time she broke free, splitting apart whatever was clinging to her body. Her lips wrenched open, and she gulped down the fragrant air, feeling her chest expand almost uncomfortably. Her body sank, and hard, pebbled ground pressed on her hips as she threw out her hands, trying to get her bearings. Dirt bit into the underside of her nails and she froze, her breathing loud and scratchy.

You're not drowning.

The placid liquid around her wasn't volatile; it wasn't trying to drown her now.

She brought her hands down, her palms cracking against the surface tension. She tasted it. Water and *salt.* Not just that, though. There were small shards of a malleable, white substance that floated on top and looked like wax.

She rubbed over her eyes, bright little shapes blooming under her lids. It looked like when she had white blood cells caught over her retinas on a sunny day and it made her feel nauseous, as if someone had stuck a fork in her brain and scrambled hard. The film didn't lift much when she blinked, seeing the darkness around her broken up by soft blue light. They crested and poured from somewhere above her.

Still.

Everything around her was still.

She was alone again.

Another dream. It had to be.

Her white hair hugged her, wayward strands pulling against her scalp as she got to her feet on wobbly knees, holding on to the edge of what she realized was a large tub dug into soil. Strength dripped from her like the water rolling off her skin and she buckled slightly, supporting herself on the bank with weak arms. Vision returned slowly and when she squinted, she was able to make out five more holes identical to hers on either side of her. Except those were still covered by white—and she imagined hers had looked the same before she broke it. Some were smooth, but some had faces and limbs imprinted in the surface, like the wax blanketed them completely save for the small nose holes she spied.

What the fuck? Aheia didn't know if they were alive. She didn't know if *she* was alive.

It smells like dianthus. But it didn't look like Keloseros. *There is earth under your fingers.* She told herself. *What do you hear?* She focused on the small streaks of light flowing down from the domed ceiling above. *Nothing.* It was silent save for her own breathing, for the small laps of water she created when her knees shifted. *What do you see?*

Smooth glass bumped into her exploring hands and her eyes snapped down, her heart leaping before she realized it was just a cup. She picked it up from the small stone it stood on, feeling how parched she was and testing its contents before gulping it down.

Plain water, no salt.

It hurt traveling into her chest, like it was trying to soothe an open wound. A muffled groan left her as some of the liquid escaped, but the cold felt good because right then, she wasn't sure that she wasn't made of cracked, burnt wood. Her stomach churned at the invasion, wracking her with dry heaves so strong that her hands lost their hold on the glass. Wet splutters filled the room, bouncing off the dirt walls as a new pain forced its way through her. It started in her stomach, infecting the rest of her like fucking poison.

She sank back into her hole, leaving the cup on the bank, clutching her chest.

Tears welled up in her eyes as she drew up her knees, white pieces of wax sticking against her fingers and her legs. They were thin, thinner than last time she'd paid attention to them, and her knees looked like carved stone with skin stretched over them. Pink lines littered her arms—healed scars. She didn't recognize those either, and it should have elicited more questions. But none of it made sense to begin with.

Her back dug into packed dirt, small roots poking her spine as she let her head tip, noticing the dark plants hanging above her for the first time. They stretched slightly, thin leaves hanging from thinner branches. They almost touched her. Like they were reaching for her.

Her bottom lip trembled as she lifted her hand forward, tears breaking the barrier of her eyes when she touched the soft cleft. Something sank inside of her. She didn't know why. But it felt devastating.

Colorful veins ran through each small leaf, a dull rainbow that almost looked like it glowed—almost looked *alive.*

It has to be a trick of the light. She thought. Plants didn't glow. At least not in her world.

Oily residue built up on her skin, and she brought it back, inspecting her fingers. They were thin too. Bony. She didn't recognize them.

Dreams. Was this just one more?

Her mind stretched, and she tried to remember why she knew without a doubt that she had been in so many before this. Why she knew it was all a dream to begin with. It felt so sure, just as the sun rising in Lyria was sure. But when she tried to sift through the last places she remembered, she came up short. Her past was becoming murkier by the moment.

Her vision faltered, everything starting to blur at the edges. Her thoughts were falling from her grasp so quick she couldn't hold them. *Wings. Blood. Water. Monsters.* That was clear in her head. But when she stepped beyond it ...

The inside of her subconscious was cracked, shards of it cutting into her like glass. Bursts of color. Mountains she'd never seen before. Iridescence. Water and a city layered with it. Or maybe just an ocean. Everything flickered—a dying flame, suffocated by clarity—the lucidity of her present. She tried to dig in her hands, but the harder she clawed, the worse the pain at her temple became and the less she could see. The colors all congealed, a black veil drawing across them, hiding the mess of strings and glass in the back of her mind until she forgot what she was looking for.

Her memory was failing her.

There was more. *There has to be more.*

Why are you fighting me? She grit her teeth in frustration.

What are you looking for?

"*Gefah khatya*"—Her head shot up—"*ya lijah*,"

Bright light flooded her surroundings, and she hissed, clamoring back. *Keloseros. The air smells of dianthus.*

She threw out her hands, but the only thing near her was the glass she'd drank water from. Trembling fingers picked it up before crashing it down against the stone on the bank. It shattered in her hand, and the hard edges burst against her skin. She hissed, the uneven glass cutting her as she wedged the big piece into her bleeding palm. Everything already hurt, this pain didn't feel any worse.

She brandished her weapon, squinting against the light, and seeing two bodies breaking it apart, two males from what she could tell.

They were colorful, just like the plants above her, soft rainbows running through their bloodstreams.

"Where am I?" Aheia croaked, the dryness in her throat throwing her into a coughing fit.

"*Ha takal bisnaha?*" one of them asked the other.

"*Where*?" she growled again, unsure of the language he'd spoken.

"Keosha," the second one said, and she didn't know if that was an answer or yet another word in a language she couldn't understand. The one who'd addressed her stalked closer slowly, and Aheia gripped the glass tighter. She forced herself upright, trying to hold the low ground she stood on.

"Put it down." The male was getting closer still, and the word was thick with a familiar accent. The colorful threads that painted his veins vibrated, a dying heart that was losing its life, the glow fading slowly until it disappeared completely, leaving him looking merely ordinary.

"Stay back." She crawled onto the bank, ready to fend off the stranger, but fear made her actions unreasonable and when he took another step, she threw the glass. *Senseless*. It was swatted out of the way easily and she'd lost her weapon.

"Shit." She looked down at her palm, the blood welling now and her vision pulsed, a soft blackness drawing around her periphery. She blinked hard, trying to strip herself of it, warm panic trickling through her when it didn't evaporate. She gripped her chest, but the erratic way her heart ran didn't lessen. She was frantic, feeling things that didn't make sense, things that weren't hers.

Her lungs heaved with the effort to accommodate the vise that drew tight around her ribs, ribbons of silk wrenching them tighter and tighter until she was barely gasping.

Her throat went dry, her mind clouding as those wisps in front of her became a tangible thing, stroking across her skin. Her lips parted in shock.

Shadows.

Her attention snapped up, a trickle of blood running from her palm and splashing onto the floor. Silence surrounded her like a vacuum when she met those eyes, gray and dark, bright orange flecks that burned bright hidden beneath.

Arioch.

His darkness melted from him, spiderwebbing across the dirt walls as they stood worlds apart for so long that Aheia lost track. It felt like a trance, like if neither of them moved or said anything, this moment would be etched into eternity. But then he spoke and her insides squirmed.

"*Out.*"

It wasn't for her. It was for the others, the ones that now scrambled to find somewhere less dangerous to be.

She swallowed the need to sink to her knees, to cradle her hands at her chest, and to break apart. Not here. Not in front of him. It didn't matter that he was made up by her mind. She couldn't. Her steps faltered as she fumbled backwards, the heel of her foot dipping down into the tub as gravity clawed at her. She yelped, anticipation of hitting the water behind her twisting in her stomach. But before she did, her body was jerked to a stop mid air. Her head lolled back, wet hair heavy as she looked down at herself, seeing his shadows wrapped tightly around her.

They held her middle, her arms, her legs, and the feel of them balmed the discomfort on her skin. She exhaled roughly, sinking back as they set her down carefully, her feet probing the prickly bottom of the pool. Arioch followed his magyck, reabsorbing it with each step and the closer he got, the worse Aheia's chest vibrated. She realized that what she'd mistaken for panic before, wasn't that at all. It was *him.*

Every step that brought him closer sent shivers through her, but she couldn't move as his eyes held her hostage. The walls were closing in fast, the room folding in half as his boots splashed the water of her pool and he joined her in the small space.

He was so steady, so completely clear in front of her. Dark shadow ink curled up the side of his throat, his sharp jaw covered in hair. It was slightly thicker than she remembered, and some of it bled onto the sides of his neck. His black curls were longer, tied back and messy, some of the strands hanging into his eyes—eyes that were currently sending lightning down her spine. Those irises were as sharp as his blades, and when they turned on her, they cut into her just the same way.

Eyes. His eyes.

Seeing his face, the little details in it, made the vise in her chest worsen.

"Are you real?" It sounded like she had cotton on her tongue.

For the first time since waking up, she let herself wonder.

He leaned closer, placing one hand on each side of her. Not touching, but hovering close enough for her to feel his warmth. The proximity cost her, her eyes welling with fresh tears as she was forced to remember what it had been like when he owned her soul. It felt the same now, and it was fucking devastating.

"You tell me, little goddess."

Her breath stuttered from her and her fingers relaxed, an unwanted hiss breaking past her lips when she felt the air against her wound at her palm. Arioch looked down between them, onyx oozing into his gray gaze as he lifted his right hand and reached for hers. She flinched out of the way, but he didn't let her find any more space, fingers swallowing her wrist. His touch *burned* and her lips quivered with the effort not to whimper when he brought the cut up between them, probing its edges softly. Blood welled up and dripped, mingling with the waxy water below.

"I don't know." The inhale on her lips was sharp and shaky, and it was all his air. It made her brain swim. His face inches from hers, and every bit of contact fed the hope that spun inside. He felt so real.

Could it be? She reached out and touched her hand to his chest, feeling his steady heartbeat beneath before trailing her fingers over the blades clasped in leather next, the sharp edges of his knives teasing her skin. It felt like a dare. She could cut herself open right here, right now. And maybe it would take away the irrational fear—fear that if she stopped touching him, stopped holding on, he'd disappear. That he'd fade.

She explored, and he let her.

"Show me. Show me that you're real." She faltered, not attempting to mask how it sounded.

Please.

She begged silently, letting herself touch the hope with the same hand she held on to that echo imprinted on her bones.

Please be real.

But he kept her at a distance, big hands gripping her waist to keep her from getting any closer. It felt like refusal. The breath stilled in her lungs. Was he just another trick of the light?

A sad noise worked itself up her throat, shame flaring behind her cheeks as his exhale ghosted across her lips, almost as unstable as her own now. It smelled like him. So much him.

"Please." It was barely above a whisper.

He cursed under his breath, the pressure between them so heavy it felt like it might snap her.

His fingers tightened, and so did hers.

The connection between them flared hot.

It was being stretched until it couldn't span any further.

And then it broke with a loud *crack*.

Her body shuddered, the sound echoing in her mind, and she thought she saw it in his eyes when they widened.

But he hid it, and this time he didn't give her a cold mask. This time, he kissed her.

His teeth pulled at her lower lip and it felt furious, like he was trying to punish her for something she'd done as his tongue pried her mouth apart. It was a lot like fighting, fighting for air, for the upper hand, for relief. But there wasn't any relief between them now, only aching warmth that kept intensifying.

His kiss made her feel that languid pull, the thing between her ribs that felt impossible, so much stronger. A thrum for every beat of her heart, a connection that shouldn't have existed, and every touch, every swipe of his tongue, every drag of his teeth, made it pulse worse. The sensations had her back bowing—the pleasure running through her in jagged lines. Her thighs spread, because she needed him closer, needed to feel every part of him, needed him to prove it. Prove that he wasn't paper thin like everything else had been.

His weight let her breathe. It compressed her and forced the air from her lungs. *Relief. This* was relief. His teeth razed a trail down the side of her throat, as his hands gripped her thighs and pulled her onto his lap in one fell motion. She squeaked, feeling the delicious friction of his abdomen against her center.

Yes.

She bucked her hips in his lap, grinding herself against his leathers as he yanked up the middle of her shirt, pooling it at her stomach.

Real.

His teeth found their way to the column of her throat and she dropped her head back to give him access because she needed more, she needed fucking *worse*. *Gods*, his tongue felt good, but his teeth felt better. She cried out when he bit her, palming her breasts and tweaking her nipple, her vision flickering in front of her as her clit pulsed and her insides clenched tightly—so empty, so desperate for anything but that emptiness. She felt helpless to the way he grabbed her, the way he ground her down hard against the ridge of his cock. Fuck, she wanted him to burn her insides, wanted him to torch every little remainder of doubt in her mind that questioned her reality.

The laces strung across his leather rubbed her so fucking good that her movements devolved into uncoordinated jerks, toeing the line between pleasure and pain.

Pain. His own personal brand of it. The kind she couldn't imagine, couldn't dream up, because it would never compare to anything else. It was the pain she remembered when he bit her skin, the kind that made her forget her own name as it sank between her legs.

Always pleasure and always pain with him.

She'd bruise savagely under his teeth, and she liked the thought of that.

It felt possessive.

A mark.

More.

She wanted to be eaten alive.

She'd been so lost, but she wasn't lost now.

"Does this feel *real*?" he growled, nipping at her lips, grazing them with his teeth before soothing the sting with his tongue, and all she could manage was a messy nod.

"What happened to me?" she asked, against his mouth, their breathing hot and dizzying.

"What do you remember?" He held her like he thought she'd run, like he wouldn't give her a choice if she decided to.

"You—" She tried to grasp at anything that wasn't blurry, reaching too far in her memory.

This time, it wasn't hard to remember.

She saw his shadows manacling her wrists; she saw herself, the tears dripping down her cheeks, the pleas on her lips as he dragged her across the floor. Heard the death blow he delivered ringing in her ears when she squeaked out the one word she'd thought would change his mind.

Honey.

He'd treated her like she was worthless.

Our game is over.

He'd betrayed her.

And she'd let herself forget the moment he gave her his warmth.

She sucked in a breath, her fingers digging into the side of his neck until he hissed, until she managed to pull back enough to look at those dangerous eyes.

"Your knife in my back," she said, her voice wavering.

His teeth were bared, his breathing just as erratic as hers as she read the truth of it all in his eyes. All those bright images, all those loud memories turned into an ocean inside of her. They were lapping at each side of her, the waves so big she couldn't keep them out. Her chest hurt, it ached, and she felt the sorrow that came with accepting her reality and she withered. Remembering her last hours with Arioch made her feel hopeless and worthless in a way she didn't expect while his words echoed in her ears. He'd laughed when she cried. He'd twisted the knife in her back when she didn't have a weapon to defend herself with.

"Not mine." The words dragged themselves down her spine and her body hummed like he'd whispered naughty things into her ear. The reaction wasn't hers, because hers was angry and volatile, the molten mess that weighed down her stomach in pleasure now eating into her like acid.

"What?" she rasped, pushing back as far as he'd let her, his arms still wrapped around her. *What the fuck does that mean?*

"It wasn't *my* knife in your back." His eyes moved across her face.

"Not literally." She furrowed her brows, trying to control her breath. "It's a figure of speech."

"Usually, but not in this instance." He shifted his weight, dipping his fingers underneath her soaking wet shirt and running the callused tips up her spine.

She jerked in his hold. "Don't touch me." It fell from her before she could decide to say it. She didn't want him to touch her because she couldn't stop from wanting to touch right back even now.

His eyebrows creased but he didn't stop. "Give me your fingers,"

He stroked across her spine as she stared him down, trying her best to summon heat to her gaze. But ice overtook it, and her fingers twitched with compliance. Her hand met his, punching up the wet fabric and when it crept under his callused palm, he guided her across the ridges of her vertebrae. Aheia's eyes widened when she felt it—a scar. It wasn't fresh, and it wasn't tender, but it *was* new.

"Not your knife," she repeated, her chest heaving with a different kind of labor.

"Ophion's," Arioch said.

"That's what happened to me? I was hurt?" It sounded soft, and she supposed it was. Because she was in the dark, while he held a light to her form.

"You were dead, Aheia."

The sound around her pulled into a vacuum, her blood loud in her ears.

What did he just say?

Her eyes cleared, and so did her mind, his words pulling her onto solid ground. The quick shift made her insides turn upside down viciously.

"Oh ... Gods." Vomit forced its way up Aheia's esophagus, the sour contents burning her throat worse than the water had earlier. She managed to move her limbs, as wet splutters broke past her lips and she spit up the liquid she'd ingested, a bitter sting hitting her nostrils.

Arioch's hands gripped her hair, dragging it back from her face, and she didn't have the strength to fight it.

Her stomach squeezed, and an undignified moan left her as she spit over and over again, trying to rid her mouth of the taste of bile. That's all it had been, yellow and watery, and now it was spilled all over the ground, trickling toward one of the other baths.

Shit.

"What the *hel* do you mean with that?" She choked, wiping the back of her hand across her mouth. *You were dead.* "Who *says* that to someone?" *Theia's sake.* Besides, it was impossible. It was *im-possible.*

She'd been ...

Focus.

Keloseros, you remember the church, you remember fighting Ophion. She drew in a slow breath. *You remember ... Kazim.* Arioch's brother. She remembered him on top of her ... his knife.

No.

It was just a wound; he'd hurt her, that's all.

But what if—

She looked down at herself, at her legs, her hands. She was bony. Hollow. She *looked* dead if nothing else.

Weeks without food.

She sucked in another breath, reaching back in her memory again. Black. It was all black. Until it wasn't—until the water invaded her vision, and her body ached with the phantom feel of the riptides. The stars, the *Shykoya.*

How did you get into that river? How did you get out *of Keloseros?*

"It's impossible."

You were dead.

Arioch's hair was longer than she remembered, and so was his beard.

She looked like a ghost.

You were dead.

A lump lodged in her throat as she looked up at him again.

"You asked if I was real. Why did you doubt it?" he asked as she sat there reeling.

She shook her head. "I'm not sure." It was the truth. The longer she kneeled here with him, the more fuzzy everything became. Fuzzy like the colors she'd thought she'd seen in the plant's vines—the other people's bodies. It's why she'd believed it had been a dream—at least that's what she thought. Or maybe she'd had other reasons to believe she was dreaming ... If that was true, she didn't remember them and when she searched, she was met with *nothing*.

"What do you remember?" he asked, in that low voice that made her insides tense harder.

"Not much," she said, sparsely. "I remember Keloseros, and I remember the river I almost drowned in." The two panes of memory were sitting in her mind side to side, separated only by the blink of an eye. "But I don't remember being *dead*. People don't just die and then come back—It's not one of those things that just *doesn't stick."* Whatever adrenaline had been coursing through her was slowly trickling out, and the world was starting to drape itself across her shoulders heavily.

"And what do you know about death?"

Her head swiveled. She'd been so wrapped up in his presence that she didn't notice the Ifrit leaning in the doorway.

Mazikeen.

The embers in her dark hair flared, her onyx dress dripping from her body like a stream. She was a whisper of her real form, the larger than life creature that had flown high above them in Keloseros and Aheia could feel the veneration in her own stare.

"Death is permanent," she breathed.

"You're proof of the opposite," Mazikeen said, her voice low and ribbed.

Aheia couldn't stop staring. "It can't be true."

"Let me show you."

Chapter 12

Aheia

Mazikeen slinked into the room, almost too tall for it. It seemed like a fire hazard amongst all the hanging vines.

"How?" Aheia asked, watching the Ifrit sit in front of them at a safe distance. She was almost three times the size of Aheia, and the height difference was even worse when she still stood in the sunken pool. But the water felt safe when the ground sizzled and cracked under Mazikeen's body.

"My memories," she said, her voice low and vibrating. Arioch and her had the same dark quality. She held out her hand, orange cracks running overtop and down her fingertips. It was a trick of that molten magyck of hers, the way the veins moved, and it reminded Aheia of how Arioch's shadows seemed to squirm on his skin sometimes.

She swallowed thickly, staring at the Djynn's outstretched palm so that she wouldn't look back to the Avarice beside her. Arioch had moved and was sitting against the edge of the tub, spreading his legs and resting his forearms against them. His fingers were inches from her thighs and she'd never been so aware of something in her entire life. It was a fixation she didn't know how to break as the pulse pounded between her legs.

Stop. She implored herself, as the Ifrit rubbed her fingertips together, small sparks filling the air. A low fire ignited and filled her palm, warping the room around it, bright and orange until soft contrast broke into the uniformity. Aheia's lips parted, and she leaned forward, her abdomen pressing into the dirt as she watched in fascination. A scene was playing out in the fire, one she recognized, but it was from an entirely different vantage point.

My memories.

Mazikeen was showing her what had happened through her own eyes. *I didn't know it was possible.*

They were back at the church in Keloseros, and Aheia watched Mithra bodies appear, colored orange but unmistakable compared to the dark dressed Nephilim. They fought, and Mazikeen did too, far above the ground. She saw herself, and she saw Arioch as the glass fractured above and large splinters rained down. She saw them getting onto Koutávi's back and barreling down into a tunnel after Kazim, Kal, and Ophion. Her heart pounded in her chest as the Ifrit's vantage point changed, and with it, the tableau in front of them. It was as if she'd swiped across her memories, and this time Aheia saw herself from far away. Kazim was straddling her back, and she remembered the panic in her chest. The silent screams that played out in the fire were eaten by the crackle of Calmani as the heat scorched the edges of her death. Mazikeen was far away, but she didn't need to be any closer for Aheia to see the dagger that Kazim plunged into her back. Dark blood pooled and Arioch fell to his knees at her side.

Dead.

She held her breath and her shoulders became rigid as she watched her likeness go still.

Mazikeen's memories bled yet again and this time, she was left staring at herself—her body laying on a black stone slab, wearing the same clothes she wore now. Oversized leathers, and a black shirt.

"Where is that?" she asked hoarsely, reaching out her fingers but stilling her movement, realizing that the fire would burn her.

"Gehenna," Arioch said, his voice a low thrum in the near silent room.

Her hand dropped.

Gehenna.

"I—" Aheia stuttered, staring unblinkingly. "How is that possible?"

Mazikeen tilted her head as the smell of burnt dirt drifted up around them, and the ground started to smoke under the Ifrit's embers. "Fate decided it wasn't your time."

"I don't understand—I'm just a Mithra," she fumbled her words. "We don't come back from the dead."

Mazikeen folded her fingers, and the fire extinguished, letting the darkness of the room swallow the orange light.

"And yet, you're here," she said, languidly.

"What about?" Aheia waved her hand through the air, trying to find her words. "What about the river?" Her eyes darted from Mazikeen to Arioch. "If you brought me to Gehenna, how did I end up *there*?"

"We're not meant to understand everything," the Ifrit said, slowly getting off of the floor.

"I'm not asking for everything. I'm asking about *my* life. *My* death." Aheia's hands shook as she pushed herself out of the water.

"It's never been yours. It's always been a gift from the Gods," Mazikeen said.

"I didn't *ask* for it; that doesn't feel like a gift," she grit out, but her anger was misplaced. She wasn't even sure it *was* anger. It was shock.

She'd died. She'd *died.* And yet she stood here.

"Give it back then." Mazikeen's embers flared. "You won't be lucky twice, I imagine."

Aheia stared at her, slack-jawed.

"What *can* you tell me?" She spun back to Arioch, who was still sitting at the edge of the pool while her thoughts skewed wildly.

"I can tell you what happened after you died," he said, resting his tongue at the corner of his mouth, wet curls hanging into his eyes. Aheia swallowed, giving the barest of nods. Anything. She'd take anything that might fill in some of that darkness in her mind.

"We left Keloseros and the Mithra followed us to Lyria."

Awareness prickled the back of Aheia's neck. "And then?"

"They fought and they lost." So vague. Everything was always so fucking vague with him.

The skin on her arms pebbled, and the temperature dropped. "And Ophion? He's dead too?"

Arioch's jaw tensed. "No."

"*What?*" Panic reared inside of her, not at all helping the nausea that hadn't fully subsided. "He's alive?"

Arioch cleared his throat, but it sounded like a growl. "He can't hurt you."

"How could you possibly promise that?" she hissed. But he didn't answer, and the silence stretched between them as realization dawned. She looked to the Ifrit and then back to him in disbelief. “He’s *here*?”

“His leash is tight.”

She fought the urge to climb onto one of the small stone benches and tuck her feet under herself. Because in her mind he was somewhere below her, and he’d know exactly where she was standing. She’d never been quiet enough to escape those ears.

“Why?” she croaked as Mazikeen leaned against the far wall, watching.

“Because he hasn’t answered all of my questions.”

“How long has it been?" she asked, her voice more quiet now, exhaustion tingeing it. "Since I—”

“Just over a month,” he said, finally climbing out of the hole in the ground. She bristled slightly when he diminished the space between them, trying her best to hold her ground as she fought the confliction inside of her. Part of her wanted to flinch away, and part of her wanted to fall into his embrace. One urge felt a lot more her own than the other

He took you back. She scolded herself. *You’re here now because you’re a mystery they can’t solve. Another thing to barter with if they feel like it.*

The clarity of their situations dribbled water across the fire in her belly, and it hissed. She was filling with smoke and having a hard time figuring out how to breathe, especially when he was just inches away now, towering over her, and when the proximity manipulated her intentions.

“You’re awake.”

Aheia jumped, taking a step away from him, hand covering her lips. Shame colored her cheeks, and she cursed the hue, feeling undoubtedly *caught* in her own thoughts.

Emryn strode inside, her critical gaze dropping down Aheia's body. *Fuck*, she must have looked like a Gods damned wreck. Meanwhile, the Syraphem looked perfect, her dark hair braided back across her head, small gold rings decorating the plait, with eyes outlined in a deep emerald green that made her dark irises stand out.

"Em—" Aheia started, but the Syraphem cut her off, addressing Arioch instead.

"She needs rest."

"I'm not tired," Aheia protested.

"Great." Emryn looked unimpressed until her eyes scoured the room and landed on Mazikeen. Her face fixed itself quickly, and she nodded at the Ifrit with respect.

"I know I shouldn't, but I really want to touch those acid leaves, just to see if they'll burn me." Lúc disturbed what little light was streaming in from the entrance in sure strides. His hair was a little longer, half of it pulled back into a bun, wearing the same leathers as Arioch.

"If anyone ever asks me to explain who you are at your core in one sentence, I'll know which one to give them." Kar rolled her eyes, arm linked with Lúc's. The empath's hair was a deep teal now, the ends dipped navy, and she wore a dress that matched.

"Look at you." Kar smiled, biting her bottom lip as Aheia's gaze shifted between all of them. "Life looks good on you."

"Oh, um—" Aheia looked down at herself, flustered, pulling the wet material of her shirt from her body. It felt overwhelming, all of them, all of *this*. And what was more confounding was how casually they treated the situation. Was she the only one who thought all of this was fucking insane?

"Fucking bad timing, I know, but we need you," Lúc jumped in, talking to Arioch. "There were another few Shykoya stragglers in Siraj's territory, and he's demanding your presence." He flipped his knife in his hands, moving his attention to Aheia. "That necrophilia joke didn't age well, did it?" He winked at her.

She huffed out stunned air. *So casual.* Was death not usually permanent here?

"I'll be there." Arioch's reply was clipped.

"Give me your hand." Emryn held out hers to Aheia, who just stared at it. "*Hand.*"

Her brows furrowed, and it took her a moment to realize what the Syraphem meant. When she did, she held out her wounded palm.

"How does it feel to be back?" Kar asked, hanging off Lúc's shoulder as Emryn drifted her fingers over the gash, and dark spirals of magyck sank into it, melding the shallow cut she'd made with her weapon. It tugged in a sick way, but it didn't hurt.

"I don't know yet," she murmured, feeling the static in the air at her words. Their energy was bright and awake and hers was fading fast.

"You remember anything?" Lúc asked, eyes sparkling. "When you were dead, did you see things? I have a standing bet with Shiron about this, but no pressure."

"I don't—" Aheia's lips thinned. *No.*

"You're healing well." The Syraphem pulled down her hand, inspecting some of her other cuts before looking back to the Avarice. "*Aistrah,* Arioch."

Aheia was starting to feel sick again, her gaze diffusing slightly. Her knees weren't all too steady either, and Arioch's warmth didn't help when he stepped closer.

"That's enough, give her some fucking space," he drawled at the others.

It was like being in a room full of armed cats.

"I'll check in on her later. I'm due in Thryn," Emryn said, as if Aheia wasn't there, heading out of the room so quick, it seemed she was thankful for the dismissal.

"Azalam—If I have to be there, you have to be there." Lúc pointed at Arioch, just as Kar shoved his shoulder toward the hallway. But before she could force him out completely, he leaned his chin on the doorjamb and taunted. "She needs *rest*, Arioch."

Her cheeks flared with embarrassment.

"You'll need rest too if you don't get the fuck out of here," Arioch growled.

Lúc smirked and winked before stumbling out of sight. A clatter and a string of curses followed and then Kar, who *told him so* in a sing-songy voice.

The Ifrit was the last to leave, after watching the entire spectacle from her corner of the room. When she did, she left behind a stretch of black earth that decorated the entire span of the wall. Aheia would remember the look she gave her, those deep orange eyes staring into her like Mazikeen was able to see everything she was trying to hide.

"Lúc mentioned the Shykoya?" Aheia cleared her throat, trying to hold on to something that made sense. She remembered the monsters in the forest, and that had been real enough. "You're going to fight them? Is that what's happening?" Formulating the questions felt awkward, but it saved her from the warmth that was still heating her cheeks.

"We'll help with whatever's needed," he said vaguely, shadows dripping from him into a thick portal.

"Wait, you're leaving *now*?" she asked, her eyebrows shooting into her hairline, gaze sliding to his magyck.

"No, you are."

The shadows had swallowed her voice, wrapping around them in a violent rush that shifted and caressed until she couldn't breathe. But they disappeared just as quickly, leaving her standing on steady, gray ground, staring at a smattering of stars.

"Where did you take me?" She twisted around.

"You're in our training compound, back near the inner city." He crossed his arms.

Her lips parted, and her eyebrows pleated. "What? Why?"

"Because your old room is occupied," he said.

"No, why would you bring me—" She swallowed the question as she realized. "You're leaving me."

Arioch didn't respond.

"I *just* got back. You've said three words to me, and you're *leaving*?" It sounded pitiful and not at all how it had in her head.

"My people are dying," he said, his words clipped.

"Then take me with you, don't just—" She crossed her arms, trying to find an angle in this conversation that didn't make her feel like a liability, like a weakness.

"No." He said it before she could finish the thought, nodding across the room, ignoring the statement. "You'll find clothing in there and there's food on the table. Eat. Keep your strength up."

Her lips parted. Was he serious?

"If you need anything, someone will be outside your door." He continued repopulating his magyck.

"Like a warden?" Her teeth ground together.

He chuckled. Fucking *chuckled.* "Like safety."

"We pronounce it differently." She scoffed, looking around at the four uniform beds. "You can't just lock me in a room because my death not being all that permanent is inconvenient for you."

"I'm not, Aheia."

"Don't try to cloak a cage from someone who knows them so fucking well. I know how they feel—what they mean. It's a cage no matter how pretty the bars you put in front of my face are."

His lip twitched, and she wanted to hit him for it, to slap that stupid fucking look right off his face. Was this a *joke* to him?

You're here because death didn't want you.

"There's no lock, and no key, little goddess."

But there are eyes.

She was left staring at the dissipating magyck when he stepped into his shadows, with her mouth hanging wide open.

"What the hel just happened?" She scoffed. *Excuse the fuck out of—* "Who the fuck does he think he is?" She argued with the wall, letting her eyes glide across the room angrily. There were four uniform beds, dresser and desk laden with food. The main door was at the wall adjacent, but there was a second smaller one that she found led into a washroom at the far side. On her way there, she cracked open the wardrobe and peeked inside.

There were a few pieces of clothing hanging on the bar, all of them white and her fucking size. She grimaced at the blatant jab.

Random room.

Separate building.

Dressed in *white.*

It was hard not to take it all personally.

It was hard not to feel like she was starting to climb back into that little box she'd known so well in Keloseros.

Not to mention how he all but ran from her the moment he had an excuse to.

She padded across the stone and into the washroom, almost screaming when she met her reflection in the mirror above the multi-sink vanity.

Gods, she looked dead still. Her eyes were harsh beacons on her pale face, sunken over high and too-pronounced cheekbones. Her throat was a thin column, and she could see the ribs on her chest when she lifted the shirt on her body. There were new wounds, pink stripes that she couldn't place. She imagined it had been the monsters, but she hadn't been in anyone's presence long enough to ask.

Arioch had left. After all of that, he left. If she'd been dead for so long, and if he'd meant what he'd said in Keloseros, why wouldn't he stay with her?

She exhaled roughly, turning on the knobs on the tub in the corner and stripping off her clothing. It felt like a safer bet than the alcove, because in the bath she could sit. And the longer she stayed upright, the more her muscles rebelled.

The water was hot and soothing, and Aheia hissed at the burn when she sat back against the sloped curve of the tub. She barely had time to settle before she noticed the darkness rolling across the water like fog in front of her. She yelped, covering her chest, but the panic that had flared dampened when she saw her.

"Hi," she said softly, watching Koutávi's form fill the room, her shadows pressing in around the wall. The space wasn't huge, but it was a decent size. The Varcolac all but swallowed it. Her exhale was warm on Aheia's face, gold gaze caressing her skin like the life that lit them was tangible.

She remembered how Koutávi had aided her in Keloseros, and her chest tightened slightly. "I'm so glad you're ok," she whispered, but it turned into a choked whimper out of nowhere. Sorrow held her just like the water did and now that Koutávi's stillness wrapped around her, tears brimmed and fell from her eyes unwanted. She covered her mouth to muffle the sound and her shoulders shook, but the large creature didn't leave. Instead, she lay down her snout next to the ledge of the tub, while Aheia lost her handle on those little pieces inside of her and fell apart. She'd let it happen here, with the Varcolac, because no one would know that she was weak. No one could hold this against her.

CHAPTER 13

AHEIA

"Aheia, you need to go!" Kal grasped her face in both hands as her eyes drifted behind him, looking for any sign of Ophion's men.

"Kal, what am I going to do?" She cried, holding onto his wrists.

"You'll live, and you'll never fucking come back here," he said, kissing her cheek. She leaned into his touch, letting herself feel his warmth for a moment before she found those strong, unwavering blue eyes.

"Iaonnis. Did he touch you?"

"No," Aheia said quickly; the thought of that brute putting his hands on her body made her stomach shudder. No, he hadn't touched her. She'd killed him before he could. Her *sýz*. It felt like hours since it happened, but it had been only minutes. Her hands still coated in his blood.

She inhaled slowly, eerily aware of the leaves rustling above her head, and of the bright sunlight streaming down on them.

"Ok," Kal said, relief relaxing his shoulders.

"How will I do this without you?" Aheia asked, her voice failing her when his brows furrowed.

"You're strong. You don't need me," he said, taking her hand and pulling her closer to the Keloseros border. The blood on her fingers stained Kal too now.

Aheia looked up at the tall wall of Brite magyck. It was imposing. She'd never been this close.

"Come with me," she pleaded, curling into his white shirt. "Please—"

"You know I can't," he said, his voice heavy with emotion.

"Why?"

"They'll find us, they'll always find us," he said. "I'll do my best to stall them, but if you don't go now, I won't be able to buy you any time." Kal looked over his shoulder.

Wayward voices drifted through the Callay Forest, shouts and screams, and the barks of Ophion's hunting dogs.

"Don't come back, don't ever come back," he said, crushing her to his chest in a tight hug, his heart pounding against hers and for just a moment she let herself sink into the thought that this may very well be the last time she saw him. It fractured her.

And the cuts only deepened when he pushed her back, those blue eyes of his dark and rimmed red with the effort of holding back tears.

"Thank you," she whispered, grasping the canvas bag hanging off her shoulder.

"Go. Don't forget me,"

"I—"

But he didn't let her finish the thought. His hands were on her waist a moment later, pushing her into the border. It felt like shards of glass were razing across her skin and she watched in horror as thin threads of light poured off of her.

Her veins shrieked as the border pulled and ate, stealing the thing within her.

No, please. This wasn't possible. *Anything but this!*

She screamed and begged anyone who was listening to spare her, to let her keep the last thing she possessed—her light. But nothing answered, and no one helped as the last of the magyck drained from her in a searing flash of hot agony. She screamed, falling onto her hands and knees, dragging herself through the liquid-like substance until she broke through the other side, sobbing, and clenching her chest at the loss.

"What more can you take?!" she cried at the blue sky, clamping her teeth as an animalistic sound broke free from her. Anger at her life, anger at Ophion, anger at the Gods for all the liberties they still took from their world even now that they were gone, fueled her.

She woke up in a cold sweat, bright stars peppering her tired vision as she rubbed her hand across her face.

She was dreaming a lot, but most of them felt like nightmares.

Breathe. Focus.

The stars are bright.

The mattress is ... kind of firm.

This room smells like rice.

One of the demons she didn't recognize had dropped off rice and beans for her last night. Or maybe it was this morning. She hadn't touched it.

Aheia tried to ground herself, sitting back against the headboard, and reminding herself of all the things she could remember, of the things that felt real, when so little did right now. Her life in Keloseros had collapsed in on her quickly, and she'd been running ever since without a moment to look back. When she finally did, it hurt. Kal had been her friend for years, and that was laying shattered, cutting into her fingers as she looked down at broken delicate curves of what had once been her world. Everything had happened so fast—learning of Kal's true intentions, watching him fight with Ophion in Keloseros, the way his allegiance shifted from one moment to the next. Or maybe that wasn't true. Maybe she didn't know what it felt like to possess someone's undying loyalty. Maybe he'd been nice when no one else had, and she'd mistaken it for more than it was.

Gods, she'd had no time to mourn her life. And now, was she just expected to move on? To let it all go? Is that what others did?

No ... Somehow, letting this fester and eat at her felt better. Feeling that burning reminded her that it had happened, that it was true.

The Mithra—no, Ophion—had sent Kal because he knew it would break her. But what was worse was the knowledge that there was no one else he could have sent. No one else she was close enough to for him to use in his manipulation.

Her breathing was shaky, and she played a silent game with herself, seeing how many tears she could collect before the dam broke anew and she soaked her sheets with the regret pouring out of her heart. Sadness started to pulse underneath the wet tracks on her cheeks, a spike of something that battled the overwhelming numb that had started to worm its way into her mind when she sat in the tub. She tried to dig at the edges, tried to widen the feeling and let herself remember Kal's soft words.

You're stronger than you know.

When you can't bear it any longer—tell yourself it isn't real. It'll help you shoulder the rest.

He'd made her feel a little more ok when nothing else was even remotely so. But those words soured until they were rotten. Until they made her stomach turn.

Aheia threw the sheets from her body in frustration, looking around for Koutávi. The Varcolac had stayed with her the entire time she sat in that tub, and after too when Emryn checked on her, but she wasn't here now. The Syraphem had forced water down her throat, and asking her questions—questions Aheia couldn't answer.

How.

What.

Where.

She acted as if Aheia was supposed to know more than she did about the time spent between Keloseros and her waking in that river. *It should have been him.* How she felt about Arioch was irrelevant. It should have been him here, asking her these questions, not his lackeys.

When Emryn seemed to finally understand that Aheia didn't know more than she was sharing, she'd left with a sparse, "Get some rest."

But Aheia's sleep wasn't restful. And it was all made worse by the stars. It had to have been a day in this room, but there was no way to know. She couldn't measure anything by the dizzying pattern outside and it was going to drive her mad.

Anxiety coursed through her now and she felt charged, pacing and pacing, unable to stop—surprised she hadn't imprinted her route into the floor. She'd stared at the door, building up the courage to use it, until the building energy inside of her jolted and she managed to grab ahold of enough conviction to find out what lurked on the other side. She went for the knob in purposeful strides, cracking it open.

"Hey again." The demon from the river—Nyco—was smiling down at her. They were holding a book spread open in front of them while Noctua, the owl, sat on their shoulder as if she was reading too.

Aheia's eyes moved around the hall, but it seemed to be just the two of them.

"You," she said like she didn't have a brain, lingering in the doorway. "You're my guard?"

"Don't sound so excited to see me." Their lips tilted into a smirk, eyes sparkling. "You'll get my heart racing."

Aheia rolled her lips between her teeth. "You've only ever accompanied life-threatening situations. Should that excite me?"

"It's early days." Their smile grew. "I don't know you well enough to answer that question for you ... But my guess is, yes."

"Oh?" She lifted an eyebrow, and her chest eased a little. They were treating her like she was her own person, not like a Mithra, or recently deceased—just *her*. "Odd choice ... for Arioch to assign you as my eyes then, isn't it?"

"Chaos can attempt to control chaos, and only that."

"*Control?*"

"See, I knew you wouldn't like that word." Noctua squawked, fluffing her wings like she didn't like the sentiment either. "But no, I'm not your guard. That sounds so fucking archaic."

"Hmhmm." She tipped her chin to the left. "So you wouldn't follow me if I walked down that hallway?"

Nyco ruffled through their split-toned curls. "Don't worry *Briteling*, you won't even know I'm there. I'm just your shadow ... something you should be used to by now, no?"

Briteling?

"Seen not heard, then?" She tilted her head, biting the inside of her cheek when they ran their thumb and index finger across their lips like they were sealing them shut.

Aheia regarded them a moment longer before dipping back inside the room.

Her heart was beating too fast. She could feel it in the tips of her fingers when she pressed them back against the wood panels of the door. The walls felt like they were closing in around her again and she took a shaky breath, trying to stretch her lungs against the tightness there.

Eyes. Everywhere.

I need air.

She padded over to large double doors that led onto a balcony, past the four perfectly similar beds, and gasped in relief as the cold night hugged her tight.

The terrace was small, bordered by an iron railing that didn't seem all too sturdy considering the height from the ground. She grasped it tightly, the purple, star-studded sky spanning the horizon, seemingly unending in front of her. The wind was treacherous out here, and if it decided to take her over the edge, it would be fate. Because the water was the reason that the wind existed in the first place. And if this river was truly made up of 'Amm's tears, as Arioch had told her all that time ago, maybe the Goddess knew what to do with Aheia if she fell.

Soft droplets floated through the air, and it reminded her of how clouds looked in Keloseros. She always wondered what stepping on them would feel like. In her mind, she pretended it would be like a bouncy bed and that they would taste like cotton sugar. But she knew the reality. She would fall through and plummet toward the ground. They wouldn't hold her, wouldn't cushion the fall, and instead she'd break her bones and lose her life.

Yet trying to step on them still felt enticing.

The emotions that were just out of reach brimmed inside of her, covered by something thick. Anger lived there, she knew that, even when she couldn't touch it. Anger at others—the ones she could never confront, hurt she couldn't return. But even though it was corrosive, biting into her bones and her flesh, her heart stayed numb. Even her tears had dried up, the remaining sorrow of Kal's memory replaced with cold ice that left her frozen.

Staring down death didn't feel like it should have. It felt a great deal less.

She let go of a shuddering breath, and when her mind cleared and her feet slid against the rock underneath, she shook her staticky head.

Not strong enough to jump, not strong enough to stay.

Her eyes skirted across the expanse of the little space around her and snagged on another balcony some rooms away. Hers was connected to it by a thin ledge of sandstone.

It was the lack of fear, she told herself, that drove her to climb across the railing toward the rock wall exterior because the thought of going back into that room made her stomach turn worse than the height she was balancing over did.

She flexed her fingers against the grooves filled with grout and tested the footpath underneath, steadying herself in her decision when it seemed to support her.

One step at a time.

The mantra coursed through her as she kept her chest toward the stone, and watched her toes instead of the river below her, continuing to inch forward. She wasn't far now, almost halfway, when a loud scree rattled her, and she slipped, grout stinging the underside of her nails.

White wings took over her field of vision, Noctua's dark eyes regarding her as the owl suspended herself in front of Aheia.

"You're going to tell on me, aren't you?" She mumbled, the owl tilting her head back and forth.

"She doesn't have to."

Another moment of almost death gripped Aheia when she heard Nyco's voice. She squeaked and wobbled, looking up toward the alcove ahead, seeing the Nephilim leaning against the railing, balancing a book on their knee.

"How did you know I'd try to cross?" she huffed, staying in her stead. *She* hadn't even known that she would, and they'd had to have come here moments after she saw them in the hallway to make it in time.

Nyco's lips pursed as their hazel eyes took her in slowly. "A hunch."

"Are *you* going to tell on me?" she asked exasperatedly.

"Does you jumping off that ledge depend on my answer?" Their eyebrow quirked, an amused smile caressing their soft lips.

"Is there an answer to that question that won't result in a lie?"

"Briteling, you wouldn't trust what I tell you one way or another, so let's stop playing with fate." They sat back on the railing, resigned, and paged open their book, steeping their attention in the story instead of Aheia.

She glanced at Noctua. "This feels like friendly fire," she grumbled to the owl, before continuing toward the balcony. They barely moved over when she finally made it across, forcing her way past them and sitting on the rough stone, planting her feet on the tiled ground.

From this part of the compound, she got a closer view of the inner city in the distance—a soft glow lining the tall buildings.

"You want to kill yourself?" Nyco asked suddenly.

"Excuse me?" she spluttered, her grip tightening on the side of the balcony. Her palms stung where the iron had pressed into them before.

"You want to kill yourself?" they repeated nonchalantly, still focused on their text.

Aheia's heart beat in her throat, and she wasn't sure why. "No," she said, but her voice didn't feel like her own.

That's when Nyco finally gave her their full attention, dragging up their gaze like it was heavy. "You know what happens when two Sirens try to serenade each other?"

"An endless circle of confusion?"

"The first ceases to harbor the ability to ensnare the second with their song because the song already lives in the other's bones."

"Which Siren am I in this analogy?" Aheia asked slowly.

"Take a guess." They smirked.

She must have been wearing her thoughts in her expression because they continued. "I have no agenda with you, Briteling. But I do need to know how closely I'm meant to watch, how self-destructive you're feeling."

"I'd prefer if you didn't watch at all," she grumbled.

They held up their hand placatingly. "I'm just here under orders of another, somewhat similar to you; so save your song for someone else or you'll exhaust yourself."

"You speak incredibly plainly, don't you." She tilted her head.

"Will you tell on me?" They flipped her words, canines poking out past their lips. She couldn't help her own smile; they coaxed it out before she realized. But when their eyes drew down, taking note of it, Aheia dropped the expression, clearing her throat and glancing over their shoulder at their book. She saw enough to know she wouldn't understand the language as they snapped it shut in front of her face.

"It's a tragedy," they said, holding it up. "A dramatic love story that ends too soon." Their eyes seemed to sparkle when they opened their mouth again. "See in this book, the romance serves as a dystopian distraction, even though the author is trying to trick us into thinking otherwise."

"How is that?" Aheia asked.

"They are focusing the audience on the characters as a diversion from the macabre reality the world faces."

"Sounds depressing," she murmured.

"I don't know." They shrugged. "You'll find a lot of forgiveness in these pages—find yourself excusing vile acts because the main character has dark hair."

"Dark hair?" Aheia scrunched her nose.

"Dark *curls* in this one." They shook out the book in front of her face.

She narrowed her eyes. "Now who's singing?"

"Come on, don't tell me it's not a little easier to forget about the monster part, when the package its wrapped in is delicious to look at." They gestured down at themself and winked.

Aheia snorted. "Is that what those hazel eyes are for? Hiding your monster?"

"You think my eyes are *prettyyy*?" Nyco pulled the last word through their teeth tauntingly.

Aheia bit her bottom lip, bumping her shoulder with theirs before they turned all serious.

"The question is, do you think they're pretty enough to forgive the monster I am at my core?"

"Well I don't know, what kind of monster are they supposed to make up for?" She asked.

"The kind that laughs when younglings fall on their faces."

She snorted, the laughter bubbling up in her throat unbidden.

We're the same kind then.

Nyco's grin returned and they tilted their head, eyes catching her mouth for a moment. "What now? What was the plan after the balcony?"

There's a question.

"Would you like to go for a walk?" she asked, resigning herself to their presence.

Chapter 14

Aheia

The hallways of the *Kaserne,* as Nyco had told her, were all made of the same gray stone. Most of them had been pretty sparsely populated until Aheia and Nyco entered a large training room that was *flooded* with demons. Most of them were training on their own set of mats; some were leaning against the wall watching, and others were sitting with weapons, sharpening and adjusting. She let her gaze drift over them, meeting a few eyes.

The center room in front of them had at least a dozen offshoots breaking up the wall. She could see them carved into the muted stone in perfect intervals around the circular structure. They all looked entirely uniform, and she wondered how they kept their directions straight when they got flipped and slammed onto the dark mats that lay across so much of the floor here.

Nyco sidled up next to her, their arms crossed as Noctua took flight, circling the room a few times before taking up a spot across the dome.

"You're one of them?" She asked them, remembering what Emryn had told her when she first arrived about their warriors. *Falkri.*

Shit, that conversation felt like yesterday. Everything did. Especially Keloseros.

"Sure." They shrugged.

"You don't know?" Aheia shot them a look.

Nyco's lip twitched, but before they could answer, their attention was drawn to the left as an enthusiastic voice called out their name. They turned just in time to catch the female that had vaulted herself toward them, her dark hair bouncing.

"We missed you last night." She leaned her chin against their shoulder, looking up at them with big, warm eyes. Nyco's gaze down at her was just as adoring.

They flicked her on the nose, their canines showing when they smiled. “Next time, Safiyah.”

"Did you just full name me? Am I in trouble?" She tilted her head, but that smile stayed.

"' Amm's sake, inside voice, you're rattling my fucking skull," another voice drifted over.

"This *is* my inside voice," Safiyah quipped at the redhead that joined the three of them. "No one forced that seventh shot down your throat, Rav." She giggled and then cleared her throat, feigning a serious expression. "Now, what have we learned?"

Rav gave her a half-lidded glance before he rubbed his eyes. "When stealing the—"

"When stealing the flag from the capitol building of the Thryn territory starts sounding like a good idea, it's probably time to call it a night. Correct. Good boy," Safiyah interrupted.

"Hey, *I* was not the one that woke up with the washroom floor tiles imprinted on her forehead," Rav griped, clutching his head like he was in pain.

"Whose fault was that?" She raised her eyebrow. "You wouldn't give me my noodles unless I ate them in the bathtub."

"You were covered in *glitter*." He groaned exasperatedly. "You were going to get that shit everywhere."

"It would have added to the *ambiance."* She rolled her eyes.

"The barracks has none. Glitter was never going to help that."

Nyco was silently laughing as the two of them went back and forth, the conversation getting more and more ridiculous until Aheia became completely lost.

"Ok, you might have had to chase me through three of the four mineral pools at Lynx last night, but I'm fine today, whereas you can barely walk." Safiyah let go of Nyco and crossed her arms. "So you don't get to bring up the giraffe incident with me."

"You are a *pain*," Rav grumbled.

"And you're flaccid."

"Fucking *flaccid*, Saffy?" He grimaced, scrubbing his tired face with a large, ring-studded hand.

"I'd call you a pussy, but it feels wrong to attribute the divine feminine to an insult. Plus, historically, those have always whipped the fuck out of you—so ..."

Aheia snorted, covering her mouth, and Saffy's eyes found hers.

"You're not funny," Rav snapped.

"*She* thinks so," Saffy said, curious gaze taking in Aheia's appearance.

"I always thought a Mithra would be all glimmery and shiny." Rav cocked his head.

"That's kind of gross. I thought you were above uninformed generalizations." Saffy shook her head.

"You want me to glimmer for you?" Aheia asked, and the redhead narrowed his eyes.

"Listen, you're three degrees from it already. Does your skin sparkle in the sun?"

"You know that's crackpot *Helren* lore, not Mithra. You're getting yourself all mixed up, genius." Saffy hit him upside the head.

"Don't mind him." Nyco grinned. "He was born with his tongue tied in knots."

"Born that way? No," Rav chuckled. "But it's been tied ever since last night."

"*Wait,*" Saffy's voice dropped to a hushed whisper. "Are you talking about the Shifter you were eyeing at the bar last night? When did you find the time to—"

"Well, you were in the tub with noodles and glitter, so I had the bunk to myself."

Her mouth dropped open, realization settling in. "They weren't friendship noodles at all, were they? They were bribe noodles."

Rav started to smirk just as Nyco reached up and snapped their fingers against his ear, and the expression turned into more of a scowl.

"Gods, *fuck*." He cradled his head in pain.

"It's too much fun." Nyco grinned in response to his glare.

"You don't get to look so happy while I'm miserable," Rav pulled out the last word, reaching out and tugging at one of Saffy's dark curls. "Come on, we're late for the devotional seminar *you* signed us up for."

"Right." Saffy's eyes lit excitedly, leaning into Nyco and nestling her forehead against theirs for a moment.

"I'll see you." She smiled at Aheia, who attempted and failed at a smile that she didn't mean. Frowning was a relief, even though she was sure she'd read somewhere that it took less muscles to smile. It didn't feel that way. And she didn't feel like smiling.

"She's trouble—you two should get along," Nyco said as the two demons left, Saffy bounding onto Rav's back.

"You know nothing about me."

"You scaled the outside of a building to avoid me. I know enough." They winked at her, and Aheia rolled her eyes.

"It had nothing to do with you," She murmured but realized quickly that Nyco wasn't paying attention to her any longer, and when she felt a heavy arm drape across her shoulders, she realized why.

"Welcome back, princess." Lúc grinned, jostling her slightly, tucking her underneath his shoulder.

"Am I?" she asked, halfheartedly. "Welcome here?"

He narrowed his eyes slowly, smile spreading. "I see why Arioch likes you." He winked. "You don't make anything easy, do you?" His tongue swiped across his teeth, expression glinting even as she scowled. Scowling had kept her safe—had kept her unapproached. But Lúc didn't seem to care, didn't move his arm away.

"You're not out in Keosha," she remarked.

"Perceptive," he said. "We're weaning off our presence."

Is Arioch still out there? The words were poised on her tongue, but she didn't ask them. It felt like blinking first.

But who was or wasn't blinking first didn't matter when a loud commotion arose across the training room. Aheia's head snapped to the far side.

"The fuck's going on over there?" Lúc barked out, and Nyco bristled slightly, those hazel eyes doing something Aheia couldn't quite read when they followed the Shifter's attention.

She squinted to the hallway across from them as a rush of demons filtered into the large dome, screaming at each other in *Lujha*. There were two females at the forefront, tackling each other and knocking down three warriors training on a blue mat near the door. Lúc's gaze was fucking furious as he watched the two rolling around on the ground, one struggling to hold the other's blade away from her throat.

"Shit, Syn," Nyco hissed, and when Aheia shot them a questioning look, they clarified. "Tei's sister. She's been having a hard time with his death."

Her stomach bottomed out. *Oh fuck.* Tei had helped her that night in the atrium. She wasn't all too sure that she would be alive without him. She might have drowned before the monsters ever had a chance to try their luck with her.

Aheia's shoulders became heavy, and she felt the blame that she carried for it. Without her, Nyco and Tei would not have lingered in the forest; they might have even gotten themselves out. Her eyes burned, and her fingers curled in on themselves, static running through her chest.

Your fault.

Sour spit pooled on her tongue as Lúc rushed past her and shoved through the throng of demons obstructing the space. Nephilim on each side jumped out of his way while the warriors that had been knocked down by the females tried to help separate them.

"What is this about?" Lúc wedged himself between the two fighters as Aheia and Nyco followed. One of them was a pale redhead, and the other a dark-skinned brunette. Neither of them met his level gaze. "Oh, come on now, you're going to make me guess? Fucking abysmal." He grabbed their knives and chucked them to the side with a clatter. "Who started this?" he asked, looking between them.

"She did!" the redhead spat, nodding at the brunette.

"Fuck you, Nameless—you started this shit when you took Tei's name into your dirty *whore* mouth," Syn hissed back.

"Why did she call her Nameless?" Aheia asked.

"She doesn't have one and refuses to pick one for herself," Nyco answered under their breath.

"Your brother was an *asshole*." Nameless reared forward, but Lúc caught her middle like she weighed nothing, dumping her back in her spot.

"You outcast *bitch*," Syn growled. "He's *dead*."

"Good fucking riddance," the redhead grinned, emerald eyes caustic, fighting against Lúc's hold.

"*Stay*," he growled, and it sounded animalistic like his jaguar was talking alongside him, his hand buried in her hair, forcing her gaze. Her nostrils flared, but then she nodded, and Lúc let her go. "Get it out of your fucking systems, but not like that." He lifted his hand to the redhead's chest and pushed her back two paces before turning to Syn. "If you're going to fight, you're going to fight."

The females looked at each other and then at him.

"You're going to punish us for fighting with *fighting*?" Nameless scoffed.

"I'm going to punish you by giving you exactly what you want." Lúc narrowed his eyes and bared his canines. "Believe it or not, it's more effective than having you try and bond over scrubbing the hallways with your toothbrushes."

Nameless almost looked surprised while Syn was staring at her like she would rip her throat from her body given a chance.

"Go on," Lúc crossed his arms, stepping back. "Trade your punches."

Aheia's lips parted, and she looked at Nyco. "Does this happen a lot?"

"Nope." They popped the *p*, watching Luc back away with crossed arms and a stony expression. "Most don't want to deal with the consequences."

These *consequences.*

"Syn." Lúc nodded at the Nephilim. "You start."

"When is it over?" the redhead asked.

"When you both stop getting up, Nameless," Lúc answered simply, voice rough.

Aheia stepped forward, noticing Syn's black bracelet as she charged back her fist and swung it through the air *quickly*, drilling the side of the redhead's cheek.

A whisper ran through the crowd as Nameless tripped slightly, supporting herself against her knees before pushing up and stepping back into place. She shot Lúc a withering look through emerald eyes and then clenched her hand, hitting Syn squarely in the jaw. The blood splattered across the mat, and the hit Nephilim staggered to the side, barely keeping her body upright.

The two of them went shot for shot until the redhead managed a blow that landed Syn on her ass, her face bloody and bruised. She spluttered for breath, a craggy split running down her nose, her chest shaking with every inhale.

Everything went still around them as the Shifter watched, dark purple eyes surveying the two fighters a moment longer.

Then he stalked across the mat and reached a hand out to Syn. She took it, and he helped her off the floor, gripping the side of her face softly. She winced as he took inventory, his gaze softening. "Get it healed." His voice dropped low, almost reassuring. The bite in his words had fallen away completely as his thumb brushed over her cheekbone.

Does he treat her differently because of her brother's death?

Syn nodded, her eyes brimming with tears as a few bystanders rushed over to help her out of the way. When she disappeared through the hallway, Lúc turned back toward Nameless, all the softness that Aheia thought she'd seen dissipated.

"Go on," he said, his voice holding a dark edge. "Finish what you started." He stood in front of the redhead, cracking his knuckles.

She bared her teeth, shaking her head. "She's done. She tapped out."

"I said it's not over until *both* of you are on the ground," he challenged, and then he turned to the rest of the demons. "There's killing the enemy, and there's fighting your allies." He said it loud enough for everyone in the large domed room to hear. "If any of you start to feel like you want to fight your allies—out of the ring, consider me your enemy."

Then he turned back to Nameless and curled two of his fingers, motioning the battered Nephilim closer. Her breath shuddered, and Aheia could see the hesitation—the shake in her hand when she clenched her fist tight and swung. Her knuckles cracked against Lúc's jaw, and his head snapped to the side, black hair falling into his face.

The energy around them shifted, and the crowd became one organism, moving closer.

When Lúc straightened, his eyes were gleaming bright purple, and his expression made Aheia think that just maybe he ... liked getting his face smashed in. His smile grew, the corner of his mouth dripping in black blood.

"Good." He leaned forward, licking at his lower lip. "You get one more, Nameless. Then, it's my turn."

She swallowed, her shoulders square as she widened her stance and delivered another blow to the same side. He stumbled slightly this time before clearing his throat to spit out the blood.

"Ready?" Lúc asked, giving the redhead a moment like he was preparing her.

The Nephilim exhaled roughly, shaking out her arms. And there was something in her actions that told of her resignation at what was about to happen.

The hit Lúc delivered knocked her back on her ass, her red hair sticking to the blood on her face. She croaked out a groan, cradling her chin, her knuckles white against the mat.

"You done?" Lúc asked, stepping over her.

She nodded furiously, hissing at the pain.

Aheia lost her focus on what was going on in front of them, staring down the long hallway Syn had disappeared into. There was a surge in her veins to follow, to explain herself to the demon and offer her apologies, but before she could, Nyco's arm shot out in front of her. She looked up, furrowing her brows. How did they know that she was about to move? Had she worn the expression on her face?

"I need to talk to her," she said.

"No, you don't." Nyco shook their head. "She's not in a space for it right now, trust me." They nodded in the opposite direction.

"I'm not going back to that room," she hissed.

"That's not where I'm taking you." They wiggled their fingers like they were expecting Aheia to take their hand, and when she didn't, they rolled their eyes. "Do you like oranges?"

"Oranges?"

"The fruit," they said slowly like they were gauging if she knew what it was.

"I suppose."

Nyco explained the layout of the Kaserne to Aheia as they ushered her down two hallways and up a flight of stairs. She was breathing hard by the time they reached the top of old stone steps, her vision peppered with little light leaks.

“Mind your head, wouldn’t want you to lose it just yet.” Nyco flashed a steady grin, holding their hands up to the arched doorway in front of them. It dipped at the center, carved stone coming to a small point, and Aheia’s jaw dropped when she cleared it. She’d been so busy focusing on not stumbling and bruising herself that she’d looked nowhere but the steps under her feet. When she finally lifted her gaze, a smattering of beautiful stars met her. The night sky was purple and blue, and there were even some dollops of red and pink spread throughout, a different vantage point to the same horizon.

A citrus grove. She stared in disbelief at the trees sprouting from the near black dirt, rows and rows of it.

"We grow a lot of our own food, the kind we *can* grow anyway, and there are a few gardens around Aljira. Some are filled with vegetables, some with fruit, others herbs. But out here, it's citrus. The Kaserne sits lower than the compound, and the loamy soil helps with the trees down here." Nyco explained, spreading their fingers and gliding them across the wavy leaves of low-sitting trees. They spanned far and wide, little, equally spaced, heavy crowned patches dotted with orange fruit.

"Why are you showing me this?" she asked, following them down the aisles of flora on either side. "Seems like extra trouble you don't have to go through."

"Maybe I'm the one who wants to be out here." They shot her a look, picking a fruit, the branches crackling. "Maybe I'm forcing you to tag along."

She narrowed her eyes and opened her mouth but before she could call their bullshit, something wet poked her back.

"Koutávi." Little prickles of excitement peppered her skin at the creature's presence. The Varcolac towered over her, but held her head bent—gaze level with Aheia's. Nyco stumbled a few steps backward, taking in the huge creature with wide eyes but wiped their expression of the surprise a moment later. Noctua came shooting from the Kaserne entrance and circled above the three of them squawking, and stirring up some of the shadow magyck. Koutávi's deadly teeth bared as she snapped her jowls after the bird, and Aheia almost smiled.

"Careful," she murmured on instinct.

"Noctua likes to instigate. She'll learn once she gets a feather pulled." Nyco backed away across the clearing, nestling themself against a tree trunk and peeling one of the oranges. A glimmering pond centered the space, reflecting the stars above, and Aheia felt the sadness like a touchable thing, slowly dripping down her. It looked so much like the reflecting pond in Keloseros that she and Andromeda would visit. Her breath was hot and heavy when she turned toward the placid expanse of water and stared at a distance, far enough away not to see her own reflection—not to see her own eyes.

Home.

Not something she understood. Never had.

A homeless, misplaced, different thing, just looking for her own freedom.

Freedom.

The word was synonymous with relief—at least it had been in her mind. But it didn't feel like she'd expected. Not like breathing at all. Suffocating instead. It gnashed in her face with cold, sharp teeth, demanding everything she didn't know how to give. Because a childhood of oppression might have sparked a flame inside of her, but it never equipped her for a life of any kind of choice in her future.

Future. Another F word that felt entirely double-edged. She was in it now, that word, living it when she'd narrowly planned for it in the past.

The thought grated across her mind invasively. A dark spot at the end of a retina-burning, bright tunnel. She'd been running toward an elusive word. The realization made her stomach twist tight. She had no reason to want to return to Keloseros, no friends left behind or family that was being held hostage—had nothing there to coax her back, threat or no threat. But that didn't change that she didn't know how to stand still here, either.

The books she'd read and the stories she'd taken into her heart had always depicted heroines with clear minds, clear hearts, and obvious motivations. When they ran, they knew where they were heading, even if they were being chased. And she'd had that for a bit, she supposed. *Aljira*. But was that still her focus? If she had the choice to go anywhere, where would it be?

Koutávi poked her back again, sliding her face against Aheia's side, and she almost started crying right then and there. The equivalent of someone asking, *"Are you ok?"*

"I'm sorry." She looked back at Nyco, letting the discomfort of her blame outweigh the difficulty of her indecision. It came from a selfish place—a place that understood that one pain, the worse pain, would always outweigh the others. "I'm sorry about Tei."

Their throat bobbed and those gold flecks shone a little less brightly in their eyes. She noticed how they fidgeted with the bracelet on their wrist, identical to the one Syn wore.

"It's not your fault." Nyco said.

"Do you believe that? Truly?" she asked, picking at her nails, and keeping her gaze down.

"You weren't the reason Tei and I found ourselves at the Asara, Aheia. It was all happenstance."

"But you lingered because of me. You could have gotten yourselves out."

"You're not responsible for his choices, or mine."

"Do you believe the same for yourself?" she asked. "Or are you trying to shoulder the blame for both of us?"

Their silence spoke volumes, but she didn't know how to cradle their hardships, could barely hold her own at the moment. They didn't need to tell her it was all going to be ok, because she knew better. She winced anyway, because she hadn't meant to push like that. Not when she saw them in their vulnerability and they *let* her. "You saved me in that river," she shifted. "You saved me from the Shykoya too. Thank you. I owe you."

"I'll keep the favor safe." They smiled softly, but it didn't reach their eyes.

"Do that. Hopefully I'll be of some use some day." She fidgeted with her fingers. "I didn't mean to prod at you like that, I think ... My mind is heavy."

"It's expected when that's where you carry all your emotions," Nyco said simply, pulling out their book again and settling back against the trunk.

"What?" Aheia turned from the pond, letting herself lean into the shadow creature next to her because she didn't know how much longer she could stand. Koutávi inhaled heavily, bursts of her breath blasting against Aheia's bare feet.

"You didn't think it was your heart, did you?" They chuckled, paging through the old paper.

"My emotions?" Aheia asked.

"Well, it starts in your mind and manifests in your gut, but apparently the poets didn't think that sounded all too romantic."

"Useless, bleeding organ." She hadn't meant to sound so bitter, she truly hadn't.

"Let it bleed with purpose, then." Their sharp eyes met hers over the red leather binding.

Aheia hadn't seen Arioch since he took her to see Mazikeen, and the loneliness was starting to become familiar. Easier than anger or hate. It felt friendly and safe, because if she kept herself tucked behind her own walls, then she'd be the only one with the power to hurt herself.

Another two days passed, at least she thought. It was difficult to figure out how time worked in this realm, especially with how heavy the weight in her chest felt now. It was hard to figure out a lot of things ...

She hid at first, under the blankets of her bed. She ignored the food that appeared on that sad little desk in the corner until she was so empty she became nauseous and forced down something manageable. Sometimes she kept it down, sometimes she lost it in the washroom, the vomit burning her nostrils.

But in the citrus grove, she could breathe. Some at least. She came here a lot while she wondered why the hel Arioch was keeping her here when he wouldn't even come to see her. Wondered why the hel *she* didn't leave three days ago.

Probably because you can barely keep your eyes open.

The exhaustion had become a heavy, almost tangible presence, and it mingled the cold and the dark that had always lived inside of her. They played with each other, while Aheia was the chessboard they used.

But at least out here, she wasn't surrounded by walls. The trees here made her feel just a little lighter, and when the shadow creature bled from between the heavy, wood trunks, and curled in a massive ball by the center pond, she didn't feel alone. Not the same kind of loneliness she felt around people. Koutávi's presence made her own feel a little bit more ok, and she listened like no one else could. The Varcolac had no obligation to her, not like Nyco did.

They were there with her every step of the way, but she'd lost the mind to speak. She had questions, so many of them, but when she went to open up her mouth, it felt like her mind took a dive down the side of a balcony. So, they were silent often, and she got lost in the stars, contemplating how real something could be when there was no measure of time to outline it.

CHAPTER 15

ARIOCH

He could feel the moments he wasn't with Aheia weighing him down, becoming heavier and angrier by each second.

Her being alive and bleeding amongst the dead owls some days ago had felt like a fever dream, and the time that followed wasn't any different. The reality of her hadn't fully sunk into him, like a truth he couldn't let himself look at until she'd touched him in that wax tub. Then the connection between them had cracked like a bullwhip, demanding his attention. It wasn't anything snapping into place that wasn't already there.

He'd watched her the entire time Maz showed Aheia their past, while his magyck bucked under his skin with the desire to touch again. It was his own personal torture, sitting on the edge of that pool and keeping his hands close enough to feel the cold radiating off her skin, but far enough to make the pads of his fingers *itch.*

He was fixated. *Too* fixated. And so were his shadows.

They whispered about her, especially now that he was away, plastering her blue eyes all over his mind.

Fuck's sake. He flexed his fingers against the stone wall of the alcove he stood in, letting the spray of hot water burn him. He'd been in Azalam, Siraj's territory, since he'd dropped Aheia off in her room because there was no way in hel he'd leave her in Keosha while he sorted out the shit with the Shykoya. The Kaserne was safe—safer than the compound even, with all the Falkri around and she wasn't fucking dying again. *That's* why he'd left her behind—at least that's what he told himself. That he was here for his people, in a part of the realm that made his skin crawl because of the Shykoya and not because he didn't know how to face the small creature that was back at the Kaserne—that he didn't fucking trust himself to be close to her.

Fuck, maybe if he said it out loud, he'd start to believe his own bullshit.

He'd busied himself with meetings, and the mundane shit he usually avoided because when it was loud, he could distract his brain. It was the silent moments that were dangerous because in those, he found his memories, in those, his shadows became overbearing.

The water running down his skin reminded him of the pearls that had glistened on Aheia's lips back in Keosha. She'd been wet all over, and he was jealous of fucking water, because it touched every part of her while he kept his fingers just out of reach.

Her tongue had tasted just like he remembered; soft and silky. It was warm and wet in his mouth, and *so* fucking demanding. Just as hungry as him. Fucking hel, he needed to kiss her again. He needed to feel that tongue in his mouth, on his skin, swirling around his cock while he fucked her mouth.

Touch.

Squeeze.

Fuck, he couldn't think.

The imprint of her soft skin remained. She was touching him when she was miles away.

His teeth bared in a snarl against the strain in his shoulders. He wanted to punish her for leaving him when it wasn't her fault, wanted to bend her backwards until she cracked because she looked at him like she wanted to do it again—leave.

It wasn't a fucking choice for either of them. That was clear; the only clear thing.

When she was dead, all he wanted was to have her back. Now, he didn't know how to be close to her. Needed too much from a creature he didn't know without anything to offer her in turn. Nothing but obsession and stomach-knotting need.

The heat inside of him rushed down his spine. He hadn't relaxed since that kiss, his muscles tense and hard for fucking hours, and nothing took the edge off. He fucked his hand, thinking that maybe release would be enough, maybe he just needed to exhaust himself. But just as his shadows hadn't been satisfied with the bloodshed at the border, he wasn't satisfied with his hand and her memory.

A fucking headache. The dangerous and blinding kind. Not just a temple pain, a fucking migraine instead.

He pressed his forehead against the coarse rock, too tall to fit under the metal spout, letting the water pelt him for another minute before he got out the spray for the second time that day and dressed to head down toward the border.

"And this will keep the Shykoya at bay?" Siraj asked, his

hands folded neatly behind his back as they stood on the outskirts of *Jahra*. The town bordering the Sephy Forest in south Azalam. Heretics were crouched low to the ground in front of them, their fingers digging into the dirt while the magyck pulsed through them and flowed into the earth below. Arioch watched as black waves shot toward the sky, purple ripples breaking through the viscous magyck like columns. Every ten feet there was a new Heretic working, webbing the fabric that wove together in bright light pulses across the length of the line in patches.

"Yes." It would take a few more days to set up the perimeter around Azalam with how much ground and magyck had to be covered. The Heretics needed to rest in the face of those complicated invocations, but they were making headway nonetheless.

"Might be a good idea to keep the border open in some areas—population control," Eros' slimy voice piped up from behind them. Siraj's brother was leaning against a broken half wall with his arms crossed, blonde curls hanging around his dark horns in greasy strings. Arioch worked hard to keep his features devoid of any reaction, even though his shadows tightened around his muscles until they sang with discomfort.

"Population control." Arioch repeated it slowly, keeping his voice cold. "Revolutionary."

He'd heard something similar from one of Eros' men. Bassam had called his own fucked-up actions *social maintenance.* But Bassam lacked a tongue and his life now.

Eros grinned in challenge, but the smile fell when Arioch continued.

"The border does need to be tested. And if you're volunteering yourself, I can have Aylee tie you to one of those trees." He nodded at the dark trunks in front of them. "We'll see if your screams and blood lure them in, and if the magyck holds up once the Shykoya are done with you."

He met Siraj's calculating gaze before tilting his head toward Aylee on his other side, her familiars slithering across her body. Salamander hissed, black, glossy eyes trained on Siraj. It almost looked like the snake was frowning with how the ridges above her gaze dipped. "More controlled that way, don't you think?"

"Much," Aylee said simply.

"My brother forgets himself," Siraj said, voice almost placating. But Arioch knew better than to believe that Siraj didn't share Eros' opinion. The brothers were always on the same page, but the difference between them was that Eros could speak his mind freely where Siraj had to train his.

Disgustingly symbiotic, the two of them. One could think it, the other could scratch the itch for both of them.

"All the fucking time," Arioch said, focusing back on the blond. His blood boiled when he thought about the limitations he faced. How much power he held in his hands, in his position, and how quickly that shit was leashed when it came to blood ties and hierarchy. Eros was a fucking disease and Arioch had been raring to burn him clean off the face of this realm for a long time. That fixation was only worsened when he sent his demons after Aheia by fucking proxy. However, Eros wasn't just Siraj's brother, but one of the Siada's *Rasmí*, a sworn-in Nephilim. Just like Tariq, Lúc and the rest of the demons that lived at the compound were Rasmí. Killing him without reason that Arioch could back would cause a fucking shit storm. And until recently, he'd tried to keep whatever fucked up version of peace held with the Siada that opposed him for the sake of the mess it would cause. But it seemed along with everything else around him, that was crumbling just as well.

"Surprised he's made it this long without losing his head." Aylee's voice was as cold as her gaze. "Or any of those limbs."

"Night's still young," Arioch shot back and this time Eros' jaw ticked and he averted his eyes.

"He thinks disrespect is an option," Aylee continued, holding up her hand and watching Embyr slither across her digits.

"Those who haven't felt what it's like to be hunted rarely fear their predator." He shot a smirk Eros' way.

Siraj laughed off the conversation. The fake kind that was cultivated in high standing houses meant to lighten heavy air. "I think you've done enough damage for one night." He redirected that expression at his brother before exchanging cautionary words with him. Eros pushed off the wall, watching the exchange with a childish smirk, like none of it fucking mattered to him. And none of it did. Because Siraj's sentence was as hollow as the intention behind it. "You can't pick your family." He shook his head disapprovingly.

"You can decide how much power you grant them," Arioch said, disgust lacing his words, eyes following Eros as he walked away from them, snaking around the Heretics lazily.

"Hmm, family," Siraj hummed thoughtfully, and Arioch caught something flashing in his eyes that sparked apprehension. "I've been meaning to drop by to discuss it with you."

"Yes?" he drawled.

"Your brother." The Siada continued. "You've told us nothing of him. Word that he's back was rumor until you confirmed it only a week ago."

"I've told you everything you need to know." Arioch narrowed his eyes.

"And we're meant to believe the Mithra took him? And then kept him for all those years without a demand? What for? It makes no sense. Why give him back now?"

Arioch rolled his shoulders. He hated that Siraj had a fucking point. Ophion held on to Kazim when he had a powerful tool in his arsenal. But not until Aheia did he show his hand.

"Trade interest," he said calmly. A lie. He'd kept Aheia's part in everything as quiet as he could. No one knew about the failed bargain between Ophion and himself. As far as the rest of Aljira was concerned, they swarmed the Keloseros church that day to bring home Kazim. And he'd fucking keep it that way. Siraj didn't need any more fuel for that fire he was steadily trying to stoke.

"Forgive me, but"—Siraj cleared his throat—"It seems ... unlikely."

Yeah, it was a fucking stretch. He knew how it sounded.

"Unlikely?" Aylee asked, crossing her arms.

"They held the rightful sovereign of Aljira at their fingertips," Siraj continued.

There it fucking is. The rightful sovereign.

Three precarious fucking words to those who looked for reasons to break down Arioch's power.

"How about you script the rest of this conversation," Arioch said, tilting his head. "Tell me my side, since you clearly already have a thought for what it is."

"Well." Siraj straightened, sanctimonious expression in place while treasonous words slipped from his tongue. "Power is motivation for every creature in this world. It drives action. Kazim's disappearance shifted the power significantly in your direction, just as Alshaytan Sahren's death did." Siraj picked at nonexistent dust on his jacket. "Oftentimes, the simple answer is the right one."

"Careful with all of those thoughts. Putting them in the wrong order can prove dangerous," Aylee said, languidly.

"It wasn't meant to offend, just an objective consideration," Siraj followed up quickly, all of the mannerisms practiced.

"I am sure Siraj isn't foolish enough to implicate me in my brother's disappearance," Arioch said to Aylee as he held the Siada's gaze. "Are you?" But it didn't sound like a question.

He'd considered Siraj's opinions on Kazim's return. He'd considered that the Siada might try to question his seat in power. But he hadn't considered being implicated in his brother's abduction. He should have. That was an oversight.

"Of course not." Siraj's eyebrow rose in challenge. "But I do look forward to hearing more about his harrowing story and what truly transpired. From him."

Arioch's lip twitched. "Of course," he repeated blankly.

"As you said, we all decide how much power to grant our family." Siraj clapped his hands together, a broad smile spreading across his lips. "I trust your stay in my territory has been satisfactory?"

Arioch didn't answer.

"Well, if you need anything else from me and *mine*."

"I know where to find you," Arioch said slowly, eyes narrowed.

They were sizing each other up now, neither of them even fucking blinking as time settled.

But then Siraj nodded, breaking the eye contact, and lingered for another few moments before he finally followed his brother down the line.

"What the fuck was that about?" Aylee hissed.

"Power is motivation for every creature in this world." Arioch repeated the words, soaking them in venom.

"He's accusing you of—"

"I know."

He knew a lot of things in that moment, which for once felt worse than knowing none of them. He knew that Siraj had found a crack in Arioch's exterior to hold on to. Kazim was a point of interest for the Siada of Azalam, and that was fucking dangerous. Because Siraj had wanted Arioch out of power for a long time, and if he believed he could somehow get Kazim into the foreground as *rightful sovereign*, he could alter the trajectory of their realm.

Aylee shook her head, but something snagged her gaze between the trees. "What's going on with them?"

"They can't track the Shykoyas' scent," Arioch said, watching the Varcolacs trail through the high grass. They'd been doing that for hours now—catching a scent and dropping it, like it vanished into thin air.

"Has that ever happened before?" she asked.

"None of this has ever happened before."

He stepped through his shadows, letting the darkness stretch and breathe inside of him—too big for him. Too much. It was hard to control the magyck when he was focused on the beam he was walking, trying to keep his world level on top of it. Worry twisted his stomach—worry for the balance that was tipping a little further each day and for his brother's place within the chaos. The air was ripe with stagnant energy—with *potential.* Potential for Siraj to gain a foothold using Kazim. Potential for a restructure within his ranks because when everything was said and done, he only held power if his people wanted him to. *Rightful sovereign.* Siraj had alluded to it, that he'd taken a place that didn't belong to him. *Fuck,* a place Arioch had never wanted.

His teeth ground as the darkness cleared slowly, bitterly.

But Kazim couldn't take it, not with the state he was in. And that's not truly what Siraj wanted anyway; he didn't want to be *oppressed* by yet another Avarice from the same bloodline. Arioch imagined he saw Kazim as an in, someone to manipulate easier than Arioch.

Potential was fucking poison.

The night smelled like citrus here, and the scent calmed the erratic jerking in his muscles. The trees from the grove were bared one by one as his shadows thinned and he let himself breathe for a moment. It had felt like that *then* too, when he visited the grove with his mother. It had been Malia's favorite place. It had been theirs.

But he wasn't here for some fucked up nostalgia trip down memory lane. He was here to see *her.* Aheia was a speck of white dropped on dark, thick oil paints, crouched by the water, drawing her fingers across the placid surface.

Little ripples floated from her.

A disruption.

That's what she was. A fucking disruption. His shadows purred just at the sight of her and he swallowed against the lump in his throat. Their reactions were so different that it made his stomach tighten. It was almost a nauseous feeling, one that had anger for himself burning a little brighter. Because *they* wanted her close, they wanted to touch, to feel, to consume. But he saw the hollows in her cheeks, the bones that were so much more pronounced now than ever before. She was withering away. A ghost.

A reminder.

Malia had been a ghost before she died. She'd stopped eating, and he wasn't sure if it had been the drugs or the lack of food that saw her wasting. Pleas, and coaxing words hadn't worked with her, hadn't saved her life. They'd been useless. So he'd discarded them a long time ago because honey might have fed flies, but corpses did a better job of it.

Aheia looked up again, and he could see how drawn back she was. Her eyes were glazed, and she wasn't looking at anything in front of her. It was detached, and he recognized it. It seemed regardless of how different they were, they shared a great deal. That numbness he could see being one of them. Except he wasn't numb anymore, not now that she was back.

His shadows slithered like they wanted to remind him that she was just paces away, as if he didn't fucking know, couldn't see her with his own eyes. The tendrils around his neck grazed his tendons and tugged until he ground his teeth together and dug his fingers into his palm.

I know, he thought in frustration. *I fucking know she's here.*

And by the looks of it, she felt his presence too.

Her fingers faltered against the water just as the pulse ran through him and the little reaction made the fire lick across his spine.

Arioch motioned to Nyco, who was sitting on the bench behind Aheia, and waited for them to leave while Koutávi stayed put. Her gold eyes pierced him and he could feel their connected magyck simmering.

The Varcolac had taken a liking to Aheia, because they shared their shadows and when his feelings toward her shifted, so did anything that held pieces of his magyck. Koutávi had gone from hunting her down at his word to protecting her for the same reason, to being here in his stead.

She was here because he'd told her to be, and Aheia was here because he'd told Nyco to bring her. A place that could be hers with a creature that gave her what he couldn't. Comfort.

He was about to ruin that for her, because it was time to revisit not just their past, but hers.

Chapter 16

Aheia

She'd tricked herself into being thankful for Arioch's absence until now, until he made her feel all over again.

Her awareness heightened with the humming in her chest. She felt it. *Him.* Just like her soul was still with him. Except this was worse—like a plea worming its way free from somewhere in her bones. Small and quivering, she and her mind disagreeing on how much she hated him once again.

When he was near, she wasn't numb. She was out of control, underlining the truth she didn't want to acknowledge.

You're not your own.

She never had been. Not when she was young, not when she was grown. Not even now. Now she was his, without a choice in the matter, connected by something intrinsic that made it impossible to understand her true thoughts and feelings.

Her hand dropped, seeing the dark shadows in her peripheral, the squirming remnants of how his presence affected her running down her spine.

Aheia looked up, keeping her chin rested on her knee because moving it higher felt like a lot. The silence between them was charged, and she'd never learned how to sit in someone's presence in silence, so she spoke instead.

"I miss the rain," she said finally, gazing across the little droplets of water she'd let dribble down her legs, soft, dark spots against the white. "I could just scream into the noise of it, and no one would know." Her throat was dry when she tried to swallow.

"You don't need rain to scream."

The sound of his voice made her shiver. Cold, she was cold now, sitting here, and this time she couldn't bring herself to look for his warmth. So, she kept her eyes down, and her words quiet.

"It's different." He moved behind her and the proximity tugged at her awareness. "Rain feels like—" Finding the right words was near impossible as her mind continued to weigh her down. "In Keloseros, rain reminded me that I was really small compared to the rest of the world, that there were more important things than my own heart, people suffering worse than me. That the trees around me had survived hundreds of years of hard weather, and that I could bear the clouds too."

Her stare slid to his reflection in the pond, as she told herself that a likeness wasn't the same as looking. Soft green hues curled underneath his gray eyes, but even diluted in fantasy, she saw it, the anger. It lived in those bright embers and it was directed entirely at her, though she didn't know what she'd done to deserve it this time.

"You really think that? That weighing your pain against the world somehow explains what was done to you? Makes it ok?" he asked, keeping his distance. It was hard to focus on him, the colors of his tan skin and hair muting and mixing together like paint.

"It makes it bearable." Her chest gave a hollow throb. So empty. Or maybe it was full.

Maybe heavy masked itself as hollow and confused the meaning. She had to swallow three times to wet her throat, inhaling all of the sorrow that had dripped from her. She choked it down and tipped her chin, keeping the tears that welled up dammed safely.

"You didn't survive a fucking thunderstorm." His words held the same fire those eyes did, and she turned hers away again because if she didn't, she'd believe the sentiment meant more than it did.

Why do you want it to? She scolded herself while desperately trying to hold on to those crumbling walls he was so close to knocking over. It seemed every time he spoke they shivered in their stead around her frail heart, and every time she tried to support one side, another threatened to crumble.

"Pain didn't start, nor will it end with me." Hers wasn't different. It wasn't special. She let herself forget that sometimes. She'd forgotten it for seven whole days with him, and it was selfish.

The renewed cold in her veins was welcome in the light of that realization. Its dark hands slithered down her spine and cooled her, calming her heart until the muscles in her face felt heavy and her eyelids did, too. It was a balm that soothed her inflamed skin when his fire licked across her mercilessly.

"Do you want it to?"

What kind of a question is that?

She turned, finally looking up at him. The real him. He stood with his hands in his pockets, eyes drawing across her features like he was seeing something there. And she hated that. Hated that when she couldn't seem to figure out how to read herself, he had no issue.

"Wouldn't anyone?" She felt a languid flicker of anger stir inside of her, heat collecting behind her eyes as she tried her best to glare and fend him off. It was hard—conjuring it.

"To some it's comfort." He tilted his chin, continuing his scrutiny of her. "They'd take the pain they understand over a happiness that is foreign. To some, letting go is invalidating the past. To some"—his eyes seemed to drop to her collarbone—"it's purpose."

"*Purpose*?"

"Something to hold on to—a pretty little lie that's friendly until it tries to swallow them." He sank to his haunches slowly, and she felt the prickle between them. "No matter how much you love the rain, Aheia, it will drown you if you let it. All of those drops will grow into an ocean and the current will rip you from the surface and force you under until you suffocate. No one will hear you scream then either."

Her name left his lips and once again, it felt like a warning. *Careful*, it echoed at the back of her mind, but the voice was meek.

"Why are you here?" she managed through her teeth, a brittle sound. "What's changed since you left?"

His eyes grew distant as he stood, his hands back in his pocket like none of it mattered.

It doesn't. She was here because *he'd* wanted it his way. Otherwise he would have apologized, would be 'proving his worth' to her. This ...

"I figured it was time to take you down to see Ophion." She watched his shadows gather behind him in a thick cloud and a familiar fear blossomed in her chest. Just his name had the power to do that, where she wished it was anger that Arioch had conjured instead.

She took his hand and let him lead her into his shadows because it felt like too much effort to do anything else. The magyck caressed her softly, tendrils curling around her in a way that was almost comforting. But Arioch undid that in the same breath, making her shiver all over.

When the darkness fell away, she stood on cold familiar cave floors, her gaze focused hard on the sandstone underneath. It smelled horrid. Stale and dirty, and fire flickered in her periphery. Jarring and labored breaths bounced off whatever walls surrounded them, and the hair on her arm stood on end.

The thought of facing the Malek that had made her life hel for so long had everything inside of her in a nauseated vise. There was more of a reaction somewhere, outrage, tears, anger—but it seemed she couldn't lift it off the fucking floor. It was worse somehow—*knowing*. Diagnosing herself without a way to fix it. Feeling how disproportionate she was without a way to level herself out.

She kept her chin down, but it didn't last long with the demon who was standing at her back. Arioch's chest brushed against her spine and their connection hummed; another thing she resented in that moment. It was ownership. And as it stood, she was being squeezed by it on all sides.

Alshaytan gripped her jaw with the rough pads of his fingers and tipped it up, her eyes dragging unwillingly across the scene in front of her. A macabre fucking sight.

Ophion was bent across a dark slab of stone, his hands manacled down, one wing stretched taut toward the opposite wall. On the other side, a jagged, burned wound ran the length of his back. It was fleshy with dried red blood crusting it while the weight of the remaining appendage pulled him at an angle. He didn't look up at their intrusion, not even when the whimper Aheia couldn't help squeaked past her lips. His shoulders and back twitched with slow breathing, but past that, it didn't seem he was registering their presence.

"Can he hear?" Aheia felt small in the Malek's presence, even now. And it became worse with time. She shrank back, and no part of her could help it.

"Some," Arioch said, the rough timber of his voice low in her ear.

Ophion's eyeballs slid underneath the lids frantically and Aheia held her breath, because if she was too loud, he'd wake up. If she was too loud, he'd hurt her. She'd always been too loud in Keloseros, even when she was silent.

"Breathe," Arioch said, stroking his fingers down the column of her throat. But Aheia held that last bit of oxygen in her lungs until her skin tingled and she couldn't go without it any longer and her pathetic gasps filled the cave around them. The Malek didn't move, but that didn't give her any comfort.

"Again," Arioch said against her temple.

There's no air here. She was sure of it. It didn't exist.

Her knees buckled slightly as she turned, unsure of where or what or who or how, eyes zigzagging across the cave wall, trying to look for an out.

Out. There wasn't an out. Her fingers shook as she grabbed ahold of Arioch's arm. She was going to fall, faint, something. Stars spangled her vision, black dots that narrowed her eyesight into a pinhole.

"Out, I need—I can't." Words shook loose frantically, wrong words. Not ones that made up a sentence.

Her heart jolted and prompted her to run, to scratch at the stone until her fingers bled if it meant she could leave this space. But before she could jerk away, Arioch's hands gripped her waist, heavy and warm, steadying her where she stood and in the next moment the darkness that had started to seep in around her spread to its completion.

Shadows.

"Breathe deep for me." Arioch was just as all-consuming as his magic. He was in front of her, behind her, inside of her fucking soul—the one that acted as if her taking it back had been some awful transgression, the one that preferred his body as a home to hers. And she couldn't do anything but try to comply, pulling in dark air in unsteady intervals until her heart evened out enough for her fingers to stop shaking.

Fuck.

And she did her best over and over again, until she was no longer gasping.

"I know you can take it deeper." His hand was on her chest, just across her sternum, pressing in at all five points while his other slid up her spine. "Let me feel it here." He flexed his fingers over her diaphragm, his thumb rubbing over her back in small circles while she watched his darkness. It was a different shade than the one she'd found herself in with Ophion, different than the one that had its claws wrapped around her throat when her thoughts punished her. Her shoulder rested against his steadying arm as they stood in silence, and he didn't make her speak, didn't ask anything else of her as the shadows thinned slowly.

When they emerged in the light, she was thankful for the sight of the room she'd started to resent. The four uniform beds, the dresser, the windows across the far wall. Her chest eased slightly, but she felt wholly unsteady, her mind stuttering. It took far too long for her to collect herself, minutes that felt like hours, and when she finally did, she couldn't swallow the experience.

Arioch tugged her toward the mattress, while her vision blurred and Aheia stared down the dark covers, because the burn in her eyes made sense when she deprived them of a break. She could tell herself that's why they teared up.

He let her stand when she wouldn't sit, and reached for a golden tray that was set on the black silk. It held a few bowls, one ghosted with condensation as the steam rose from the rice and meat within, another filled with white raspberries, and a third that held a myriad of little green vegetables. The spit welled up on her tongue as she stared it down, like an adversary.

"What do you like?"

His words felt almost numb now.

"What?" Her mind was mush.

"To eat."

"I uh—I don't know." She cleared her throat. What did she like to eat? "I'm not hungry."

Arioch reached a heavy arm past her to snatch up one of the raspberries, meeting her eyes as he held it up to her lips. She shook her head.

"Aheia." It was a warning, one that shot lightning strikes down her spine, one that conjured quiet little alarm bells at the back of her mind.

"*Dey peynjao.*" She repeated it blandly, her stomach knotting further.

"And I'm not in the fucking mood. Eat the damn berry." His nostrils flared. "It's like bargaining with a youngling."

Her eyebrows furrowed, but she kept her mouth shut.

"*Aljah,*" he cursed, gripping her chin with one hand and shoving the raspberry past her lips with the other. She jolted back, trying to shake off his hold, but squishing the berry against her teeth with her tongue in the process. How fucking *dare* he. She chewed it even though all she wanted was to spit it back in his face.

"It's not bargaining when you're not offering something in return," she said finally.

"It's food Aheia, I shouldn't have to." His jaw ticked. "You should want to stay fucking *alive.*"

Her neck flexed as the air shifted between them.

You should want to stay alive. Right ...

Her fingers twitched at her side and she rubbed them together in a nervous habit, feeling the anger he conjured bleed through her. *Anger*. He called it back so easily when she had a hard time finding it on her own.

Arioch watched her, and she wished he didn't. His stare was something she felt incapable of holding. But then, she felt incapable of holding a lot of things. Her weapons were heavy and her muscles were screaming.

Taking the next piece of fruit between her teeth felt almost mechanical, because today she'd pick her battles. It sat sour in her stomach, like an intrusion once it finally settled. Battles seemed silly after seeing the remnants of the war she'd waged all her life manacled to dark stone in some nondescript cave.

"What was wrong with him?" she asked, unwillingly remembering Ophion's face. "He was ... twitching."

"He's busy fending off the rats," Arioch said calmly.

"What?" *Rats?*

"Nightmares," Arioch said slowly. "A way to kill him without killing him. He'll spend the next hours getting eaten slowly."

"Why?" she asked, her knees feeling unsteady. "Why are you keeping him alive?"

"Death has to be earned." The look he gave her did its best to melt through the suffocating layer that wrapped around her. "The suffering he's caused has to be repaid first."

Her breath whooshed from her lungs, and her sad little heart couldn't differentiate his intentions. It took them and pretended they were for her, *her* suffering. Why did she reach for anything that felt like kindness, even if it wasn't meant for her? Why was her soul so fucking hungry for heartbreak?

"Why not barter with the Mithra?"

"I've never been interested in bartering with the Mithra." Her jaw tightened, the layers of that statement stacking. "I'll bring you back down when he's recovered enough to talk," he continued, as if the reason they'd left the cave hadn't been her own inadequacy.

"Recovered?" she asked, wetting her throat, watching Arioch dig in his pockets and retrieve something in a closed fist.

"He'll adjust." He opened his fingers, letting the contents clatter to the floor. Small white pieces of bloody bone—*teeth.*

Aheia's jaw trembled, and she felt herself tug forward in sick fascination. She crouched down, reaching out an unsteady hand while Arioch moved past her and sat on the mattress.

The ridge of a molar depressed the pad of her finger, and her skin pebbled. The blood transferred onto her and she looked down at it, mesmerized. Ophion's blood. She'd never touched his blood before. But he'd had his hands coated in hers.

Her bones started to feel nonexistent, and just as she questioned if she'd be able to get herself back off the floor, Arioch hauled her up. He took her hand and wiped her finger on his black shirt, distaste twisting his features.

"How did you do it?" she asked, her voice thick and coated with something that made her sound hoarse as he picked up another berry and held it out to her.

"With my hands." He gripped the back of her left thigh, keeping her between his legs while he fed her the fruit. Shivers wracked her. *With my hands.*

Those hands, the ones that held berries between them delicately. He could crush them without any effort. He could crush her, too. And the thought of it shouldn't have felt so inviting. The weight of him shouldn't have enticed her the way it did, not when he was such a complication. That didn't change how her mind conjured flashes of red blood dripping off his fingers as he pulled teeth from her stepfather's mouth. It softened her resolve, the tiny, strong parts of her that remained, leaving the lonely version bared. The one that wanted to throw her hands at something that would undoubtedly cut the life out of her if she gave herself over.

Hatred did nothing to ebb the way her soul lit, the way his touch felt, the way he could quiet her mind in a completely different way. It was that lure of distraction that had her reaching for his hair, feeling the soft curls between her fingers and marveling at his height seated in front of her, almost eye to eye even now. *Soft*. One of the only soft parts of him.

"You need to eat." The sound of his voice matched the static in her veins, his hand nowhere near the food now.

"Feed me then, *majte*." They weren't her words. They belonged to whatever simmered between them. But it didn't matter, because in this painful moment, the two sides of her were on the same page.

His reaction was delicious. The calm on his face faltered. A crack in the marble. The vein at his temple pulsed with the strain of his jaw and Aheia felt a stripe of something warm blister through her. Elation. Elation at his response, watching white knuckles on clasped hands.

"Don't call me that while you hate me." His eyes dropped to her lips, and she wet them instinctively.

"Did you expect me not to? Hate you?" And she'd meant to say it lightly, but as soon as the words left her, the weight across her shoulders doubled, and the sadness that had been so numb before cracked through. Her vulnerability crashed into her with full force. "You took me back." She spilled the hurt that felt like an open wound being prodded. "You didn't—" *stop. You'd said you'd stop if I asked you to.*

It was the part that ached the worst, and the pain robbed her words.

She wasn't prepared for how much it would cost, to say it out loud, how much everything would shift. Cold teeth dug into her sides as his body became all hard, rigid lines in front of her. She wanted to dig her hands into his flesh to find nerves that would shake his exterior, that would make him bleed, because she couldn't be the only one with an open wound. She needed him to lose something the way she'd lost. Kept losing.

Over and over again. Little parts of herself. When would it be enough.? When would she disappear completely as strips of her skin were pulled from her body to clothe others?

Hatred. She felt it between her ribs. Resentment too. Resentment for the things she remembered. His words, her malleability even now, the way her heart seemed to beat for him after everything that happened between them—after getting back the things he took. Her soul was somewhere in the threads of her being, and yet it didn't feel like hers. It purred and hummed where Arioch touched her—writhed and slithered, making the distance between them stomach curling—like her own essence wanted out, wanted back to him.

It was as if that helfyre they'd shared molded them into one disastrous thing. Or rather, had braided her to his side in a body that housed a pleading soul.

Was it just her that felt this? This fucking fire, this need, this obsession?

She'd wanted so badly for this, for *him* to be real when she first awoke, and now she wished he wasn't. Because if it wasn't real, then she could keep losing herself without the heavy ramifications of the past. She could give in to him without feeling like so much less when she did.

"I took you back. I could have done worse." His breathing matched hers, but it was his words that stole the air around them completely.

What? The need for his distraction shifted. He was *fighting* her? After everything, he was pushing back? Her lips parted and she felt that anger blossom worse.

"Excuse me?"

Chapter 17

Arioch

"*You could have done worse?*" Aheia repeated in a huff, baring her teeth.

"Did you think you were more important than Kazim?" Arioch asked, feeling the spite in his veins. "That I would find out about my brother being *alive* and not do *everything* in my power to get him back?"

She bristled, and he could see it, the hesitation that slipped through her mask before she returned that practiced look to her face—like she was realizing and actually understanding, for the first time that there had been a fucking reason for his actions.

"I don't give a shit. You should be *groveling* for what you did, Skotá," she spit.

"Apologies don't mean a fucking thing," he said coldly, and he meant it. They were fucking worthless. They'd never gotten him anywhere. "It's just words said by people who want forgiveness and can't figure out how to earn it."

"They mean something if they *mean* something," she countered.

"You want me to lie to you, then? Tell you I regret what I did?"

"You're an asshole." Her eyes snapped to his as he stood from the mattress, renewed flames licking at her gaze. Her hands fisted at her sides and that blush crept down her neck. He felt her—just the tiniest little thread—her turmoil. It was hate. Hate for a lot of things; him, life, but most overwhelming was the kind that burned for herself. There was so much self-hatred inside of his Aheia, he didn't know how she was standing upright.

"It's just words, Aheia," he drawled, keeping that smile in place because for every moment he held it, she hardened a tick further. Hardness was strength, it was resilience. And it wiped out that hollow, lost look on her face.

"Gods, you keep saying my name like that." She stepped away, crossing her arms. "You use it like a threat. Something to be dragged through the mud in anger."

His throat went dry.

His tongue was heavy with endearment, but he couldn't use it, not when she looked at him with empty eyes and the barest flicker of resentment. A flicker that should have been a fucking bonfire because he'd used her and he needed her to make him suffer for it.

It's what he reached for, the heat he recognized, buried under the dissociating side of her. She'd shown it to him before when she held a knife to his throat in his dining hall, when she spit venom from her tongue, when she dug in her nails. That's what he fanned, because those emotions would incinerate the numb kinds. He wouldn't let her drift and if that meant playing the villain for her, he'd gladly do it. Because at least she spoke when she was mad. At least she was alive, even if it was corrosive. Being kind didn't have the same effect.

"Is there a question in that statement?"

He picked up another piece of fruit and took a step toward her, relishing how she flinched back even though there was nowhere to go but the wall. He liked that it seemed instinctual for her to back away from something that wanted to fucking eat her alive.

"Why am I here?" She fixed him with a glare. "If all you do is say my name in anger, why am I here?"

If the aim hadn't been to infuriate her, he would have told her about what it had felt like when she'd died on that brittle, white ground. He would have told her how long he'd held on to her even after her death, how often he went to Gehenna when he hated being in the lower realm—how he wanted her here because he *wanted* her here and he hadn't felt that for anyone in a very long time.

But he didn't say any of those things. Instead, he watched her anger blossom and blister like a flower catching fire in the silence he fed her and then he made it all worse.

"Because I get bored," he said it calmly, but it felt like he was biting it through his teeth as he diminished the space between them and her white hair bunched up against the wall. "It's why I gave you seven days for your soul, Aheia. It's roughly when I lose interest in my toys." The words were chosen harshly, but they weren't a lie. "I'm not bored with you yet."

She inhaled sharply as he reached for her jaw and squeezed, the fire inside of him burning just as hot as hers. Aheia bared her teeth and shoved at his chest, except her fingers twisted in the fabric, her nails pricking his pecs instead of letting him go after the impact.

That's it. More. Give me more.

"Get your hands off me," she grit out between her teeth.

Arioch looked down between them, watching her tits heaving, her little body pressed in tight, hands wrapped up in his shirt.

She was staring daggers now and the sharpness of them made his shadows vibrate.

He was hungry. So fucking hungry that it was almost desperate.

"You first."

A pleat creased her eyebrows as she blinked, snatching back her hands like he'd burned her. But he didn't let go, he'd never let go again. Instead, he forced her head to the side so that he could drag the flat of his tongue down her jaw. That floral impossible fucking taste branded him as she froze, a soft pink line blushing her complexion under his touch.

"I'm not your toy," she said breathily, nostrils flaring but despite her words, her body shivered against his, and he felt the echo in his veins, felt her lust as his stroke for stroke. She wasn't pulling away even though she had enough space to. And then she fucking pressed into him—just the softest amount, like she was chasing his tongue as he flicked it over the corner of her mouth. But it was enough to spur him on, to start a new game just because he wanted to see what she'd do.

"Aren't you?" He pushed harder, stoked that fire. "You respond so fucking pretty when I play with you."

"Disgust. That's the response," she huffed out, but it was more of a whimper than anything, as he let go of her jaw and brushed his hand down the side of her neck. She didn't look at him, didn't move one inch, when he touched her body, a long line that framed her collarbone, her shoulder, her bicep, all the way down to her waist. They both watched her skin pebble, pink bursts of color blooming in his wake.

When he rounded her hip she gasped, and squirmed, pressure swiping against his cock in the most delirious fucking way.

"If I keep picking up full trays of food, I'll start forcing it down your throat instead." He dropped his voice to a growl, not bothering to address her words.

"You're not coming near my throat," she hissed.

"Next time you waste my food ..." He rubbed his fingers across her soft lips, the image invading his mind: her on her knees with her lips parted for him. "I'll come down it." Her mouth parted in shock and he took the opportunity to push the berry he'd been holding between her teeth. Anger shone brightly in her eyes as her hot breath coasted across his skin. His fingers touched the wetness on her lips when she closed her mouth, and his shadows jerked violently, flickering his vision. She coughed and spluttered, gripping the fabric over his chest again, trying to chew the food.

"Through your nose, Aheia. Wouldn't want you to choke." He trailed his thumb and caught some of the juice dripping down her chin, sucking it off as she swallowed his mouthful, red splotches peppering her neck. He taunted her with her name, because volatile meant alive. And if she wanted something to hate, something to punish and tear apart, he'd give her just that. He'd keep her angry, to keep her mind here.

A cut youngling loved knives, and he'd never run out of blades for her.

She opened her mouth, but her answer muffled against his ears when he felt the stabbing pain in his palm. He knew what it was before he glanced down to see the black dot forming. The *Shayṭān* were ready for their audience. They had shit fucking timing, and they were moodier than Aheia. If he let them wait, there was a chance they wouldn't see him again for weeks out of spite. Everything in this world operated on their timetable.

Thick ink bubbled onto his skin until it formed a circle at the center and his fingers flinched against the pain.

"And now you're ignoring me?" She scoffed, forcing her arms between them to cross them over her chest.

He grit his teeth, pushing himself away from her and it took more effort than he wanted to admit.

"I have somewhere to be." He flicked his tongue against the underside of his teeth. "Don't get into any trouble, Aheia. Stay put for me."

Fuck, he really hoped she took it as a challenge. Because that's exactly what it was.

His feet dragged over the rough rock of Gehenna, Aheia's gem tucked in his palm. His shadows simmered as he watched himself approach the Shayṭān, his favorite cryptic fatekeepers, with a leather bag in hand. The oracle had only let Arioch see them once—the first time he'd ventured into the underbelly of Gehenna. The first time they'd pulled him here.

Their form between the dead rock was black and viscous. A large, slimy beast with long appendages. They'd shown him the gold threads of fate then, the ones that lashed across their tongue and let them speak only when the words and knowledge fell inside the lines of what destiny would allow them to tell—allow him to know. He'd spent many fruitless visits since trying to learn about things he wasn't meant to learn, being turned down each time with that droning silence.

Now all he saw was himself, because they lent him their sight.

"Last time I came—"

"You were empty-handed." The disjointed voice floated around him.

He watched his own movement, dangling the leather pouch he'd brought off his finger because down here, he saw through their eyes.

The oracle nodded, at least it seemed that way, and Arioch flattened his palm, holding out the bag like a cube of sugar to a horse. A long, slick arm reached toward him and slung around the leather, bringing it close.

"You couldn't give me any insight about Aheia last time I was here. You told me she was a question without an answer."

"And nothing has changed." The Shayṭān opened the pouch and reached inside, pulling out a dried, nectar-soaked cricket. The oracle crooned contently, an eerie clicking noise echoing around them before crunching the candy between its teeth. "Young sovereign, there's much for you to learn. The questions in your mind have answers, but you won't find them before you walk the path that leads you there. We do not deal in shortcuts."

Arioch pinched the bridge of his nose.

"Ask us," they continued.

"What is the point?"

"Or don't." Another cricket disappeared with a crunch.

They're enjoying this. He grit his teeth with the effort to keep himself relaxed. Down here, his shadows felt a lot more stretched, and all they wanted was to travel topside to see Aheia.

Alright, your way.

"What can you tell me about this stone?" he asked, holding out the lápis.

"Come closer."

Arioch stepped forward when the oracle beckoned him, standing on the uneven ground, feeling the air becoming warm around them. It was thick, and its smell was old—air that had been living underneath rock for eons.

He presented the crystal like an offering.

"A binding stone," they said, voice deep, their arm drifting over the small gem.

"A binding stone?" Arioch narrowed his eyes. "Binding what? Magyck?"

The oracle only nodded.

What?

He hadn't questioned Aheia's lack of power when she was with him in Aljira, because no Mithra would be able to use their given gifts in his realm. But he hadn't for a moment thought that she'd lost it before crossing his border. If the Shayṭān's words were meant how he'd interpreted them, had she been near mortal even in her home? Fuck, this created new questions that made his head spin. If she'd been truly powerless—bound—how had she shocked his realm with something powerful, something he'd barely held together with his shadows all those weeks ago when the Mithra first came to claim her?

He watched himself, literally seeing his face change with the realization. If this was true, then she hadn't had her magyck on her run across Lyria. She'd made it to Aljira without any help.

Did she know?

No.

If she'd known about the stone, about it being a bind, she wouldn't have offered it to him in their trade. It was too precious.

Fucking hel.

"Could a stone like this tether someone to life? Keep them from true death?" he asked.

"It's possible."

He loosened a harsh breath, caressing the thing with his thumb. It had gone from useless to important in the span of moments.

"How old is the bind?"

Maybe it had been created just before she escaped, maybe it had been a punishment. It made the most sense, even though all of it still stroked him the wrong way. Because she hadn't been powerless here. The opposite.

"Time is irrelevant."

His jaw tightened. "The rock being broken—does it mean the bind is broken?"

The oracle nodded.

"Is the suffocated magyck returned, then?"

They shook their head.

What the fuck?

"That doesn't make any sense."

The bind broke with the rock but she doesn't have her magyck back.

"Because you don't understand it, or because it's untrue?"

Fuck's sake.

"The thunderstorms in Lyria, the fire that lights their homes, the connection to the Gods that plants and fungi can provide, may have been explained by the mortals, but that does not make them any less magyck. You look for answers because you fear things that you don't understand. Cease trying to assign meaningless words to simplify something that could never be simple."

"Everything's a riddle with you," he growled, frustration lacing his words.

"You want clarity? Stop looking." A brittle crackling filled the air. "And don't come back, not until you know you can."

Chapter 18

Aheia

When he left, she sank to her knees, her fingers digging into her thighs.

Fuck. Fuck. "Fuck," she groaned, the air hammering in and out of her in shallow gasps. Her soul spasmed and her body, traitorous bitch that she was, responded with vigor, making her all jelly legged and messy. She pressed her forehead against the stone, her elbows quivering. Arioch might not have had a soul glyph to stroke to his sick heart's content, but somehow it didn't seem to matter. It felt like the small discolored patch of skin still existed, except now it was assimilated into his bloodstream and hers just as well.

Did this feel the same for him? She wanted to know, but she couldn't bring herself to ask. It was offering up too much when she was on the offense.

The shadows he'd stepped through so casually were still dissipating, and that black made her see red. Her fingers twisted into the shirt at her side as she pushed upright, her knees brittle against the stone. He kept leaving, and she kept losing a little part of something when it made her crumble.

He wanted her to *stay*. Not stay with *him*—stay *put*. Eat. There for him whenever he felt like visiting. Demands, demands, demands. The warmth he'd stoked in her chest spread down her limbs until her fingers prickled with it—blood returning to a lifeless arm.

Fuck him.

No. She wouldn't stay. Not when he wanted her to and not when Ophion was somewhere below her feet. The thought threatened her throat with bile, but she swallowed it and grimaced. *Don't think about it.* She couldn't let it be real. She needed to pretend it was just another nightmare because right now, the thought of the Malek being alive, even if he was restrained, even if he was *wingless,* made her want to stop in her tracks and swaddle herself in a blanket. She'd never get up again if she did that.

Instead, she grabbed the tray of food and opened the door to the balcony, throwing the entirety of it over the side. The gold bowls and fruit twisted through the air and splashed into the roaring Asara River below as she padded back inside, holding on to that waning stream of adrenaline that leached from her veins. She wrenched open the wardrobe, the door hitting the opposite wall, and growled at the color choice. *White. White. White.*

Was that what she'd be reduced to here, too?

Fuck's sake.

The anger burned bright now, and she let herself feel it, let herself hate Arioch for leaving again. Hate him for wearing dark shirts and being born with gray, hypnotizing eyes. Hating him for everything she could manage to tack on to his name.

But for all of that, she hated herself more.

Because she hadn't wanted him to leave. Even after he degraded her like he did.

Get your shit together.

She wiped the back of her hand across her eyelids, rubbing furiously and rolling her shoulders like it might force out the weakness in her veins. And then she made a plan. A haphazard one. One that had maybe two whole steps to it, but a plan nonetheless.

Getting dressed was the first point.

She decided on a matching set of leathers that both tied at the front and stuffed her feet into thick, white boots. Then, she braided back her mane, and secured the end with one of the leather straps that was tucked on top of the tallest shelf.

When she finally ridded herself of everything Arioch touched, she stalked back to the balcony and let those pieces fall as well. She watched them growing smaller and smaller until they disappeared, the wind whipping free loose strands of her hair.

The second part of the plan was fighting everything he'd asked of her. That's as far as this rage, soul, lust, and anger-fueled dizziness inside of her brain reached. She was impulsive right now, and she knew that. But *knowing* what she was about to do was pointless and insane, didn't equate to not doing it for sane reasons.

She wouldn't just sit here at his beck and call. If he wanted to be around her, he could come get her.

Her eyes drifted to the small walkway that connected her balcony to the next as she considered that Nyco would be outside of her door again. She needed to avoid their attention to get out of this fucking place. She was under no delusion that she was escaping this realm, not now, not with zero knowledge of how to actually breach the border or where she'd go after, but that didn't mean she had to *stay put* here.

She walked to the far end of the balcony, and this time teetering over certain death felt more precarious when she balanced on the thin beam.

Maybe it's the shoes. She couldn't feel the stone on her feet, couldn't curl her toes into the grout.

With determination and frustration on her side, she made it across quickly, climbing onto the next balcony and squeezing inside. She looked around, no Nyco in sight, only a few Nephilim that looked at her sideways.

She was painfully aware that she wouldn't blend in here like she had when she snuck out of Ophion's house. It had been much easier to hide when she didn't stand out and could just steal one of the Dioscuri maids' robes before ducking amongst the expanse of white in the streets. It was how she'd started hearing about different schools of thought. It was how she'd come to learn that there were groups of rebels that didn't believe in Ophion and his teachings. But she found quickly that *rebel* was a generous term in the small circle. The people who gathered were not particularly loud, especially not when exposure threatened them. They were too scared of death to truly make a change. But at the time, it had felt like *something*, like the defiance she needed to keep going.

Aheia focused on her feet, trying her best to blend, well aware that she stood out like the first snowflake on a dark night.

Nyco had given her a sparse run down of the Kaserne's layout and most of that information bled together in her mind because there were way too many offshoots, but she'd tried to remember where the vortexes were located. She thought they'd spoken about a very distinct stone mural that was carved into the wall next to the red *alusca* plants last time they passed, offhandedly remarking that a vortex into the city was down the right spiral staircase. Or was it the left?

Fuck.

She stood in front of the artwork, pretending to admire it while her eyes slid furtively to each option.

Left.

Right.

Left.

Hopefully.

She darted down the staircase, keeping her hand clamped on the stone railing and almost stumbling twice in her hurry. Her heart was thundering in her chest, and she whipped her head over her shoulder every so often, feeling the eerie prickle of eyes on her back even when no one was there.

She exhaled in relief when she reached the bottom, met by a swirling, dark gray wall. The vortex she'd walked through with Emryn at the compound had taken her into the city as well, and this looked identical. Aheia didn't know where it led, but once again, that scarcely mattered. She was suffocating in that room because Arioch had taken up space there, and when he left, he took that space with him. It was a quarter of the size it had started with.

Her breath was warm and heavy, and the quick trip down the stairs had stolen much of her oxygen. She was weak, having to clutch her knees for a moment to calm herself down. Her body screamed at her to just sit down, to stop moving.

Instead, she pressed her eyes shut tight, pushed herself up, and took a step forward. She didn't watch the magyck eat her, only felt it—felt the water like consistency, felt the shift in cold, *cold* air around her, felt the earth move under her feet.

Her nostrils flared and she let the freshness sting her lungs. The cold always had a specific smell, like a bite. But something different was mixed into it here and she could see it in the dark behind her closed eyelids—fire. She smelled fire and burnt wood.

"Woah." Her lips parted when she let herself see the landscape in front of her.

She was standing in a town square with a small fountain at the center. It was broken, split down the center, and stale water puddled inside. Buildings surrounded her, some made of brick, some made of wood, but nearly all of them dusted in ash. Pieces of it drifted through the air as she took a step onto the old cobblestone. Broken beams were propped up on the house to her left, fresh lumber that had been placed next to a structure that resembled a clump of charcoal more than a house.

It was eerie and quiet. Abandoned. A ghost town. Where was everyone? What had happened?

There were pieces of clothing scattered too, some of them smeared with black. *Blood.* Aheia crouched down, hovering her hand over a small, pink shirt. There were strawberries printed on it, and large holes ripped into the side.

"Get lost?"

"Shit." Aheia grabbed her chest, when her heart leapt into her throat as if her hand could keep it in the correct cavity.

Her eyes darted behind her, but she knew who it was when she heard their voice.

"How did you find me?"

How had they found her *so quick?*

"A shifty Mithra hurrying down the hallway tends to stand out." Nyco cracked a grin, leaning against the old rock that bordered the vortex.

She returned her eyes to the shirt on the ground, not bothering to try to hide herself with her arms as was instinct. Because the white pigment of her skin wasn't much different from that of the fabric that covered her.

"What is this place?"

"You've been here." They looked around. "You woke up here."

Her lips parted as she searched for the name of the town. "Keosha? What happened?"

"The Shykoya," they said simply.

The monsters.

Aheia looked across the charred buildings. She'd known about their attack, but these buildings ... "These homes, they're burnt. Shykoya don't have fire magyck, do they?"

"No. The fire was sparked in a panic. Sometimes the mindless fear is more dangerous than the threat itself," they said, standing in front of her and stealing her attention. "You know what that feels like, don't you?"

"What are you trying to say?"

"Just attempting to work out what you're going to do next." They lifted an eyebrow.

I'm leaving. It was on the tip of her tongue. Her own reaction to that statement was unsettling. It was a lie—one she hadn't even said aloud. But her body acted like it was a separate thing from her mind, like it couldn't read her deception and it fought her as if she meant it. The words elicited a violent throb in her chest—a revolt. The thought of staying felt like drinking poison but the thought of leaving felt like dying from its effects. Death either way.

They clicked their tongue. "If it helps"—they pointed behind her—"that's the direction of the Kaserne." They jerked their thumb over their shoulder. "That way is the inner city. And"—they gestured to the heart of the burnt town to their right—"if you pass the square, you'll get to the Sephy Forest. It's your best bet if you want to disappear." They started circling her slowly. "However, it's also the birthplace of the Shykoya and Syka, and about another two dozen deadly creatures that could rip your ribcage from your body before you even realize they're near you."

Nyco was calling her bluff without her actually bluffing.

"Now, the border," Their hazel eyes glinted in the moonlight. "Is cut off by the Asara. So, unless you have a way across it, you're shit out of luck. The River might look beautiful, but that doesn't make its rapids any less treacherous. Besides ..." They shrugged, shoving their hands in their pockets. "The border's glamour would set off alarms, and I imagine you wouldn't get far into the shroud before you got yanked right back."

This realm is a prison of mass proportions.

"What will it be?" They held her eyes.

"You assume I'm trying to escape."

"Aren't you?"

She pursed her lips, weighing her options. She didn't know if she could trust Nyco, but everything here felt like a gamble, so what was one more?

"No." She glanced down at herself and then with a voice that wasn't as strong as she wished it had been. "I just ... I needed to not sit in that room for a while."

"Well." Nyco's eyes narrowed slightly, and she readied herself for them to usher her back toward the swirling magyck, to tell her that she could just sit in the citrus grove and pretend, or worse—take her back to the room. "That I can help with."

Her eyes snapped up.

"I was getting bored of that hallway, anyways." They shrugged, keeping their hands stuffed in their pockets and dragging their feet across the ground slowly, off toward one of the small alleys on their right.

Aheia just stared, slack-jawed. She hadn't expected that. "Wait." She jogged after them. "Where are you going?"

"Ah." They tipped their chin toward her, white curls falling into hazel eyes. "I can't tell you that."

"Why?" She crossed her arms, but hadn't stopped walking.

"Because you've scaled a building twice now trying to get away from me, which means you don't trust me. I don't think me telling you where I'm heading will aid that any."

What?

"Are you trying to kill me?" she asked seriously.

"If that was a plan, I would have already done it. The whole town is a crime scene. It would have been easy to add one more body to the ash." They shrugged again, and she supposed that was the truth. Either way, she didn't really need much convincing. Going somewhere new, somewhere that wasn't the Kaserne—she'd take the opportunity for it even if it was suspect. That pesky voice that usually tried to keep her from poor decisions and *alive* was buried somewhere Aheia couldn't hear it.

"Fine." She fell into step, letting her arms drop again.

"You look tired," Nyco said after a moment, weaving through the puddles.

"You have a way with compliments," she huffed.

"I do, Briteling, but you don't want my compliments." They grinned. "I imagine you don't like me very much at this moment,"

"Depends on where you take me."

The two of them cleared another square and dipped down a second alley, heading toward the star-studded horizon beyond it.

They walked in silence for a while, and it was just fine with Aheia. She was busy taking in the sights around her as they left the burnt buildings behind, generally trying to forget her reality while she was at it. The Asara cut through their path, forking out and away from them, the riverbanks bordered by thick protective rocks. There was a small bridge that seemed much too thin to be safe that arched over the wild water. Aheia remembered faintly what it had felt like to be ripped under by the unrelenting waves, a cold chill prickling her spine that didn't leave her until she stepped onto steady ground on the other side.

The streets here seemed more chaotic, not as straightly drawn as she'd seen them from the window at the center of Aljira the first time she'd been in the city. The stone roads were different, smoother, and the buildings were huddled much closer together. There was smoke in the air, a myriad of different colors that came from the establishments here dancing across it as it rose into the sky. There were carts with vendors lining the right side of the street, and whatever food they were selling smelled overbearing.

"Is this still Keosha?" she asked, cocking her head as they dipped down a side alley, away from all of the commotion.

"Nope, the river breaks up Keosha and Thryn."

"How come that vortex opened into Keosha? Do you have vortexes for every—you call them cities here?"

"That vortex is set to the outlier town we were just in—a small unnamed hovel bordering the forest. It's there because it's where our efforts have been needed most. The gate gives us quick access, but it can be shifted as needed. Keosha is the whole territory and is made up of a bunch of smaller cities and towns. Kamaria is in power there, the Siada for that portion of Aljira," they clarified.

That's right. Aheia remembered meeting a few of the Siada.

"How do they come into power?" she asked curiously, feeling her chest ease the longer they walked. Females had never held positions of high standing in Keloseros, not in that way.

"Well, it used to be bloodlines, but we're slowly coming out of that era."

"Why?"

"Alshaytan Arioch has made many changes, a political voting system being one of them. The existing Siada don't support it, of course, at least not the ones who only hold their power because the right has run in their families. The ones who care about their territory and do their best to see it flourish aren't as irritated about it."

"How does the system work?" She'd never considered such a thing. In Keloseros, it was all bloodlines.

"Well, each territory holds its elections when the time comes and the Nephilim that live there can choose amongst different candidates to represent their territory. Some play fair, some elicit enough fear to sway the vote." They pointed her toward what looked like a huge dead end—three buildings rising up in front of them. "So far, all the ones Arioch appointed when he took over for Alshaytan Sahren have been voted back."

She blinked. "Why would Arioch want that? Wouldn't it be easier to control his people if he didn't provide them with a choice?"

If he didn't give them a voice?

Nyco looked at her sideways. "Yea, it would be."

Aheia let herself consider that. "What about him? Can he be ..." Her eyebrows crinkled. "Voted out?" She wasn't sure if that was the right wording.

"Not as such. His role is more difficult to replace, but at the end of the day, if a majority of the Siada had reason to break down his rule, they could attempt it."

They looked at her sideways, and Aheia opened her mouth to ask another question when a familiar voice sounded in the distance.

"Nyco, you're *so* late!"

Her head whipped forward, spotting the two demons she'd met a few days prior at the far end of a dead-end alley. Saffy had her hair tied back, but a few black curls hung down into her eyes. Her lips were painted dark blue and the scraps of clothing that matched the color wrapped around her body like water.

"Late?" Aheia asked Nyco as they tugged her forward by her elbow. "Were you already coming here?"

They only smiled.

"That whole idea of self-preservation is really wasted on you." Rav looked over at Aheia, grazing down his near naked chest with purple nails. The redhead wore a netted shirt with his leathers, eyes rimmed in thick charcoal. "Did you think about whose bed she warms before you decided on bringing her?"

Aheia had to hold back the hiss on her lips as she spoke. "I do not warm his bed."

"He's just jealous," Saffy said in a mock whisper. "Ignore him, I do."

"She found her way here almost on her own; who am I to stop her?" Nyco grinned, but their eyes stayed on Aheia.

"Isn't that exactly your point?" Rav nudged their shoulder. "To stop her?"

Aheia's eyes widened. "Will you get into trouble for this?" She didn't need to hear their answer to know they *would* get in trouble and it would be her fault, because she left and they were meant to watch her. She'd been so focused on somehow getting out of her building and then staying out once she made it that she didn't let herself consider anyone else in the equation.

They clicked their tongue and rolled their eyes. "*Arrê*, you couldn't force me to do something if you tried, Briteling." Then they turned to Saffy with a pleading look. "Will you *distract* him?"

Rav rolled his eyes as Saffy jumped onto his back and Nyco linked their arm with Aheia's.

"Fucking exhausting," they muttered.

She let Nyco lead her forward, *toward* the dead end, which made no sense.

"Where are we going?" she asked again.

"Just wait."

"I'm not fucking running you the whole way," Rav bit out, readjusting Saffy. "You'll break my back."

"I thought your little Siren whore did that last night." She sniggered.

"You're a bitch when you're celibate," he snapped back.

"It's kind of like being hangry, but I don't get to eat for thirty whole days," Saffy groaned.

"Why is she being celibate?" Aheia asked Nyco.

"Saffy likes a challenge," they said, resting their tongue in the inner corner of their mouth. "This month it's something about connecting with her inner self—"

"I am *trying*," Saffy interjected over her shoulder, "to get to know who I am, alright? And"—she looked at Aheia and bristled slightly when Rav jostled her—"I'm trying to be more intentional, less transactional." She waved a hand through the air.

"Do you even know what that means or are you just reciting it from that yellow book you keep under your pillow?" Rav chuckled.

"Now you're definitely running me the rest of the way, asshole," Saffy grumbled.

"Running?" Aheia asked.

"Stick with me," Nyco said, much too casual.

"Stick with you *where*?" She was exasperated, but that emotion didn't stick around as she watched the two Nephilim in front of her *bleed* into the seemingly solid wall. *Another vortex,* she realized.

"Hel." Nyco's canines glinted ominously as she paid closer attention to the old carved stone. At the top, in rough etchings, she read '*Lasciate ogne speranza, voi ch'entrate.*'

"Wait—" She balked, but Nyco wasn't letting her back down.

"Hesitation killed the cat, Briteling," they said without answering her question.

"I don't think that's how it goes—" she yelped as Nyco yanked her forward with them. Her world turned on its axis when the magyck lapped at her sides, cold outside air replaced by something damp and heavy.

Hel. That's why they hadn't told her where they were going.

Alarm bells sounded in her mind as the darkness swallowed her and spit her out on the other side unceremoniously. She stumbled forward, gulping in mouthfuls of air.

There was no light.

"Nyco!" she gasped, because they weren't holding her now. The word echoed, along with screams, yelps, hollers, and laughs that drifted all around her.

She twisted and turned, random flickers of light *whooshing* past her—fire, and bright blue orbs. She caught teeth and smiles, caught bodies running, hair whipping in and out of sight, all too quick for true recognition. It felt like one of her dreams until a flame appeared in front of her face, the orange dancing across Nyco's hazel eyes.

"Don't let the darkness eat you," they said, their voice a low purr before they took off in front of her.

"Oh my *gods*," Aheia wheezed, falling into a jog. "What is this place?"

"I told you, it's hel," they threw over their shoulder.

"This is *not*—" Aheia squeaked, stumbling over a rock when another pair of demons dashed past her with their own torch.

"Sure it is. You saw the entrance, didn't you?" Nyco asked, voice echoing. "It was carved to match the description in the mortal's religious tales—to liken what they believe the gates of hel look like. The inscription above it—*Lasciate ogne speranza, voi ch'entrate*—it means roughly '*Abandon hope, ye who enter here*' in one of the mortal languages."

"A joke?" She huffed, latching on to Nyco's hand.

"Legend has it the Nephilim in the past plucked mortals from their homes and ran them around down here—scaring them shitless and betting on the outcome."

"What kind of outcome?" Aheia sucked air between her teeth. She wasn't cut out for running, let alone talking through the experience.

"Who would go insane first, who killed to survive, who sacrificed another—that type of shit. It's most likely where the mortals got the idea for what hel is like to begin with, all because of some blood sport."

Aheia picked up her pace as best she could, stumbling against the ground under her feet. Her legs rebelled against her, a reminder of the food she didn't eat before she left as her vision peppered in little light leaks.

"Stay close, Briteling. You could get lost for hours down here—days and weeks if no one looked for you." The firelight licked at their eyes.

"Why are we running?" It was barely a sentence, mostly just breath.

"To pay our respects to those who came before us," they replied steadily.

The noises around her grew and built with the bodies that slipped past, the tunnel opening up further, connecting to many different branches. Demons jumped off the wall and sprinted on all fours, metal glimmering in the light as they rounded a corner, some of them running into each other, others tackling the ones in front of them. Aheia's breath came in an exhausted huff, a stitch lacing her side as she spotted the first light that wasn't fire or Solas gleaming in the distance. It was red, floating on clouds of thick smoke that bled toward them from a large opening in the rock wall.

The closer they got, the more boisterous it all became—deep pulsing music sounded, the kind that conjured images of dancing amongst dark trees, of secrets dripped in gold goblets and blood spilled across spider-riddled underbrush. It smelled of frankincense and myrrh but mixed with something wet and salty. Time slowed with them as their running fell away to slow steps, sweat pearling against Aheia's forehead. The thick air bewitched her senses and sank into her pores like it wanted to pull her near and hug her tight in its embrace.

Her jaw dropped when she and Nyco walked into the light-flooded room ahead.

You're fucking kidding me.

Aheia's mouth parted, her eyes drifting lazily across dark red lights streaming down across countless dancing bodies with flashes of blue breaking up the deep hues.

A church?

The ceiling was tall and vaulted, and there was red glass that stretched against the stone sides even though there was nothing past it—just more stone. It was as if this place had been carved into the hardness and built as though it was outside. She couldn't see much past the crowd mobbing the front, as Nyco turned around, walking backward, and coaxing her deeper. Their smile was fucking delinquent, and their eyes almost black under the red light. Demonic.

"Come on, Briteling," they purred over the music, bodies enveloping them slowly, arms and hands sliding across them, hair and feathers, leather and lace.

Chapter 19

Arioch

Kazim's return wasn't a secret, not since a few loud mouths had spread the word, but that didn't mean Arioch wanted it to be a talking point. His brother's re-emergence made things difficult, and he held onto that because if Arioch focused on the complications that could arise and the political discourse it was already starting to require, he didn't have to pay attention to the fact that his brother couldn't look him in the eye.

Kazim's hair was hanging into his face—so much longer than Arioch had ever seen it as they sat across from each other in his room. The loose spirals went past his shoulder blades now, curls pulled almost straight by their weight. Arioch and he looked similar—that's what others had always said. But he'd never seen that. Kazim was taller, his eyes darker. His features were sharper, and his frame broader. But that hadn't helped him then, when they were young—the healed-over skin on his forearm was a reminder. That wound hadn't been Ophion's doing. His brother's scars were more familiar to Arioch than the rest of his appearance.

He watched Kazim's eyes, the gray that bordered his black irises, so completely opposite of his own. At one point in their past, he would have recognized himself there, in the similarities. But not now. They were strangers.

He didn't know what they'd done to him in Keloseros, but what was clear was that he'd starved.

The ink that was written across almost the entirety of Arioch's body used to look the same on Kazim. Now it was just a few sad wisps slung around his shoulders. He was drained, empty, just as Aheia had been when she came to his realm first. It seemed Keloseros dealt in starvation and it didn't discriminate in who it stripped bare. He'd tried to fix it the only way he knew how, found a willing soul and offered it to Kazim. But that had resulted in a vicious reaction. He'd attacked the young male, tried to rip the head clean off his shoulders, a wild look in his eyes.

"You finally have what you wanted," he rasped, blood rimming his fingernails as the demon who'd bared his soul convulsed on the floor. "All that power."

Arioch's shadows whispered in his ear.

Vicious fucking words.

"I never wanted this," he hissed, the statement covering so much more than just power. *He didn't want any of this.*

"You fought like you did," Kazim said, slinking back toward the mattress in a disjointed pattern.

You fought like you did.

Sweat prickled at the back of Arioch's neck. Guilt. So much of it. It found him so easily now when it never had before. It was fucking needles against his insides.

Coming here was his own fucked up form of self-flagellation because this room, his brother, those reminders, cut open old scars every time he did.

Kazim's fingers were cradling a metal cup. His eyes were far away, and Arioch didn't know how to speak. They just sat in silence while he tried to temper the memories that he'd been able to swallow much easier before he saw Aheia's eyes when she was hollow, before his magyck became so loud that he didn't have enough fucking hands to hold all of the threads cutting into his organs, he had to choose which ones would draw blood while he held the others at bay in cut-up palms.

He watched the chair in the corner, because Kazim wasn't the only painful part of this fucking room. He could see it too easy now, Malia's dark curls draped over the leather, the shivers that wracked her, the concave of her cheeks, the unsteady way she held her knees, making herself small against the wingback.

Her eyes were vacant toward the end, and they'd stared past Arioch at the stars like maybe they were talking to her. Her mind rotted before her body did. And when he was little, he didn't understand. Why would she do it? Choose a drug over them.

He'd hated her for so long because she'd been his only safe haven. She'd been the only thing that felt like home in that cold, suffocating house. And she'd decided to drift, instead of fighting, instead of staying. She hadn't loved him enough to bear the pain of her reality for him, or for Kazim.

She'd stopped eating. She'd stopped doing anything but sitting in that chair—the black leather one still nestled in the corner of this room because he couldn't let it go. She'd shrunken into herself, drowned. And then one day she'd taken too much Nerium—enough to permanently steal her away to whatever world she'd sent her mind to a long time ago.

He wondered if he existed in that alternate universe or if he was no different from Sahren. If she wanted to escape Arioch just as well.

He'd hated her for it. He'd hated her until the day she died. The day he found her on the floor with foamy spit dripping from her mouth. He'd never forget it. Her frail body, the way her skin stretched across her bones like a thin sheet.

When she died, Arioch had forgotten how to hate her. And that's when he learned what it felt like to live with regret he couldn't strip from his bones. He could scream it into the voids of Gehenna, he could tear into the flesh of his enemies with atonement on his mind. But nothing would ever change that she'd died because he hadn't done enough. Hadn't been important enough, *loud* enough.

She chose Nerium over her offspring, and he hated himself for it.

"Do you think about her?" he asked. "Malia?"

"Don't," Kazim said, his voice quiet. But Arioch watched his eyes shift to the chair like there was no question about it. He'd been older and had known her longer. She'd been a softness to him in a world where everything was cut from rough stone, just as she had been for Arioch. Maybe even more so.

His heart squeezed, remembering the day of her death, remembering the moment Kazim smiled at him for the last time. They'd sat on the balcony, throwing burning flowers into the Asara below for hours, because where some burned their sins, they'd burned their hopes.

All the while, their mother was fading just a floor above them.

"Make a wish, little brother." Kazim's scarred lip tilted, and he remembered that moment like a tangible thing, holding it in his clasped hands in front of him.

He wished everything was different.

His eyes burned as he let himself look back to his brother, the whites of his eyes bloodshot. Little, red veins spider-webbed toward his irises like he hadn't slept in too long, his cheeks just as hollow as Malia's had been, as Aheia's had been too. His throat felt tight, like someone had stuffed leaves down his esophagus, and he couldn't figure out how to temper his shadows when they slithered between his muscles, not now.

"I failed you," he said to Kazim, standing from his spot in the corner. "It's all my fault. I failed you in a lot of ways and I can't seem to stop ..."

Kazim shrunk back slightly, as if Arioch had made a quick movement when all he did was take one step.

"I'm trying to understand—"

"*Awa' enjala,*" Kazim grit through his teeth, dark eyes still focused on the cup in front of him, the pads of his fingers pressing against the metal so hard that a yellow ring cut across his nails.

"*Natye.*" The word broke in Arioch's hands as he walked toward his brother. No. Fucking *no.*

"*Jia—*"

Arioch gripped his arm, but Kazim reared back, and it sent the water flying.

"Get it off of me." Kazim's voice was panicked, his nails scratching against his skin, lines of white turning to black as it split. The water splashed as he tore off his shirt, wild eyes staring past anything in front of them. He scrambled back until he hit the wall, throwing away the wet fabric. His chest rose and fell quickly, his palms sliding at his slick skin over and over again.

Arioch followed him, gripping his brother's cheeks and steadying his gaze. Kazim ground his canines, shoving at his shoulders, but Arioch was stronger even though his brother was taller—forcing his eyes for the first time since he'd come back.

"Talk to me, fucking talk to me. I don't know what to do, how to help you. Tell me."

"I don't want you here. I don't want to see your face," Kazim spat, drops of spit landing against Arioch's chin when he spoke.

"*Why*?"

"Because it's all I see when I close my eyes," he hissed, his nose wrinkling in disgust. Tears rimmed his eyes now. "You and our father over and over again."

Arioch furrowed his brows.

"It's all he let me see when they—" His words wavered, and he paled, his skin becoming near gray. Arioch watched Kazim's stomach jerk, his arm slinging across his mouth and he dry heaved into the crook of his elbow.

He let go then, and his brother doubled over onto all fours, retching. His knuckles were white, skin pulled tight across his ribs as his back convulsed.

"When they what?" Arioch's voice was hoarse, his eyes burning. He didn't want to know, and that was his shame to bear. But he asked anyway, barely managing the question.

Kazim choked and coughed, his forehead hitting the floor as he tried to catch his breath. His arms were shaking, fingers inches from the starlight that cut across the stone in front of him.

"Your face," he whispered at the floor. "Always your face." His voice was hoarse, his body sinking into itself. "Joke's on them; I saw your face regardless."

Arioch's stomach tensed as his brother's words faded into incoherent slurs, words he couldn't make out between numbers that he repeated over and over again.

He stood, forcing himself into Kazim's washroom.

Because it's all I see when I close my eyes. You and our father over and over again.

The door shut behind him and he gripped the edge of the vanity while his shadows slithered uncomfortably, seeping onto the old rock in the pools. His eyes burned as he faced himself in the mirror: a fucking mess. He could see his insides as if he wore them on his skin, the burns, and cuts, and bruises, and slashes from years and years of life, years of fighting his own family. It was covered by his magyck. It was why he'd always taken so many souls—for a long time, he'd consumed more than he needed to. But he could see it, nonetheless. The black didn't cover shit, not to his eyes.

A fucking road map. He hadn't failed Kazim when he was dead, he'd failed him when he was alive.

"Please forgive me," he whispered against his brother's forehead. Blood dripped down his temple and mingled with Kazim's—his face barely recognizable after their last fight. He'd won, and Sahren had lashed his brother for it. "Please forgive me."

He turned on the sink and splashed water onto his face. It didn't do enough, didn't clean him, and he thought that nothing ever would.

He let his magyck wrap around him, walking through it and into the old wing below. He stood, looking at the burn marks on the fireplace he should have torn down. He remembered Kazim's screams when Sahren forced his hand into the flames after yet another loss to Arioch.

He couldn't be good enough. He didn't deserve forgiveness, yet he was furious at the lack of it. He let it twist his insides until he tasted the bitterness on his tongue.

"Don't you look like a ray of sunshine." Lúc was standing at the far wall, with his hands in his pockets.

Arioch shot him a look.

"You know what I think?" The Shifter asked, pushing off the old stone.

"Generally."

"That there's more fun ways to torture yourself than *this.*" He nodded past Arioch at the fireplace. Lúc had been with him for the worst of it; he knew everything there was to know about his past.

"Got an alternative in mind?" he asked, trying to loosen the tightness in his shoulders.

"That little tail you put on Aheia sent their owl." Lúc's smile glinted. "I think you'll like this."

Chapter 20

Aheia

The music was loud and pulsing. Aheia could feel it inside her veins, moving with the beat of her heart while it stole her thoughts, and the crowd around her fed the anonymity. No one here paid her much attention, and she felt like she could just bleed into the background without having to try at it.

She was dancing with Nyco, unable to help the smile when they twirled her body in a way that didn't at all match the songs playing, as lyrics she couldn't understand had her trying to sing along regardless.

Saffy had brought her a pink, sparkly drink, which was too sweet, but that didn't matter when it only took a few sips to make her mind wobble all over itself. The liquor cut apart those rigid boards that were keeping her shoulders squared, and when those snapped, she felt the relief. It was a physical reaction to something intangible, and she wanted more of the same. She wanted to melt further until she was nothing but a puddle because puddles didn't have to face their realities or make decisions they didn't know how to make.

Puddles could just puddle.

Aheia blinked hard, her vision flickering slightly as the lights around her changed colors. Red, white, a deep blue strobing in a way that made time feel like it was stuttering. Her hair was sticking to her body to the point of discomfort until Nyco swept the braid over her shoulder and held it away from her sticky skin as they walked to the far side of the church.

"What are all of those pages?" Aheia asked, pointing at the ripped-out, ancient-looking paper that was plastered across the wall.

"It's a novelty." Nyco grinned. "Those are from the, umm—*Agía Sahnta*."

"What is that?"

"It roughly means—religious texts." And then they leaned in pointedly and gestured up the wall, eyes glittering. "These very specifically are from the mortal's books."

Aheia's jaw dropped.

Holy scripture.

Pages of it covered half the space, red circles outlining specific passages, and caricatures bordering the sides—flames and white flowers. Some held signatures, some held notes, and others had full oil paintings across them.

Nyco tugged on her mane like a rein when she froze to stare at the walls, and she bumped her shoulder into theirs with a reciprocating smile on her face. She couldn't help herself down here with them. They had a way of easing some of the tightness. Nyco and the liquor.

They made it to the far side of the bar, to the cluster of Nephilim she recognized, and Aheia caught the tail end of a conversation. "Keep your mouth shut, or I'll go to your bunk and eat out your female," Saffy snapped at the male in front of her, and Aheia snorted.

Apparently, that was the wrong reaction because Nyco looked almost stoic.

"We don't laugh at that anymore," they said. "Not after last time."

The demon Saffy was talking to looked ready to throw blades with how his gaze simmered in her direction.

"You're kidding," Aheia's eyes widened, and Nyco shook their head.

"Don't look at me like that—I really *am* joking. I'm celibate right now," Saffy shimmied her shoulders with a mischievous look on her face and ran a finger down the male's chest. But he shoved her off, disappearing into the crowd behind him. Saffy tipped her chin and groaned, following him, while Nyco hopped on the bar, pulling a blonde Nephilim between their legs.

His hair was braided across the top of his head, and the sides of his scalp were shaved and inked. He leaned into Nyco, gripping their thighs, and where Aheia would have felt like an intruder any other time, she just watched, her skin prickling.

"You two are so pretty," she said slowly, biting her bottom lip. "Like unicorns, do you have those here?"

"The big-horned horses?" the blonde asked, raising his eyebrows, decidedly not taking her comparison as a negative. He leaned against Nyco's chest, biting the fabric just above their pec, drawing a hiss from them.

"One horn. *Uni*," Aheia sounded it out.

"No, but we have horses born with three—they stick out across their spine, making them unrideable. Do I look unrideable?"

Aheia choked at the absurd image that was conjured in her mind. "*Hmmno,* the ones I'm thinking of are all ethereal with one horn on their forehead. I've only ever seen them in our forests at—" She swallowed the word that came up unbidden. *Home.* Keloseros wasn't her home, hadn't felt that way when it was still supposed to be—before she left. Her contentment dragged into the pit of her stomach and soaked in the pink-colored liquor that now felt like a bad idea. The pink wouldn't look pretty in her body. It would become all brown and gross, and that was what soaked the comfort that anonymity had brought her, her shoulders becoming incredibly heavy once again.

How did trepidation swallow happiness in mere moments when it took so long to build it?

"I have to use the washroom," she lied and waited for Nyco to point her across the way at a large alcove that fed into a tunnel. It was a means to get away without them following.

She nodded, rubbing at her temple. It was starting to ache as the time around them did conspicuous things, just like when she'd been dancing. Everything felt too slow, too warm, too much. Aheia got her bearings as ...

... Nyco leaned into the blonde, catching his lips between their own in a kiss.

... Saffy slinked back to the group, her expression looking pained.

... The Nephilim on Aheia's left laughed loud and boisterous at whatever happened in front of them.

Too much.

She blinked hard, shaking her head, and pushed off the bar, threading through the tightly wound crowd of dancing demons. Teeth flashed in her periphery, and black eyes watched. Eyes everywhere. Always eyes. Why couldn't she escape those?

The alcove Nyco had pointed her toward came and went, and Aheia kept walking along the wall. The stone was rough but cool against her fingertips, starkly contrasting the humid, hot air around her. The more she looked, the more nods to both the Mithra and the mortal religions she found around the ceiling above her.

Frayed white wings were hanging everywhere, feathers falling around them as if it was magyck, their number on the wings never dwindling, while blood dripped down a few spots against the walls. Bright red lights were strung, outlining columns and the spire in straight fluorescent lines, with white boughs of dried dianthus hanging in in between.

Seeing those flowers made her stomach leaden, and she held the phantom smell of them in her nose. It was a sharp scent that almost burned with cleanliness. It took her right back to the white pews in Keloseros, the marble that had hurt her knees after hours of kneeling, the bright light that didn't temper through the glass overhead. The discomfort that had started at the bar swelled, and it became hard to swallow her memories.

But then she saw something that stopped her in her tracks. Her own reflection on the adjacent wall-- the entirety of it covered in mismatched mirrors.

Her blue looked back, but under the deep red lighting, it seemed almost black. Her lips parted as she watched herself, the liquor in her veins manipulating her surroundings enough that it looked like she was staring down a different creature entirely. Her reflection tilted her head, and those black eyes watched as a thin smile spread across her face. Was Aheia smiling? She couldn't feel her mouth, but she must have been.

Her feet carried her closer on their own accord, and she lifted a finger, feathering it across her eyes slowly, too aware of the skin of her own body. It didn't fit. It had never quite fit, and now wasn't any different.

"What the fuck are you?" The voice was slimy and slurry, coming from somewhere behind her. Aheia whirled around, almost touching the male that had spoken. He was standing much too fucking close, his dark hair hanging into yellow eyes. Well, eye. One of them was swollen shut, with a fresh scar healing across it.

"Excuse me?" Aheia couldn't help the distaste on her face. She fucking hated being approached on a good day. This was *not* a good day.

"You don't look right," *Scar* said, clutching his drink between thick fingers.

If her stomach hadn't already knotted, it would have at that statement. *Disgusting.* She tried to squeeze past him without another word, but a second male stepped into her path, the two demons acting as a fleshy wall.

"Let me through," she said, narrowing her eyes.

"Now, why would we do that?" The second Nephilim said, tying his dark blue hair into a ponytail. Aheia could smell the dampness rolling off of him—not the pleasant kind that came with dirt in the forest when it rained, but like water mixed with sweat.

She backed up, trying to put distance between them, but there wasn't anywhere to go.

"You that white everywhere?" *Blue* sneered, catching a spiral of hair that had come loose from her braid between his fingers and tugging lightly.

A small sliver of panic lashed the back of her neck. She didn't like being cornered, and right now, she didn't feel equipped to get herself out of it if she needed to. She had no weapon and wasn't sure screaming would get anyone's attention.

"Are you this stupid when you're sober?" She tried to push away his hand, but he held on so tight that all it did was pull at her root.

Scar laughed, taking an almost impressively long drink before he hiccuped and sloshed some of its contents onto the floor.

"What gave you the impression I wanted to hear you speak?" Blue pulled at the strand again, and she was forced to bow her head slightly. "No one's interested in what you have to say."

"Stop asking me questions then," she ground between her teeth, staring at the stained shirt covering his chest while he restricted her movement.

"I don't need the answer. I plan on finding out for myself."

"Like hel," Aheia spit, shoving against him and gaining just enough room to see the movement behind him.

"I think you took a wrong turn, Briteling."

Her eyes found Nyco's hazel, and where she'd felt irritation when they followed her to Keosha, their voice elicited nothing but fucking relief now.

"This yours?" Scar grunted at them, nodding to Aheia.

"*This yours*?" Nyco quirked an eyebrow. "Why use many words when few do trick, right?" they snorted. "I mean, I wasn't expecting an intellectual debate, but you didn't even use a verb."

"Get the fuck out of my face," Scar hissed, bending down toward Nyco.

"Oh, so you *do* know about verbs."

Blue smirked sourly, speaking before his friend could. "The *halfbreed* uses his words, so he doesn't actually have to *do* anything." He gave Aheia's hair another tug as she felt the clinch in her chest over how he was speaking to Nyco. She jerked back, the pain at her scalp cutting into her as hair loosened from it.

"I suppose I was foolish for thinking words meant anything to the likes of you. Words like 'no' and 'stop.'" They tilted their head, looking at Scar like they were sizing him up, brushing off Blue's insult like it never happened.

"He's learning." Blue's grin stretched, and Aheia's teeth clenched. The adrenaline started to feel like needles under her skin and she let it feed her strength, managing to yank herself away from the distracted demon by pinching the hair at her root to dull the pain of his fingers still holding on hard. He was left standing with a few of her strands, but she was free.

"*They*," she corrected him in an angry hiss, managing to get herself upright, and meeting Nyco's gaze. Their lips twitched but they shook their head like they were telling her to drop it.

"Who gives a fuck?" Blue chuckled, letting Aheia's loose hair fall, before rubbing his fingertips together. "You tell the halfling to turn away before *he* gets hurt." He grabbed her chin instead. "Don't worry, you don't need him, you're about to have a good time with us."

She growled, clawing at Blue's wrist when he held tight, managing to tear into his skin enough to make him bleed and drop his hold.

"Dumb fucking slut," Blue's nose twitched, anger replacing any kind of smugness he'd held before. He reared back his hand, ready to strike, and Aheia flinched, bracing for impact. But before he could hit her, Nyco grabbed ahold of his hand and twisted it behind his back in one fluid motion. The Nephilim struggled, his shoulder wrenched back at an unnatural angle, and Nyco bracketed his throat, forcing him to the floor. "She's not your horse or your mother; don't try to fuck with her," they said into the demon's ear, bending his wrist so far it looked about ready to snap.

"Get the *fuck* off of me," Blue snarled.

"Really should have left your fucking assault tonight at shitty words," Nyco hissed through their teeth, their voice dropping to a growl.

"Why's that?" Blue struggled, but even though he was bigger, he failed at getting out of Nyco's hold.

"Because shit behavior I could have let slide, it would have cost you a bruised wrist at most. But he won't like that you touched her hair."

He?

"He?" Blue asked just as Aheia thought it.

But the question spasmed in her mind and faded quickly as she felt the shake in her fingers. That's where it started, working its way up her arm until it reached her chest. The warm echo that reminded her of the thing she'd been trying to escape, the proximity she didn't know how to handle when there was a reason for it and much less now that there wasn't. Her back hit the mirror because she needed the support as she met Arioch's gaze. He was bleeding through the crowd of dancing Nephilim with Lúc, all of the demons near them shrugging out of the way and *staring* like they couldn't quite believe their eyes.

The two of them commanded the room's attention without even trying, and they had Aheia's, too. She couldn't get herself to look away as they diminished the space, the vise in her chest stringing tighter with every step.

"Oh fuck," Scar hissed, frozen where he stood.

Fear flamed in Blue's eyes as he looked up at the tall Avarice approaching him, and he ceased struggling. Nyco was transfixed, too, but their attention was drawn to Lúc, those hazel eyes watching him carefully.

"You're still standing. Why?" Arioch said to Scar, whose hands were raised placatingly. It wasn't a question. Aheia's back squeezed against the mirror when something molten and disruptive prickled against her spine as she watched Arioch smile at Scar, a feral fucking expression. "*Down*."

Her own knees buckled at the command as the male fell to the ground unceremoniously, his hand sliding on the dirty floor.

The Nephilim stuttered something she couldn't understand between his teeth, and Arioch lifted his brows just as Lúc stepped between them and kicked a heavy boot at the side of his leg. Aheia jumped as Scar fell to his knees, and the Shifter stamped his foot on the back of his neck, laying him down further.

"Nice and low, sweetheart," Lúc purred, pushing down until the male's cheek smashed against the sticky wood. "Kiss that floor."

"That's where you fucking belong, as far as I'm concerned." Arioch shoved him to the side with his boot. "If you even fucking twitch before we leave, I'm taking your spine as decoration," he said coldly.

"I don't think either of them came here with one." Lúc grinned, pulling out a curved blade and drawing the pad of his finger over it.

"Take him to the bar," Arioch told Nyco, nodding to the far wall as he reached for Aheia. She dug her teeth into her bottom lip, weighing her options as his hand floated between them. *The demon you know over the demon you don't.* Her mind purred and she gave in, reaching for him. His eyes dropped down her body, taking inventory and then he moved his fingers to the back of her neck. It was a soft touch, not at all what she was expecting.

"What are you going to do?" She asked as they passed the parting demons ahead, her heart in her throat.

Arioch didn't answer, only stroked her vertebrae with his thumb. One at a time.

"Please, I didn't do anything." Blue choked out when Nyco threw him against the bar top, his fingers bracing on the edge.

"I didn't ask you to beg," the Avarice said, adjusting so that Aheia was tucked against his chest.

"—I didn't know."

"Didn't know what?" he asked, every word he spoke vibrating against Aheia's spine.

"That she was spoken for."

"I don't speak for her. Now stop wasting her fucking time and keep your mouth shut until she tells you otherwise."

Stop wasting her *time.*

Blue's jaw locked, and his eyes trained down at the wood. Aheia could see them glazing, could see the tears welling up and she felt her own breathing become heavy as the demon at her back shifted.

"Take it." Arioch unfastened one of his knives and brought the hilt up in front of her. "Go on, helfyre."

"Take *what*?" she asked, her voice unsteadier than she liked.

"What he owes you," he said calmly. "His hand."

The music around them sucked into a vacuum, and she could feel the involuntary twitch of her lip.

"He touched my *hair.*" He'd done no more than the presumptuous males she was used to.

"Did you want him to?"

"Are you really asking me that?" She met his eyes in the mirror next to them because ignoring them felt just as weak as twitching under his gaze.

"I know the answer; I just want you to tell me."

Her brows furrowed. *Games, games, games.* Always games.

"No," she grit out.

"Then you have every reason to take his hand for it. He just had none to lose it." Arioch held the handle of the blade to her chin and tipped it. *He had none to lose it.* It sounded a lot like *he made his choice.* "You think that's where he would have stopped?" He continued, eyes dropping to her lips. "Your hair?"

Light leaks licked at her vision as she looked back to the demon across from her, sweat dripping down his temple.

You think that's where he would have stopped?

She couldn't fucking breathe.

The blade hovered between them ominously, and her fingers itched. She wanted to take it. *Holy fuck.* She *wanted* to take it.

"I didn't do anything," Blue tried again, and this time Arioch answered.

"Yeah, I *saw,*"

Aheia's stomach plummeted. Of course, he'd seen. How much had he been there for? Why hadn't she noticed his presence? Or maybe she had; maybe that's what fed the way her skin stretched before.

"What's it going to be?" The Avarice waited for her answer.

Chapter 21

Aheia

Aheia was scared of who she might become if Arioch kept handing her blades. Because she didn't know what she was capable of. Last time, she'd taken a life. This time ...

Arioch's lips tilted in challenge.

Her heart pounded in her ears.

Blue's fear called to her as the sweat dripped from him.

... This time she'd take a hand.

She reached for the knife handle, her chest heaving as the cold gripped her limbs. She couldn't breathe, but maybe monsters like her didn't need air. After all, that's what she was. This was disproportionate. The demon had touched her *barely*, and insulted the fuck out of Nyco, but it hadn't gone any further.

That didn't change how badly she wanted to do exactly what Arioch told her to.

He leaned back against the bar, letting her pass him, but those eyes never left her. She could feel them like fire against the side of her body as she approached Blue. The cowering demon looked very different now than when he towered over her before.

"Lay down your arm," she said, watching him look behind her like he was searching for a way out of this. It spurred her anger. Did he think that Alshaytan would change his mind and take the knife from her hand. "He's not going to help you." She looked over her shoulder at Arioch, who watched her every move. "He likes this."

Blue's jaw ticked, and his eyes returned to her before he peeled his fingers from the wood slowly.

Aheia raised the blade, running the flat of it against the small cuts she'd managed with her fingernails, and Blue hissed, his breath just as erratic as hers.

"Please," He begged quietly, and the word slithered underneath Aheia's skin. Her legs felt like jelly, the fire in her chest spreading through her arms and fingertips. This was a lot of power. She'd rarely held this much, and it felt like the liquor before, permeating her mind.

"I didn't ask you to beg either," she said, tilting the blade until the sharp edge depressed his skin.

Blue's lips parted over gritted teeth, and he looked *desperate.*

"I want to hurt you," she said under her breath, words just for the two of them. "But I have a reason for it. You wanted to hurt me too," she continued, watching Blue carefully. "What was yours?"

His eyes moved between hers quickly over and over again, like maybe he could find an answer there, something that would save him.

"You think I owe you my body? That you somehow have a right to it because what—you're stronger than me, and *taking* it would be easy?" She continued because she knew he wouldn't have anything to say to her.

"I--" He stammered.

"Nyco was right, words are hard for you, aren't they?" She narrowed her eyes, pressing down harder, just enough to bulge his skin and discolor it white. He choked out a gasp, his fingers flexing, and Aheia looked back toward the mirror, meeting Arioch's gaze.

Fire. All fire. He watched her with fixation.

"I'm sorry, I—" He started but Aheia cut him off.

"Great point." Her eyebrow lifted. "I think you owe Nyco an apology." She nodded their way, catching a glimpse of their curious expression.

Blue looked back and forth between them.

"Come on, you were so good with your verbs before," she coaxed, pressing the knife in harder. "Say 'I'm sorry for ruining your night.'"

Blue spluttered, turning his head toward Nyco and rushing out the words while Aheia kept him on razor's edge.

"Water and bridges," they sent Aheia a wink, and crossed their arms.

"Did that do it for you?" She asked Lúc. "Felt a bit disingenuous."

"That was fucking embarrassing," the Shifter said, flicking the metal of his piercing with his tongue.

"My thoughts." Distaste layered against her tongue thickly as she dropped the knife, clattering it on the bar beside him. "But since you did what I asked, I won't take your hand." Venom laced her words. "You can do that yourself."

Doing it for him would have been a kindness.

Blue looked down at the blade while the red light around them made his eyes look like voids, his jaw feathering, and then he redirected his attention to Arioch.

"I didn't know she was yours." He tried one last time as Aheia backed away, feeling her proximity to the Avarice behind her.

"You think that's what this is about?" Arioch asked, and Aheia watched him in the mirror. His jaw flexed, and so did that vein at the side of his neck. There was something focused and dangerous splitting his features. It wasn't calm, though he sounded it.

"Well—"

"Consider her nameless and faceless." His hand fisted on top of the wood bar, and Aheia caught it, though he relaxed his fingers a heartbeat later. "You touched her when she asked you to stop, and that's all the reason I need for my decision."

Aheia's lips parted in sick fascination as Blue lifted the knife from the bar and brought it to his wrist with wide, wild eyes, pearls of sweat dripping down his temple. She could see the way his fingers pressed, the way his skin stretched taut over his hand, and the slight tremble in his elbow right before he pushed. A scream tore itself free with the splitting of his skin, and Aheia held her breath as the black blade disappeared into his flesh. The inky blood poured, and she glanced up at the mirror again, Arioch's expression stealing what was left of the breath in her lungs. Violence was etched in every line of his face, but there was something more behind it—molten and caustic.

"He barely fought," she said out loud when it should have been an internal thought.

"Refusing would have forced me to do worse." Arioch's voice was all gravel.

"What? Kill him?" she asked, still mesmerized.

"No, *not* kill him."

Blue's cries were guttural, and he only made it an inch in before his hold on the blade slipped, and his legs quivered, threatening to drop him on the floor. Nyco was at his side a moment later, steadying his shoulders. It looked like they were supporting the majority of his weight as his bloody fingers twitched uncontrollably.

He'll die. He's losing too much blood.

Arioch's hand curved over Aheia's hip, and she stumbled back in surprise, hitting the rugged expanse of his chest. She chanced a glance at the mirror again, but Arioch wasn't watching her this time; he was completely focused ahead, like pulling her close had been a subconscious move. Aheia's body hummed with the feel of his, the echo between them flittering like an insect as she readjusted, her ass rubbing against his groin. She froze, feeling him there, the laces, the leather, the way he was unforgiving and hard. Her throat went dry as the warmth dripped from her abdomen into her thighs, and she scolded herself because that response was off-limits. But that didn't change how it felt, how she had to *fight* to not rub her thighs together while Blue tortured himself in front of her.

He screamed again, and Aheia's vision blurred slightly, watching him trying to sever the bone.

Arioch had given her a choice—an opportunity for revenge instead of taking it himself, and there was something in that knowledge that softened her when she should have become more brittle in the wake of it.

Blue was puffing out his cheeks in an effort to breathe, but his whole body was shaking, his fingers slipping and failing like his brain was fighting his actions. And it was the third time he lost control of the weapon that Arioch stepped around Aheia. He gripped the demon's knife and forced it the rest of the way in one brutal push. The bone cracked, and skin tore, Blue's wrist severing completely as he collapsed against Nyco and cradled his stump to his chest, gurgling screams drowned by the music.

Aheia could barely speak as the wounded male screamed and sobbed, another aiding him with a rag until the crowd swallowed them both, resuming their dancing and talking. The show was over, and it didn't seem to affect anyone else.

Lúc grinned, passing Nyco and casually hopping onto the bar top, straddling it while Arioch's hands kept Aheia in place, wedged between the wood and his body.

Her blue eyes met his, and the expression there was all fire—the silent, scorching kind.

She watched Arioch's reflection while Lúc pulled out a few glasses from behind the bar before leaning down again and snatching up a bottle. The male that had poured Aheia's pink drink protested, but one glance from Lúc shut him up.

The Shifter poured four glasses and shoved one at Nyco, whose eyes flickered down to it before returning to Lúc's. They shook their head apprehensively.

"Suit yourself, but I recommend a little mind-numbing before I get ahold of you for bringing her down here," Lúc said, shooting back his liquor and propping up his knee on the bar, leaning his arm against it.

Aheia was ready to interject, but Arioch raised one of the glasses to her mouth before she could say anything. The smell fucking singed her nostrils. It smelled like him. Like something that might poison her, so different from the clean dianthus in the air.

A little mind-numbing before I get ahold of you. He and Lúc spoke the same words in a different language. He didn't have to say it out loud.

Her eyes met his as she parted her lips and let him tip it back because it would help skew her reality further.

Ugh.

She fought against the urge to wretch.

It is *fucking poison.*

And it burned. Just like Arioch did.

After taking his own shot, he sat the glass down next to her, bracing his hands on either side of her body. "I'm not sure I was expecting this," he said, finally, his voice coarse.

"You kept leaving me alone. I was tired of it," she said with as much edge as she could manage as the fumes of the liquor evaporated to the roof of her mouth, feeding her mind. "So I left."

Arioch's lip twitched as he leaned into her ear. "You want my attention, Aheia?" It sounded like a taunt. He kept her tucked tightly against his chest, her stomach pressing against the bar as he pulled out an inhalant and ignited a flame in front of her face. Her eyes flickered to the fire when he leaned past her temple and dragged in a rough inhale, the cherry burning bright before her eyes.

Yes. The answer wasn't all hers. It was born from the echo that begged for his proximity, and it was painful because it wedged her worse than he did against this bar.

"What I *want* is ..." She hissed, feeling the heat against her skin like a threat. Tonight had been about distance, about pushing the fucked up boundaries Arioch had set for her. So she kept going because she needed to know what he'd say when she told him— "I want out of Aljira."

"Oh?" His inhalant sparked just like the embers in his eyes. "Where do you *want* to go?" he asked, keeping the razor edge, the smoke sticky against her skin.

She froze, the haze clouding around her.

"*Where* do you plan on escaping to?" he repeated. "Keloseros? Lyria?"

"I—" She swallowed, her legs quivering. "Lyria," she lied because she wouldn't tell him that no part of her had worked that out.

"No."

"Keloseros then," she bluffed as he gripped the side of her neck.

"No."

She bared her teeth when he forced her head to the side, inches from her mouth now-- the real version, not the reflection she could be as strong in front of. "You made a choice. You fought *with* us in your realm. You fought against your people—and I told you then what that meant."

Her chest rose and fell too quickly. "I took a way out. That's all."

"It wasn't the only way out," he challenged. "I gave you two."

If you fight with us, you leave with me. If you decide to go back to the Mithra, I will make sure you leave this church alive.

"I couldn't stay," she said, and everything inside of her sank. Because there had only ever been *one* option. How the fuck would she have existed in that place? She would have been alone, and who knows what they'd have done with her? The next Mithra in line for power wasn't any better, and she didn't have a home, not even a house. She would have been kicked out of Ophion's, or worse, *kept.* Her stomach tightened worse, and tears started to collect. *No. Stop.*

"No, you couldn't," Arioch's voice interrupted her racing thoughts. "Because you're not weak, are you, helfyre? A weaker creature would have run back to what's familiar."

The smoke caressed her lips, and she tipped her chin slightly, feeling his breath against her.

"That's why you're not leaving Aljira."

She was starting to get whiplash from the way he seemed to defend her honor before taking it a moment later.

"You're taking my choice from me," she hissed.

"I'm giving you an answer to a question you barely want to look at." Her chest rose and fell quickly. He was right. She didn't know what she was doing and didn't feel all that capable of looking at the options that presented themselves.

"And if I run?" she asked. "I've crossed your border once. I can do it again."

"I think I'd enjoy hunting you," he said, the smoke drifting from his lips and framing his face as if he were on fire.

"I've been hunted before. I got away then, too," Aheia challenged, but it was becoming more and more breathless.

"I thought we cleared up exactly what happens when you compare me to lesser creatures." His movements were too calm, too calculated, when she was a wobbly mess. She felt helpless when he twisted her hips so that her back dug into the wood, and she was forced to look at him properly. "I'm better than them." His lips grazed hers when he spoke. "I'll catch you."

"And then?"

"What do you think I do with my prey when I catch it?" he asked, sending static pulses through Aheia. *Tear it apart.* Fuck. *Eat it.*

Gods, she felt out of control. She felt *frayed* and didn't know how to twist those threads back together.

He brushed his mouth against her cheekbone before speaking into her ear. "Are you picturing it?" he asked, his voice deep and coarse. "How you'll scream when I do?"

Heat slithered down her spine as he turned her so that she was flush with him, his hand still curled around her throat, narrow oxygen supply thinning further. Her chin tipped, and her lips parted. She couldn't help it. Her body was a nerve, and he was pawing at it.

"How I'll hurt you?"

Her hand shot to his arm because his hold on her neck was becoming punishing. She was thankful he couldn't see her face because her lids fluttered shut, and her lips parted. Every word fed the fire he'd lit, making her feel more and more out of control.

Dear Gods, what is my damage?

"How you'll beg me to stop when all you want is *more* because pretending *I'm* the monster—pretending you don't have an out with me—gets you off?"

Her thighs pressed together, and she dug her teeth into her bottom lip to silence the whimper that wanted nothing more than to spill for him.

"How you'll cry, and you'll fight, living in the delusion that those scratches you're trying to land on my skin are there in defiance of me and not for your own pleasure. How you'll tell yourself that there's a reason for your motivations—try in any way you can to make what happens between us feel less dirty, less *fucked up.* And you'll blame me while I take *everything* you have to offer for myself, and then, when I decide to let you,

you'll come so fucking hard that all of those thoughts wilt away." He growled, pulling back enough to look at her.

His eyes were hungry, burning--a promise of pain she didn't know she could handle.

Fucking hel.

"Can you see it? Because I can."

"You're making big assumptions," she managed, her nostrils flaring.

"I don't make assumptions." He brought the inhalant to his lips again and took another drag right in front of her eyes.

Aheia bristled, her fingers digging into his skin, realizing too late that her grip wasn't helping her cause. That it showed him just how tight she was strung.

"I already know the answer. I just want you to tell me," Arioch repeated his words from earlier in a taunting tone, the flames inside her roaring. Anger, need, and all of the things that were out of her control tonight melted into one maddening thing.

No. Aheia told herself fiercely, trying to temper the fire consuming her. Fuck, she couldn't think. Everything was dizzy.

"I don't forgive you," she said instead, but she wasn't all too sure who she was telling. She needed herself to hear those words too, *really* hear those words, because maybe, if she did, she could calm herself down.

"I didn't ask you for forgiveness."

He took the power of the statement right out of her hands. And it was the part of her that needed to know why. Why didn't he want her forgiveness? Did it mean so little?

"But it doesn't matter either way, does it?" His body pressed into hers. "Because the distraction I'm offering you is better than my hollow words. I could give you something you can't give yourself, and you wouldn't have to talk, think, *decide*." Her heart pounded. "You could fall into yourself, and no one would see, not in my darkness."

"You would." She shifted her hips in an attempt to find any kind of space between them, but regret shadowed the action. Because he bared his teeth, and her abdomen pressed against the hard ridge of his cock, his laces rubbing against her soft belly.

"Always." A hollow throb wracked her, and the blood rushed against her ears so loudly she could barely hear the music. "You can't hide from me."

It was so fucking unfair that he saw those things when she'd wrapped them so tightly into herself. How did he keep fucking *seeing* the raw rubbed parts of her?

He reached for her and pulled her mouth apart roughly with the callused pad of his thumb. Then his lips touched hers, and the smoke curled between them, warm and wet. She sank. Slow and deep, her eyelids drooping slightly as she let it all consume her. The smoke, the liquor ... him. And while she couldn't feel her happiness anymore, she also couldn't feel the dread or the heaviness. His eyelashes brushed his skin, and she watched the red lights cast shadows across his features, wholly fucking demonic.

"I hate you." She exhaled slowly, letting the smoke roll from her lips. She hated Arioch for being right about her, for the connection between them, and for that Gods damned control he kept.

"Show me, helfyre." He leaned in close. "Fight." And for a moment, she thought she saw something new flicker in his eyes. "*Take*."

I can't think. Aheia almost said it out loud in a desperate gasp. Her heart was beating so loud she imagined that anyone in earshot might hear it, might know the secret that lived between her ribs. That whatever this was made her feel alive.

There was enough room for her to take a step sideways, to slide out from under him, and he followed her when she did. She stepped back for every one of his, and his lip twitched. His eyes flicked down to her legs before he advanced again, and she stumbled, keeping the same distance between them. All the demons that had crowded them parted as he backed her to the far side of the bar again, her back hitting the wall. The same corner as before, but a completely different feeling.

I think I'd enjoy hunting you.

She wanted that, even though it made her feel *less*. The thrum inside of her couldn't be ignored, and she knew it wasn't her, not entirely, but that didn't change the fact that this was something new to focus on when the reality she faced had her reeling. She wanted the pleasure and the pain, and right now, down in this church with him, it didn't matter that she didn't forgive him. If she was honest with herself, she preferred it this way. The imbalance kept a barrier in place.

She swallowed thickly, but the adrenaline was already spiking her veins, her body trigger-happy. Every second that elapsed made her more jittery, the beat of her heart racing faster, the warmth that pooled in her abdomen heavier.

"Now, give me my answer," he said, taking another step, and her fingers twitched against the rock. This time, his voice sounded a lot less composed. Like he was strung over the same bow she was, just waiting for the release. "Yes, or no."

I'm not bored with you yet.

It's just words, Aheia.

No one will see.

Fuck. Him.

"Yes." The word left her before she could give her mind permission.

Crack. The same feeling from the wax bath. A demand, hot and intrinsic. *Leading.*

His eyes dropped to her lips, and they were so sharp she felt them like a physical touch. The inhalant fell from his fingers, and he crushed it under a heavy boot, almost closing the distance between them. Almost.

"How do you stop me?" he asked as she pressed herself back into the rock, feeling the jagged edges against her skull.

"I don't want to stop you,"

All or nothing. She wanted all or nothing.

He clicked his tongue, black wisps creeping into the gray of his irises. Like his shadows were twining his vision.

"You might," he said slowly, and there was no trace of humor in his features. *You might.* What the fuck was he going to do to her? "Pleasure comes at a price."

"Pain?" she choked out.

"Trust."

Her jaw snapped shut tight. Did she trust Arioch? Not really.

"What's your safe word?"

She chewed on her lip. It would cost her to ask the question in her mind. "You'll stop even if you're punishing me? Even if you want me to hurt?"

"Yes," he told her, holding her eyes with his.

Did she trust him? *Enough.*

His tight grip was exactly what she needed because her own control was too heavy on her shoulders. If he could hold it, manipulate it, bear it for a little while—make a choice she couldn't get herself to make, take it from her so she wouldn't feel weak—it was worth it. And she trusted him enough for that. Even though she didn't trust him with anything else.

"*Honey.*" She swallowed the bitter aftertaste the word conjured, flashes of his shadows binding her wrists filling her vision, words he'd said to her before he dragged her back to Keloseros, pressing against her mind. But they dissipated when he let the smoke curl from his lips like he was on fire and tipped his chin.

"Run, Aheia."

Chapter 22

Aheia

Run, Aheia.

She scrambled against the church wall, her nails scratching over the rock as she slipped from between the stone and his body, taking off toward the far side of the room. She dipped into one of the cold, dark hallways with no idea of where she was going, tearing around the tunnels frantically. She squealed, hearing his footsteps, much too slow, much too calm. Like he didn't even need to run to keep up with her. His nearness lingered like her own personal shadow—she could feel it against her skin even now as the darkness swallowed her so completely that she had to feel her way along the rock.

Her side stitched as her lungs screamed and sweat built up against the nape of her neck.

She hadn't missed running, had done so much of it, and it had been her least favorite activity in all of these realms. But running from him ... That felt different. It was the danger, the anticipation, the anonymity the darkness offered that made this feel alive and exciting. She wrapped herself in it as her steps faltered, as the part of her that wanted him to catch her became heavy and dragged her down. She fought against the pain in her legs, trying to keep pace, but her breath was starting to fail her, and the void in front of her was playing tricks on her. She thought she saw openings only to smash against another slab of curved, hard rock. Adrenaline prickled down her neck as she ran into yet another dead end, feeling something soft brushing against her shoulder. She yelped, jerked away, and ran in the opposite direction with her arms stretched in front of her in hopes of not hitting the stone. But instead, her palms collided with soft fabric, and her forehead hit a wall of imposing muscle.

"*Ahh*," she squeaked, squinting, and trying to make out anything in front of her. But before she could decide on her next move, another touch wrapped around her ankle, and her world turned sideways. The magyck pulled at her mercilessly, the floor bruising her shoulder when she fell, barely catching herself.

"That was sweet," he purred, his palm replacing his shadows in a tight grip.

She twisted in his hold, anxiety sending her blood hurtling faster, her limbs flailing while she tried to find leverage around her.

She kicked out, wrenching out of his hold, her hands scraping against the ground as a broken groan slipped past her lips with the effort it took. The cobbled rock gave her the hold she needed, and she managed to pull herself away, her knees bruising as she crawled. He was stalking her slowly; she could hear his footsteps.

He could see her, and she couldn't see anything.

The only sound in this hallway was her frantic breathing and the whimpers she couldn't hold on to. He was close, and she was completely turned around. She didn't know where she'd come from or where she could escape to. Her head whipped back and forth in an effort to locate him, but it was impossible with the echo around her that every little movement made.

And then she felt his hands again. This time he skimmed her body over the dirty floor, her knees and palms stinging with the burn. She yelped, fighting against him as he pushed a massive hand between her shoulder blades, forcing her cheek against the ground while he leaned across her.

Gods have mercy. Her lips trembled, the hunger in her veins impossible. It was addicting, and it was devastating. Because it meant accepting that she wanted him to have her control. That it was too heavy, and she needed him to take it. And worse ... that she trusted him enough to hold it.

Her heart was jumping up into her throat as his hand left the center of her back. He stroked down her vertebrae like she was a cat, and it was almost soft, but that thought felt foolish when he hooked his fingers in her leathers and yanked. The pants were lined, but it still burned, grazing over her skin when he shoved them down around her thighs.

"Fuck, squirm just like that," he rasped, finger squeezing and massaging her inner thigh, spreading her cunt from behind. And it was obscene even when she couldn't see. "Just. Like. *That.*" The warm air licked across the wetness, forcing her to feel just how turned on she was. Even her thighs felt fucking soaked, the exact spots he touched with his hands.

"Now that I have you back"—his voice was gruff in her ear—"I'll bite how I want to."

She held her breath, her lungs spasming in her chest. For a moment all she could do was hear—hear his breath, the sound of his leathers, hear the ricocheting noises from somewhere deep in the caves. But the entire world shifted as he rolled her onto her back, the cold ground poking against her thin skin.

She yelped, but this time he gave her no time to adjust, his hot breath stroking against her neck and his teeth replacing it a moment later.

Yes. She couldn't help it. The word echoed in her mind as he dug into the side of her throat relentlessly—hard enough to leave an impression but not hard enough to break the skin.

Oh fuck, that felt good. She pressed her eyes shut tight. Her teeth clenched so hard it felt like she might never open them again, while her fingernails dug into the cold ground in desperation.

"I want to feel every inch of you between my teeth." He pushed on her stomach to keep her from sitting up, nipping a line of marks down her body. Every bite made her world light up in the darkness, the pinpricks of pain making her clit throb, and her hips rock in the search of friction.

"Careful, or you'll make me think you want it," he growled, hauling her closer. "That you're *letting* me bury my tongue in your sweet little cunt."

"I don't." She choked out the lie, fraying at the edges. "Fuck, I don't want this. I don't want you."

He chuckled, his fingers parting her pussy for him. "Is that why you're so fucking soaked for me, Aheia?"

The word no was on the tip of her tongue, but it devolved into nothing but groans as he dug his teeth into the side of her cunt hard. She cried out, pain zigzagging from the site right back to her clit and she bucked in his hold.

What's wrong with me? She was helpless, as he licked across his bite, soothing the pain before dragging his tongue up her entire pussy, eating her feverishly. She was boneless and wound tight in the same sentence.

Her back arched, the pleasure knocking through her so hard her lips wrenched apart and all she could do was feel. This was exactly what she needed. For however long he'd give it to her. Fuck, the flat of his tongue did things she couldn't picture in her mind. It was messy and sloppy, and his teeth grazed at her clit with intention. She jerked in his hold, riding her cunt against his face, his beard rubbing over the sensitive skin of her legs. He growled, and the vibration rumbled through her entire body in a sick shiver.

"Tell me again it's not what you want. Fucking *stop* me, or keep your mouth shut and take what I'm giving you."

She whimpered, but it was the only noise she managed. In the darkness around them, she wouldn't deny it.

"Only a brat until I make you forget how to breathe properly, aren't you?" he growled, thrusting his fingers inside of her roughly.

He spread his fingers, her walls widening around him, wider and deeper than she expected, just fucking stretching her until she was frozen underneath his body.

She cried out, too full, stretched too Gods damned tight. It didn't matter how wet she was, how much that pleasure sparked at the base of her spine and dragged arousal into the pit of her stomach—this *hurt* and she wondered if it ever wouldn't.

She inhaled dirt, fingers gripping between the seams for the stones above her head tightly as he played with her, pain and pleasure colliding into each other.

"Remember how I treated you?" he asked, stroking inside of her with a tight curl. She choked on the breath in her lungs, words far from fucking possible. "How worthless I made you feel then?" Her heart sped up, hurt twisting her gut at the memories he forced. "Do you feel worthless now, Aheia?"

Fury bubbled in her chest and even though the darkness was too heavy to see where his face was, she threw her hand out in front of her anyway, trying to hit something, any part of him. But she only swiped air, while he undid her slowly.

"You're mine to use however the fuck I want, aren't you?" he pushed through his teeth. "So desperate for anything I have to give."

"I'm not desperate for you," she gasped as he stretched her pussy. "I hate you."

"Say it again." He pumped his fingers harder, rubbing that spot inside of her, making her legs shake. All of the pain turned to molten pleasure right then and there. Every bit of it. "Get angry for me, little goddess. Really nice and fucking angry."

"I hate you," she whined, knowing how weak it sounded, but it didn't matter right now. It was too fucking good. She could barely manage to think. And it was just his Gods damned *hands.*

"Yea, remember that when you come all over my face."

"Sick f-fuck. Why are you doing this?"

"Why?" He added another finger, his calluses grazing across her swollen insides harshly. She cried out, her eyes burning with tears she wouldn't let fall. "Because I want you to feel how much you need me." She spasmed, tilting her hips. *More.* "Feel how wet you are, feel how close you are to coming for me even when you hate me. Even when you think the fucking worst of me. You might want to kill me, but that doesn't change the fact that your little cunt knows who owns it." Aheia's muscles pulsed around him, hugging him tight over and over again as her orgasm teased itself closer. "I'm going fuck you like this until none of your movements don't remind you of me." His thumb swept across her clit in messy circles and she almost lost it there, little stars starting to fissure her vision. "I could have anything I wanted from you—couldn't I? As long as I stroke you just like that. All mine. Something pretty for me to ruin."

Shit.

"And even if you had someone else between your legs—"

She ground her teeth, her fingers pressing into the stone below her in hopes of any kind of leverage, because she'd lost her hold on everything else.

"You'd be digging your teeth into those lips to keep from moaning my name, because no one else can make your needy pussy come like I do."

Fuck. Fuck. Fuck.

"*Kanys ajos den borej na sas kanyja na to niostaha afto ejktos elenchyo.*" The words rolled off his tongue like honey, the accent fluid as if it was his first language. But it wasn't. It was hers.

Good Gods.

"And if you ever let anyone else touch you like this, taste you like this, I'll hunt them down and you'll kill them for me."

She felt him shift, felt his arm disappear from her abdomen for a moment as he parted her legs further, hooking them across his shoulders.

Her hips twisted, but there was no space for movement and the air punched her throat as she felt him bury his face between her legs again—felt his nose and his chin, as he slid his tongue from her ass up to her clit and she choked on a cry of pleasure that sounded so much like her demise.

His attention was furious, like he wanted to eat her alive, like not an ounce of proximity was enough.

When she opened her mouth to fight him again, he pushed against her abdomen hard and everything that had so eagerly built up on her tongue died down. She lost herself in the pleasure and the pain he gave her, her cheek pressing into the floor, hot tears and spit pooling and dripping from her. The darkness held her, and he cut into the brittle her safeties with ease when it had taken her years to build them. Brightness burst around her, lightning shooting down her limbs as the orgasm he forced hit her, knocking her into the ground hard.

"*Gods, fuck*!" she cried out, nondescript words falling from her lips—the wrong language, the right language, maybe not a language at all, and then his name. It sounded like a plea, but she didn't know who she was pleading to. Because down in this cave, nothing would help her. And she wasn't all too sure she wanted it to.

But he didn't give her time, not to think, not to catch her breath when he pulled her up by the back of her neck, fingers still buried deep inside of her. "What did I say, Aheia?"

"So many things," she whimpered.

"*My* name. Not theirs," he growled, pinching her cheeks and squeezing them together. Nerves crawled up her spine and sparked against her skin as she remembered.

If you take their names into your mouth again while it's me between your thighs—

"They have nothing to do with your pleasure."

"I-I," she fumbled, the words barely sounding like anything past sounds as her tired brain tried to reach for more than a half thought.

"Your come"—he leaned into her ear, running his nose against her temple—"is dripping from my tongue. You better fucking remember who you worship with yours."

She swallowed, anticipations heightening her already buzzing state as his shadows thinned around them and amber light streaked through the darkness. They were back in his room, on the black silk-covered mattress. Aheia inhaled sharply as his weight left her and she fell back against the pillows but Arioch was already getting up, standing at the side of the mattress and towering over her ominously as she scrambled to push herself up. But as soon as she did, his magyck slithered from him, assaulting her arms and her legs. Tendrils wrapped around her tight, like black manacles that pulled her right back down.

"What are you doing?" She choked, spread wide enough as the leathers around her thighs would let her, her arms tugged above her head.

"You want to feel good?" His eyes devoured her, and it didn't matter that he'd had his fingers, his tongue, inside of her in those tunnels. She'd been exposed then, but it was nothing like *this*. "I'll give you that. I'll make you feel good over and over again, until you can't find the energy to push me away." Embarrassment burned her cheeks as she looked down at herself, her stomach tensing when yet another black tendril slung across it, weighing her down. She was completely trussed up and there was no way out, no wiggle room. "Until no part of you confuses exactly who holds your pleasure." Her stomach sank into the fucking mattress as he flexed his fingers.

"Count for me," he said, his eyes watching her pussy carefully as two more tendrils twisted up her legs.

"Count what?" the question was strangled in a gasp when she felt the magyck stroke across her clit.

His eyes held a deadly edge when he finally looked at her. "Your orgasms."

Chapter 23

Arioch

"Five," she cried out, her arms straining against his shadows.

Five.

Her legs were shaking, and the silk beneath her was drenched as she came for the fifth time.

And he hadn't touched her yet, not with anything but his shadows.

"Please—" she was crying, dripping in sweat, and spit, and come, while her arms fought against his magyck when he stood and circled closer. Hooded eyes stared up at him, and as with everything she did, it was laced with the war she was fighting. "Please not again,"

Fight or run.

She liked to do both.

She'd run from him tonight in more ways than one, and chasing her was becoming his new favorite thing. That and the softness he forced out with his shadows, the kind that had her wanting to fall into the mattress and take everything he had to give. But on the other side of that docility loomed something dark and volatile. He could feel it rippling through his magyck as if it was his own, and it drove the need to push her further until he couldn't see straight.

No more numb bullshit.

His cock pulsed against the seam of his leathers at the sweet way she begged. Watching his magyck play with her, feeling her through it, was fucking maddening, but seeing her ruined for him was worth every bit of torture.

Her movements froze when he got on to the mattress and crawled over her—tight and rigid.

"Does it hurt?" he asked, sliding his fingers against her cunt without any warning. She bucked her hips, rotating them just as he released her from his magyck. She hissed, pulling down her arms, before a defeated groan slipped past her lips.

I'm going to savor this, savor forcing my cock into that abused pussy.

"Yes," she grit past her teeth.

Good fucking girl. Look at those claws.

"Tell me, Aheia," he purred, pressing two fingers against her clit.

She cried out, her anger faltering as her forehead fell against his shoulder.

"It hurts," she whimpered, breath uneven and broken.

All fucking mine. This was his. All of it.

"Not yet," he whispered softly, nuzzling the side of her temple. "But I'll make sure it does."

He continued lazy strokes against her, and learned her reactions, noting what movement did the most damage, feeling her carefully as she buried her face in his neck.

"No, please. No more," she begged, her voice shaking.

"Damaged little thing," he said, rubbing his thumb across her clit in tight little circles, until she whined, and renewed tears tracked her cheeks. "Look how pretty you respond."

"Oh m-my f-" she stuttered, her back arching, sweat trailing between her tits.

Lightning ran down his spine, watching her whimper. He wanted all her sounds, to draw them out and figure out what made her voice tremble the way he liked.

"That's right, let me hear you."

He sank two of his fingers into her pussy and they groaned in unison, her hot flesh splitting for him as he curled them against the walls of her abdomen. His relief prickled down his spine just as her pleasure coiled her tight. It was getting him off, seeing her little cunt swallow him.

Fuck, he needed to be inside of her. He wanted to fucking rut into her until she was screaming his name, until she forgot hers.

He rested his forehead against hers as she sobbed, keeping up his pace.

"You make everything h-hurt," she gasped, squirming helplessly.

"Just fucking wait, little goddess." His lip twitched into a dark smile as he unlaced his leathers, and she watched, a mixture of fear and excitement bright in those blue irises. His little creature was conflicted. Wanted this but didn't. He could feel it, could see it, and he planned on making it so much more complicated for her.

She liked to make him the villain between the two of them. He didn't know if it was because that's how she wanted to see him, or if it was because she still felt that fucking shame over what got her pussy wet. He could play either role for her, but he'd figure out where all of the twisted little needs came from. What fucking trauma they stemmed from.

Spit dripped from her lips as she sat up, trying to pry his hands away, to stop him. But instead of doing just that, he pulled her underneath him, pushing his pants down against his hips.

He dragged the head of his cock through her folds, feeling the wet heat lick at him as she wiggled her hips, a mixture of trying to swallow him inside and finding distance between them.

His skin broke out in pebbles, across his back—a reverberation that bristled from the base of his neck all the way down his spine and his arms. Every inch of him vibrated.

Aheia froze, her expression cracking. He saw it in her gaze first. The color of her eyes diffused, light blue, dark, darker, bleeding, and twisting until they were midnight. His midnight. A mirror of his realm outside.

She was his impossible creature.

His fucking thing to play with.

His Aheia.

But his shadows wanted her just as badly. They bucked and twitched when she was around, when she wasn't. They worshiped her, and it was blinding. It became his intention, and it didn't matter where it was born from. Because the sun was still real when the moon took its place.

He pressed her legs apart further, and she dug her fingers into the silk, eyes snapping down between them as he notched the head of his cock against her entrance. Her glossy lips parted as he sank inside of her slowly. *So fucking tight.* So swollen.

"You'll kill me," she croaked, pushing her legs wider.

"Not before I'm done with you," he growled, pulling out the few inches he'd fed her. "And I've barely fucking started," His lips quirked into a smirk, watching the anger flash across her features. *Fuck,* he liked her angry. Such a bright flame. And he wanted her to burn him.

She was never made for me. This was not meant to happen. They fit, but they didn't, not at first. Her body wasn't made to take his cock, but she did such a good fucking job of it. And he wasn't meant to have her, just like he should have never held her soul in his body. He was stealing something and ruining it. *I'll make her fit me.* So that no one else would ever feel good enough. Because that's what she was doing to him. Her pussy was molten and tight, and her skin cold, even covered in warm sweat.

She was dripping all over his sheets, her arousal splotched against her thighs, and he still barely fit. He pushed back inside, harder this time, deeper. Her back bowed, her lips dragging over his chin as she threw her head back while he moved inside of her with deep strokes.

Her hips rolled, her breathing interrupted by choked moans, and her eyes almost closed as she lost herself. It was the most beautiful fucking thing he'd ever seen.

"Not yet, Aheia," he growled.

"Fuck I—I cant."

"I better not feel this little pussy come." He slung his arm around her waist, and lifted it off the mattress, so he could hit that spot that made her eyes roll to the back of her head.

"Fuck, please. Don't stop." She was begging the ceiling, her lips parted. But he didn't give her the comfort of focusing anywhere but on him, of escaping what was going on between them, of imagining it was somewhere, some*one* else. He grabbed the back of her neck, bringing her close so that his teeth grazed her lips when he spoke.

"I better not fucking feel this"—*thrust*—"lit-tle"—*thrust*—"pussy"—*thrust*—"come."

"*Gamisyeno maljka.*" Fucking asshole. She hissed, but the edge was nonexistent.

Heat seeped through him at the insult. Fucking *brat*. He grit his teeth, and rolled her tired body onto his chest so she straddled him instead.

"Shit. Please—" Her words were swallowed by a disjointed groan.

"Fuck yes," he cursed, pulling her hands behind her back until her torso bowed and that white, pullable hair pooled on his legs in a messy braid. Her tits bounced in his face as he met her movements with his own, watching her stomach bulge when his cock filled her. She was taut, without much room to move, every muscle spent focusing on the angle he forced her into.

Fuck, he wanted to see just how far he could stretch her, bend her, rearrange those fucking insides. He splayed his hand over her abdomen, feeling himself move inside of her and pressing down enough to make her cry out.

Maybe I should *let her pray when I fuck her tight cunt, when I have my fingers inside of her, when I force my cock down her infuriating fucking throat.* Maybe he'd pretend the Gods that would never hear her were watching them and see the shame cross her face when she imagined it.

Life was too long for shame—he'd meant that when he told her, but there were ways of spinning that feeling, of making her crave his twisted version of it just like she craved his cock while she hated his guts.

"You think they hear you now, your Gods?" He drove into her hard while he rubbed his thumb over her nipple and rolled it between his fingers. "You think they see you crying, stretched around my cock and losing your pretty mind over how good it feels?" He couldn't stop now that she was wrapped around him again. It felt too fucking good.

Her pussy clamped down tight when he spoke and he thought she liked the idea even as she whimpered the word *stop*. It was so breathless and choked that he wanted to make her say it over and over, just to hear how hard it was for her.

I'll never get enough of this.

"Ask them again." He tugged at her arms harder, bowing her further. "Maybe they'll hear you if you just *believe* hard enough."

"*Stop*," she gasped, "you made your point."

No, he fucking hadn't.

"And what point is that?" he taunted her, taking the thick rope of hair behind her and wrapping it around her throat, while he slowed his movements, just enough to let her speak.

Her hips bucked on top of him, and her shoulders twitched like she was trying to free herself.

"You're the one making me ..." She swallowed, the blush across her breasts deepening. It didn't seem like it was possible; she was already bright fucking pink. He let go of her hands and she collapsed forward, barely holding herself up on his chest while he kept a tight leash around her throat. She sat there with his cock buried inside of her, a mess of white hair covering her face until he readjusted and propped her chin onto his fist, forcing her eyes back to him just how he knew she hated. She hated it because she couldn't tell him the truth, the things he already knew because he saw them in her gaze; he already fucking *knew*. But he wanted to hear it from her lips.

"Making you what?" he pressed, tugging at her braid, as she gasped for air.

He watched the shame spread, and he felt all of her thoughts in his bones. *I shouldn't like this. I shouldn't want this. I shouldn't be here.* That fucking word. *Shouldn't.*

"Making me come." She bared her teeth, and so did he.

No more prayer, not to anyone but me.

"What else?"

"I—I don't, *fuck.*" She huffed her exhale, testing her limits with the noose around her throat.

"Your Gods won't help you," he growled. "They'll watch you get dragged into hel rather than hear your pleas. They've done it once before." He worsened his hold, feeling the pulse around his cock when he did. She liked when he stole her oxygen, too. "Don't waste your breath on them when I only allow you to catch it while you scream my name."

Sweat glistened her skin, and her shoulders shook as she held herself up, her eyes soft. That pretty defiance was shattered somewhere on the ground now, leaving her pliable. It was so fucking worth it, breaking down the brat inside of her because this? This was fucking addictive. He liked her words, liked when she fought him, fought others. But that made the moment she gave over her control so completely that much sweeter.

"You want more?" he asked. "You want me to show you those stars I see in your eyes?"

She nodded messily, her pussy throbbing around him.

"Ff-fuck."

He watched her carefully as he lifted her off his cock, cold air wrapping around his hot skin. Aheia whined and his lip twitched. *Greedy.*

He was fucking greedy, too.

"Then ask *me*," he said, moving his hand around her hip, dipping his fingers inside of her again.

"Please, Ari I want more. I want everything." Her words were all but slurring together.

Everything. His shadows grazed underneath his skin, a shiver working down his spine.

He spread her arousal between her two holes as he let go of his shadows for the first time since he'd tortured her with them. They wrapped around her legs and her arms, applying just enough pressure for her skin to bulge in between the tendrils, and her eyes snapped up to his. He liked that expression on her face. Something almost fearful, like she realized what she'd asked for in that moment.

He pushed two fingers against her ass, and he kept them there. "I told you what would happen, didn't I, Aheia?" He massaged the tight hole, dragging his darkness over her clit and down to her pussy. "If you called for the Gods again while I was the one fucking you." His chest hummed, and he pushed harder, feeling her ass swallowing his fingers slowly, drawing out a long, guttural moan from her lips. "And if you don't use your word, I won't stop until every part of you is full of me."

Aheia's hips pushed back against him, and then she nodded, her bottom lip drawn between her teeth.

"Breathe in deep," he told her, and when she did, he adjusted, sinking his cock inside of her cunt again. *Fuck*, he'd never get used to that.

"*Shit.*" She huffed out the same breath roughly.

"Again." He stayed still this time, watching her inhale deep, feeling her contract around him. Then he told her to do it one more time, and when she did, he let his magyck replace his fingers, pressing into her ass slowly.

Her hold on him tightened, nerves flaring in her eyes for a moment, both of them rigid against each other. Another tendril of his darkness dipped from her thigh between her legs and stroked across her overstimulated clit as he rocked his hips slowly. A broken little moan vibrated from her and her head fell against his chest. She clenched down tight, gasping, but he could feel her pleasure, and he hadn't expected how much fucking restraint it took. He had to focus hard, on her reactions, on how she felt, on what happened between them, so he didn't lose the handle on his magyck.

Black spots bordered his vision, and the shadows inside of him whispered, coaxed, and razed their teeth across the cords of his muscles with need. They wanted more, and they were vicious. They conjured images of her little body marked up under his knife; her flushed skin splitting against the blade, as he lapped up her blood. Every part of her just *them* while she was suspended in so much darkness that she'd never find her way out again.

Aheia cried out, letting herself fall against his shadows while the magyck between her legs started to move deeper, stretching wider. Arioch blinked, ridding his eyes of the darkness slowly, watching the skin on her arms pebble as her body went rigid.

He was fucking fighting for air right alongside her, his shadows slowly slipping from his control and curling up her throat toward her lips. She opened up for him without prompting, drool dripping from her tongue when she licked and sucked a tendril into her mouth like the greedy little whore she was for him.

She was full, so fucking full, her mouth, her pussy, her ass; everything was him. And it wasn't enough. He wanted more, wanted to permeate her skin with his shadows and swipe them against her heart, feel it beating for him, feel it run from him when he scared her. He wanted to have his hands in her chest and feel her fucking blood, twist his fingers so tight that she'd never move again without remembering his presence.

Her hair was still coiled around her neck and he held on tight, while three parts of him fucked her at the same time.

"Who holds your mercy?" he growled.

"You," she cried out against his shadows, as he thinned them enough for her to speak properly. He wanted to hear her because it was her words that slowly unlaced him.

"Please, yes *please*, fuck, please," she choked, her words running into each other as her back bowed and her legs trembled.

"Yes please, what?"

"I want"—she tipped her chin—"Please make me come."

He could see those walls closing in around them, around her, as he leaned in and whispered it in her language.

"*Ylea gia mé,*"

"Ari—" She sounded panicked as her body spasmed around him.

"That's right," he groaned, working her harder, deeper, faster. "My name. Scream my name when you come, or we'll have to do it again and again until you get it the fuck right."

Her body twitched, her pussy contracting around him tightly as she cried his name. His shadows purred, and pulsed alongside, and it took those blue eyes on his to pull him right over the edge with her. His come filled her cunt while his shadows spasmed and fissured like she'd undone them just as much.

Time didn't feel real as they lay there just breathing, his cock and his shadows still buried deep, his release dripping down from her pussy and onto his abdomen.

"You did so good," he said hoarsely, wrapping his hands around her thighs and holding her while he moved his shadows from her ass. She hissed, her forehead dropping to his chest as he repeated the treatment, and pulled out his cock. She moaned, as he rolled her onto her back, squeezing her ribcage with his hand before trailing his fingers down. Her legs spread when he got to her waist, and an approving growl vibrated through him. *Good.* She spread her legs just as instinctually as she backed away from him. A fucking duality of mass proportions.

"Fuck, that's pretty." He wet his lips as he looked at everything he'd done to her. The bruises on her arms and legs, the scratches there too ... the bite marks. All his. All *fucking* his. He spread her pink pussy for him—glistening, and puffy.

She raised onto her elbows so she could watch better, her blue eyes dark while the pink in her cheeks deepened. It looked a lot like embarrassment.

"I'll wash up," she mumbled, starting to roll to her side, but he hauled her up to his chest instead, winding a heavy arm around her waist as they settled back against the pillows. He caged her close while his other hand trailed back down to her pussy. She squeaked, her hips jerking when he pushed his come inside of her with two fingers. "Don't you fucking dare."

"No—" She squirmed, fighting harder, looking up at him with alarm. "You can't—" A soft groan disrupted her words as he slid his thumb over her clit.

"I *can't?*" he growled, curling his fingers and watching her spasm, her thighs clamping down hard. "I can do whatever the fuck I want with this pretty little pussy. I thought we cleared that up."

"Fuck you," she gasped, her fingernails digging into his shoulders. "You can't come inside of me like that." Those words were punctuated so perfectly with little gasps that he almost didn't hear them. "It's dangerous."

"*Dangerous*?"

Her eyebrows pleated, her face so fucking flushed that it looked like the color might become permanent in her cheeks.

"I haven't taken any"—she caught her breath—"*precautions* in months."

He ran his tongue across his teeth. "You don't have to worry about that, Aheia."

"Not worrying doesn't exactly count as contraception."

He slid his fingers from her cunt slowly, watching her tremble for him. "No, but the herbal shit I take every three months does."

"Excuse me, what? You take an *herbal*?"

Most males, unless they actively wanted offspring, took the herbal. It did nothing but suppress the shit inside of them that wanted to procreate. "You're surprised?"

"Yea, I ..." She cleared her throat. "I've only ever heard of anatomically female Mithra taking any kind of contraception. None of the options were very comfortable."

None of the options were very comfortable. Of fucking course, the Ćist would try to strangle the part of the equation that could have a youngling every nine months and not the one that could reproduce over and over again within a single damned day. *Archaic.*

"It's easy, I just swallow." He brought his fingers to his lips and sucked off their come as she shoved at his chest.

He inhaled, feeling all of the space in his body, feeling how *calmly* his magyck rested against his muscles. Like for once, his shadows were sleeping.

What are you, little goddess?

How did she hold him in the center of her palm like she did?

"Don't—" she said suddenly, eyes flicking up to his. "You won't hurt Nyco, will you?"

"Nyco's a good warrior," he said. He liked how she tried to protect them—she'd forced that fucker in the bar to apologize to them with his knife instead of to her. It was the hottest fucking thing Arioch had seen in a long time. That and how she spoke to Lúc right after. That shouldn't have done shit for him like it did. But it was how she fell into that vicious side of her so fucking effortlessly that got his blood pumping. Did she know that there were such defined sides to her? That she toed a line?

Her chin tipped, tired eyes suddenly not so tired anymore. "What are you saying?"

"What I've been saying since we first met, Aheia. I know what goes on in my home."

She narrowed her stare. "You knew about tonight?"

He didn't answer.

Her brows furrowed. "Nyco's been reporting to you?"

Let her do what she wants but watch her, indulge her, keep her safe—That's what he'd told Nyco the night she came back to them. He didn't like the idea of restraining her unless it was against his bed with his leather and shadows. Contrary to what he'd told her, he had no plans to restrict anything about her. She'd had enough of that and fuck, she glowed when she was defiant. He wanted to give her something to defy. He'd put rules and barriers into place to see exactly what she'd do with them. Nyco was a safety.

"Everyone reports to me," he said, letting her feel his fingers, tracing them down her bruises until she squirmed.

"Stop," she hissed, but her nails dug into him, pebbles breaking out over her arms. "I thought you wanted me to stay put?"

I wanted to see what you would do.

"I'd prefer it," he murmured. *I want you alive and safe, and those two things are different no matter how similar a shade you paint them.* "It's easier to keep you breathing if you stay close."

She scoffed, rolling her lips between her teeth. "But Lúc—" Her eyes widened, and he knew what she was thinking of. The Shifter's threat.

"Will he hurt them?"

Her compassion for the Nephilim was sweet.

"Nyco will be fine, Aheia."

"And me?" she asked.

"What happens next is in your hands."

"Is it? It feels a lot like it's in yours. And if you squeeze any harder, I'll suffocate."

"You can't suffocate sunshine," he said, feeling the echo between them.

"Darkness tends to do exactly that." She yawned, resting her head against him again, her heart slowing. "Snuff out light."

Not his, and not her. He stroked across her hair, as her breathing evened out. When she was submerged in his shadows, she was a shining fucking star.

Chapter 24

Karyme

Kar woke up with a heavy swell of emotions weighing her into the mattress. The anxiety wasn't hers, but that didn't mean she felt it any less.

Dark vines hung from the ceiling, thick and green, the moonlight cutting through them and casting small shadows over her face. Maya's limbs were draped across the empath's belly and her head was resting against Roux's furry back, his snout curled into Kar's side, eyelids moving quickly with whatever dream had him in its hold.

'Amm's sake.

She hadn't meant to stay the night after picking up the eyrid for Arioch at Lynx, but she'd gotten more than a bit side-tracked and the evening ended up running into this morning quickly. Her arms stretched above her head as she took inventory of her muscles before slowly untethering herself from the two Shifters that were sleeping around her.

Fuck, my legs.

So sore ...

She pushed off the mattress and picked up her discarded dress that had somehow landed on the lamp next to the wash-room. Then she pulled it over her head and sat at the gold vanity near the door, rummaging through the drawers to see what Maya had to work with.

One of the gold receptacles at the back held some loose charcoal, and she swiped it on with a small, red brush, watching it dust her cheeks. It covered the creases under her eyes that the exhaustion of the last couple of weeks had carved into her face.

Emotions were running high, and it became hard to disassociate—which was the most difficult part of her existence on a good day. Feeling foreign sadness or even rage was second nature. It was almost hypnotizing—so easy to sink into, like a warm bath. But separating from it all, rising above it, and forcing that practiced smile ... That was muscle work.

She let her eyes close for a minute, basking in the darkness behind them, a darkness she'd grown comfortable with. A safe haven. The only place she could be alone.

Where others saw their thoughts and their streams of consciousness brightly painted against their insides, she faced nothing but black, empty space. Imagining an object as simple as an apple, for instance, was near impossible. She couldn't hold on to the likeness of it. Even when she conjured the picture of its waxy, red skin in her mind, the curve of the stem, the gleam that light would throw onto it, there was static wrapping around it.

When she tapped into someone else, however, the emotions played a symphony. Sometimes they were colors, and sometimes nothing but pangs that lit up her nerves—the experience varied from creature to creature.

She didn't know why it was colors when she pleasured the Shifters in the bed behind her, but gut-wrenching pain when Arioch had handed her the bag of margaritári right before they traveled back to Keloseros with Aheia. But *feeling* wasn't new to Kar, where Arioch was concerned. He always *felt.*

She conducted. That was her existence—feeling the emotions of creatures who didn't understand themselves.

Her abilities had been passed down through her mother's lineage, but she was the last empath to be born in her family and the last alive, too. That was another facet of her existence that varied from other Nephilim. Where her brothers and sisters were immortal, her and all empaths' natures saw their own lives cut short. She would die eventually, and no one truly knew why. There were a few ideas about it—that the intake of emotion and energy was effectively killing the cells that would normally just keep regenerating, but there was no true proof behind it.

She didn't mind.

Kar was intrigued by the finality of time—it didn't scare her.

There was a beauty in death to her, a comfort to its cradle.

She slid the straps of her dark green dress into place, letting them hang loosely off her shoulders. Her eyes weren't right. They were tinged pink from the tears that may or may not have been hers. The faint red color that had somehow stayed on her lips complimented her dress, and the jewelry that danced up her ears, down her fingers, and across her neck and wrists glinted to draw attention from the things she struggled to hide. The hoops dangling in her lobes were etched with wards that were meant for luck and protection and held small snake vertebrae in the center. Her sister had made this pair for her before Kar left Thryn—her family's territory—even cleaned the bones herself.

Kar chewed the inside of her lip, her chest pulling with a small burst of sadness at the thought of her sister.

"Are you ok?" A groggy voice drifted toward her and Kar met Maya's dark juniper eyes in the mirror, feeling a string of pleasure shift in her abdomen when she saw the Shifter's ruined face. There was something about smeared makeup on pretty creatures, especially when Kar was the reason for the way the white powder smudged.

"More than." Kar smiled, standing to readjust the dagger and her four strategically placed hair pins across her head. They were sharp enough to take out another's eye ... and had twice before.

She laced up her black boots and kissed the thick, hanging vine that twisted across the top of Maya's ornate gold mirror before plucking one of the dark navy leaves from the stem.

"Thank you, beautiful thing," she murmured, rubbing her fingers over the *helichrysum*, the sister plant to Achlys. A layer of oil built up on her skin, the fresh scent prickling her nose as she brought up her hand and dabbed it behind her ear. The plant's secretion soaked into her skin and numbed her brain slightly, her vision becoming waxy as it dulled everything in her mind.

"Stay," Maya pleaded, pushing up slowly, the red silk bedding pooling around her hips.

Kar's pulse hitched, and she felt the warmth curl into her abdomen as she wet her bottom lip. The Shifter's taste was still on her tongue, and it was getting hard to remind herself that Emryn was most likely already outside waiting for her.

"Was that a demand?" Kar asked, standing from the chair slowly. The Shifter's eyes followed her movements, captivated. That's all it took. Kar's proximity. It made the little wolf squirm and melt, and it was too powerful, too addictive.

"N-no," Maya stuttered, her full lips parting as Kar levied her knee against the mattress, her dress spilling over the bed.

So submissive, so absolutely fucking bendable.

She crawled across her, watching those deep green eyes look up through white, curled lashes. It matched the delicate cream tattoos all over Maya's body, flowers blooming against the side of her neck and across her collarbones. Kar knew how far the tattoo reached, how the Shifter's entire ribcage was a forest, and small mushrooms bloomed on her hips. Nightshade was inked on her inner thigh, and small Achlys that rounded her ankles like bracelets. She knew because she'd trailed every line with her tongue, and remembered the way the wolf had come apart around her fingers when she nipped at the tips of the belladonna that was just inches from her cunt.

Emryn's waiting.

She repeated it three whole times before the words became sounds without meaning.

"Try again," Kar said, looking down at her, eyes half-lidded.

"Please," Maya's voice was meek. "Please stay."

Much better.

The Shifter's fingers twisted in the sheets and Kar could see the desperation, could see how badly she wanted to touch. But she knew better than that. Bad girls didn't get rewards.

Kar darted out her tongue, just a swipe across her lips, coaxing out one of Maya's whimpers. The sound tingled between the empath's legs like glow moss that lightened in the dark.

Just one more taste.

Little blue streaks painted her vision, the same blue that had filled her eyes last night, mingled with Roux's pleasure that manifested like an extension of her own. She'd been a canvas then, filled and covered with color and sensation. It was fucking beautiful, but it could be just as dangerous. Because it opened her up, and every time she fucked someone, they got a part of her, just as she got a part of them. It was an exchange.

Emryn's waiting.

Fucking hel, she should have taken a *caravan* instead of asking the Syraphem to pick her up.

Emryn's w—

The Shifter pushed up onto her hands, brushing her mouth over Kar's.

—waiting.

The thought stuttered as Kar opened her mouth to taste Maya's air. It smelled like liquor and sleep and there was the faintest hint of grapes there too—the scent she leaked into the air when she was turned on. The Shifter saw an opportunity when Kar hesitated and acted in a way that the empath would have punished if there had been the time—nipping at her bottom lip. Her leftover lavender lipstick mixed with Kar's red as she bit softly, like maybe if she latched on hard enough, she wouldn't leave.

A groan vibrated through her and her eyes rolled to the back of her head. Fuck, it felt like bubbles bursting underneath her skin, the lust and need that swelled inside at the wet heat that enveloped her. Some Kar's, some not. All of it consuming and near impossible to cleave apart. Her clit throbbed, the back of her neck on fire with the desire to give in, to take what she wanted.

Roux stirred lightly, his fur rubbing against the side of Maya's arm, but he didn't wake as Kar gave in, dipping out her tongue. Maya wrapped her lips around it eagerly, pain tugging at the root when she sucked.

She felt so—*Gods, she's soft.*

Maya broke away from her mouth to gasp, and Kar watched the glaze in her eyes deepen, watched how her neck flexed when she tipped her chin, watched her lips quiver with her inhale.

So needy.

She leaned in, tugging at the wolf's bottom lip with her teeth, teasing out more blue streaks. They outlined those perfect tits, that ink, the curve of her thick thighs, and the stretch marks across her belly.

Fuck it.

"One more," Kar purred, running the pad of her thumb over the bud of Maya's nipple. "I want one more,"

One more orgasm.

One more just for her.

"Yes, Gods, *yes*." Maya nodded frantically, her palm shooting up to her mouth to muffle the sound she made when Kar trailed her fingers in a soft line down her stomach. The empath clicked her tongue in warning, just as the Shifter realized her demand and corrected desperately, "I'm sorry. I meant please, *please*."

"You sound so pretty when you beg for me," Kar whispered, kissing the edge of her jaw.

"Anything you want, tell me and I'll do it, just please touch me," Maya whimpered.

Good wolfling.

Kar's pulse hammered inside of her, and she felt it fucking everywhere as she crawled back enough to sink between Maya's legs, seeing the blue streaks jump against her skin in time with her heart. She traced her palms up the inside of the Shifter's thighs, sliding her thumbs down the sides of her pussy and pressing down lightly. *Fuck*. She groaned, watching her glisten and squeeze—so gods damned wet already.

A soft moan escaped Maya, and her eyes looked almost panicked as she dug her canines into the back of her hand, eyes shooting to Roux who was still sleeping next to them.

"I want to hear how good I make you feel," Kar said, razing her teeth against the belladonna again. It had become her favorite flower and it would stay her favorite until she left this room and everything would end between them.

"But—" Maya choked on her next words when Kar slid one finger inside of her slowly. "Oh, shit," she hissed, her back arching. Her breasts bobbed with the movement, and Kar couldn't fucking look away. She rubbed her thighs together against the mattress, needing friction, needing—*fuck, anything*. Because seeing the pretty female above her writhe made her own pleasure swell.

She watched the wolf carefully, the little shivers that ran through her when she pushed her middle finger deeper, when she curled it and rubbed against the inside wall of her abdomen, the way her hips bucked when she did it again.

"How do you know exactly—Gods," Maya choked, her fingers twisting up the sheets. "Right there, fuck please, right there."

Yea, that's fucking it.

Kar salivated at the way her pussy bulged slightly around her fingers, entranced by the way her muscles hugged her. Her arousal soaked down her knuckles and dripped onto the bedding, making it dark red when Kar leaned in, licking Maya's silky flesh. Her taste was fucking branding. The grape ran all the way through her, sweet and musky.

"Take what you need, Maya." She hummed against her, a hard edge in her voice as she sucked the Shifter's clit into her mouth. "Fuck my face."

The wolf's legs tightened around her temples at the command, her weight settling forward as she ground her pussy down on Kar's mouth in shaky movements.

"*Fuh—*" the Shifter choked when Kar got done licking the third letter of her name against her cunt, her thrusts becoming rough inside of her. Maya jerked out of her hold, a cry of pleasure muffled against her hand, and the empath had to clamp her forearm over her abdomen to keep the wolf underneath her. The sound of wet skin on skin filled the room, her fingers drumming into the female in hard strokes that landed against that same spot over and over again until Kar felt her unfurl slowly.

"Come for me," she said, sucking her clit into her mouth again and circling it with her tongue. Maya's walls fluttered when her orgasm rippled through her, come spilling out between the empath's fingers.

Fucking hel. Kar moaned, lapping at Maya's cunt, tasting every bit of her release.

Blue. Everything was blue.

"Gods, you're good at that," Maya gasped against her hand, her body slowly relaxing back into the bed.

A bead of sweat trickled down Kar's neck, and every part of her felt fucking on fire. Her timing was shit sometimes. She was going to feel that for the next few hours.

Kar slid out of Maya's pussy, and rocked back on her heels, feeling her heartbeat thrum between her legs. She cleaned off her fingers, which did nothing to help deter the lust that held her in its warm grip and pushed herself from between the wolf's legs.

"Please don't leave," Maya begged. "I want more of you and—and Roux will be such a good boy if you stay," she whined, keeping her hands at her sides because she knew better.

"You know that's not how this works," Kar whispered, climbing over her and dipping her tongue into Maya's mouth, sharing her taste. "Go back to bed."

The Shifter frowned, but the helichrysum seeped into Kar further, dulling out those bright emotions invading her space.

Maya was a fun distraction, but nothing more.

"Are you coming back?" she asked, as Kar got off the bed on shaky legs, snatching the leather bag she'd come here for last night from the floor.

"Eventually," she said without another look, leaving the room and the Shifter's emotions behind.

She made her way through Lynx's winding hallways, one of the establishments that Siraj owned in Azalam. It employed mostly Sirens, some Shifters, and the odd blood-sucking Helren that pulled security while the Sirens danced.

She descended into the lower levels to get to the outside and passed a few Nephilim that had stuck around. There was a veil drawn across Lynx, one that the Heretics had woven together. It bewitched its patrons and took away their awareness for time, ensnaring them in all the pleasures it could offer. It's why Kar wore opal beads in her bracelets, wards against the magyck.

The smell of bacon and coffee became stronger the further she walked, and she followed it through toward the Ambient room.

Water cascaded down the dark walls and collected in small pools across the expanse of the floor. Dark orange flowers bunched in various places outlined paths between the pools, and soft light broke through the knitted vines overhead, made to look like dusk in the mortal realm. At the far end of the room, Kar saw a few of the Sirens that worked there huddled around one of the low gold tables that was piled high with food. They were a rainbow in front of her: dark green, light red, blue, and purple, each hue a different gift, each color an insight into who they were.

"Karyme!" Khai stood from amongst the others, and the use of her full name grated across her like knives.

She plastered on the smile his words deserved—the sharp and unequal kind—and followed the thin path to where they were sitting. Khai held out a cup, a shit-eating grin steadily in place on his light red features. His dark maroon hair was braided back across his scalp and fastened at the nape of his neck in a small bun.

"It's been a while," he said as Kar took it with a nod in thanks.

"Hmhmm," she mumbled into the coffee, letting spit well up on her tongue as a barrier before she took a sip of the scalding liquid. Khai wasn't always at Lynx; he pendled back and forth between different establishments as needed and the others were no different.

The Siren let his gaze travel for a moment, taking her in, and landing at the leather bag that hung at her side.

"A while since Ari's visited, too." His tone was suggestive. He was fishing. And he knew Arioch didn't like that nickname, not on the wrong person's lips, anyway.

"You think Alshaytan makes house calls for something as simple as holdings?" She rustled the bag.

"He used to."

She let the words drift between them for a moment, resting her tongue in the inner corner of her mouth. "He used to do a lot of things," she said, keeping her voice airy. "You're not one of them anymore." And the subtext was loud and clear. *Let it go.*

"I'm well aware," Khai fired back, a sure smile in place, but Kar felt it—how undoubtedly unsure he was. He was hurt. Streaks of little red clawed at her vision and she blinked, feeling the hum of the drug working slowly and erasing them for her. "It was a mutual decision."

She let a slow grin split her face, lips still close to the cup. "Is that what happened?" One of the other Sirens offered her a plate, and she picked an apple from the bunch, winking at them before looking back at Khai. "How interesting."

No one lost interest in Arioch. It was never their choice to end things with him. Not from what she'd seen.

"Well, you know"—Khai shrugged, eyes darting down to his own food—"Sirens aren't for everyone and some can't handle us."

Kar bit the inside of her cheek. Laughable.

"Dignity, Khai. It comes with acceptance and carefully picked words."

His eyes narrowed and his mouth opened, but he ultimately seemed to let go of his thoughts instead of baring them—which, for Khai, was unusual.

Lúc had described him as 'pretty voice, good head, and mouthy as fuck.'

Mouthy as fuck was right. Arioch clearly had a type. The opposite of Kar's. She wasn't into brats like he was.

"Good luck tonight," she said to the group of Sirens, hearing the hum of their music in the air, and feeling its pull as she handed her coffee cup back to Khai.

Late. You're so late.

"Will we see you again soon?" Khai cocked his head.

"Not before Alshaytan needs next month's takings," she said, curving her lips.

With that, she passed him, biting into her apple and stepping into the cool morning air.

The street was busy—this part of the city always was. She squinted, feeling the leftover pounding of her hangover as she spotted Emryn leaning against the building on her left. Her eyes were trained on the border, almost small so far off in the distance.

"Thanks for getting me," Kar said, taking another bite and then waiting a breath to decide if the apple would stay down, or try to claw its way back up her throat. "You look tired."

"I've spent the night working over Aheia's blood for the antidote. None of the fucking serums like it, and it doesn't make any sense. It's destroying them. Like it's Gods damned acid."

Kar's brows furrowed. "Have you ever seen Mithra blood act that way?"

"That's the trouble." Emryn shook her head. "I've never used Mithra blood for anything. Everything at this point is guesswork."

"It's strange." Kar took another careful bite. "Holding so many questions without anyone to ask about them, isn't it?"

Emryn scoffed. "Everything feels strange these days."

Kar glanced up at her. Emryn didn't often share.

"Something's making me feel uncomfortable. Something in the air, Kar. It's been like this for too long. I don't understand it."

Kar nodded again. She supposed maybe she'd feel it too if she wasn't busy feeling everything else as well. Emryn looked down, and when she did, Kar realized she was still wearing her smile, which she quickly wiped off her lips.

"We're all dealing with a lot," she said, trying to swish away the taste that smile had left in her mouth. It had become such a practiced look that sometimes she forgot to take it down. "Sometimes that demands more than we're prepared to offer."

Emryn looked at her for a long time, her thick curls braided into two plaits that hung on either side of her head, a few loose waves framing her face. Her brown eyes were hard, but Kar could feel the energy in her veins, could feel her heart. Emryn hurt, and she didn't know.

But that was something Kar couldn't tell her. Because the reality was that Emryn hurt a lot, but didn't seem to realize it was hurt. And maybe ignorance was bliss.

"Your eyes are red," the Syraphem said finally, her voice taking on a cool tone.

Kar blinked a few times. "Something in the air," she said, letting the implication rest between them.

Emryn only held out her hand so she could tuck Kar into her chest before her strong wings started to flap and they shot up into the early morning stars.

They landed at the center of the Kaserne, on a black square stone that hovered separately from the rest of the building. Around the edges, there was an abyss that every Falkri learned to jump across when they first joined. It was just far enough that it took practice, and there had been many deaths in the past. The Syraphem had the advantage of their wings here, but in the ring they would weigh newer trainees down.

The slate was quiet today.

Kar took care to let go of Emryn quickly, knowing she didn't like to be touched for long bouts, and started her running jump, clearing the abyss.

The wind played with her hair, and she breathed in the dampness that rose from between the rock curling itself around her. It smelled like the inside of a cave, of perpetual night, or waters that lingered on rock walls. *Home.* She smiled again and meant it this time, loving the cool caress. It was a memory, clearing the chasms for the first time. The elation she'd felt then had been hers and hers alone.

The square of halls that ran around the middle training ground was trimmed by columns and occasional doorways. Emryn and Kar walked through the one that led into the large, oval-shaped building to their right. The barracks and other common rooms populated the top floors and more training grounds spanned below. The structure was tall, but it was the underground that went far further. In the hotter months, the cool hallways offered a break from the warmth that seeped into the realm.

The center building had large padded floors, bordered by round mezzanines and was busy with Nephilim training.

When they entered, the air changed slightly. The few warriors that were battling on the mats didn't miss a beat, and it was apparent who had been with the Falkri for a longer time. Because the recruits still bristled slightly when any of them walked by, especially Emryn. But it wasn't just them who changed with their entrance—the Syraphem changed too. Her demeanor became fortified, and her emotions locked themselves away so quickly it gave Kar whiplash. She stood taller, and her face would betray nothing to them; it never did. Kar handed off the leather bag with Arioch's coin to Emryn before heading toward the side of the room where Lúc and Tariq were sitting.

The Shifter jumped up when he saw them, snagged Kar's hand, and threw her over his shoulder. She squeaked, fisting the fabric against his back, and couldn't help the laughter bubbling up in her throat.

"Put me down!"

"Ask pretty." Lúc hummed, squeezing her thigh.

"Put me down, asshole."

He chuckled, dropping Kar onto unsteady legs, before twirling her, the dress she wore hugging her with the speed of his spin. "Shit, Kar." His nose twitched. "Who the fuck are you wearing all over your face?"

Kar slapped his arm, swallowing the urge to wipe her hand over her mouth. She knew there wouldn't be anything there; it was just that Gods damned nose.

"She smells sweet." His canines glinted.

Kar rolled her eyes, burrowing into his side anyway as he wrapped her into a hug. Tariq was lying on the bench by the entrance, seemingly asleep with his arm draped across his face. Both of them looked worse for the wear, but that wasn't out of the ordinary. They tended to treat sleep more like a suggestion than a hard and fast rule, kind of like flight speed limits and liquor consumption labels.

"*Ant aljah,* Lúc! That's mine!" She pinched the fabric on his chest, realizing what shirt he was wearing. He'd rolled the sleeves, but she recognized the black and white splotches. It was one of her favorites, oversized on her but snug against his shoulders. It rose just below his belly button, leaving a ribbon of pale skin between the fabric of the shirt and the thick, baggy pants he was wearing.

"These too." He hooked his fingers underneath the collar and sneaked out a string of pearls that sat close to his neck.

Kar's eyes widened, and she hit his arm. "Stay out of my closet."

"Not a chance, little one." His smile was blinding, his tired eyes mischievous.

"If you get blood on any of this, I will hurt you," she said seriously, fixing him with a stare that didn't feel all too intimidating from her stature in front of him.

"It's like you know what I'm into." He swiped his tongue across his bottom lip and pushed against his silver lip ring, before letting go and sitting back down next to Tariq.

"Don't encourage him," the Leviathan's lazy drawl sounded, evidently not asleep after all. "I'm fucking tired."

"I can find someone else to fuck if you need a break," Lúc said, pulling out his curved blade and swinging it around his finger.

Tariq kept his demeanor cold, looking up at Lúc from where he lay, but Kar saw the falter in Lúc's knife. The way he almost cut himself.

"Try me, Lúci. I like watching you fuck."

The moment was thick, and Kar let her eyes roam across the small audience they'd gathered. Most of them were still training, but some of them cast furtive and interested glances.

"Gods damned tease," Lúc grumbled, not so subtly sliding his palm across the seams of his pants before readjusting in his seat and leaning his head back against the wall.

Kar rolled her shoulders against the swell of emotions that the helichrysum was trying to dull. Lúc always felt like a lot—more than any of the others. She'd never met anyone who held more inside of themselves. It was warm and hard and encompassing, and it had taken her a while to get used to. He played at being emotionless, but she knew better.

"If you don't care, you won't get hurt." Lúc told her that after the first visit with her brothers when he found her curled into a corner of one of the hallways at the compound. He'd wiped her tears and called her small before stealing her necklace and making her chase him through the halls until she couldn't breathe, let alone remember her family's vile words.

He'd been stealing her necklaces ever since.

Emotionless. Something so far from what Lúc was. She'd seen past that smile and felt his soul on her fingertips back when she couldn't control it—knew he was trying to save her from what he felt because he never learned how to be ok with it all. He'd villainized his heart.

Kar had learned early on how dangerous it could be when a creatures insides were maligned simply for existing. Because nothing was more scornful than instinct when it was stripped of importance and buried alive.

"Where's Shi?" she asked, shaking off the lingering energy as best she could.

"He just finished his daily devotional with some of the others."

"Which *means,*" Tariq said, getting off the bench, running his hand through his messy black hair while the Shifter watched his shirt slip up above his waistline with hungry eyes. "I'm late. We're due in Azalam. The border is almost completely drawn up out there, but Arioch doesn't trust Siraj and Eros with the Heretics."

"I wouldn't either," Kar said.

"I'll see you later." Tariq gave Lúc a lingering look before he slipped past Kar, snatching the fabric of her dress between his fingers and tugging. "I like this."

She smiled, letting her hand trail across his waist as he passed, feeling the warmth of it.

It was comfort.

They felt like comfort.

Chapter 25

Aheia

Every part of her ached.

It's what woke her. That and Aroich moving around the room.

Her head pulsed slightly and her tongue was coated in whatever strawberry and sugar turned into after hours of sleep. Her stomach was heavy, and her esophagus burned with a sour taste.

The idea of getting up and moving about felt like a wet blanket. So instead, she let her eyes part just enough to see past the brush of eyelashes, throwing a white film over everything in front of her. Those beautiful stars greeted her, and she wondered if it ever wouldn't feel like an odd sight. *Timeless.* That's what this realm echoed in its threads. Timeless. Something she'd never understood, even before she'd lost her magyck to the border, even when, in theory, her life had still been unending.

"How long have you been awake?" she croaked, stretching out her arms.

Arioch was standing at his fireplace fully dressed, wet curls bound back at the nape of his neck. He sat down a gold cup that had steam rising from it as he paged through a folder in his hand.

"A while,"

"*How*? We just went to sleep."

His lip twitched as she looked down at herself. Theia's sake, *what*. She was smeared in drying spit and come and who fucking knew what else. Dark feathers stuck to parts of her like she was a swan Shifter and she could see the mattress through the ripped silk.

What the—The bed was ruined. Her eyes widened. When had they torn the sheets? The *pillows*?

Arioch set down his folder with a soft thud on one of the side tables near the seating area and picked up a bowl before joining her on the mattress next to a pile of clothing that sat on the edge.

He picked out a slice of banana and held it to her lips. "It will help."

"A banana is going to fix my life?" she asked around the bite, chewing it too long. No part of her wanted to swallow.

"It'll help you retain water." He handed her a glass from the bedside table. She took it from him and drained it. "You need to eat."

"I'm fine. I'm not hurting that bad."

He touched her thigh, massaging his massive fingers into her muscles, and she flinched.

"Liar." His voice was deep and gravelly, and it shouldn't have affected her the way it did. But that's what he did, *affect* her.

"Where are you going?" she asked as he picked up his holster and slung it across his chest.

"I have a shit ton of meetings."

So domestic.

"I'll be in Keosha all of today." He latched the leather. "But I plan on being back early tomorrow."

"What for?"

He hesitated a moment. "The rebuild of the outlier town, the shelters in Thryn that are housing the Keosha Nephilim, and the wage strike that is getting out of hand in Nori."

Aheia blinked. She hadn't quite expected him to answer. Nor for it to sound like such ... *politics.*

"And what am I supposed to do?"

She waited for him to tell her to sit tight, prepared herself for disappointment, but instead he reached for her clothing and dumped the cotton in her lap.

"I have something in mind. Get dressed."

She washed off quickly and put on the soft pieces of white clothing he'd brought her. They were comfortable, but no part of her was warming up any more to that damned color. She wound her hair into a thick ponytail, and then followed Arioch out of the room.

They walked through the halls of the compound together, and her mind wandered, trying to understand last night and how she felt about it. She was sore as fucking hel, but she'd liked it all too much to regret it and supposed that maybe starlight wasn't as sobering as the sun.

Something about that tight grip of his was enticing, even if she didn't *want* to admit it to herself. He was volatile, and impulsive, and he'd taken a demons hand for touching a strand of her hair last night. Her chest fluttered and she scolded herself for that too as she wondered if maybe he would have fought to keep her in Keloseros if she told him she wouldn't come back.

You shouldn't want that. The voice was groggy, but it was back anyway.

Her mood soured slightly, but didn't have time to fester as Arioch steered her through two double doors at the end of a hallway and Aheia balked. She was facing tall, book-studded walls that were broken up with windows spanning from the floor to ceiling.

A library. Well, a room of books. Were there enough here to constitute a library? *There have to be.*

There were countless words—countless stories that populated these shelves, stacked high enough to warrant a balcony halfway up the wall with a ladder attached. There was an archway across from them that seemed to lead down to another floor, the marble columns around it bordered by more books.

"Why did you bring me here?" Aheia gaped at her surroundings.

"Because Aljira is new to you," he said, sliding his thumb over her bottom lip. "Learn about her."

Aheia didn't have the words as Arioch ran his fingers down a strand of her hair, the one that framed her face and still felt the phantom touch of the demon who'd groped it last night.

"Escort her back when you're done, will you?" He said it over her head and Aheia whirled to the right, seeing Shiron sitting on one of the window benches. But the demon didn't look up, just gave one quick nod. By the time she turned back, Arioch was already disappearing into his shadows, the darkness roiling softly. Her face burned at the reminder of last night. She'd never be able to look at his shadows the same way.

She turned her attention to the room, needing to distract herself from the blush spreading across her cheeks that made her want to sink into the ground when she looked over at Shiron. He seemed wholly unbothered, sitting with a dark, leather-bound book. The Solas orbs above were held by multiple gold chandeliers, coloring the space in soft amber hues.

"Wow." She hadn't meant to say it, but this was more books than—than she'd ever seen. In Keloseros, she'd been allowed to hear stories from Andromeda when she was young. But once that time passed, once she could start reading herself, she became restricted in her options save for the books she'd snuck from Ophion's library when she was sure no one would catch her.

She'd never had a choice in so much material.

"You read?" Shiron asked, standing up from his spot.

"*Gjóssa*," Aheia said. "Yes, my mother taught me as much as she could, and I'd sneak away and sit under the windows of the schoolhouse where they educated the males."

Shiron's lip curved, but his gold eyes stayed hard as he walked past her, moving one of the ladders to the side and sliding his fingers against the leather bindings in front of him. Aheia followed, tilting her chin to read the spines, but most of them were in glyphs she didn't understand.

"What are these?" Shiron handed her two similarly sized books and she separated them, recognizing the mortal common language scrawled atop one, and the Lujha glyphs on the other.

"The same books. You'll need to learn how to speak our language,"

Her eyes shot over her shoulder where Arioch's magyck was still slowly dissipating.

"Why?" And she knew he wouldn't understand what she meant. Because the question she was truly asking was—*Why would Arioch want me to?*

"So that you know what Emryn is saying when she insults you from across the room," Shiron said without any humor in his voice, before passing her and grabbing a few more books on his way to the middle tables.

She rolled her lips between her teeth, running her hands across the leather.

The common language book on top read:

The History of Aljira

"Did Arioch tell you to give me these?" she asked over her shoulder.

"Yes."

"Why would he do that?" She turned as the Leviathan met her gaze.

"What does it mean to you?" he asked finally, after a long silence.

What does it mean to me?

Keeping her in the dark would have made Arioch's life easier. If she didn't understand Lujha, he wouldn't have to go out of his way when he wanted to lie to her, be secretive or push her away. He could simply dip into a tongue she didn't understand.

But he wanted her to understand.

He wanted her to understand *them.*

She bit the inside of her cheek, thankful that Shiron didn't ask for an answer as he passed her and spread the books he'd collected on the nearest table.

"Lúc asked me if I saw anything while I was dead, that he had a bet with you over it," Aheia said finally, meeting him at the center of the room. "I'm assuming you would have gotten paid if I said yes?"

Shiron almost smiled. "I would have."

"Sorry to disappoint." She bit the inside of her cheek. "I didn't walk through any special places, didn't see my old life flash in front of my eyes, I just ... I blinked." She fanned her fingers across the wood top. "I blinked and I went from getting killed in Keloseros, to attempted murder by the Asara river."

The Leviathan chuckled, a warm, deep sound. "I guess I won't hold it against you."

Her eyes darted back and forth between his. "Is that what you believe, then? That souls live on after death?"

"Not quite."

"Oh?" Her eyebrows lifted as Shiron leaned forward in his seat.

"The soul is important in most belief systems. In mine, it is one of three parts that amalgamate each creature that lives in this world." He pressed down two fingers against the wood top. "It's the spark of life that the Gods gifted us."

Wait.

Aheia's brows furrowed, watching his hand. "If that's true, how is Arioch alive?" The Avarice didn't have a soul.

"There are a few schools of thought, but at the end of the day, the most likely answer is that an Avarice's genetic makeup doesn't require it."

Interesting.

"Alright," she said slowly. "If the soul is the first of three, what are the other two?"

"Soul," Shiron drew his fingers from the spot on the table in a long diagonal line toward Aheia. "Body and the energy within"—He halted in his tracks right in front of her before tracing back toward himself in a large triangle shape—"and consciousness."

Her brows furrowed

"How is consciousness different from a soul?" Aheia asked. She knew the term, but never in relation to the afterlife.

"Well, your soul may have ignited the fire inside of you but it's air that stokes those flames. Your consciousness is your thoughts, your personality, everything that makes you, *you*. That's why you still had your feelings, and your own mind, when Arioch took your soul." His eyes met hers again. "I believe *that* part of you continues on after death, stays aware in one way or another."

Her mind was racing as she considered the Mithra and how differently they viewed everything.

"What I was taught"—*what was shoved down my throat*—"was that the soul lived on after death and that it would ascend as long as the life lived was pious and followed the Gods' teachings and rules." That oftentimes meant the teachings of the Epísmos that was in charge. "But I saw so much violence ... All the beings I've been around lived like sinners just to die as saints—as long as they confessed their wrongdoings before their demise, all would be forgiven then."

"What I've found is the ones that dedicate too much life to the salvation looming on the other side of death have become blind to what any of it truly means," Shiron said slowly opening the book in front of him.

"Salvation," she said slowly. "You still think it's real? Even now that I tell you there was nothing waiting for me on the other side?" She wasn't challenging, she was just curious.

Shiron squeezed the beads around his neck. "I believe in the things that have bared themselves to me."

"You've seen the Gods?" Aheia scooted closer, eyes wide.

"Most of us have in one way or another." Shiron lowered his voice, a soft smile on his lips.

"What do you mean by that?" Aheia tilted her chin.

"I saw 'Amm just last night." She jumped, shooting a glance over her shoulder to see Lúc strolling inside, hands stuffed in his pocket. "Probably because her stained glass likeness was staring back at me while I had that small priest bent—"

"People need to mind their own salvation. But none of them ever do." Shiron interrupted with a click of his tongue, annoyed, and Lúc grinned mischievously, letting his eyes drift over all the books laid out on the table. "Mortals believe in hel, but they think Gehenna is some sort of eternal damnation when all it is is a resting place. There are no torture chambers, no punishments doled out by different demons—"

"Like we have the numbers for that," Lúc snorted, pulling a piece of paper across their table and scanning it for something. "Though I would be first in line if we did."

Shiron continued without missing a beat, "Aljira and Gehenna are tethered. They always were, because 'Amm was instrumental in both of their creations. But they are not the same. Aljira is not hel, even though mortals and Mithra alike perpetuate that belief. Our people have done nothing to deserve the stories told about them."

"Mithra think Arioch holds death at his fingertips," Aheia regurgitated.

"Don't we know it." Lúc's smile spread. "Where do you think the term *Alshaytan* came from?"

"Alshaytan? Isn't that Lujha?" she asked.

Lúc tilted his head. "Well yeah, but Lujha originated from one of the mortal languages that existed before the Gods found Lyria. It was adapted, sure, but it's why words and even phrases can be understood both in Aljira and certain parts of the mortal world. It was the Mithra who decided to instill fear by using their word for devil to name our sovereigns—well, a derivative of it. It was smart." He shrugged.

"Hold on, Lujha is an adaption?" Aheia scrunched her nose.

"So is Gjóssa," Shiron said contemplatively.

"No, it's not."

"Think about it, princess." Lúc propped up his arm. "If the Gods only spoke Calmani, why don't we all speak it?"

Shit. She'd never thought about it that way. "What language is Gjóssa derived from?" she asked curiously.

"It's in one of the history books; I think it starts with a *G* as well." Shiron frowned for a moment, like he was trying to remember.

She mulled over the information. The title Alshaytan was given to him by the Mithra and the mortals. But then ...

"His title—" she said with disbelief. "Naming him *devil* gives him more power. Why would they do that? It deifies him to the mortals."

"They had to." Lúc's smile dropped. "If they didn't deify him, they couldn't deify themselves."

Power really is everything to some.

"The Nephilim race was always doomed. There was no narrative in which we weren't evil in the mortal's faerie tales. Not when we were"—he crimped his fingers in quotation marks—"led by a demi-god that deals in death."

Aheia nodded slowly. "You say you all suffer under the brands that others have imposed on you when you seem to thrive in the wake of those accusations," she challenged.

"If they were going to make us out to be the villains in their perfect story, then we were going to lean into the part. Because if there is something clear beyond any doubt, it's that perception held by such masses becomes reality." Lúc leaned his forearms against the table, glancing at her sideways. "Light. Demure. Quiet. *Sweet*," he said the last word with an infliction that had Aheia's stomach dropping. Misconceptions about her. "If everyone already believes the worst, we might as well play while we're at it."

"You're smarter than you look." She tilted her head and Lúc snorted.

"It's all steeped in false tongues and lies spread a long time ago." Shiron shook his head. "At the end of the day, I think regardless of what religious texts a creature follows, many of the beliefs are similar. But it's easier to wage war on the back of semantics."

"How often do you go amongst the mortals? The Mithra would have us believe it's incredibly frequent—that so many of you are trying to corrupt them," Aheia asked.

Lúc shook his head. "I don't mind making the little critters tremble, but overall, the mortals are awfully dull. Plus, I don't know how they stand the sun. It's migraine-inducing after a night out."

Shiron sat up a little straighter in his chair, scanning the page he was on intensely.

"I suppose the same didn't go for Arioch's brother. He always held a fascination," Lúc continued, slipping his knife free and twirling it around his fingers.

"Kazim liked mortals?" Aheia asked.

Lúc nodded. "Yea, it drove him to do the one thing that their father wouldn't forgive."

Aheia raised her eyebrow in question.

"He fell in love with one of them."

"A *mortal*?" The disbelief was thick in her voice

"Sealed his death right then and there. Well"—Lúc shook his head—"Not death, I suppose."

"What happened then?" She breathed.

"Arioch confronted Sahren about Kazim, and the bastard didn't even try to hide any of it. He laughed in Arioch's face and clapped him on the shoulder, congratulating him on cementing his spot as the next rightful ruler."

"How does that work? With immortals?" she asked.

"It's more contingency than anything. Every Alshaytan to date has died, either at the hands of another or their own, save for a few that handed off power. Proper succession didn't matter in the end because after Arioch killed Sahren in the old wing for what he had done to their family, there was no other blood alive to take over rule of Aljira. It fell in his hands then and there." Lúc rubbed a hand across his face. "Fuck, the way Arioch tore that asshole limb from limb was brutal."

"How?" Aheia asked.

"Lúc," Shiron snapped, but the Shifter continued, dropping his voice.

"Arioch had help killing Sahren that day; it wasn't entirely him. It was something much darker, much more powerful, something that lives inside of him, and I think he holds on to very tightly." Lúc cracked his knuckles. "One would have thought that Manāt's Gods damned cage cracked with how he was acting."

"His shadows?" She asked.

"You should ask Arioch about that," Shiron said calmly, still steeped in the text of the book propped up in front of him.

"I'm not surprised you haven't talked about anything of substance." Lúc played with his lip ring, his eyes glinting. "I'm sure it's hard trying to get to know each other while his *magyck* is all the way down your throat."

Fuck's sake. Aheia was flustered, her fingers twitching under the table in an effort to combat the blush that was undoubtedly coloring her cheeks. "You'd know, I'm sure."

Lúc barked out a laugh, rubbing the back of his hand over his eyes. "Gods, you two are similar sometimes."

"Oh?"

"Both brats."

She balked. "Excuse me?"

"That's all the more dominant archetype is, isn't it?" Lúc winked. "A brat with a control issue."

Aheia huffed out a sound she didn't quite recognize, biting the inside of her cheek against the pressure in her chest. "You know him well."

"Hazard of living with someone," Lúc said, leaning back casually making Aheia wonder about how the Shifter had been at the compound? "Were you here for everything that happened with his father?"

The glint she'd seen in his eyes darkened. "Just." Lúc's jaw tensed, his features looking near serious all of a sudden. "I'd just—" He cleared his throat, shaking off whatever he was going to say, and Aheia noticed Shiron looking up from his reading for a moment, watching Lúc carefully.

"You'd just what?" Aheia pushed.

But when Lúc looked at her he was smiling, and she got the feeling that was his own mask. "You know, this is not my idea of fun." He rolled his shoulders, his tone changing completely.

"Wait—" Aheia turned, but the Shifter placed a hand on her shoulder, keeping her facing the table. "If you learn our language, let me know—I have some really fucking filthy books I can show you." His teeth flashed at her before he left, twirling his knife around his fingers.

"Did I say the wrong thing?" she asked when he left.

"He doesn't like to speak about that time in his life." Shiron shot her a heavy look. "Lúc still believes his past is something stationary. He'll figure out for himself that it'll follow in his wake like a shadow until he decides to face it."

"And you?"

Shiron turned over the page, dropping his gaze down. "I'm steeped in mine as we speak."

"Lúc gave me shadow advice once too." Aheia's gaze softened. "It seems this entire world revolves around them."

"Oh?"

"He told me not to believe the lies told to me by the light—that its brightness casts the most vicious of shadows."

Shiron only stared for a minute before his face broke into an exasperated grin and he shook his head. "Little shit reuses all my best life lessons."

They spent the next few hours with books, most of them silent. Aheia started comparing the language and took little breaks to read over translated history. Eventually, Shiron escorted her out even though she'd pleaded with him to just stay put. She didn't want to disturb him, but she also didn't want to be watched. When they left the library behind she realized that she didn't know where Shiron was taking her in the first place. Would it be the room at the Kaserne? Arioch's?

She cradled the two identical books Shiron had given her tightly so that she could work on the language on her own time. It felt off, carrying them through the halls, and she had the urge to move them behind her back countless times, even though that wouldn't do much to hide them. It was the thought that Shiron had somehow forgotten she'd had them and would take them from her, even though he'd been the one to hand them to her in the first place, that plagued her.

"There are facets to this building, and it takes a little while to learn," Shiron said, walking a few paces ahead of her. His strides were so long that she had to double her steps to match his gait. "Where we are now is sort of open to anyone. It leads into the old wing and stops there. Adjacent is where most of us stay. You've been there obviously; you've been in Arioch's room."

Aheia felt her cheeks flush.

"If you go up that stairwell"—he pointed to an opening to their left—"you'll find a vortex to the Kaserne. If you take it down, you'll get to the hall. It's where all the court events take place. It's busy most nights with demons swearing fealty, asking for favors, dancing, wagering, you know ..." He rattled off the list with a flick of his wrist before he hesitated. "Or ... I suppose you didn't, but you do now. The hallways are a bit tricky and tend to shift slightly, so keep that in mind and watch them closely."

"Shift?" she asked, glancing at the immovable-looking walls.

"Everything is a little more alive than you might think here, including the buildings—if they were built with magyck, that is. Most of the old structures defer to simple rock and mortar, but anything built past Sahren's reign was erected with the help of Heretics."

"How alive, exactly?"

Shiron shot her a glance that she'd almost slotted as amused. "Enough to sometimes play with whoever's in its halls ..."

She was starting to feel a slow headache at her temple, realizing that nothing would ever have a clear answer here.

"Wait, where are you taking me?" She asked when they passed Arioch's door.

"Your room."

"I don't have a room."

Shiron looked over his shoulder, and his expression looked as if they shared that headache that had started in the library. Before long, he stopped in front of a black door that looked the same as all the others. He nodded towards it.

"This is mine?" she asked, looking around the hall. "I didn't know ..." *I didn't know he was giving me a room.* Butterflies dragged their soft wings across the inside of her stomach.

"Go on." Shiron nodded.

She depressed the handle and pushed inside, the butterflies dying almost instantly.

"If you're hungry, there's usually food in the room down the hall," he said.

But she couldn't focus on him anymore as she stepped inside.

Every fucking surface was white. The bed was white, the canvases on the walls were white, and the Gods damned wardrobe was white.

"*Skotá*," she growled to herself when she found the clothing and that was white too. There were leathers, shirts, dresses, tucked into the wardrobe drawer all of them that Gods damned color that she'd been trying to escape.

"Is that what you want?" she hissed to no one at all. "A *Mithra*?"

She stomped over to the mirror in the bathroom and stared down her reflection. She was angry, the female looking back. Maybe she'd always looked like this. Maybe she'd hidden it. Because her features weren't soft like they'd been before. They were sharp now, and she held her own shadows in the dips of her bones. Aheia blended with the color of her clothing, and the longer she stared, the more unreasonably angry she got. It was bubbling up in the pit of her stomach and spreading through her chest.

She supposed she should have been grateful for all of this, and somehow that thought made it all worse.

When she passed the closet on her way out of the washroom, she kicked the door shut with her foot.

Fucking males. The same. All of them.

Chapter 26

Arioch

His head was pounding as he walked into the common room and poured himself a shot. It was a dark liquor morning.

"How was Keosha?" Emryn asked from her spot at the table, picking away at a few berries.

"As good as can be expected." He let the drink burn as his magyck twisted and squirmed inside of him like it wanted to punish him for not seeing Aheia immediately upon his return. Arioch felt heavy, and his shadows were full. Too full. Like his body wasn't enough to house them. He refilled the glass and brought it over to where the others sat, Lúc and Tariq wedged around the gold tabletop across from the Syraphem.

"Ophion still mute?" Arioch massaged his temples, trying to find relief for his headache.

"Ish," Lúc glanced up. "Mumbling nonsense. He can't form words quite yet."

He'd let it get out of hand last time he was down there. He hadn't meant to maim him beyond speech for that fucking long. But he'd thought of Aheia and Kazim, over and over again, and he'd ... he'd lost it. It all became worse when the Malek played fucking stupid, told Arioch he knew nothing about any binding stone. That's when he'd taken half his teeth.

"Aheia needs to learn to fight." He shot his eyes back to Emryn. His little goddess had to have some notion of self defense, afterall, she'd made it across Lyria. But she wasn't eating the way she needed to, and it would diminish her muscle unless she started taking care of it—of herself. She'd become strong and lethal. He'd make sure of it.

"I can find some—"

"You," he cut her off, and just as she opened her mouth to undoubtedly protest, the door to the common room flew open, and Aheia rushed inside, her face screwed up in anger.

"She does like to storm into places, doesn't she?" Lúc quipped, leaning the back of his head against Tariq's shoulder, watching lazily.

What now?

"Is this what you want?" she barked, gesturing down at her body, and the expanse of white that covered it. "You keep giving me the Gods damn color, is that still how you see me?"

"Fucking sit and eat Aheia," he growled, the pain at his temple worsening. "I don't have time for this."

"Sit. Stay," she growled. "*Eat*. I'm not some trainable pet."

His jaw ticked. "You don't give yourself enough credit."

Her lips parted, her eyes staring daggers through him, when Emryn's cold voice broke between them.

"Is it difficult, that entitlement of yours, or does it come as second nature?" She looked at Aheia, her chin leaning against the hand she had propped up against the table.

"Excuse me?" Aheia's brows pulled in tighter.

"Well, you seem to think the clothing, the food, the room you have here is barely good enough for a common dog and that it's somehow beneath you." Aheia scoffed. "Consider yourself lucky, *Ĉist.*" Emryn shook her head, already done with the conversation, and picked up her goblet.

Arioch tsked. "*Natye.*" He pulled out the word slowly, shooting her a warning look.

He was fucking tired today, and this wasn't helping.

"What did you call me?" Aheia growled.

"For a dog, you have shit ears," Emryn laughed.

"*Traveske,*" Tariq chuckled, watching the Syraphem with amusement.

"What? I'm supposed to be *nice*? When she trashes everything she's given? Mind you, nothing she's earned." Emryn shook her head, the goblet clattering on the table as she stood. "*Jah alay.*"

"*Trashes everything she's given?!*" Aheia regurgitated even though the Syraphem was already out the door. "Is that what you think I'm doing?" She snapped at Arioch. "Gods, don't pretend any of this is a *kindness.*" She exhaled roughly, dark red splotches peppering her neck. "All you want me for is to feed into your sick fantasies. Dress me up the way you want, remind me of my place and then fuck that idea you have of who I am in your head."

The frayed knots that held his control slipped.

"Fuuuck," Tariq murmured on his left.

Aheia straightened her shoulders, inclining her chin slightly. She was playing at strength, but the way she faltered imprinted itself in her features.

"*Pretend.*" He turned the word over in his mouth. "You'd know all about that, wouldn't you, Aheia."

"What the fuck is that supposed to mean?"

"It's all you fucking do. You *pretend* like you don't fucking love this role, the one where I'm the monster you need me to be, and you can be *good.* A good, poor misplaced thing, taken advantage of—you can stay *white.*"

"I *don't,*" she hissed, as he stood, dropping his napkin on the plate.

"You'll keep the image you want—the damaged little creature that's here against her will, here fighting tooth and nail and no one will question it—not when your body is covered in *my* bruises and bite marks. But I know if I slide my hand between your legs right now, your cunt will drip all over my fingers, begging for more, begging for what a monster can make you feel."

"You know *nothing* about me or what I want. I'm here because you won't let me leave."

"You haven't tried very hard." He narrowed his eyes. "You haven't tried *at all.*"

"Yes, I have. Two nights ago—"

"Fuck that." He shook his head. "*Two nights ago,* you were dancing and drinking with my people. Don't *pretend* it was some grand act of defiance."

"Because I don't have the means to leave. I don't have anyone. I don't have family ... people ... anything," she bit out.

"Don't throw that at me like it's my fault. You don't even *try.* Because it would be too simple, letting yourself be happy. You'd rather sink into your heaviness because it makes you feel something. Anything. Isn't that right? You're holding on to the fear and the pain because you don't know who you are without them. You're afraid to let them go because then you might have to actually live a life that isn't rooted in hardship." He took another step. "Happiness scares you, and anger and sadness are familiar. It's an age-old story. You're not special."

She backed away, and it was like she didn't remember that he'd always fucking follow, no matter how much she tried to put distance between them. He matched her stride. "But I'll tell you a secret." He gripped her chin, the venom acidic on his tongue like it might burn her skin if it touched her. "The thing that's scaring you most—the size of the world and the dark little urges that sit just below your skin, the creature you might become if you stopped stifling her—is something you'll never outrun. If you keep trying, you'll find new places, fuck new people, numb the pain in different ways, and then you'll circle right back. The thing that's chasing you lives in your chest and if you don't fucking accept it soon, you'll run yourself into the ground."

He barely had time to let go of her face before she shot out her hands, nails dragging over his cheek. The slap tore open his skin and his shadows fucking purred. He let her hurt him, stabilizing himself against the wall with one hand, as another sharp crack hit the side of his face.

It was a fucking high, seeing her like this—seeing the darkness lick the walls of her irises. And his magyck shivered down his back, like whatever nonverbal thing that passed between them was exactly their language.

An angry, breathy groan left her and Arioch squeezed his fingers into his palm—a wholly subconscious reaction, every inch of him staticky with the noise she made. It was unequivocally his favorite fucking sound.

He watched her close her eyes, and turn her chin away as he pushed away and returned to the table, the agony in his mind growing. He hadn't meant to vomit up every single thought he'd had about her. He was fucking tired. And his exhaustion hadn't been her fault. But he'd taken it out on her anyway.

The silence stretched, and he was eerily aware of her presence—Tariq staring from across the table, and Lúc was smirking like an asshole, staring at his cheek.

The scratches on his cheek pulsed with his heartbeat, with the echo inside of his chest when she crossed the room. He didn't know what he'd expected, but it wasn't for her to grab ahold of his chin and stand over him. Her cheeks were flushed, and her eyes were a dark blue. She looked fucking furious.

"You speak of running like that's not all you keep doing. It's why I was sitting in that room in a separate building and you kept leaving me, wasn't it? Why I've spent more time with almost all of your demons than I have with you." She looked down at him. "You don't know how to deal with any of it, because *kanys ajos den borej na sas kanyja na to niostaha afto ejktos elenchyo.*"

Arioch grit his teeth, looking into those blue flames above him.

"You asked me to come back in that church in Keloseros, and I did. For you it might feel like a lifetime ago and you might have made peace with everything that's happened there, deciding for yourself that you're not in the wrong, or wouldn't do anything differently—but I'm standing at the beginning. Or rather, the end—the one where you took me back to this." She thrust out her forearms, shoving her healed scars into his face. "I'm waking up every day remembering it as yesterday when you cuffed me with your shadows and dragged me across that white ground. So, I'll be as *entitled* as I fucking want because I'm living with the reminder of it every. Fucking. Time you make me feel like a Mithra. Every time you make me feel *different*." Her nostrils flared. "My world changed overnight while yours never stopped turning."

"Fucking hel," Lúc whispered.

"You have a fucking nerve thinking you get to analyze me when you won't look at your own shit. When everything you do has a double meaning, or serves as some kind of Gods damned test. You want me to be who *you* think I am?" Her hold became tighter. "You don't get to try to build me into what you want now that I'm here and I'm not what you thought I'd be. I am not battling my demons only to be killed by yours in the process."

She let his chin go, shoving his face away and then reached past him toward the table.

"Here's what it feels like to live in your hands," she growled, tipping the jar into his lap. He reared back when it hit his leathers, glass shattering around them when she smashed it on the marble. "Uncomfortable and fucking suffocating."

"Who knew she possessed so many words." Tariq snorted, getting up from his spot on the floor, and tugging Lúc up with him.

"Their foreplay is getting scary." The Shifter grinned, picking up a berry from the plate and tucking into Tariq's side before they headed for the door, leaving Arioch and Aheia staring each other down in an empty room.

Chapter 27

Aheia

She was standing on her own fucking island, and she'd never learned how to swim. She'd die on this stupid mound of sand because the water around her was dark and deep and there were monsters licking their teeth for her under the surface. Though watching Arioch's expression made her want to dive in and swim a pretty backstroke amongst them.

The black lines on his face were starting to turn red at their edges, and she felt the blood cooling on her fingertips. She chewed on the inside of her cheek, watching him wipe the back of his hand across his lips. Angry eyes sparked as he looked at his leathers. Thick, dark honey was dripping down his legs and onto the floor below him. He pulled his shirt up, enough to get it out of the way, a thin layer of his toned stomach peeking through.

She was angry because everything she'd said was true.

She was angry because everything he'd said was true.

She was angry because no matter how mad he made her, the broken bits of her that were so fucking terrified of being abandoned had her standing here suddenly unable to speak. And she feared that if she somehow *did* manage to open her mouth, nothing coherent would escape it. So instead, she crossed her arms and went to walk past him with every intention of leaving the room. But before she could, he slung an arm around her waist, and hauled her back.

"I'm not done with you yet." His voice was gravelly, as he tangled his fingers at her neck. Aheia stumbled, holding on to his arm for support. "Get on your knees."

"Fuck no," she hissed.

The small vein at his temple pulsed, his teeth grinding and then those bright embers burned into her and he closed his fist, pain tugging at her scalp.. "I like your obedience, little goddess, but I don't fucking need it." Aheia fought the whimper that lodged in her throat. "On your fucking knees," he growled, squeezing her tight, the pain of his fingers zig-zagging through her until her legs shook. She winced, her hand shooting to his wrist, trying to shove away his hold, but his grip was iron.

She exhaled through her teeth as he pushed, and she wasn't strong enough to keep herself upright.

Her knees hit the stone painfully.

"Now, clean off your mess," he spat towering over her.

Her eyes drew from his honey-coated leathers up to him.

"*What?*"

He sank to his haunches in front of her moving his hand from her neck to her chin, dark curls hanging into his eyes. She dug her fingers into her thighs, ignoring the little sparks that ran through her, that hadn't stopped since she'd started yelling. It was touching lightning. It felt alive, just like running from him in the caves had.

Her chest rose and fell hard, her stomach full of lead.

"Don't make me ask again."

"You're not asking." She hissed, spreading her knees.

"No." He looked down between them. "There's two ways this can happen, and you have your choice between them." His shadows curled around her hands tight, like a hard, real restraint. She squealed, pulling against the tendrils, but they wrenched her wrists behind her back savagely, while he kept her chin tipped, straining her neck. "I can guide you down my body with your hair in my fist while I keep you restrained, or you can do it yourself."

No part of him held any amusement, no part of him suggested that he was joking. Every part of her in turn was hurting. Her muscles were still exhausted, her mind sluggish, her lungs ... failing her. She ground her teeth, wiggling her fingers, and testing for any slack as her shoulders felt the sting of the angle he held her in.

She wouldn't give him the *pleasure* of forcing this from her.

"Fine," she jostled her shoulders when he pulled his magyck from her and stood.

She rose up on her knees and gripped the side of his legs to keep steady. Then she leaned close, darting out her tongue to scoop up some of the honey. It lit up her taste buds, warm leather and sweet, glossy sugar. She swallowed, repeating the motion, lapping at his leg like the dog she told him she wasn't.

"Eyes on me," he snapped and Aheia complied angrily. She could feel the heat against her skin and knew she'd find uneven patches of a red blush there and the awareness of it made it worse. Her hands were shaking slightly, but she tried to mask it in the grip she had on his legs, the taste of the leather twisting into the honey. It was bitter and sweet, but beyond that, it tasted forbidden and fucked up. She could feel him, his muscles flexing when she touched his thighs, and it fanned all those little embers he'd lit a long time ago, forcing them into a simmering pyre. She ran her tongue across his laces, keeping her eyes on his as she felt his cock twitch against the fabric. Her core throbbed like it was fucking responding and it made her so Gods damned angry.

The honey was starting to bite into her. She'd never had so much of it, and the more she swallowed, the more her tongue stung. She flinched, grazing it across her teeth in an effort to scrape some of it off, but it was branding her, just like he was. They'd fought evenly until he forced her down. Now everything was disproportionate, just how she was used to.

You can't do this. You can't just sit here on your knees like this. Her heart hammered in her chest and panic flared. Because while the voice in her head told her no, her body purred and fought to stay. It was tearing her down the center, and she couldn't think. Could never think around him. The echo between them strummed, and it fanned all those little embers he'd lit a long time ago, forcing them into a simmering pyre. Would it burn her alive if she let it?

The air in her lungs turned to short gasps that she tried to mask with big inhales, but she couldn't calm it down, dropping her hands from him and rocking back on her heels.

I have to get out of here.

She pushed back on her heels, but he sank back down in front of her again, still fucking towering over her. "Where do you think you're going?"

"I'm leaving. I'm not just going to--"

"Did I say you could?" He wiped her bottom lip with his thumb, tasting some of the leftover honey.

"I don't give a shit," she hissed as he moved, wrapping his hands around her waist. She looked down frantically and yelped when he picked her up and forced her onto the gold table behind her. Bowls and food got pushed around by her body as Arioch bent down and cupped her legs, spreading her apart. Aheia's hands braced against the precious metal below, her chest heaving.

"What do you think you're d—" she started, but before she could finish, his fingers were at her lips and he shoved a little red berry onto her tongue. She inhaled sharply, her teeth clamping down on instinct. It was sweet and a little sour, bursting against her taste buds. A green one appeared just as she swallowed, and he fed it to her before she could catch a breath.

"If you keep refusing the food I try to offer you, I'll have to feed you in other ways. And I'll fucking do it until you're begging for the honey you spilled today," he pushed through his teeth as he halved a blood orange next, and fed her a piece of it.

Holy fuck.

She took her time chewing it and while she did, he brought up the remaining half and squeezed it tightly, the red juice dripping onto her shirt. She jolted, her hands flying to the fabric, eyes wide as he repeated the treatment on her clothing until she was splattered full of different reds and oranges.

"That's not mine." She choked in a breath, her stomach rebelling against the amount of food she was forcing into it.

"Is this better?" he cooed, running his hands along her rib cage. "You like red, Aheia? Because that's all I ever get to see when you're around. Fucking *red*."

She glared, watching him pull back and slowly pluck each ring off his fingers.

"Hold these for me."

"What—"

He pulled her lips apart mid sentence and dropped each ring into her mouth.

Saliva gathered, coating the jewelry as it moved inside of her, the taste of metal spreading. She fought a whimper, her core empty and pulsing, her nipples straining against the ribbed and wet fabric. Her tongue rolled around the intrusion, slipping through the holes and stacking them slowly.

"I don't like when you put words in my mouth," he said. "But I do like seeing yours occupied." Arioch leaned down, grazing his teeth across her breast, sucking it into his mouth with her shirt still on. She let out a muffled cry, her fingers clawing against the table.

"Now fucking look at me, and listen," he growled, sneaking his fingers into the laces of her waistband and pulling them apart slowly. "I'm not dressing you the way I do for my own sick enjoyment. White might have muted you before, little goddess. But here you stand out in it."

Wait ... what?

She blinked, eyes wide, while he loosened her leathers and yanked the pants down her legs. A muffled noise left her, the cold tabletop pressing against her naked skin.

"And you're not meant to be hidden," he continued, discarding the clothing and spreading her legs again.

Good Gods.

Her heart beat against her windpipe, every part of her aching as Arioch trailed his tongue up the inside of her thigh.

"As for the room," he said, biting her skin before sucking it into his mouth until it hurt, until she leaned into the sting he caused in hopes of relief. When he finally let her go, a bruise was already starting to form. "I don't know what you want, what you like. That's why it's white. It's so you can change it to what feels good for you. You can do whatever you want with it, strip it bare, dump color all over the place for all I care."

She breathed hard as he held her gaze, brushing his knuckles over the silk between her legs.

"Am I clear?" he asked.

She nodded slowly, the rings getting heavy.

"Good." He wet his bottom lip, looking down between them. "Now, you interrupted my breakfast, and I'm fucking starving."

Spit dripped down the side of her face as he gripped her undergarments and ripped them down the center. The sound filled the quiet room, the flimsy fabric discarded with her leathers as he dove down, his tongue sliding against her cunt.

She almost swallowed a Gods damned ring. *Fuck*, how were his words so hard and his tongue ... his *fucking* tongue. How was it so soft? She tipped her chin, rolling her hips against his face as he ate her in place of his breakfast.

She squealed when he yanked her against him in one thorough slide and hooked her legs over his shoulders. Wetness seeped into her clothing from whatever the fuck she was laying in but none of that mattered. Nothing would ever matter again while his face was buried against her pussy.

His hand moved from her hip down between them and he pushed two fingers inside of her while he sucked her clit into his mouth. Her body jerked as the pleasure ran down her spine and into her abdomen, collecting behind a dam that was ready to spill all over Arioch's face. She squeezed his temples when he curled his fingers, hitting that spot inside of her over and over again while his tongue did things that shouldn't have been fucking possible.

"There you go." He grazed his teeth against her clit, teasing her orgasm closer. "So trainable."

Stars exploded behind her eyelids and whatever sound came from her throat was unrecognizable. The pleasure slammed into her, just as demanding as he was, and letting it consume her felt better than anything else had in a long time.

The scruff of his beard scraped across her sensitive legs as she convulsed, the rings pressing back into her throat. It took everything Aheia had to focus on not fucking dying while he stroked her through her orgasm, a satisfied growl rumbling from him. *Gods damn.* His lips were glistening—no, the entire lower half of his face was soaked.

Her chest heaved, her nostrils flaring to get in as much air as she could when he pulled back. She was shaking while he was steady, helping her up slowly before bringing his palm to her mouth. "Spit."

Her resolve crumbled further, and she did as he asked, messily pushing the rings off her tongue. They clinked together, spit stringing across them when he pulled away, her saliva reflecting the Solas above. But he didn't set them down, didn't clean, or even dry them off. Instead, he slid the sticky metal back into place on his fingers. A mess of her spit and her come now coating his hand.

"Why did I give you white?" he prompted.

"Because—" She'd lost her edge. She'd lost the anger she'd stormed in here with, the anger she was so thankful for at the time. Embarrassment replaced it, and she could feel her cheeks reddening. She was spread bare for him, and yet, repeating his words felt more intimate, more disarming. "I'm not meant to be hidden."

She'd never known how to handle his kindness. Not then, not now.

"Good girl," he whispered, reaching for her leathers and helping her put them back on. The wetness between her legs felt uncomfortable now that she didn't have a barrier between her and the fabric, and she tried to readjust as he scooped up the discarded undergarments and shoved them in his pocket.

"That was exactly what I needed." He groaned, rolling his shoulders.

"What *you* needed?" She blinked.

"You don't know your favorite foods, but I know mine."

I know mine. Fucking. Hel.

Her eyes widened as he stretched past her to pick up a grape and plopping it into his mouth. She watched his lips close around it, still wet from her arousal, still slightly red-tinged from the effort, a few dark splotches peppered across the base of his neck and around his ink. Seeing him come undone because of *her* taste alone, over what he could make her feel, over *her* pleasure and taking it as his own ... It was intoxicating.

His lips curved, and she realized she got lost in him for just a moment too long when he stood.

"What are you doing?" she asked, as he reached across his back and pulled his black shirt over his head in one tug. Her eyes dropped to his broad chest and down to his abdomen, shamelessly carving along the muscles that disappeared into the waistband of his leathers like a Gods damned arrow. His arm flexed, shadow ink slinking across with the movement as he held the soft fabric out to her.

"Changing your colors."

Oh. Her cheeks heated further.

Changing your colors.

Her heart tripped over itself as she took it from him with shaky fingers and slipped inside its warmth. It was almost down to her knees, warm, and it smelled like him.

His gaze dropped down her body slowly, more predatory somehow, now that she wore *more* clothing. Or maybe it was because it was *his* clothing.

Arioch sat down on the cushion next to her, holding out his hand to her so that she could climb off the table with her boneless body.

"What do you like to eat in the morning?" he asked, staying close.

"I—I don't know," she said, and the words rolled from her too quickly. It caught her off guard, that question.

There hadn't been a lot of options in Keloseros. Not for her, at least. "Anything but oats," she said finally, wrinkling her nose. They were mushy and bland and had been a staple in her life for the longest time.

"I don't like oats either." He reached past her, sliding over a black, empty plate. "You won't know what you like until you try it all," he said.

He loaded up a helping for her, and the more spoonfuls he added to the monstrous pile of food in front of her, the more her eyes rounded.

"That thing is the size of my head."

The eggs looked ghostly, the yolk covered in a thin layer of white, layered on top of a mountain of rice and crispy meat that looked glazed. There was an assortment of berries in the gold bowl on the left and three chalices on her right, filled with different juices and water.

"I'll split at the seams."

"If I haven't torn you apart, neither will this." He smiled, and she swatted after him halfheartedly, completely caught off guard by how *pretty* he was when his lips did that thing. Was he always that pretty? She chewed on her lip as he moved her from his lap onto her own cushion.

It felt odd, this exchange. She wasn't used to the part that came after fights. Wasn't used to fights that let her voice her side, no matter how vicious the opponent. Now that the anger had abdicated, she felt fidgety again. They were somehow back on level ground, except she seemed to have forgotten how to walk.

So, instead of talking, she picked up a fork and speared a small piece of meat.

"I want you in my bed at night and at my table in the morning, Aheia," he said in between bites, not sparing her another glance. Apparently, she was the only one who struggled to find her words.

"Your bed?" she breathed, chewing the spicy meat. "Why?"

"To sleep," he said lazily, taking a long drink from his glass. Her heart thrummed, forcing her to feel those vibrations everywhere. She swallowed the food unenthusiastically, as the air around them thickened. "What else would we do in my bed, Aheia?"

"F-fight," she choked out.

His smirk spread, and his eyes dropped to her lips.

"I'll fight you all night if that's what you want." His fingers rounded her inner thigh and squeezed. "It's what I do best."

Instead of saying anything else, she plopped a strawberry into her mouth and tried to ignore the weird shudder her stomach gave, like now that it was used to not eating, it didn't understand the food.

"Shit, I almost forgot." He reached into his shadows, and when he brought it back, he was dangling a familiar gold leg holster on his fingers.

She stared at it in disbelief as he rotated her cushion toward him and slung it around her thigh, pulling it snug before retrieving the matching knife from his shadows as well—the beautiful gold thing he'd given her—the knife that matched the dress.

Her eyes trailed down toward the blade between them.

"You want me in your bed at night, and you're giving me a weapon. What makes you think I won't use it?"

"Don't flirt with me like that when I'm already hard for you." His voice was thick and sinful.

"You *like* that idea? I thought you wanted me to be good," she said, too quietly.

"I prefer you violent." She blinked at him for a moment, those words doing nothing to calm her down. "So try it, helfyre. But use one of mine." Arioch ran his tongue across his teeth and she thought she caught something flash in those dark eyes, something young as he tapped his own blade.

"Why?"

"I'd rather you not use my mother's blade against me while you're riding my cock."

"I'm sorry, *what*?" She coughed around a berry that tried to go down her windpipe.

"You heard me, little goddess." He dragged the words through his teeth, but with a smirk this time as he stood, hooking his hand in his leathers.

"You gave me your mother's blade?" She got up, wincing at all of the shit in her body that hurt. There was less that *didn't* hurt. "*Why*?"

"Malia used it a lot; you seem just bloodthirsty enough to do it justice."

Her mouth opened and closed like she had exactly two brain cells left and rubbing them together was starting a fire instead of sparking words.

"Was she--"

"Don't ask me about her," he interrupted. "I'll lie to you."

"Why are you telling me that?"

"So that I don't have to."

Is that endearing? She tried to figure it out for herself without much luck.

"And your brother? Will you lie to me about him, too?"

His stare hardened. "I can't give you answers I don't have."

"He's here?"

He nodded tightly.

"How is he?" she asked instead.

"He's—" Arioch's jaw ticked. "Surviving."

The room felt heavy now, and she recognized the feeling. She'd felt it herself many times, but heaviness had always been hers then. This was his. "What happened with the wage strike in Nori?" She reached for what little information he'd given her yesterday in an attempt to push them in a different direction.

For a moment, she thought she caught something like surprise in his eyes. "We came to an agreement. Their demands were reasonable, but the Siada in charge of Nori didn't want to chance how the decision might influence the rest of the territory."

"Hmm," Aheia considered. "Is it going to?"

"Every decision does." He grabbed a piece of cantaloupe. "It'll be an adjustment for the treasury and a cut to the Siada's earnings unless he can work out the dead air in his garment district, but that's *his* problem. The demons who live there shouldn't get their wages cut because the one in charge couldn't pull his shit together." He readjusted his laces slightly, biting into the melon. "If half the demons in Nori can't afford eggs at the end of week market, something is grossly out of balance."

She didn't know what she'd expected, but it certainly wasn't that much insight.

"You don't have people to handle something like that?"

"The important things you handle yourself." He ran his fingers through his hair, and Aheia watched the underside of his triceps flex. "Feeding my people is important."

Feeding my people is important. So it wasn't just an obsession he had in regards to her.

"Speaking of—" He picked up another piece of fruit, looking ready to leave her behind once again.

"Where are you going?" she asked.

"Work."

Nerves prickled the back of her neck because the next words out of her mouth felt like she was climbing out on a ledge.

He walked that ledge when he went down on you while explaining his reasoning for being an asshole.

Her shoulders tensed.

Fuck it.

"Take me with you." She cringed slightly, hiding the look that wanted to crawl across her face, just waiting for him to shut her down. The ledge felt breezy and unsafe now that she stood on it. She decided then and there that she did not like asking him for things.

"Alright."

"Really?" For a moment she thought she'd misheard.

"Eat, and get cleaned up in your room. I'll have Nyco show you the way when you're ready."

"Nyco?" She quirked her eyebrow.

"You like them," he said simply.

CHAPTER 28

AHEIA

She took her time in the water, letting it wash across her body as the steam billowed around the washroom. Her stomach was full and her joints sore, and the thought of getting dressed and leaving the room was decidedly heavy. But she fought the way her mind tried to blanket her energy, fought against the numb, because she knew the potential of what was on the other side of her door. Fire and ice, both painful, but alive.

After toweling off, she pulled half of her hair up into a knot and fastened it with a leather strap she found in her vanity. The white wasn't as bothersome in the bathroom; she blended here, and it was easy to feel indifferent about her own eyes in the mirror when they simply looked like floating orbs.

She sifted through the clothing in the wardrobe and the animosity she'd felt toward the white had dissipated a great deal since breakfast.

You're not meant to be hidden. Every time she thought about those words, her cheeks heated.

The leathers she chose had a metal seam with small teeth that zipped up in the front and for a brief moment she worried that it would catch the delicate fabric of her undergarments. There were two cutouts where pockets might have been, making the waist a leather band that the leathers hung off of almost like a belt. On top, she picked a matching white, strapless corset. Except it wasn't very tight, and closed with the same metal seam as the pants—with bones down the front to hold its structure. She finished off the look with a pair of heavy boots that gave her at least another two inches in height.

The gold knife was last. She fastened the holster on her thigh and let her fingertips explore the ridges while considering how one sentence could change the tone of a story. It felt like a small gesture when Kar had strapped the knife onto her leg all those weeks ago. Now it felt priceless.

Nyco was squabbling with Noctua outside of her door when she emerged, wiggling their fingers in front of the owl's face.

"So, you've been singing," Aheia said slowly.

"Have I?"

"Telling Arioch about me?" She raised an eyebrow. Of course they would. It was naïve to think that they'd simply trail her without reporting back but she wanted to see what they'd say anyway.

Noctua tilted her head to the side entirely, blinking at Aheia.

"The important things, yes," they drawled, stroking through the owl's feathers.

"Like?"

"Like ..." They matched Aheia's stance across the hallway. "That you may or may not have run off into the city without any protection."

"Hmhmm." She held back a scowl when that inner voice of hers purred, *protection that came in handy*. "Why did those demons call you halfbreed?" she asked, remembering that moment.

They rolled their eyes. "The more dense fucks out there think it's an insult."

"What kind of an insult?"

"It's meant to insinuate—" They drew across the delicate line that split their face. "That my family lineage was bred with—" They chuckled.

"With what?" she pressed.

"*Wyvern.*"

"With a dragon?"

"Wyvern."

"If we're splitting hairs ..." Aheia blinked in disbelief. "Are you?"

They gave her an exasperated look. "You really think that's possible? We're not talking Shifters here—full-sized danger lizards." They flashed their canines. "No. I'm nothing special."

Aheia huffed out a laugh. "Right, plus, I suppose wyvern don't *really* exist. I mean, some have said to have been spotted out in the Badlands, but—" She stopped her ramble when she noticed their stare.

"That's pretty," Nyco said, eyes dropping to her lips.

Aheia covered her mouth and cleared her throat. She hadn't meant to smile.

"Why do you do that?" They tilted their head.

"Do what?"

"Correct."

Aheia's shoulders stiffened of their own accord. "I don't."

It was an immediate response, one that didn't feel so much like a choice but another mask instead.

In that moment, it felt important to hold Nyco at arm's length, even if everything they'd ever said was anywhere but an arm's length away.

"I'm not judging you, Briteling." They held up their hands. "I've seen it before, your traumas and your safeties in response to them. I get it."

She crossed her arms over her chest. Did Nyco tell Arioch things like that too? Insights that felt lethal in the wrong hands?

"What else have you told him?" She steered their conversation back.

"That you are, in fact, capable of smiling. Though admittedly—" They ruffled their hair. "I didn't mean to tell him that. I was just shocked when I saw it first. Can't blame a wyvern halfbreed for letting it slip."

"That's important?" she asked.

"You smiling? Do you think it's not?"

No. She dropped her eyes to the side of the hallway, tracing down the black marble column.

"Why you? Why does he send you?" She continued her line of questioning. *Because you like them.* That's what Arioch had told her. But was it that simple? Could it be?

"He didn't tell me." Nyco shrugged.

"Is that the same?"

They tilted their head.

"As you not knowing?"

Nyco always seemed to know.

They rolled their tongue against their bottom lip, flashing their eyes to the ground with amusement. "I could guess."

"What would that guess be?"

"You smiled." They cleared their throat. "And to some, it's important."

The vise inside of her tightened, and it left her wondering how good things could hurt a heart just as much as bad things. Different pains, but debilitating nonetheless.

The hall that Nyco had taken her to was *busy.* Music played and there were boughs of red smoke curling around demons that sat at tall, gold tables. It seemed most of them were meant for different sorts of games, outlined by dark, plush couches, while columns separated the shared spaces into three. The center was one long hall that led towards a wall of windows.

Arioch was sitting on what she could only describe as a throne—tall and simple, just black marble, slightly bigger than the average chair, chiseled with clean lines. His eyes were hard and dark, and even from here, Aheia could see those hot embers burning. It was the only part of him that betrayed his emotions; the rest of his muscular body leaned back in a show of nonchalance.

Aylee was sitting on the armrest next to Arioch, her snakes slithering around her limbs like they always seemed to be, as Aheia and Nyco spilled past the Nephilim that had formed a large circle around whatever was going on in front of Alshaytan.

There was a demon at the center, and he looked rough, bruised, and bloody, barely standing while a few others congregated behind him—one female with dark skin and blue hair and a male that was supporting her distraught body as she sobbed into his side. The sound was sharp, pulling at Aheia's heart, so broken and desperate that her eyes started to burn.

Arioch didn't look at them, turning to Aylee and exchanging a few hushed words instead. She nodded, her gold jewelry making soft clinking noises when she jumped down from the throne, her black dress hugging her curves. She walked past Lúc, the white snake hissing its little pink tongue in the Shifter's face. Her heels sounded against the marble as she circled the bloody demon in front of them.

"He won't admit to anything," the blue-haired demon ground through her teeth, disgust lacing her words.

"They never do," Aylee sighed casually, those eyes of hers now a dark and demonic blue when she darted her gaze across the Nephilim's body. The more time that passed, the more he squirmed, readjusting his stance. Aheia noted the tremor in his hand, and it looked as though he was holding back an instinct that told him to go for the knife that was within reaching distance at Aylee's side.

"You didn't do a thing wrong, did you?" Aylee asked slowly, her red lips stretching into something feral. Lúc matched her expression, watching her intently from his spot next to Aheia. There was a spark in that purple-tinged gaze now, and it almost looked hungry. But it didn't feel like it was for Aylee—instead, for what she was doing. He looked like he was appraising, like he wanted to play with his food too.

"That's truly what you believe, isn't it?" She hummed. "That you did what those little eyes asked you to."

"N-no," the Nephilim stammered, his voice too unsteady as Aylee came up behind him and leaned into the nape of his neck.

"You took what belonged to you, that's all," Aylee murmured. "You like younglings," she quipped, and Aheia's fingers twitched, feeling the disgust sink deeper. Acid filled her stomach at the new expression on his face. *Lust.*

Meanwhile, Arioch's expression was unreadable. He was sitting there, arm leaned against the side of his throne, wholly unfazed.

"Hmhmm," Aylee cooed, running her red fingernails over his arm. It almost looked reassuring.

"No—I, that's not—" He choked, his words cut off by a garbled sound when the blond moved her hand. Aheia watched, unable to look away as she trailed her fingers down his abdomen and to the waistband of his pants.

"You like them young and helpless ..." she said almost breathily, her hand sinking further until her palm rubbed against his groin.

The demon groaned, tipping his chin as she squeezed, and Aheia's eyes traveled to the blue-haired female just behind him. She was burying her face in the neck of the Nephilim next to her as angry whispers filtered through the crowd around them. The male with his arm around her stared at Aylee, his balled fists shaking, the anger pouring off him in waves, face red with restraint.

"Is her blood still on your cock?" Aylee asked, keeping her hand in place. "Should we check?" And then she huffed out a humorless laugh. "Is that all it takes?" she continued. "Just the idea? Just the reminder of how it felt to hurt her?"

The female sobbed loudly.

You like them young and helpless.

"No," Aheia whispered in realization, turning toward the throne again. Arioch's eyes were on her this time, calculating and heavy. Too heavy. She swallowed against the lump in her throat, watching him give a brief nod—not to her, even though his attention was on her—but to Aylee.

"No, please—"

Aheia turned back toward the scene in front of her.

"Shhh," Aylee hushed, unfastening his waistband from behind. "It's ok, this won't hurt." She tip-toed up to his ear. "That's what you told her, right?" Her hand shoved into his pants and he huffed out a breath as she gripped him.

"Do you believe me?" she asked, pumping her fist once, black fabric moving across her knuckles. "When I tell you the same now?"

Lúc took a step forward, his eyes the darkest purple Aheia had ever seen, his smile gone.

Aylee grinned to herself, but it was vile. It was the kind of smile that lived in the darkest parts of someone's heart. The true kind.

She looked across to Aheia as she freed the demon from his pants and a foul, cold brush of ice slid down her back.

He was hard.

The blue-haired female collapsed.

Aheia couldn't breathe.

Then Aylee moved quick as lightning, drawing her knife and slicing it through the air. Silver blurred and black blood gushed as his skin split, and the Nephilim doubled over, his hands flying to his groin, leaving Aylee standing behind him, holding his bloody cock in her fingers.

Aheia's stomach lurched, and she had to focus her entire being not to cover her mouth with her hand as Lúc hissed, his teeth bared. Everyone else went silent. Everyone but the demon on his knees, choking and spitting up blood, a puddle of it forming under his body, spreading toward them slowly. Aylee dropped her smile as she crouched down next to him.

Another sob broke through the air, but this time, the female was watching, her red puffy eyes fixated on the spectacle. Her pain and her anguish devolved everything so much further. But there was something else, a sliver of strength that decorated her features now.

Pain is the same everywhere. It didn't matter what creature, or what realm. Pain was yet another constant, just as revenge was. She could see that plainly now.

Aylee gripped the demon and forced his chin as he sobbed and coughed, his dark eyes looking up at her like she was a God, like she held his life. She squeezed his cheeks, widening his already gaping mouth, and rammed his own appendage inside until he choked on it, his skin paling more and more by the second.

Aheia inhaled sharply, the only show of emotion she'd allow herself as she felt something amongst all the outrage—something she'd been looking for in the cave with Ophion but hadn't been able to find. *Righteousness.*

"You'll be erased. Not even your memory will stay in this world," Aylee hissed to him, gripping the shirt at his neck so he stayed upright when his head lolled to the side and his hands dropped from the bloody gash that was still dumping blood. "Your death is meaningless and the Gods will not take pity on you."

Aheia absorbed her words and watched the faces around them. Few were shocked, most were resigned and angry as Aylee dipped her left hand into the demon's blood and made quick work of drawing a few black glyphs onto his skin. Then she kicked the body aside and turned toward the blue-haired female. Aheia circled the room slowly, weaving around the demons in front of her to watch Aylee and every little movement she made. The demon reached a hand for the female, who took it with shaky fingers and let Aylee pull her close. She spoke hushed words in Lujha, touching her forehead with her own. The male stepped next to them and did the same, the three of them sharing a moment while Aylee spoke. Aheia couldn't understand the words, but she wished she did. She wished she knew what in any language might have been comfort for something like this.

Then Aylee pulled away and walked through the black blood on the floor, back toward Arioch. She leaned into his ear, and he gripped the side of her neck when she did. It was intimate, but the kind that didn't ask for anything in return. Alshaytan's gaze slipped for a moment like he was lost in thought and then he nodded, dropping his hand.

"What did she say to them?" Aheia walked back toward Lúc, gripping his arm.

The Shifter didn't look at her. "She helped ease the pain."

"And the glyphs? What did she draw?"

"Damnation," He said, his tongue swiping across his lower lips, his eyes sparkling. He was transfixed on the thick stretch of blood.

"Was it their child?" Aheia asked against her better judgment. "That he—"

The demon's jaw set. "It was."

Heat prickled the back of her neck, and the lead in her stomach only became heavier at his answer.

"What will happen to him?" She redirected her attention to the dead body that was now being dragged from the center, painting the marble.

"They'll string him up at the center of their territory," Lúc said.

"He's not taken to Gehenna?"

"In time. But until those limbs rot, until his blood looks like ash against his skin, until the ravens pick out his eyes. He'll serve as a reminder."

"But isn't it more painful that way?" she asked. "That family will be forced to remember this every time they see his body." She looked up at Lúc.

"Everything has a price. The cost of this message is public knowledge of the pain caused. That sick fuck's pleasure cost his life. The revenge that family sought cost giving the power to carry it out to someone else,"

"Why?"

The purple in Lúc's eyes shifted and danced. "Balance, princess. Not one thing in our life is given without having something taken in return. No one is meant to hold that much power. All we can do is learn how to live with the pain we're dealt, how to make it work to our advantage." She watched him run his knife across the white lines of his knuckles absent-mindedly.

"Is that what you do?" she asked. "Make it work to your advantage?"

His eyes watched the blade, but he didn't answer.

"You wish you'd been the one to do it, don't you?" she asked. "Kill him." Aheia said slowly, and it was far from a question because the answer was written in every line of his being.

Lúc finally met her gaze. "Yes."

"You enjoy it." Yet another question masked as a statement.

"Yes." He grinned and there was something dark about this smile. "The Gods enjoyed it, otherwise they wouldn't have murdered so many of their offspring. If that's worship, then I'm as devout as they come," he said slowly, dropping his voice, eyes drawing a line down to the floor.

Aheia followed his gaze, seeing a white disruption slithering across the floor. One of the only stark color changes here besides her, and it came in the form of a thin, long, white snake. *One of Aylee's serpents.* It was slinking through the black blood, and Aheia bent down when it curved around her feet. In Keloseros, snakes had been a bad omen, but she'd played with them anyway out in the fields. Those had been covered with splotches though, little black and brown ones that made them look like cows.

The snake wove between her legs, just long enough to draw an entire circle around her when it quirked its head and looked back at her with beady eyes. Its tongue tasted the air, smooth scales rippling over the skeleton when it moved.

Aylee was still standing with Arioch, but her calculating eyes were turned to Aheia, as she played with the fire of a lighter, holding it to her nails and letting them catch the flame.

"Seems she likes you," Lúc smirked. "That's Embyr and"—he looked up to Aylee, Embyr's black twin coiled around the Nephilim's arm tightly—"that one is called Salamander. They're Aylee's familiars."

Aheia's lip twitched, and she ventured out a hand, keeping a few inches of distance between Embyr's nose and her skin. The snake flicked out her tongue again before she snapped at the air, just shy of Aheia.

This time, Aylee grinned and shifted her eyes away in amusement.

"Is she venomous?" Aheia asked, pulling away.

“Very,” Lúc said, “But most things are here.” Then he looked at her with the same look he carried when he spoke about killing. “You’re in our world now. You live on the tongue of a fanged monster. Try not to get swallowed.”

CHAPTER 29

AHEIA

Days passing felt odd, because for once she wasn't counting the kernels in her sand glass. It was almost a blur, and it was hard to keep track of how long she'd been in the lower realm. She followed suit, eating when the others did, and getting her mind in tune with their schedule as much as possible, even as the stars fucked with her perception. Arioch and her had devolved into something wordless and messy. She was tangled in his sheets at night, but his days were busy and hers were ... open-ended. Though she'd gone with him a few times when he left the compound, learning more about the political structure of Aljira, how deep he had his hands sunk into certain issues and how he handled and delegated them. The surprise at how easy it was to spend her time with him didn't lessen as more of it passed, nor did how odd it felt that he offered to bring her *everywhere*. Well, nearly. Places that she'd have never seen in Keloseros, not unless she snuck away to see them herself. Aheia had even joined them for one of the markets down in the inner city and she'd learned that each territory provided different foods and goods. There was a lot of trading and bartering, and at the end of that day, she'd filled half of a journal book she'd found at the library with notes about it all. The pages were thick and there were no lines, and she liked that too, because she'd never known how to stay inside the lines anyway.

Arioch was at the border for maintenance—the only place he didn't bring her when she asked. He wouldn't be back until late tonight, or maybe early next morning, depending.

She stood at the edge of the pond amongst the citrus trees, crimping her toes around the edge when Kar nudged her shoulder with hers.

Aheia jumped, almost dropping the blood orange in her hands. "Kar, you scared me."

The empath smiled. "I'm told you're not partial to the clothing you're wearing." She tilted her head. "You tired of that color yet?" she asked, a soft lilt to her voice.

Aheia looked down at herself and pinched the white fabric between her fingers.

"Gods, yes."

"Come on, then." She nodded towards the Kaserne. "Let's fix the fixable."

Aheia's mouth fell open as she stepped into the empath's room, which was essentially just a huge hexagon wrapped in windows, tapering at the top like a spire. There were globes of Solas hanging in the air amongst thickly painted canvases, and long colorful strands of fabric woven across the walls. Plants climbed the windows, some green, some black, and some a deep purple, snug against the panes like they were feeding off the stars just beyond the thin sheets of glass. The headboard of Kar's bedframe was a deep orange velvet studded with variously sized pearls, while the mattress was filled with different blankets and throw pillows, of all colors and patterns. There was a large wolf splayed out on the covers that roused as Kar fell next to it.

"I told you to go home, and I meant it," she said, her voice stern. "I don't like repeating myself."

The black wolf jumped from the bed, heavy paws landing just in front of Aheia. It came all the way up to her hip, those red, dark eyes watching her carefully.

A Shifter.

"Who was that?" Aheia asked when the animal left the room.

"No one important." Kar shrugged her shoulders.

"*Wolves,* Kar?" Aheia raised an eyebrow.

"Great cuddlers," she said simply.

"Do you ..." Aheia rolled her lips between her teeth, realizing she'd started that sentence without thinking. Kar and her weren't that close, and the question felt—

"Do I fuck any of them while they're animals?"

Aheia's eyes widened. *Yeah.*

"No." She shook her head. "But by how uncomfy you looked just now, don't ask Tariq and Lúc about what they do with each other. Well, that's a good rule of thumb in general, actually." Aheia's lips parted, but Kar jumped off the bed and continued, "If I were a more possessive Leviathan, I'd say it's my closet. But pretty much everyone but Shiron and Arioch borrow my shit." She pointed toward a door across the room, smiling bright enough to crease her eyes and dimple her cheeks. Aheia wondered if it was the little beauty marks that differentiated her true smiles from the practiced ones. She'd seen both versions.

She followed Kar into the closet, her eyes wide as she took in all of the colors.

There was a rainbow of fabrics hanging from the walls, gold and silvers glinting from between the folds of delicate materials—pearl and gem adorned dresses hung on thick gold hangers. She couldn't help but gape as she sat on the large green cushion at the center of the room, the velvet soft against her skin.

Kar started pulling articles of clothing from the wall and throwing them over her arm. "Some say too many options make life more complicated." She skipped over to Aheia, cradling a bunch of fabric, and sat down next to her. "I think that's only true if you have a limited imagination."

"I suppose mine's limited then," Aheia muttered, feeling overwhelmed at the bounty of choices here.

Kar smiled. "Only because you're looking at the painting as a whole, which can be daunting." She pulled a long red dress from the pile by the sleeve. "Start small—what's your favorite color?"

Aheia's eyes widened. *Favorite color.* What was her favorite color? She'd never had many colors in her life, never thought much about it. The blue sky above her always felt a little too bright and intrusive, but maybe it had been the sun that truly spoiled it for her. The gold-framed paintings in her old room were beautiful, but that felt like the wrong answer to a question that shouldn't have had a wrong answer. *Is gold a color?*

"I'm—I'm not sure," she said quietly, realizing that this truth made her feel just a little more sad, a little more incomplete.

"I love a good blank canvas," Kar said, a slow smile stretching her features. It wasn't the reaction Aheia had expected. "Come on, we'll work backward. Forward is overrated anyway."

"Is it?"

"I was born backward, and look how incredible I am."

The empath flitted out of the room before returning moments later, holding what looked like a light beige folded tarp. She spread it out over the floor, covering half the space haphazardly and fanning her limbs at it like she was calling it good.

"Where did you get that?" It was huge.

"I make my own canvases," Kar said, "Now, in the bottom few drawers"—she waved her hand toward a tall dresser—"I have a ton of paint in there. Go grab some bottles!"

Aheia got up from her seat and followed the direction Kar was pointing at, fishing out a few bottles.

"You have a preference?" she asked.

"Yours," Kar said simply.

Aheia picked out a few, cradling the red, blue, pink, orange, and a couple more until her arms were full.

"What is this for?" she asked, kicking the drawer closed with her foot and heading back toward the empath.

Kar shrugged, smiling up at her from her spot on the floor. "An art project. Come, sit with me."

Aheia did, dropping all of the bottles in front of them as carefully as she could.

"I really like this orange," Kar said, reaching for the unlabeled bottle. "It kind of reminds me of the sunsets we don't have here." She popped the splattered cap open and squirted the paint between them. Aheia yelped, shuffling back as the orange splattered thick and goopy. Kar giggled, dipping her fingers into the color, drawing a few lines from the center, and spreading the liquid into the likeness of a sun.

"Go on, pick one you like." She nodded at the other bottles.

"You want me to—"

"Paint with me." Kar lifted her chin.

"I thought we were picking out clothing."

"Can't run before you walk, can you?"

Aheia wasn't sure if she understood but reached for the paint anyway. She opened up the royal blue and scooted back on her knees, turning it upside down and glancing back at Kar, who was watching her with an amused look on her face.

"Kar, I'm not sure that—"

"Go on." She grinned wider, circling her hand through the air.

Ok.

Aheia squeezed, and an involuntary squeak left her lips as the blue glopped down in front of her.

"Oh my Gods." She covered her mouth. "What a fucking mess."

Kar laughed, throwing her head back. "The stress in you over this is delightful. It's *ok*."

"But it might leak through." Aheia chewed on her lips, setting down the bottle and sort of lifting the canvas a little. She could already see it seeping into the fiber—it would leave such a mess. How would she clean—

"So?"

"Well, it'll get on your floor," Aheia tried to explain what she was worried about. "It'll *ruin* your floor."

"What a broad word." Kar reached for the red and uncapped it. "You say ruin, I say elevate."

Aheia's chest shook with a suppressed giggle—the involuntary kind, the kind that was brought on mindlessly.

"So that's what that feels like for you," Kar said, eyes sparkling.

"What?" she said through the fingers she was hiding her mouth behind.

"Something other than worry and anger."

Aheia's smile dropped, but Kar didn't let her sit with the blank look on her face for long, dragging her knees through the orange in front of her instead and dumping a glob of red on Aheia's lap.

"Kar!" she screeched, her hands dropping the blue bottle. The empath dipped her palms in the blue and the red without paying her any mind and then clapped them against Aheia's cheeks with a wet splat.

Her mouth popped open, her eyes wide. And then they both devolved into laughter, Kar pulling Aheia down into the mess of colors below them.

Her arms smeared through the wetness, streaks of it following her movements, and when she pushed up on her forearms, she saw that the different color choices they'd made had mixed into an unfortunate brown. The empath lunged for the pink bottle that had rolled off the canvas and opened the top, splattering it Aheia's way. She caught most of it on her palms when she threw out her hands, but the rest landed against her chest with a wet thud, clinging her clothing to her body.

She tasted it on her tongue and she wrinkled her nose, reaching behind her blindly until her fingers found another bottle. She uncapped the yellow, and lunged after Kar, targeting her back when she tried to crawl away, the paint streaking everywhere.

Aheia grinned; she couldn't help herself. Kar's face was covered in colors, the pigments running into each other and obscuring the dark tattoos across the bridge of her nose. It was comfortable. She didn't remember the last time she'd felt comfortable like this. It was as if she could wrap herself up in the Leviathan's arms without a second thought behind the action. The realization had her pulling back, her grin falling.

"I don't know you," Aheia said, the air changing slightly.

Kar tilted her head, drawing her lip between her teeth, and chewing on it lightly. "And?"

"I shouldn't feel this close to you, should I?"

Kar splayed her arms wide, and ran them through the wet color on the floor. "Most do."

"Is that an empath thing?"

"Or maybe it's because I'm a fucking delight." She shot a glance up at Aheia, a wicked glint in that ever-changing green.

"Does it make you uncomfortable?"

She'd asked it before her mind could reprimand her, tell her the question was much too forward. She didn't want to ruin this, and the need to preserve whatever she and Kar shared in their small bubble of colors in that infinitely fleeting moment felt more important.

Leave it to you to run your mouth.

Kar stared at her for a long time, so long that Aheia started to fidget.

"I-"

"You know." Kar propped herself up on one elbow, and when she finally spoke, her voice was contemplative and her eyes matched. "No one has ever asked me that."

Aheia's jaw tightened slightly.

She knew the feeling.

"I suppose I don't mind," Kar said, but her gaze slid to the ceiling and stuck on the orbs of Solas that were collapsing in on themselves. "I feel comfortable around you, too. And that's not an empath thing. Because your insides are a fucking mess and it should give me a perpetual headache."

They spent another hour like that, pulling out even more paint until most of the canvas was covered, and so were they. Aheia had told Kar about the small *braje*—white, bear-like animals with curled horns—that lived in the Callay Forest and Kar had talked about a building near the outskirts that was both a museum as well as infested with venomous spiders that could kill you with one bite.

"You've been?" Aheia balked.

"Yea, the adrenaline high is out of this realm."

"Weren't you worried about dying?" She asked.

"If I was worried about dying every time life got dangerous, I would never leave this room." Kar shrugged and then her demeanor changed when she looked at the drying paint on her body. "Anyway, I think that I'm starting to crack—you want to get cleaned up?"

Aheia looked down at herself. "Yea, I think I know how to get back to my room from here."

"Don't be silly, I have a perfectly gorgeous washroom right through there," Kar pointed to a green-painted door across from them.

"But—"

"Come on, I'll pick you out some clothes to tide you over," she chirped, jumping up and looking down at their handiwork. Aheia followed the empath when she led the way, leaving behind colorful footprints.

The washroom was incredibly similar to Arioch's, except there were countless empty, gold frames hanging all around the walls and plants that seemed to come from *inside* the marble. Kar bent down to rummage around in one of the cabinets underneath the marble countertop as Aheia tried her best not to take up space. She watched her pull out a plush towel and throw it onto the vanity before turning on the water in an adjacent alcove.

"Let me loosen some of your knots first, it'll be easier to clean that way," Kar said, eyes darting over the towels again like she was making sure she'd remembered them, before slipping behind Aheia. The empath busied herself with the mess that was Aheia's hair while she looked at herself in the mirror. The steam collected around the edges slowly, blurring the background more and more the longer they stood there. It was as if the glass was frosting over, distorting the blue of her eyes that stared back, hidden amongst splotches of color. She couldn't remember a time when she'd been this colorful. And she didn't know if it was something that she could have done herself. The empath had shared her colors with Aheia, and she considered that maybe that was what it took. Another's color.

Kar pulled a brush from a drawer next to her and laid it on the marble before moving her hand to the hem of Aheia's shirt. She kept her eyes on the Dioscuri as she lifted it over her skin slowly. Aheia didn't mind, letting Kar maneuver her clothing and then her hair, working the bristles through her knots.

"I look dead," she murmured, the truth slipping free as her eyes drifted down to the hollow of her neck, her breasts, and the xylophone of ribs below them. Skin and bones.

"You were."

The words reminded her of everything she'd been trying to avoid, everything that she'd been distracting herself from.

Dead. How? How had she truly died when she stood here now?

Kar's hands stilled at her back, and she fixed her with a hard stare. "Your body is doing its best with everything it's been through," she said, meeting Aheia's gaze in the mirror. She wasn't smiling now, and her demeanor was anything but sunny. It was the same shift Aheia had seen when she spoke to the Shifter. "You'll eat"—the back of her neck felt hot, and her stomach tightened—"You'll drink water, you'll be *kind* to yourself." She pulled out the word, pointed expression on her features. "And that's all you can do. You're perfect at every stage of your journey, Aheia. We all are," she continued, splaying her fingers through the once white strands. "The size of our bodies has nothing to do with our worth. They're simply a vessel for our minds."

Aheia rolled her lips between her teeth. "Thank you. No one's ever said that to me."

Kar smiled quickly, her cheeks dimpling and her voice almost lyrical as she threw the brush onto the marble. "Alright, rinse off so you're comfortable. I'll leave you some clothes. There's a bunch of fruity-smelling gels in there that you can use—whatever you like."

When Aheia finished scrubbing the paint from her body, she stepped into the washroom with her towel tucked, finding a few dark navy pieces folded on the counter: a pair of cotton pants and a ribbed shirt with built-in support as well as undergarments. She pulled on the bottoms and they were almost her size, though they hung off her hips a little too low. The top was comfortable too, and the material seemed to breathe with her. Lastly, she secured Malia's gold knife around her leg and looked at the distorted reflection of herself in the mirror. Her colors were muted now, not so stark, not so brash, mixed with the navy on her body. She liked how she looked when she was diffused.

There was a ridiculous pile of clothing at the center of Kar's closet by the end of the day. The empath had pulled any and all pieces that might fit Aheia, who lost track after the seventeenth pair of differently nuanced shirts.

"No, actually, I think this lavender—" Kar picked up one of the hanging plants that sat on top of the closet shelf next to a hat rack. "Would be gorgeous if we just weave it into your hair." She darted across the room again, and Aheia was getting breathless just watching her. "You can wear this dress with it." She fisted something tiny and lacy. "You'll look like a goddess. *Oh*—" She dropped both the plant and the lace before rifling through a drawer below her. "I think I remember—there was something, *aha*!" She pulled out a plaid skirt from the back and waggled her eyebrows. "I was going through a phase with this one, but I think it would look so good on you."

Aheia huffed out air. It wasn't quite a laugh; it felt too heavy for that. It was more like unsure exhaustion. Her skin didn't fit when Kar paid that much attention to her. The genuine way that the empath got excited about dressing *her* had her eyes burning and it felt so silly, but she wasn't used to that. It was odd, trying to understand how to handle the emotion of it—something good that felt so anxious instead.

"Where did you get all of this?" Aheia asked, trying to sound lighter than she was, running her hand down a satin dress that was laying across her knees.

"We have beautiful garment districts here," Kar said, adding the plaid to the pile next to her. "Feel free to try any of this on. I'm going to grab us some food, because it's getting late."

"Is it?" Aheia asked, eyes shifting to the glass above her..

"Time flies ... and all that." Kar smiled thinly and Aheia made a show of going through the clothing all around her even though no part of her had the energy for it. The painting had drained her, and the warmth of the shower even more. And even though it had been days ago now, she still thought about the blue-haired female who'd lost her youngling. Her sorrow was imprinted on the back of Aheia's mind. True sorrow. Why did it feel so familiar to her own? She was disgusted at herself for comparing it.

"Thank you." Aheia nodded, waiting for the empath to leave before she let herself sink into the fabrics and curled into a ball. All of it was beautiful, and she was grateful for Kar's kindness, her willingness to share so many of her precious things.

She wondered how heavy the empath's own life blows had been to make her that kind.

Bright lights tore at her mind, nightmares rushing through her so quick she couldn't remember a single frame as she gasped and shot out of her sleep. She choked down the nausea, cold air licking across sweat soaked skin, everything hazy.

"Hey." Soft hands stroked down her arms. "You're just dreaming."

Kar's green eyes were filled with worry, standing out against the darkness of the room. When had she fallen asleep? Fuck, she hadn't meant to.

Aheia was flustered, realizing they were in the empath's bed when the last thing she remembered was the pile of clothing.

"You dozed off, and I figured sleep was one of those things that might be hard for you to come by, so I didn't wake you." She smiled.

"What time is it?" Aheia asked, rubbing her eyes, feeling the sweat all over. *Fuck,* she was a mess.

"Close to morning now, but not nearly late enough to necessitate getting up,"

The velvet around her felt damp when she padded her hands over it, and her eyes darted down around her.

"I destroyed your pillows." Aheia panicked, rubbing over the soaked pink fabric. "I'm so sorry."

Clean up your mess.

"It's ok," Kar said calmly.

Can't you do anything right?

"No, I *ruined* it." Tears pricked her eyes, as she rubbed the velvet over and over again, only smearing the wetness.

Every inch better be spotless.

"Aheia." Kar gripped her hands. "It's alright, really. I'll wash it."

"What if it stains?" She crumbled, and she knew it was too much, that her reaction wouldn't make sense to Kar.

"Then I'll throw some color on it, and hang it on my wall," she said, her thumbs massaging Aheia's pulse points. "They're just things. Replaceable."

Aheia tried to even out her breathing as she settled back, but her chest was starting to hurt with the effort. *Just things.* How could she tell Kar that *things* had always felt more important than her in the past?

"Try to get some rest, because ..." Kar chewed on her lip for a moment. "Emryn's going to meet you at the Kaserne in the morning."

Aheia almost choked; one shock traded for another. "What for?"

"She'll help you get your strength up."

"Since when?" She furrowed her brows, nerves prickling her skin as she remembered her last interaction with the Syraphem.

Kar didn't answer and Aheia hated seeing the tense of the empath's shoulders—imagined she felt a streak of discomfort that ran through her. *Oh Gods,* she'd probably kept Kar up with her nightmares, too. "It'll be fine. You'll do fine. Everyone's horrible at first."

"It's not that—" Aheia started. "Emryn doesn't like me."

"No, I suppose she doesn't."

Aheia was almost surprised at her candor.

"But you have to understand," Kar continued. "She's slow to trust. Once you have it, she'll wage a war for you, but getting to that point, it doesn't just *happen.*" She waved her hands through the air. "You are kind of the same in that area. You're probably more alike than either of you would like to admit. Emryn protects herself with the poison in her veins. She wasn't born with it; none of us are. But survival hardens."

"You think that's what I'm like?"

"I think you're still deep in survival mode," the empath said, and that shut Aheia up. "And someone telling you to *'stop'* being in survival mode doesn't really cut it. I get that." Kar shrugged and Aheia supposed that she didn't remember a time when she wasn't. "I know it has to come from you, be a choice *you* make, and I hope eventually you do."

She relaxed slightly, letting her muscles loosen as much as she could manage against the mattress, and Kar laid down next to her.

"Do I know how to replace one nightmare with another, or what?"

Aheia's lips twitched, and they steeped in silence, watching each other without words for a long time, until sleep took them both.

When she woke up a second time, Aheia was doused in shadows. Or so she thought. When she blinked the sleep away, they disappeared as well, and she chalked it up to another dream as she looked over to Kar, who was curled so close they almost touched foreheads.

It felt ok.

So she closed her eyes again.

"I'll take you down," the empath chirped after having fed Aheia more food than her stomach knew what to do with. She'd also given her a pair of navy leathers and boots to wear with a matching top, before she braided Aheia's hair into a thick plait.

"What are the odds of getting out of this?" Aheia asked over her shoulder, picking at her own nails. She was thankful for the opportunity; she just wasn't looking forward to the Emryn part of the equation.

"The same as hearing Arioch saying *please*. Come on." Kar just shrugged, jumping off the mattress.

The hallways looked different this morning, and that thought made Aheia do a double take. Those plants right outside of Kar's door hadn't been there yesterday. *Had they?* Or that piece of art? Kar looked at her in amusement as Aheia remembered what Shiron had said about the halls playing with whomever walked them. "You'll get the hang of this place soon—we all did."

We all did.

Aheia didn't know why it felt like such a foreign concept that the only constant here was Arioch, that all of them had been new at one point or another.

"Why are *you* here?" Aheia asked. "I mean, do you have family?"

"I do," she said, her voice light. "My family is here. My blood lives in Thryn—one of the territories to the west."

My family is here.

"I don't understand."

Kar smiled at her tightly. "We can't help who births us. I'm sure that's not a hard concept to grasp."

"Well, no." Aheia tilted her head while the empath continued.

"My mother is in charge of one of the large greenhouse complexes that populate the territory. She has her hands in the export of certain herbs that are only able to grow in the star soil near the Sephy Forest and my father is on Farah's board of Rasmí. On paper, they are wonderful people—and that's what they're good at. Keeping up appearance for the outside realm." She shrugged. "I haven't had it as difficult as some of the others. I can still see my family and it's more of an annoyance where Lúc ... well—" She shook her head, and blinked as if she hadn't meant to let that slip. "Some of us have had it worse," she finished. "Shiron likes to remind us that we have a choice. He says *'the blood of the covenant over the water of the womb you were born from'*. I think that Leviathan has picked each and every one of us off the floor and murmured it into our ears when we couldn't remember it ourselves—when we'd stepped too far into our past and couldn't see the future anymore."

Aheia repeated those words to herself. She liked the idea of that, that family was a choice.

"You don't think the Gods were deliberate in their placement of each youngling?" It was something that her mother had told her during the worst of times ... That she was exactly where she needed to be. But it had never felt like much comfort.

Kar's eyes narrowed sharply. "I think the Gods have a plan for each of us. I think that we are placed in deliberate hardships so that we can become who we are meant to be. If I didn't believe that, I think I'd lose my faith."

"Deliberate hardships?"

"Yes, I think that we are all born very similar, but it's our experiences, our traumas, and who we are around that shape us. It doesn't make it all right or much more bearable—but it feels like a gold lining—that the pain we've suffered came from an ancient place foretold a long time ago. It takes it all out of our hands." Kar shook her head. "Thinking about it that way helps eliminate second-guessing, that no matter what choices I made in the past, they were the choices I was always meant to make. And I'm thankful, honestly, because if I hadn't gone through what I did, I wouldn't have ended up here, and I would be an entirely different Leviathan. Besides, I like to think that for the Gods and the fates to collaborate on my personal pain, I *must* be something important. Why spend the time otherwise?" She flashed Aheia a dimpleless smile.

Believing in the Gods didn't come easily. Aheia still didn't know where she stood with it all. She'd made a good show of pretending back in Keloseros, because she'd had to. Since she left, she hadn't much found the will to pray, and it didn't help when Shiron said that he'd seen the Gods, that everyone had in their own ways. Because she hadn't. They'd never shown their presence to her before.

It wasn't about their existence; she knew that Aether, Manāt, Theia, and 'Amm had walked this world eons ago, that Manāt still rested within it. It was about the doubt that speaking to them would make any type of difference now that they were dead. Especially if Kar was right, and they had planned each of their lives and hardships eons ago. Because how fucked was that?

In their almighty power, why would they want someone to go through so much suffering? Why wouldn't they create the person exactly how they were meant to be from the start? Why force them through skin shaving and bone crushing instead?

Gods ... a novel idea that lets others excuse their reality.

But she wouldn't tell Kar that. It didn't matter what she believed. And if faith gave the empath strength, who would she be to try to dismantle it with her own thoughts?

Chapter 30

Aheia

"Thank you, you've been so nice to me," Aheia told Kar as they walked into one of the training rooms at the Kaserne.

"I'm kind, not nice. Nice would be sparing you this experience." Her grin spread, her eyes darting toward Emryn, who was waiting for them. "Have fun," she quipped, heading back the way she came from.

Aheia rolled her lips between her teeth but the Syraphem didn't pay her any mind, cleaning a dagger at the other end of the room.

The silence became uncomfortable quickly, and Aheia fidgeted, passing the weapons tabled on the left and making her way closer as inconspicuous as she could. She picked up one of the heavy broadswords, drifting her fingers over the beautiful metal work and levying its weight.

"You're weak, so we'll start with strength training before we move on to actual weaponry," Emryn said, and Aheia almost jumped when she took the sword from her hands roughly. "And as a rule of thumb, don't touch other warriors' weapons without asking. It's basic manners—which I know you don't have, but try."

Aheia tamped down the irritation that flared. Fighting back wasn't going to make this any more pleasant.

"Stretch out your limbs first," Emryn said, showing her a few basic movements. Aheia copied them, and the barest of effort made her heart pick up its pace. She didn't think that this part was meant to steal her breath, but here she was.

"Now, sit against that wall."

"Sit?" *Against the wall?*

Emryn rolled her eyes, her wings flaring slightly as she showed Aheia what she meant—literally sliding into a seated position against the stone.

Aheia walked over and mimicked her.

Oh.

"Lower," Emryn drawled.

Ow, fuck. She'd thought the stretching was hard. Fuck's sake. She'd never been this weak. But then she'd never been so mortal either, not before she left Keloseros at least. She'd also never died before ... The list was getting ridiculous.

"Why am I doing this?" she asked, and she hated how it sounded. She had meant it genuinely, wondering what exactly this would benefit, but it came out wrong. Even Aheia would have been annoyed at herself for her tone of voice.

Why can't you just say the right thing?

"Strength training. It's in the title," Emryn said, unamused. "I need to see what you can handle before we get into it."

Aheia nodded and felt like an idiot for that, too. *What an answer.* She steeled her back and her legs, feeling the burn in them both quickly.

"You made it across Lyria alive," Emryn said, picking at her fingernails. "How?"

"I had my knife," Aheia said, every word feeling heavy when she needed to focus on the way her legs were already starting to tremble. "I hid well."

Emryn nodded slowly.

"Where did you get the knife?"

"Why?"

"Because I want to report you to the proper authorities for your possession of it," she deadpanned, crossing her arms.

Aheia grit her teeth. "It was—" *Iaonnis'.* "I lifted it off one of the guards," she lied. Because telling the Syraphem that she fell into possession of it when she killed the male she'd forcibly been married to felt like an overshare. That and the fact that Aheia was still hazy on how exactly she'd managed it in the first place, black spots crowding those memories in her mind.

"You know how to use one? A knife?"

"Not well." Aheia fed the Syraphem enough honesty to hopefully even out the lie. Besides, Emryn would find out quick how uncoordinated Aheia was. "Enough to stay alive."

"We'll see."

The seconds dragged by slowly, her knees buckling, and feet slipping against the stone over and over again.

"Up," Emryn barked. "Keep your knees at a ninety-degree angle."

"I'm trying." Aheia huffed, her fingers curling into fists.

"Trying won't cut it," Emryn said simply. "Trying might well get you killed one day. *Do* it."

Aheia scoffed, her heart hammering in her chest like it thought they were both in peril.

"Are you getting back at me for something?" she grit through her teeth, too flustered to differentiate inside thoughts from what she said out loud. *Shit.*

"This is not a punishment. I don't care enough about you to put that much thought into my actions—this is doing what

Arioch asked. To help you. So if you don't mind keeping your mouth shut unless you have something useful to say, it would make both of our lives a lot easier."

Aheia's jaw locked, and she pushed her head back into the marble, trying to find some sort of relief for the pain in her legs until her neck sang just as badly.

Doing what Arioch asked.

Emryn circled closer, regarding her with discerning eyes. Then she pushed the tip of her sword against Aheia's stomach. "Here." She prodded lightly. "This is where you need to tense, not your spine."

She tried to adjust, but no part of her body wanted to listen to the commands in her brain as her vision flickered. She was lightheaded, and she wished she'd eaten more as she flexed her abdomen. But no matter how hard her muscles worked, she kept slipping across the floor, eventually losing her footing, her tailbone bruising against the stone.

"Take a breath, and then do it again," Emryn said coldly.

Aheia inhaled, feeling tears stinging her eyes.

No, don't you dare fucking cry, she lashed at herself, crawling up off the floor. Crying wasn't going to do shit, especially not in front of Emryn. The Syraphem's strength flustered her, making all the words she tried to line up in her mind sound wrong. So she kept them to herself and focused on how many muscles she didn't know existed in her body until this very moment.

Time felt so incredibly slow while she was suspended here against an imaginary chair, and the only way Aheia could measure it was by Emryn's movement around the room. First, she sat on the table, then she walked to the other side, and Aheia watched attentively as the Syraphem circled her fingers over the ink on her leg, coaxing a real dagger from her tattoo. It would never not mesmerize her, watching Emryn dip into her very skin to pull out metal.

"I didn't mean to upset you," Aheia managed as her limbs shook, and the sweat dripped down her nose. "At breakfast."

Emryn didn't answer, just leaned against the wall.

"I meant to upset *him,*" she tried.

"You know, this isn't some cute bonding experience." The Syraphem pinched the bridge of her nose. "I'm busy. Really fucking busy." Her hand flexed. "Do you think I give a lot of one-on-one lessons? I don't." She exhaled slowly, as if she was trying to calm herself down. "Why do you think any of us are spending our time with you? The goodness in our hearts? Your fascinating mind?"

"I—"

"You think Kar has the time to dawdle through hallways and play with paint? That there isn't something more important she could be doing? That Shiron sat with you in that library for his own health?"

Emryn shook her head, a joyless laughter on her lips.

"Why do you think any of us are trying to help, hmm?"

Aheia grit her teeth, the pain in her legs distracting her from the ability to string words together. But it didn't seem that Emryn cared to hear them anyway. She just cared to tell Aheia exactly what was on her mind.

"He asked us to. He *asked* us to make space for you—Gods can only fucking glean why since you don't want any part of it. Arioch knows that training might not make you comfortable, but it damn sure makes you better and that's why *I'm* here. So next time you tell me about all the ways you're trying to make *the sovereign of this realm* pay for whatever it is you think he owes you, remember that this is *my* home, and he is too. I will never be on your side, not until it aligns with mine. Upsetting him upsets me."

Then she turned away again and Aheia slipped onto the floor, her hip bone smacking against the rock. She hissed, pushing up on tired arms and reassuming her position with clenched teeth. It was a fucking slap in the face. It was sobering.

He asked us to make space for you.

Why? Why did he go through the trouble when he'd told her she was just a pastime. A pastime he was possessive of, sure, but a pastime nonetheless. She imagined he'd always had a pretty tight grip on his toys, even as a youngling. Didn't seem like the sharing type.

Emryn was right, but that didn't mean Aheia was wrong. She'd sit here and take the physical pain, but she wouldn't take the rest.

"Tell me you'd be different—if you were in my shoes," Aheia asked, fighting the strain in her knees, fighting the tears that were burning her eyes now. "Tell me you'd take what seems like kindness at face value when nothing in your life has ever been kind. Tell me those things and I'll keep my mouth shut."

Emryn regarded her with those hard brown eyes before she folded her knife back against the dark skin of her leg and it melded, becoming a tattoo once more. She walked over to where Aheia was sitting and sank to her haunches.

"No, I wouldn't." And for a moment, Aheia thought there was a softness to her words. "But I wouldn't whine like you do either. If you don't like something—change it, fix it for yourself. Don't lean on Arioch for everything and then act like you don't want the crutch. It's embarrassing. Commit to something—your role, your words, your thoughts—and do it. Don't pretend one thing and then contradict yourself entirely."

Aheia sucked in a labored breath. She hated how the Syraphem's words cut right through her center, prodding at her insecurity. Because Emryn was right about that, too. She was right about everything she'd said to her, no matter how harsh her delivery had been.

He asked them to.

"Get up."

She glowered at Emryn, who was already across the room, picking a towel off the table.

"Two minutes; get some water, and then we'll start at the top."

Aheia clamped down on the defeated groan that wanted to crawl its way up her throat.

At the top. Aheia was scared shitless at the prospect of what exactly that meant.

Wall to floor, floor to wall, Aheia was doing poses that had her considering all of her life choices that had brought her to this exact moment. Right now she was crouched low, her arms spread wide, holding two small sticks that she'd laughed at when Emryn first handed them to her. But now they were heavier than rocks.

They hadn't spoken again, save for occasional instructions, and this time, Aheia was grateful for the silence. She couldn't defend herself against truths she wasn't ready to analyze. And she didn't want to attack Emryn, not yet, not until she could line her words up in a way that didn't make her sound like a stuttery fucking mess. She didn't know what it was about the demon. But that sharp gaze and her unmitigated use of logic made Aheia fumble. She knew she'd finish this conversation in the tub later with an imaginary Emryn, and she sure as shit would sound comprehensive then.

Her inner voice rolled her eyes and turned her back at the thought.

"We're at the hall today." Lúc strolled in, dressed in nothing but loose black pants, and he seemed to be sweating just as much as Aheia.

She caught his gaze across the room, her muscles spasming in the pose that Emryn had left her in, feeling her already sore legs tremor. Lúc slapped his towel against Aheia's shoulder and then walked over to Emryn with a smile.

"We?" Aheia huffed.

"Not you—you look like you're about to pass out." He grinned. "You're shaking,"

"You're an asshole," Aheia spit back before her mind could formulate anything more thought out.

"Touchy." He tilted his chin, pushing against his lip ring.

"Sorry, I thought we were stating obvious things." Her words came out rough, but she didn't care.

Lúc chuckled, leaning into the Syraphem, and exchanged hushed words in Lujha.

"You're done for the day," Emryn said after a few more heartbeats, and Aheia collapsed onto the floor, dropping the stupid sticks so she could catch herself. "You can do most of those stretches yourself. Once you last longer than twenty seconds on the plank and wall sits, find me. We'll move on then."

Aheia fought the urge to spit out the iron taste on her tongue. *Great.*

"You put her through the wringer?" Lúc laughed somewhere in front of her.

"No, it's the same shit we teach the younglings when they turn ten years of age."

Embarrassment flared under Aheia's skin, but she didn't dare say anything.

Lúc laughed before reaching out a hand. "Come on, princess."

She got up without his help, dusting off her leathers.

"It'll get easier." He grinned.

But Aheia was focused on Emryn, who was already on her way out the door.

"Thanks," Aheia yelled after her, but the Syraphem didn't look back.

Lúc regarded her slowly, running his hand through his hair. "It feels ten degrees colder in this room."

"I thought hel was supposed to be hot," Aheia said, wiping the spit from her chin with trembling fingers.

"She hasn't put you through hel yet." He crossed his arms. "She wasn't *just* being a dick. The younglings train pretty intensely. It'll only get worse from here."

"Yeah, I know." Aheia sent him a sideways look and left him standing there as she went for the water spout across the room, her legs barely cooperating. Emryn's training being hard wasn't the problem. She was actually excited at the prospect of knowing more, of combating her clumsiness, and understanding those large pretty weapons on the table—especially the double-bladed sword. But she'd rather get there without Emryn and her hatred for Aheia's existence.

"Can you find your way back to the compound without help?" Lúc asked, following her.

"I'll be fine," Aheia said. "Where are you going?"

"The hall, you were there a few days ago. Just politics." He waved his hand through the air.

"Politics—*you*?" She raised her eyebrows. "Wait, do you file cutting off some demon's reproductive organ under politics? Because if you do, then that makes a whole lot more sense."

"It's not a daily occurrence, believe it or not." Lúc grinned like he wished it were. "I imagine today will be on the dull side, but being Rasmí, it comes with the territory—a necessary evil."

Rasmí. Kar had mentioned it earlier.

"What is that word?" Aheia asked. "Rasmí?" She leaned underneath the stream of water, gulping it down.

"There's not really a translation for it. Rasmí are branded, sworn into loyalty, and willing to do whatever is asked of them." Lúc twisted his bicep, tapping a finger against a glyph on his forearm. It was two moons, one large crescent, and a smaller one nestled within. "We all have our roles, but at the end of the day we carry out whatever Arioch's court needs."

"You all bear that symbol?" she asked.

Lúc nodded.

"Does he?" If he did, she hadn't seen it.

"His sacrifice is different," Lúc said, his eyes gleaming.

"What is it?"

"Well, for starters, *this* is not ink." Lúc flexed his muscles. "It's blood."

"*Blood*?" She gripped the Shifter's arm and turned it, looking at the tattoo. "It looks the same as your others."

"Black ink, black blood."

Aheia worried her bottom lip, imagining that process.

"You haven't seen his back, have you?" Lúc grinned. "You must fuck really vanilla."

"*Arioch's* back?" She drifted her touch down the glyphs that ran down toward his fingers.

Lúc's smile twitched. "You'll find our initials on him."

"In ink?" she asked.

"Carved. Where do you think the blood for these tattoos came from?" Lúc leaned in close. "We cut our initials into his flesh and collected it."

"Each of you?" Her eyes widened.

"Each of us."

"Ow, fuck," The pain in her muscles manifested at her lower back like phantom knives on her skin.

"It's not so bad."

"You're not the one on blade's end."

"I usually am, princess." Lúc's smirk was mischievous as he winked and backed away from her, heading out the same door as Emryn.

Aheia found the way back to her room alone, and she was surprised at how empty *alone* felt in this instance. There was food on her desk, like there always seemed to be, and she wondered if it was magyck or if there were kitchens at the compound.

Her stomach clenched tightly at the sight of the plates and she remembered how weak she'd felt with Emryn. She didn't want to feel like that again.

There were a few peeled eggs on the plate and she reached for one, biting into it at the center, making sure she got some of the yolk. She'd forgotten how much she liked eggs when she'd managed to get her hands on them in Keloseros. They'd only ever tasted good to her like this–the scrambled version was rubbery and felt wrong on her tongue.

When the egg seemed to stay down, she took another bite, sprinkling salt on it this time. Her stomach gurgled, as she reached for a small, white raspberry and bit into that at the same time. Sweet, almost pear-like.

She licked her lips, finishing off a few more pieces of fruit before cleaning herself up and changing into something comfortable. When she opened her wardrobe this time, she was met with a rainbow of color--all of the pieces Kar had pulled from her own closet.

He asked us to make space for you

Emryn's words were rattling around her mind as she left her room and crossed the small distance to his, because her own bed was still too white for comfort. She crawled onto the large empty mattress in the dark, barely able to lift the blankets across her body as her eyes fluttered shut.

Don't pretend it's something it isn't.

But that voice in her head was quiet when her chest hummed with warmth and here between the blankets, she wouldn't try to swallow it. For the first time in a long time, she'd let herself feel it as she drifted off to sleep.

Chapter 31

Karyme

Aheia's energy felt heavy even after Kar left her. It wasn't altogether negative, but it still unnerved her and stuck around longer than others did. Her turmoil reminded the empath of Emryn, of inner unrest that had been written off as normal years ago, even though it wasn't. Both of them felt like raging oceans.

It took stepping into the old wing, the coarse rock, Sahren's old quarters, for all of that to die down. But that didn't mean quiet. The ghosts of memories were burned into the walls here, and they tasted sour. Saliva pooled on her tongue, but she swallowed it, continuing up the stairs across the way while the Solas orbs disappeared and darkness took over. The stars shone into the halls, throwing long shadows that seemed to walk in her wake, the turquoise Asara lighting the way alongside them.

There was something unrestful slithering underneath her skin and it didn't quite feel like her decision to be here, yet here she was, standing in front of Kazim's door.

Arioch forewent guards as security and had asked for magyck instead. Emryn's wards were burned into the old stone. She'd enchanted the walls, and opening the door served as an alarm that would wilt whatever totem she'd chosen to impose the magyck onto to alert her.

"Why are you worried?" she whispered to herself, reaching for the doorknob, trying to dissect the sense of dread inside of her.

But before she could touch the cold metal, a hand gripped her shoulder.

"Kar," Shiron said quietly, pulling her attention back, "What are you doing?"

She hadn't felt him approach.

"I'm going in," Kar said simply, grabbing onto the doorknob.

"Like hel. Not by yourself." Shiron's fingers moved quickly, holding her wrist in place, and Kar narrowed her eyes at the demon in front of her.

"This isn't like you."

"Then it should make the situation clear." His voice was harsh, his emotions painting wisps of dark red around her vision. It felt like hands on the side of her head that pressed harder little by little.

"You know I can handle myself, don't make me feel like I can't." Kar softened her expression, a well-practiced look, though no part of her felt soft.

"That's not what I'm saying."

"Wait here. Please. I can't have your feelings suffocating me."

"They won't."

"They will."

Shiron had worked hard, the hardest, to control them around her and she knew it was taxing; she saw the strain on his features. But if he was failing in his control now, it would be non-existent if he went into this room with her.

"I can't tell you what to do."

"No one can," she said sweetly.

His shoulders slackened slightly as he exhaled. "No fear." He dropped his chin and let go of her wrist, returning his hand to his devotional achlary instead. In that moment, she could see his age, those extra fifty years he had on her printed in the lines at the corner of his eyes.

She let herself smile big for him. "Never."

His jaw tensed slightly, that amber gaze alive with unsaid things, things that were meant to stop Kar, but wouldn't.

"I'll be on the other side of the door," he said instead, stepping out of her way.

Kar nodded, appreciation for the demon in front of her winding its way tightly around her heart before she twisted the knob.

She swallowed, stepping inside, straightening her shoulders as the lock fell into place behind her, the light from the hall disappearing. Her breath caught as she let her gaze coast through the space. Every piece of furniture save for the bed was piled in front of the tall windows, cutting out much of the starlight and darkening the surroundings. The nightstands were stacked on the desk, the chair was thrown on top of that, and it looked like the sheets had been torn from the mattress and hung sloppily across it all.

Stepping inside meant feeling the heaviness of the room—the heaviness of the demon sitting on the mattress. When Kazim's dark eyes fixed on her, her steps almost faltered. His hair was long and messy, and his body was lean. There were cords of muscles in his arms, but he was slim.

The room held a static charge that she recognized—the kind that could be masked as crippling anxiety, or debilitating fear. It stirred and churned in her stomach until she had to swallow the bile that rose in her throat and threatened her tongue.

But she wouldn't let him see that. She kept her chin tipped and her stride purposeful as he continued to watch silently. There was a weight to his gaze too, heavier than most words she'd encountered from others.

"Why did you barricade the window?" she asked, tilting her head, hand sliding up the foot end of the bed frame. She breathed through the surge that rolled off of him and her hand shot to her chest involuntarily, her nails digging in.

Fuck.

The pain throbbed, and the answer to her question about the windows seemed glaringly obvious.

He doesn't like any light. Not even the stars.

Kazim stayed quiet, his fingers twisting a scrap of what might have been his pillow case at one time.

"Are you soft?" he asked finally, bringing the fabric to his nose. "Everything here is soft."

It felt like a threat, or maybe an insult.

She stepped closer, through a patch of starlight that had made it past his barrier, and felt the flinch he didn't let himself show her. But it ran through her nonetheless, like cold fingertips, streaks of broken black splattering her vision.

"You don't have a handler." His lip twitched as his gaze fell down her body.

Kar brushed off his words, though his voice lingered, gravelly and thick.

She smiled. "Do I need one?"

"Don't all animals?" He tilted his head. "Or maybe you're not so wild anymore." He hummed. "Just a docile little *mashkah*."

Kazim's brittle exterior was meant to keep her away, but Kar couldn't help see past this form—nothing but a roiling, dark creature when his skin fell away.

Against her better judgment, she stepped closer yet, kneeling at the foot of the mattress.

"You don't speak to him," she said.

Kazim didn't answer the implied question.

"He worries for you." She didn't know Arioch's brother. Didn't know what made him tick, what would rile him or spiral him ... what would fix this. So, she had to tread carefully.

"Arioch doesn't worry for anyone but himself. I'm surprised he's fooled you this long." Kazim leaned on his hands as he crept forward.

She couldn't help the slight strain in her jaw as she held her space on the edge.

"Does he toy with you too, hmm? He always liked weak things, found them endearing." He said the words so softly they sounded as if they were meant to be whispered in her ear. "They make him forget that he himself has never been strong."

Kazim wanted a reaction. He wanted to hurt because he hurt. She'd encountered it often. It was not an excuse, but the energy inside of him gave her pause, nonetheless. Healing would take time, and it wasn't a word she'd ever dare speak out loud around him because he'd take it and eat it until there was nothing left.

The pain inside of her became muddled, twisting and melding into something messy. She hurt because he hurt.

But maybe she hurt because Arioch hurt too, maybe she hurt because everything that had happened to Kazim—even if she didn't know exactly what—was something she wouldn't wish on her worst enemy.

"*Algah qymat, Mashkah.* Look at you ... So. fucking. fragile," he said in a thick voice while those invasive eyes slid down her body.

A steady heat curled itself around the back of her neck as she breathed through the feelings that weren't quite hers and he prowled closer, his features shadowed. He looked so much like his brother, except he didn't. There was a harsh brutality that underlined every straight line in his face.

"So fucking breakable." He spoke it like a promise, so close now that she saw the scars on his neck, the ones that had healed across his eyebrows, and his upper lip too. The dagger at her thigh felt warm, like it wanted to remind her of its presence as he hovered just above her. He was still on all fours, while she kneeled.

A huge fucking beast. Not at all his brother.

Instinct told her to leave. But instead, she reached for him, and she didn't miss the surprise in his eyes when she did. Those pupils became barren wastelands, like he realized what she was in that moment, what magyck she possessed.

His lip twitched in disgust as her hand touched his skin and took the brunt of fucking everything inside.

It drilled into her. The pain, the whispers, the shadows, the fucking void.

"Hollow," she said, swallowing the waver in her voice. "Your words ... your heart ..." The intensity built with his proximity.

"*Heart.*" He rasped, "You assume I have one."

Kar inclined her head, her eyes focusing on his as she opened herself up to him, pulling at the dark sludgy haze that floated just out of sight. It was like a vacuum, slow at first and then all at once.

Gods ... that ...

Her muscles tensed as she crept inside of him slowly, feeling what he felt, becoming enveloped by the hollow throbbing, and the gut-wrenching pain that hid in the shadows under his eyes.

How could any one creature feel this and ... *survive*?

"That's enough," he growled, grabbing a hold of her wrist.

"I can take it," she said through gritted teeth, sweat beading on her forehead as he squeezed her.

"Can you now?" he purred, pulling her in. "Let's see, Mashkah."

Hollow.

She gasped, her chest feeling like it might crack under the pain that was radiating from him. A broken little squeak worked its way past her lips as he leaned down, his nose inches from hers, his eyes so hard she thought she might cut herself on the broken edges of gray. His stare forced another cold wave of sadness into her, filling her until she couldn't breathe, silent screams pressing against her eardrums.

Silent screams... how does it hurt this bad ... how can he hear ... how can he—

His fist tightened, and he loomed over her.

"I'm hurting you and I'm not even trying to," he said, slowly drawing his eyes across her features. And then the angry expression on his face turned almost amused.

Heat flared across the back of her neck. "You're not." She tried to keep her voice measured because even the anger gave him some little part of her.

"Lies look ugly on you," he said, his smile widening, and something dark fissuring through his irises. He let go of her wrist, gripping her thigh and pulling her beneath him in one rough sweep. She yelped, twisting in his hold, gripping at the mattress as panic surged through her, her very own fear.

His body came down on top of her, the heavy weight of his chest against hers driving her into the mattress as he compressed her.

"Don't make this so easy," he hummed against her temple, his breath hot and sticky.

She shoved her face against his, diving for the knife at her leg, but he was faster. His hands wrenched her wrists back, one of his large paws enough to vise both of hers.

He looked down between them, watching her writhe for a painful moment before he wrenched the fabric of her dress up her legs.

No.

She squirmed and kicked, but every movement only seemed to spur him on, as he forced her legs apart with his thigh, ripping the satin.

And that was all it took to elicit anger instead of fear.

Bastard.

She dug her nails into his hand and rammed her knee into his stomach. He grunted, faltering enough for her to slip one arm free, but recovered too quickly and restrained her hand again, forcing his knee down on her hip so hard she gasped for air.

"Better." He chuckled menacingly, wrenching her wrist down at an angle that made her shoulder scream in pain. She grit her teeth, fighting the groan that desperately wanted to free itself. Shiron was outside. He'd help. But she didn't want that, knew if she tried, she could get herself out. But part of her held back, part of her needed to see what Kazim could do first, what he could *take* in turn.

Her limbs shook as she clawed after his face with her free hand, catching a grip on his hair and pulling as hard as she could. He hissed, his head tipping against the strain, and she pulled harder, feeling loose strands rip from his head. But it didn't do enough and a moment later, his hand slipped between her knees and forced them apart again.

"No," she hissed, her voice caustic, bucking out against him. She could feel weakness in his hold, enough that if she wrenched down and to the side, she could free herself. But something in his chest had its grips on her and she couldn't pull away.

"That's so fucking useless," he growled as he gripped the handle of her knife, pushing the dress up around her hips in the process. He almost sounded angry. But it wasn't anger at her attempt to grab the dagger. It was different, she could feel it. "Blades are a fool's reliance,"

And then he pulled it from its sheath and grazed it over her thigh long ways, scraping against the soft hairs on her skin. She stilled underneath him as the metal traveled higher, her heart hammering in her throat.

"Should we see what your insides look like?" he asked, watching his hand instead of her, his eyes glazing slightly, another surge of his emotion forcing silent tears down Kar's cheeks. They were unwanted. They always were. And the pain she cried for wasn't her own. "I think you might scream for me if I split your skin with your own blade." A lump in her throat swelled until she couldn't swallow. "Or maybe that's not what scares you the most." The blade slid across where her hip met her thigh. "Maybe it's what I'll do to you at knifepoint instead." His eyes rose to hers again, something foreign and dark clouding them. "Does that scare you? That I'll part your legs and fuck you until you bleed with your own blade?" he crooned. "All because you weren't strong enough to hold me back." He dragged the tip of her blade over the black fabric between her legs and her vision flickered. Everything was blurring, everything was confused and hot and cold and fear and so much pain, none of it hers and all of it getting worse by the moment. "I'll send you back to him bruised and torn. And he won't care, will he? He won't even flinch when he sees you can't walk, sees the blood dripping from your cunt."

She caught her breath, lost in trying to sort through the barrage of layers that threatened to suffocate her, but there was something within the thrumming storm that speckled her vision black, something that felt hollow once more. *Words, heart, hollow.*

His threat, *hollow.*

It was a gamble. But—*it doesn't fit.*

"Do it," she bit out, before digging her teeth into her lip repeatedly, trying to pull herself back into her mind, tasting metal on her tongue. She made it hurt worse, feeling the clarity return. "Do fucking *something.*"

The pressure of the blade between her legs disappeared, and relief washed over her. But the relief didn't last long.

Ow, fuck. Ow, fuck.

"Watch," he growled, gripping her chin and forcing her head to the side so that she had to look at the wrist he manacled.

Her fingers twitched, a blinding pain running up her entire arm and into her chest when he squeezed, and then—*crack*.

This time she couldn't dampen the scream, because he was crushing her bones. Her chest snapped shut, the dull aftershock of his emotions ringing in her ears as she wrenched herself away from him, blindly pulling herself across the mattress. His weight on top of her disappeared, and her body fell onto the floor, her head hitting the rough stone. She cradled her wrist, her uninjured hand shaking as the pain throbbed, and her lungs worked to keep her level.

"Fragile," Kazim spit, sitting on the edge of the bed and leaning his elbows on his knees just as the door to the room opened, dim light flooding across her. His lips drew back for a second, and she saw his leg move away from where the amber touched the darkness, but he fixed his expression quickly, his black hair hanging into his face, smirk back in place.

"*Mawahjar!*" Shiron dropped to his knee next to Kar, pulling her off the ground by her shoulders and inspecting her wrist and her torn clothing.

"Times up." Kazim hummed, grin widening. "Pity ... so much more to crack."

Shiron's head snapped towards him, and a moment later, he was across the room, driving his fist into the side of Kazim's jaw. The sound of his knuckles connecting with bone turned Kar's stomach, and the emotions that spread through the room forced bile into her mouth. It was too much and she couldn't hold it. Her brain was buzzing, her heart galloping, her wrist smarting, and all she could do was turn to her side and lose the contents of her stomach onto the floor next to her.

No. Gods.

It felt like a caravan had run her over right after someone funneled a bottle of liquor down her throat. And it wasn't her wrist but Kazim's noise inside of her chest that kept her on her side, sour vomit splattering across the floor.

Kazim's laugh shattered her further. It was maniacal as Shiron hit him again and again.

Kar managed to look up just as Kazim ripped the achlary from Shiron's neck.

Shit.

The Leviathan backed off long enough to grab the string off the floor. It hadn't completely broken, just snapped.

Shiron's breath was uneven as he looked down at them for a moment like he'd forgotten about Kazim, who spit his blood onto the floor.

"Shi," she managed through gritted teeth, "come on." She gripped his arm, his eyes still glued to his hands.

Shiron let her lead him back slowly, but she never once took her eyes from Kazim, whose teeth were outlined in blood.

"You never once told me to stop, Mashkah," he said, the smile pulled into the wrong proportions in front of her eyes now that his emotions became him completely. "Not once."

She managed to get them outside of his room, gripping Shi's shirt as she pushed him back against the wall. Her wrist was killing her, but the waves coming off of the Nephilim in front of her worried her more. This wasn't like him.

"I need to go," he said hoarsely, looking at that damned achlary, and not once at her.

"Shi, what the fuck?" she groaned, trying to focus when her wrist was on fire.

"Go."

Kar jumped, wheeling around. Arioch was standing in the hallway, staring at Shiron.

"Now."

She looked back at Shi, who finally broke his fixation with the stones. He nodded, his teeth clenched, knuckles white under strain, painted black with blood.

"Ok," he said, his voice dragging across a grate, sounding like it might fail at any moment, and then he slipped from her grasp and past Arioch.

What had just happened? Why did Arioch send him away? Why did he seem to know something she didn't?

Her pulse spiked at the expression on his face, at the fury. But she held strong, grasping her side against the stitch that threaded her, while she forced her hand down despite the pain.

"What the fuck are you doing, Karyme?"

"Excuse me?" she asked incredulously, her voice wavering.

His nostrils flared, and he took a step closer, a wall of shadow and heated anger. "You don't go in there."

"Why?"

Arioch's fingers found the back of her neck, the connection intensifying his emotions. He bared his teeth, bending down so he was mere inches from her face, pushing her back into the wall and tilting her chin so she was forced to look at Kazim's door. She could smell blood and liquor, and death—so much death—on his lips when he spoke, the embers in his eyes flaring furiously.

"What's in there should scare you." *What, not who.* "Why? Why did you go in there?" he asked.

And she didn't have an answer.

"I thought I could help." That was the truth, even if she wasn't completely sure how.

Arioch's jaw clenched tight, and then he looked down, seeing her fingers shaking around her wrist that was already discoloring.

His face paled, the shadows under his eyes becoming darker until he looked corpse-like.

She wanted to say so many things.

He's an open wound.

He's pieces of glass underneath bare feet.

"What did he do?" he growled, not relenting his hold.

"I'm fine." She exhaled through her nose, though it was shaky and she definitely wasn't.

He shook his head. "Get yourself fixed. And don't come back here."

Her grip tightened on him as she rose onto her tiptoes to keep from choking and the anger blistered under her skin. Hers.

"You're not allowed to hate me like this," she said, her voice thick.

His chest vibrated with an animalistic sound, something that was so much more like his shadows than him.

"Then *listen*." His voice matched.

"You're hurting me," she said quietly.

"Don't. Come. Back." The words were harsh and messy, like it took great effort to speak them.

Then his grip loosened, but he stayed close, his eyes softening just enough for her to notice. His jaw tensed and relaxed, the vein at the side of his head pulsing while his curls hung in his face. This felt worse than the anger.

Her heart wept because his did too. Everything hurt, and the tears that returned to her eyes felt like fucking acid.

I won't lose you.

It radiated off of him in Gods damned waves.

His jaw clenched, teeth still bared as his thumb caught the wet track on her cheek, and rubbed it into her skin.

"He's not right. He's unpredictable," he said finally, exhausted eyes looking past her as her forehead rested against his chin.

"So am I," she said, closing her eyes for a moment, even though she hadn't felt dangerous in there.

Blades are a fool's reliance.

He was right. He should have never overpowered her like that—shouldn't have been able to.

You never once told me to stop, Mashkah.

Arioch let go of her, but his chin still rested against her temple. She let herself sink into him for a moment. It felt like an apology. And then he squeezed her neck one last time and strode past her and into Kazim's room.

Chapter 32

Kazim

His head was pounding, and the blood was cold against his skin. But that kind of pain was numbing. He couldn't rid himself of the smile on his lips, not even when Arioch came back.

The stars' light was eerie, and he'd forgotten. He didn't remember them being that bright, didn't remember them burning into his retinas like they did now. But nothing felt the same. Not even home.

Home. A fucked up word that didn't mean anything anymore.

This room, these hallways, Arioch—none of that was home.

This felt like pebbled flesh under a rusty knife.

He blinked against the dark floor, but he couldn't see out of his right eye, and there was darkness bordering his vision everywhere he looked. It ate and feathered, and sometimes he didn't know if his eyes were closed or if the darkness had finally eaten him alive. He'd asked it to so many times before and it had never obeyed him then.

He couldn't tell if he was awake much of the time. The only times he could be sure was when he walked into familiar nightmares. Vivid retellings, but in a blur that showed him the unreliable narrative going on in his own mind. But then he woke up and Arioch stood in his room, and that was a nightmare. Except when it wasn't.

He couldn't move from his spot on the floor, and he wasn't sure how long he'd been there. The empath had just left. Or maybe that had happened in another lifetime. None of it mattered. He still felt unnerved by her feel against him. He'd hated every second of it, every touch he gave her. It had taken everything inside of him not to lose the contents of his stomach across her chest.

Disgusting.

Arioch's presence loomed, and Kazim avoided his face. Because he couldn't look at it, not without fucking convulsing, not without choking on vomit that was just liquid because he couldn't keep down any of his food. The vomit that leeched against his tongue tasted wrong. It was a rotting sweetness that wrapped the inside of his mouth in a film, which scrubbing hadn't taken off. Instead, it had taken off some skin on his gums and tongue. The blood tasted better and he let the hot water and soap burn the wounds after he was done.

He didn't know how to be and didn't want to try anymore.

Arioch was talking, but his words were just sounds as Kazim stared at the sliver of starlight that cut across the rock just ahead of his feet. He felt the phantom burn of it against his skin when he imagined it touching him.

Burning.

Melting.

Becoming.

She had his shadows.

Kazim remembered what she felt like so vividly, and his knuckles turned white against his legs as shivers racked him.

Disgusted.

She was the reason he'd screamed after months of choking them down—when she pulled his magyck from his bones and ate at it like it was fucking candy.

And then he couldn't stop screaming.

Talking felt like trying to push words past the blade of a knife shoved deep against his trachea.

The little remnants of what used to live in his body slithered down his spine in a sad reminder. It felt like it wound along every pronounced ridge of his vertebrae and onto the floor. Like the last of the magyck left inside of him was running from him too.

His teeth clattered, but he hadn't been cold since he'd woken up in this room, with these stars, these people. The opposite. He'd been burning up.

Tears were dirty, and they felt like oil against his skin. His fingers started to twitch, and he dug them into his wrist until the sharpness of the pain distracted him from the memories that lived on repeat in his mind.

Black blood.

Red blood.

Loss. Loss. Loss.

Our favorite.

His teeth bared against the sickness roiling his stomach.

Arioch's face was distorted now, and Kazim wasn't sure how long he'd been in this room with him. He seemed to be waiting for him to talk, to tell him something—tell him what he needed.

Need.

What he needed was for him to leave him the fuck alone. Instead, he'd been sitting across the room with his hands folded, just watching.

Kazim hated when they watched. He didn't want him to fucking watch anymore.

Her eyes beckoned now.

Those threads within them watched him across the room, and that was the only part of her he remembered. Those eyes. They were embedded in the wall, watching his every move. His bones locked as he stared unblinkingly. Two round orbs protruded from the stone. They followed him everywhere and maybe they were spying on him even now. He couldn't be sure this was real. There was still time for reality to unwrap itself in front of him, for it to show its face. Just another cruel joke, Ophion twitching and pulling at the strings in his mind until his brain bled down the sides of his head.

This isn't real.

This isn't real.

This isn't real.

"You don't touch them." Arioch's voice was distant and all he could see was the empath struggling against her knife. Her face was blurring too, it kept blurring, and then it was—

"Do you hear me?" He was in Kazim's face now, forcing him to look in his eyes. The gray he'd been avoiding.

"What it must be like to live on the side of your love instead of your wrath," Kazim spit, tapping his fingers against the floor.

One.

Two.

Three.

Three times. And then three times more. And then three times more until it was over.

Arioch exhaled roughly and it shot a shiver down Kazim's back. It sounded familiar. He could see the crooked smiles. The sweat.

"Kaz—"

"Get. out." He felt it roll off his tongue in a jagged bark.

Chapter 33

Aheia

Aheia woke up to Arioch getting dressed.

"I have an errand to run," he said, handing her half of a puffy pastry wrapped in a napkin. Her vision was still blurry as she chewed on her cheek, settling back against her headboard. He looked tired. Had he slept? Her side of the bed was the only unmade part and the sheets next to her were cold. She picked at a piece of the flaky dough and watched him pick up his holster from the side table before shooting her a glance. "Are you coming?"

"You want me to come?" She couldn't help feeling that flare in her chest, the small balloon that had been so empty for so long, inflating slightly.

"Always." His lip twitched, that gaze sinful as it slid down her body. Pebbles erupted across her arms, and her thighs squeezed together on instinct.

Fucker.

She left the food on the nightstand, and peeled off the mattress on sore legs, darting toward the washroom. After managing her mane and washing her face, she shimmied on some loose fitting draw string pants and a matching shirt that Arioch had handed her. The set was orange and she couldn't help but grin at the floor as she tied the front. *Orange and new.* This wasn't one of Kar's, this was hers.

Arioch was sitting at his desk, shuffling around papers when she headed toward the door, poking out her head. Kar and Aylee walked down the hall just as Aheia left the room. Aylee had her arm slung around Kar's neck, who was picking at little berries in her palm while Salamander used the empath's shoulders as a resting spot.

"We're out of that stuff I like in my coffee, so we're gonna jump over to Nori, because they have the *best* syrups at that little market in their downtown," Kar chirped, her smile dimpleless.

"There are fifty-three other options in that green cupboard." Arioch came up behind her and Aheia could feel him against her back.

"I'm hyperfixating on lavender right now, and if I don't start my day with it, I might as well go back to bed and try again tomorrow." Kar shrugged.

"What is that?" Aheia asked Kar, noticing the discolored skin of her hand when it caught in the Solas. "Are you hurt?"

"I was." Kar smiled, but it didn't reach her eyes. "It's numb now,"

"What happened?" She furrowed her brows.

Kar picked up a raspberry. "Mishap with one of the animals." She shrugged. "I have this tendency to believe I could approach bears and they'll just feel my energy—that they'll see it and understand that we're the same. That they'll let me near them unscathed."

"Bears?" Aheia asked, confused. "I didn't think there were bears here."

Aylee's lip twitched, but she didn't look over at her.

"We have everything." Kar held her finger out to Salamander, stroking its chin comfortably just as the door across the hall opened. Nephilim Aheia didn't know, peeled from the dark insides, each one wearing less than the last. Two females walking arm in arm, both of them with flaming red hair, and blue, smeared lipstick, came first. The one held her shoes in her hand, and the other hid a giggle behind her palm when she saw them all standing there. They were closely followed by two males, the latter carrying his shirt in his hands. He was decorated with colorful ink that left no patch of skin untouched on his chest. He grinned, and his cheeks dusted in a soft blush as he slung an arm around the pink-haired male with three nose piercings that trailed him.

Aheia's eyes widened as she watched the procession, one by one, each looking a little worse for the wear, until Lúc stepped out of the darkness, gray sweatpants hanging loosely off his hips.

"Don't—" Lúc held up his hand, grimacing and rubbing the heel of his palm into his temple before any of them could say anything. "I don't want to hear it. Not a single word."

"*Shah lahry.*" Kar grinned.

"If you ever see me ordering that cinnamon liquor again." He winced, shuddering, his abdomen contracting slightly. "Slap that shit out of my hands."

"Not on your fucking *life*, Lúci." Tariq bled from the darkness, leaning into Lúc's side, his hand on the door frame lazily, dangerous grin on his face. Aheia didn't know if he owned a look that wasn't threatening. "You get all soft and b—" He finished the thought in the Shifter's ear, who swallowed thickly, pulling at his lip ring. There was no shame lost between any of them, everyone standing there like it was a normal occurrence, while Aheia's stomach dipped, and her fingers felt the urge to fidget.

Her eyes darted up to Arioch's, who was leaning his shoulder against the wall, his hands in his pockets. *Six.* She bridged. *That makes six Nephilim.* That felt like a lot of moving pieces to keep track of.

Her face heated at the thought, at the unwilling montage that her mind created when—

"You're trying to kill me," Lúc groaned, shoving at Tariq's chest, his cheeks a soft pink now.

"Was that the sword swallower? Doesn't he work the Ren district?" Kar glanced over her shoulder at the demons that were almost out of sight now.

"Yea, and he needs a raise." A slow smirk crossed Tariq's face.

"I hate that you're not in pain," Lúc grumbled, as the Leviathan tucked him into his side.

"No, you don't. Who else would feed you?" he purred, running his fingers through his hair and steering him down the hallway that Kar and Aylee had come from. The empath snorted, bumping Tariq's hip with hers as they passed.

"How does that work?" Aheia asked before she could tamp down the question.

"Which part?" Aylee lifted her eyebrow, and Aheia rolled her lips between her teeth for a moment.

"Lúc and Tariq, they're together?" She looked for confirmation. "But they—"

"Taking pleasure from multiple places and people doesn't diminish what they have with each other. Actually, I've never seen two people so in tune." Aylee shrugged. "It takes a lot of communication." She waved her hand through the air like it explained the rest.

Oh.

"Wait," Aylee asked, amused, eyes flicking back to Arioch. "Don't tell me you two fuck *just* each other? That's not like you." Her blue gaze glimmered as Aheia looked up at him.

That's not like you.

Those gray eyes held hers, nonchalant and calm, but her blood heated under her skin. She hadn't considered it, hadn't thought about his preference, but now it's all she could focus on.

"I'd catch that river before it runs away with itself." Kar smiled at Arioch before she nudged at Aylee. "Come on, I'm going on multiple hours without caffeine, and I'm about to turn into a demon."

Salamander's tongue tasted the air, a soft hiss emanating from her as the two Nephilim headed back down the hallway, Aylee telling Kar, "How do I tell you this, Kar, I don't think it's the lack of coffee."

"Is that what you like?" Aheia turned, chewing on her bottom lip as his pulled into a soft smirk.

"I like a lot of things," he said, backing her into the doorframe, his hand bracing above her head. Her lips parted, and her thoughts dripped down until they burned in the embers that lined her abdomen. She once again couldn't help the barrage of images that flooded her, her brain stuttering on a response for him as she considered the options. Did he want to fuck other people? Would he get bored of Aheia if that's what he preferred? Was that what Aylee was insinuating? Or did he prefer sharing? Did he want to share her? It didn't seem likely with how he acted when others touched her. Or maybe he wanted to keep her to himself as a novelty, something he wouldn't share with anyone else. If Aylee had, in fact, meant *sharing* and not diversifying his affairs, then did he want more? Would he want others to join them while he kept that ridiculously tight leash on her actions? Did he like getting fucked by—

"Am I speaking?" he asked, and her blurry eyes snapped back to his. "In that scenario you're building in your mind."

Her jaw tensed. "No, you're fucking."

"Who am I fucking, Aheia?" he asked as she folded her hands behind her back and held on to the marble column. Maybe the stone would lend her strength.

"The sword swallower," she rushed out to mask the fact that in that shameful moment, he'd been fucking Lúc in her mind. *Stop.* It had been something about seeing the Shifter all soft and ruffled. She'd only ever seen him strong and loud.

"Interesting," he purred, his tongue wetting his bottom lip. "You're all pink," he said, his voice too deep. Normal thoughts weren't possible when he did that. And when he brushed his fingers across the bridge of her nose, she almost lost her hold on the wall. "Does that idea get your pussy wet?"

Her nostrils flared, her chin tipping on instinct.

"No."

"*Kajha,*" he said, his voice low and quiet.

"What does that mean?"

"That I know your fucking thoughts. So save yourself the trouble of lying about them." His eyes dropped to her mouth for a moment, before he pushed back, cold air swirling between them. "Come on, helfyre, I have somewhere to be."

Aheia's skin was still completely inflamed as they walked through a large stone archway surrounded by a thick fog that ate at everything around them. It was eerie, the buildings here ghostly and dark. There was no light, save for what little of the starlight breached through the heavy moisture.

"What is this place?" she asked, a shiver working its way down her spine.

"*Valhara*."

"Is it a ... territory?" she asked slowly.

"A town."

"It's so—empty,"

"No one lives down here, not anymore," he said, ushering her forward on the path that led between the building. The homes had shingled roofs, and the walls were overgrown, like nature was trying to swallow the infrastructure back into its belly.

"Why?" she asked as he led her down a side alley. It was unmarked, no different than any of the other ones, overgrown with vines hanging overhead.

"Because of the fog. It's swallowed the town for centuries, and that kind of coverage took a toll on the minds of the Nephilim down here."

Aheia had always liked clouds and fog back in Keloseros. She liked how they both hid her in their own ways. Sometimes she even pretended that beyond the white boughs that were her surroundings, everything ceased to exist. That the little spot of earth she'd stood on was the only true, real spot in her world. No more Ophion, no more sun, no more closed doors.

But she supposed that wasn't an idea that would be comforting to most.

"The fog"—Arioch ran his hand through the air— "was laid across the city by 'Amm."

"What for?"

"It's said that Theia walked across these grounds and met 'Amm here on the day they encaged Manāt in Gehenna. That this is the birthplace of the first few notches that threaded together the prison he exists in now. The fog kept their plans hidden."

"*Here*?" Aheia asked as Arioch rested his hand on her lower back, and led her up to a tall, crooked house that was *covered* in plants. They grew from the cracks of the old building, almost like fur on an animal, the broken windows and the unhinged door bordered by the thick clusters. Arioch reached for a vine and picked a few twigs of the discolored flora.

"What is this?" She asked, touching the waxy skin. It was dark blue and splotched with white, almost like it had been splattered with paint.

"*Soma*," Arioch said, wrapping the few leaves he'd picked in a piece of cloth and shoving it in his back pocket. "They call it the god plant."

"They?"

"The ones who believe its origin," he said, reaching between the thick vines and drawing back a smattering of leaves. Below, the rock was carved with symbols that looked a lot like protective sigils. She couldn't read the runes within, but the markings tugged at her memory. Where had she seen them?

"It has to do with 'Amm and Theia, I'm guessing?" She quirked an eyebrow.

"The kind of magyck expended by the two Gods that day didn't just lay in the air. It created a byproduct that leached into the soil," he said. "Valhara is the only place in the realm that sprouts this very particular plant."

"Why are you picking it?" she asked.

"If ingested in this form, it will kill a creature faster than any other poison, but when it's cooked down, it splits and there is a film that can be extracted and used as a healing agent."

She considered how many things in this world were split by the duality of life and death. Soma could bring both; it just took the right touch to manipulate it in either direction.

"What for?"

"I ran out," he said simply, his tone suggesting that there was no chance in hel that he was elaborating.

"That's all we're here for?"

"Yeah, that's all." He let his eyes drift up the tall building for a moment, before nodding her down the paved road that led around it. She passed the side, letting her fingers drift over the lush navy leaves and consider its past. It was odd to think of the possibility that something so powerful might have once, long ago, stood in the same place as her.

"Is it dangerous?" Aheia asked, tilting her head. "The fog?"

"No, not to us. It's a barrier, a shield more than a weapon."

They passed by a few more spindly pathways until they melted out into a clearing. The air was slightly more transparent here, and Aheia gazed up at yet another odd building, off in the distance.

"What's that?" she asked, squinting. She could barely see its walls bleeding through the fog, dark, colorful glass stretching around the outside.

"Have a look." Arioch nodded forward, the dense air swirling around them into small circles as she followed the thin, stone path. It was lined with little green clovers, and for a split second Aheia pretended that it was greenery that covered water. What if something lived within the depths? If she fell from the path, would she get swallowed? Why did the thought prickle excitement over her skin?

The smell tugged at her heart. It was similar to the petrichor in her realm when it rained, the aroma of dirt mingling with water. Except here, it was laced with something else, floral and bright. She wanted to bathe in it, and drink it down until it followed her wherever she went.

The closer they came, the clearer the fuzzy edges of the thick stone slabs came. The entrance was carved into the side, down a slim set of stairs that fed right through an attached hole in the wall. Arioch trailed her quietly as she ventured inside, weaving around the hallway's soft swoops until they arrived at the large center room and Aheia stopped short, a soft gasp on her lips.

Chapter 34

Arioch

The moonlight was streaming in through the stained windows of the building, making 'Amm's likeness look ethereal in the different panes. Her skin was dark blue, soft glitter spread through the tempered glass that shone. Her long, white hair was curling around her features, her hands clasped in front of her, delicately holding onto a light blue orb, like a small moon that was shining out around her. She was surrounded by different shades of purple, blue, and white, the triangled glass cutting the dark pillows that lined the space into pieces. Her larger than life depiction was balanced by the statue that Arioch had tucked Aheia behind. She hadn't looked up at its face, just as she hadn't noticed the dianthus in the air. If she did, she'd recognize the Theia worship that those demons in front of them were partaking in.

The Brite Gods were just as interwoven in their history as the Dark ones and there was devotion for both across the realm. There had been for centuries. The Nephilim in front of them now thought they were secretive, that Arioch didn't know about the amalgamation of Brite and Dark texts they'd used to create their faith. And they hid it for good reason. In Sahren's time, they would have been strung up by the border with their innards presented to the stars as penance for following anyone but 'Amm. Arioch couldn't be fucking bothered with who believed what when he believed nothing. Nothing but the true things—how the creatures in this realm were fiercely loyal and how anything could be powerful if it was given the opportunity.

But Aheia wasn't paying attention to the details that would have given any of those things away because she stood transfixed, staring at the naked bodies in front of them.

"*What is happening*?" Aheia hissed under her breath, eyes darting back and forth between the building spectacle and Arioch. There were at least a dozen Nephilim all across the room, in various states of undress tangled up with each other.

"What does it look like?" he asked languidly, brushing his nose across the crest of her head.

"An—" She cleared her throat, squaring her shoulders. "An orgy?"

"Is that word hard for you?" He raised an eyebrow, resting his tongue in the corner of his mouth.

"No, I—" Aheia swallowed. "*Shit*," she whispered, getting sidetracked by the demons closest, the three males that were playing with one female.

"Worship comes in many forms," he said, letting his lips tilt in the slightest way.

"Worshiping what?" she asked, enthralled by the Leviathan who had her face buried between the thighs of a Syraphem.

"Bodies that they believe were a gift from the Gods."

"*Oh*." It was soft. "I never thought about it like that." She shook her head. "We were always told that pleasure like this was not to be indulged in, that we were capable of it as a test of our strength and belief. Not feeling it would honor the Gods, would prove to them that we were worthy of the salvation—of ascension after death."

Arioch's stomach twisted. *Fucking hel.* That kind of starvation was nothing but control over bodily autonomy held by creatures who should have never gotten their hands on it.

"I wasn't very devout." Aheia dug her teeth into that bottom lip, glazed eyes reflecting Nephilim in front of her. "Them telling me that I *couldn't* made me do the exact opposite. I snuck out of that sermon with bruised knees, and pulled one of the chambermaids into the forest with me, just to get right back on those knees in the grass."

Her throat bobbed, the softest movement, but it made his palm itch. And he didn't deny himself the placement, sliding it over her delicate skin, and wrapping his fingers around her neck. Her pulse was erratic, running like it was trying to escape him, and that fucking little gasp when he squeezed. Fuck. His cock swelled in his leathers at the sound.

"I liked seeing her pleasure. You know? I liked the idea that what I did"—her lips glistened—"mattered. That I made someone else *feel*."

His body warmed at the idea that his little heathen had been defying what she thought her Gods wanted from her. His Aheia liked pleasure, and she'd been willing to risk damnation for it long before she understood death.

"There's this moment," Arioch murmured, against her temple, offering something in turn. "Can you see that look in his eye?" he asked, watching the male on his knees staring up at the other. "It's almost pleading—like he might do anything to keep this all from ending."

Aheia nodded, her chest rising and falling a little faster.

"There's something in that desperation." He slid his hand down across her stomach, grazing her abdomen with his knuckles. She shivered against him, fingers bracing the stone in front of her tighter. "I really fucking like seeing it."

"You like them desperate for you?" She was all but panting now.

His lips twitched into a smile. He liked *her* desperate for him.

"Tell me what you're thinking," he said instead, his voice low against her ear.

"I—"' She wet her bottom lip, buying herself a few seconds. She might have lied to him at any other time, but she didn't look capable in that moment. He saw the same thing he felt reflected, saw it in her mindless focus, the dark pupils that filled those blue eyes to the brim, the glaze that distracted her heart from her mind. It was a heavy heat that burrowed so low that it snuck into his bloodstream, one that loosened his tongue. If only she knew—if only she knew how much power she had over him. He might have been with the tight grip, but she held him without even touching and he'd never in his life been so fucking fixated on something.

"I like the attention," she whispered, pressing her throat into his hand a little harder as the moans and the sounds of breathless pleasure intensified around them, ricocheting off the wall. It seemed subconscious, but his reaction was anything but. It took a tight grip on the stone next to her to keep him from sliding it between her legs. He needed to know what was on her mind, and in this instance, he was hopeful for a genuine answer. But she would shut herself off again, he feared, if he did anything but stay that perfect statue behind her.

"I like how they all focus on each other in the same measure ... It"—her gaze drifted across the bodies—"It feels so calming,"

She likes to watch.

He liked watching, too. The rise of her chest, the flush on her cheeks when her breathing became quick. And it was unsettling, the realization that the bodies in front of him did nothing compared to the blush on her face. Did nothing compared to just one little gasp from between those pale lips. *Fuck me.*

She was bright in a sea of dark, like she always was but more now than ever.

Her eyes shone the lightest blue, and the flush on her skin was a soft pink.

Those two colors painted his insides. Blue and pink.

He was pulled back to this morning in the hallway. How she'd looked at him when she asked him about what he liked. He'd meant when he told her he liked a lot of different things but with her ... The thought of another demon having their hands on her made him aware of his teeth and how much he wanted to dig them into flesh. It was possessive anger, but that shit was twined with the idea of how pretty she'd look used like that. And it would be his choices that made her come, his direction that made her lose her fucking mind. That much control made his cock throb.

Sweat pearled at the back of his neck with the restraint; restraint to keep his shadows from her, restraint on his mind, his movements. It was the control he was forced to hold every day in all areas of his existence, but it had never been as hard to maintain as when he was in her presence.

Another swallow and the movement against his palm had lightning shooting down his spine. Just imagining the feel of her throat around his cock, her hot mouth, her tongue, the way she'd stretch for him.

Fuck.

And then she leaned back just enough to touch her shoulder blades to his chest. He screwed his eyes shut tight, feeling the shards of the impossible bond they'd shared thrum between them.

"None of them are thinking," she continued finally, her voice barely above the sound her own breath made when she inhaled. Her eyes pulled away from the others and when they met his, his shadows trembled between his muscles. It was the kind of movement that didn't feel natural, didn't feel good. But it was also the kind of movement that had an addictive nature woven into it. He wanted to keep feeling that. "They can just be ... and they're not embarrassed by what they want." She faltered, her chin tipping slightly.

"And what do you want?" he asked, sliding his hand from her throat to her collarbone. He hadn't asked her that, not truly. Not since she came back. He'd *told* her what she wanted and part of it was because he knew the question was difficult, but he wouldn't deny that the other part was about him. He'd been too scared to give her the freedom she needed. Because at the end of the day, he wasn't good enough to keep precious things.

"I just—" Her tongue swiped over her bottom lip. "I want quiet."

His exhale was heavy and warm. *Quiet.* She spoke the words like a secret.

"You said you could give me what I asked for ..." She reached for his shirt, gliding her fingers across his abdomen, and it drew a line of fire where she touched, even through the fabric.

“Anything I asked for.” Aheia pressed against him ever so slightly, and he let her walk him back until he hit the rough rock wall. He inhaled sharply, her blue eyes watching him from below white lashes as she tugged at his laces, running her palm down the length of his cock. “Give me that, give me quiet.”

CHAPTER 35

AHEIA

Arioch told her he liked desperation, and he had Aheia's in that moment. She was warm and buzzing and all she wanted was to *worship* along with the rest of them.

His leathers were warm and soft, but that ridge that ran down his seams was hard as rock. The feel coiled her stomach tight with the reminder of how it felt to have him fuck her, of how his intensity felt.

Damaged thing, she scolded herself. He was right about that. Damaged because she shouldn't want it like she did, she knew that. But she'd lost a real reason to deny it to herself. If the only repercussion that loomed on the other side of this messy fucking thing between them was pain, she could handle it. She'd trade that for the pleasure he offered, for the quiet and the distraction.

"Show me what it looks like when you martyr yourself, Aheia."

Bright embers burst and popped just underneath her skin, her entire body vibrating because of his words. She nearly hit the floor right then and there, her knees wobbling with her own weight.

But she kept herself upright, massaging her hand over his cock, watching with delight when his neck flexed. She was mesmerized by that vein that ran the length of it, the tick in his jaw and the movement in his hand. They all reacted before the rest of him did when he was affected— the first sign of slipped control.

"You're no God," she breathed, honing the last of her edge toward him.

"I'm worse." The fire in his eyes matched hers, the moans and pants around them stoking it brighter as he brushed his lips against hers. "I'm real." Her chest caved. "And I hold a lot more power down here than they do."

She whimpered. She couldn't help herself and it felt like sadness. Because she wanted to believe it. That he cared enough to give her what she asked for.

Her body sank slowly, her feet resting at the edge of the statue behind her as she pulled open his laces with shaky fingers. Not until she touched his skin did they steady themselves, something like relief eating the tremors in her shoulders. He was warm and heavy, his soft skin stretched taut across his hard length when she pulled him free, and glided her palm over the top.

Her throat went dry for a moment, faced with his size. It was delusional, questioning if he'd always been this big, but this was a whole other vantage point. She turned her eyes back to his, so fucking tall that she had to stretch as far as she could on her knees to reach him.

He was watching her like the rest of the room didn't exist when she darted out her tongue, catching the pearl of precome that collected at his tip, and swallowing the taste. That vein at his throat became more pronounced, and it urged her on. She explored slowly, trailing her tongue up the length of him, while she kept fingers wrapped tightly around his base.

His reactions were intoxicating and she added a new favorite to her list when the muscles contracted over his abs. She wanted them all, wanted to see what each movement would elicit, watching with pleasure when she flicked her tongue up the underside of his head and he bared his teeth.

"I'm going to fuck your little mouth and you'll take it because you do such a good fucking job at defying your Gods," he growled, fisting her hair in a tight grip.

The air squeaked from her lungs, the warmth in her abdomen seeping between her thighs.

They were playing again, and she liked this game. It was shameful, but in this moment, the shame burned the right spots. It made this worse and somehow worse was better.

Flutters erupted in her stomach, melding her pleasure with his, the ground pressing into her knees sharply, as she clenched her thighs together, feeling the empty pulse between them when she took him into her mouth. She sucked him deep, the oxygen cut from her lungs as she gagged, spit dripping between them and onto the cobbled floor.

His groan fed her, a frenzy building inside her stomach. She needed his pleasure. It felt like hers.

Her chest heaved as she drew back, licking him from base to tip, before her hand smoothed back across his abdomen and down between his legs. She massaged his balls, squeezing lightly before sucking the tip of his cock back inside of her mouth, feeling his hand grasp her hair hard.

"You don't know the power you hold when you're on your knees for me." His voice was guttural, and it made her entire body light up like Solas. It felt powerful, just like when she'd walked the marble as his pet all those weeks ago. She may have been on her knees for him, but it felt like this time, she was the one holding his mercy.

She let her lashes flutter, holding his gaze as she swallowed against him.

"Do that again." A string of curses rolled from his lips, and she did, swallowing while her vision pulsed with the lack of air. Her fingers massaged his balls and stroked his length like her fucking life depended on it, and even though he was the one fucking her, *she* felt like the greedy one between them.

She squirmed, her throat contracting while she choked around him and his fingers tightened on her hair. Discomfort lit up her scalp and tears streamed down her face, mingling with the spit as he forced her down, hips driving back into her throat relentlessly now. He was taking, but she was too.

"Fuck, your tongue—" The words slithered through her like praise, and the cotton of her pants soaked with her arousal. "It's worth damnation."

She moaned, taking him deeper, until her throat ached, until her jaw did too. She'd bruise fucking horribly, and the thought of that fed her even more.

Desperate. She was desperate for it.

"Just like that," he grunted, his cock thickening on her tongue, the awareness in her chest heightening. Fuck, she wanted this. "I'm going to fill that pretty mouth." His strokes became harder and jagged, his cock hammering down her abused throat until his release spilled inside of her, thick ropes of it painting her insides. He kept her down on top of him and she coughed and choked, feeling some of his come slide down her face and onto her chest as he twitched and pulsed. She couldn't get enough of him like this, his chin tipped in ecstasy, every body part rigid and mindless. She'd done that, and she wanted to do that again.

When he eased up on her hair, she pulled back slowly, keeping her lips tight around his length, her tongue sliding against the underside of him and cleaning him off.

She barely had the chance to swallow before he picked her up off the ground and sat her back against the ledge of the statue behind her. And then he crowded her body, dragging the flat of his tongue up her chin and cleaning off the come that had escaped her.

Holy fuck.

She gasped, and when she did, he licked inside, spreading his taste between them, lips and teeth fighting for dominance as he stole her breath. "Fuck, my come tastes good on your tongue," he said and she almost lost the handle on the stone. Fucking *mercy.*

Her spit-soaked palms smeared against the rock, her legs boneless as he pulled the cotton pants she wore down her knees, his teeth keeping her close to him as her bare ass hit the cold stone. He only pulled back to discard the fabric, hungry eyes dropping down between them.

"Spread your legs for me, show me what's mine." She could barely pull in her breath now, her chest heaving with the difficulty to catch it. "Show me what I bargained for."

Good Gods. She never thought she'd crave being used like this, being degraded like this. And she should have fought those words, should have *wanted* to. But at that moment, his grip felt secure. It felt anchoring when nothing else did.

The cold lapped at her feverish skin as she splayed her thighs slowly, the blush in her cheeks burning.

"Let's see how hungry this depraved little pussy is." He took her right hand in his and guided it down between them, stroking them both against her heated flesh before he pushed inside of her. Arousal squelched around them, dripping down their knuckles, and the back of her skull hit the cold statue. "Oh *fuck*." It tumbled from her lips soft and hoarse, her knees starting to tremble at the way they stretched her, at how the pleasure turned into a molten thing, warming the ice in her veins. The whimper she let go turned into a sob when he pulled out, leaving her empty again.

"You want me to fix that ache, little goddess?" He brought his hand to his mouth and licked it clean. "Make you come all messy for me?"

She nodded feverishly, her wet hand slapping back against the stone ridge for balance.

"Use your words," he said, his voice filled with gravel as he unlatched one of his knives. "I want to hear you."

"Yes," she gasped, as he brought the weapon between them. *That's a blade. He could filet you six ways till tomorrow morning,* her mind hissed like she'd lost it completely. And maybe she had lost it, but hadn't that been what she wanted?

"You can do better than that,"

"Please," *I need you*. "Make me come." *Make me feel something.*

His eyes warmed further, and if she didn't know better, she would have called the expression on his face pride. But then he dragged the knife down her stomach, just the lightest amount of pressure, and her gaze followed it, hot bursts peppering the back of her neck. He could cut her, he could split her apart any way he wanted, carve his name across her leg, and she'd be helpless to it.

Her thighs trembled slightly as she tried to hold on to her sanity. The tunnels came rushing in and she remembered how it had felt for him to bite her—how the sharp sting of his teeth had made her lose herself. She'd wanted more of that then too, but hadn't known how to ask for it.

She needed the pain. Somewhere along the way, sensations had gotten muddled in protection of her sanity. Pain no longer felt like pain. Pleasure no longer felt like pleasure. Not exclusively. And this—whatever the fuck was happening now—excited her.

The tip of the blade depressed her thigh and the needling against her skin shot right between her legs, making her cunt throb again.

"Do you trust me?" he asked, the black in his irises seeping into the gray, as he slid his fingers up against the flat of the blade so he could manipulate the pressure.

Do you trust me? Her lips parted, and her limbs became rigid. The metal warmed as he pressed and her heart stuttered in her chest.

"*Fuck*," she gasped, feeling the shock of split skin lashing the nerves in her leg. He hadn't moved a single muscle, his fingers stone still on top of the knife, keeping it pushed down on the cut that had formed at the tip, red blood welling and dripping. *You make everything hurt*. She'd told him and he'd smiled at her. *You have no idea.*

"You're crawling into bed with a demon. And you should know what that means before you look at me with those eyes."

Her chest heaved with effort, and her legs shook with the potential that wound between them.

"It means I'll make you bleed and sob before I let you come. I'll watch you beg me to stop while I stroke my cock, because your tears get me so fucking hard. I'll lick across the gashes my knives decorate your skin with and coat myself in your blood before I fuck your tight little cunt, because I like your pain."

Run. She told herself. *Fucking run.*

"I'll take every inch you give me, and I'll ruin it, because that's all I'm fucking capable of—I'll make you hurt until you don't remember what it feels like not to." He breathed, and she leaned into it, like his air would keep her alive. And then his voice dropped.

"Just me." His tongue swiped along the ridge of his teeth before he bent down and sucked the cut on her thigh into his mouth.

She cried out, her fingers digging into the stone. *Ow, fuck. Shit. I don't know how to—*

"*No one,*" he growled, her blood on his lips, his eyes all black, "will hurt you except for me."

It felt layered and veiled. Degrading but not. Possessive. A promise and a threat to the thought of anyone else touching her.

"Trust me," he said hoarsely.

She nodded, even as she started hyperventilating. *Yes.* She trusted him with this. And maybe that was the most foolish thing she'd ever done. But the pleasure he offered was louder than the worry in her mind. *Damaged.* This shouldn't have brought tears to her eyes, it shouldn't have made her lip tremble, or that Gods damned balloon inflate in her chest. Because *this* wasn't endearment, so why did she keep tucking it away as such.

"And your pain?" Her voice was small when she bared her thoughts to him.

"You can have it, if that's what you want." Arioch growled, bringing the knife to her mouth. "Now get it wet for me." He dragged the carved metal hilt of his blade down her lips, parting them slowly. Hot breath misted the cold surface as she licked her tongue up the intricate design without any fucking hesitation.

The pain at her leg flared when he pressed two fingers against the wound before rubbing her blood across the spit-soaked handle.

Her heart was in her throat, watching with hooded eyes as he rotated the weapon and slid the cold, wet metal of the hilt down against her entrance. *Fucking hel.* The noise she made was undignified, and so was the way she rolled her hips, chasing him back when he circled the knife just too wide from where she needed him.

"You know how many lives this blade has collected?"

Her windpipe squeezed as she watched his hands, her nostrils flaring with effort to draw in air. He looked too, his thumb igniting eight thousand little nerves in her clit when he rubbed over it. "What a fucking sight." Her thighs flexed in excitement as the hilt probed her entrance. "I'll remember this—you wrapped around the handle, my come dripping from your mouth when I take it to another demon's skin."

His other hand pressed her thigh apart even further and then he pushed the weapon inside of her slowly, inch by inch. She gasped, her knuckles whitening. It was straight and hard, and the ridges rubbed inside of her already aching cunt.

"Yes," she gasped, her breath shuddering out of her as he pumped the knife.

"You want my shadows and your cunt drips for my blades. Who the fuck were you ever pretending for—who were you trying to convince you were anything else but this? Dark and twisted and so *fucking* perfect."

She squirmed and moaned, desperate fucking sounds, but she couldn't help herself. He held her in his palm, and she wouldn't mind if he crushed her as long as he kept making her feel like this. He was right about that too when he'd accused her of it. She was starting to fall into obsession with the fever.

The hilt of the knife was unforgiving. *He* was unforgiving as he angled it, rubbing the inside of her abdomen with too much precision. Like he knew exactly where she needed him.

"Such a greedy filthy fucking thing, aren't you? Tell me how it feels." His pace was punishing, and the bulbed handle hit that spot inside of her in a way that *hurt*. But it was pain that built with the pleasure, and she found herself gasping for more, choking on her own breath as her body wound tighter and tighter.

"Like salvation," she moaned, dropping her head back against the stone when he closed the distance towering over her.

"Where the fuck did you come from, Aheia?" he asked, his curls hanging into her face as he held her face in his hands, forcing their foreheads together. And this time when he used her name, it wasn't in anger. This time, it was in worship.

"Don't stop!" she cried out, much too loud, her orgasm moments from sweeping her under. She couldn't care less if they were found out, if anybody saw. None of it mattered, as long as he let her come like this.

"I won't stop until you soak this statue, little goddess,"

And that was all it took for her to shatter apart, her cries echoing off the walls, joining the cacophony of pleasure around them. He held those shards. He'd held them before, kept holding them for her. And every time he gave them back, they felt less like hers.

Chapter 36

Shiron

The flames bent around the metal, licking at the molten silver as it bound and melded with the obsidian and tourmaline orbs of the protective achlary Kazim had broken from Shiron's neck. The heat of the fire beat into him as he shook, keeping the tired *Zynair* back from the edge. It was the part of him that no one but Arioch knew about. The half of him that had fed off of fear so many years ago—the half of him that was suppressed by the necklace he clung to.

His blood was pumping fast, while the skin across his body felt stretched to capacity and itched. Damn, it itched. He extinguished the flame in front of him, sweat trickling down his temple as he thrust the achlary into icy water, burnt steam billowing back into his face. He'd fixed the Damascus, restored the loops, but his insides squeezed against the thought of donning the heavy necklace.

The idea of putting it back into place around his throat made his stomach cramp. But the pain in his gut he could handle, it was the whispers at his temples that were driving him mad. The whispers weren't vicious. He wished they were. They were coaxing little moans. Temptations that knew how to manipulate because that's what he'd been once. He'd been those voices, eaten others' fear and pleasure while they thanked him for stripping the flesh off their bones.

His eyes burned because the guilt in his veins was barely an echo. It should have been loud the moment he felt those flames inside of his chest. And the shame just as well. But those things were drowned out in the sharp pricks that awoke under his skin. It was like a poison injected in his bloodstream, carried through him slowly and deliberately, snuffing out everything that made him inherently good.

The beads in his hand trembled as he brought them out of the bucket, his knuckles yellow. Water droplets fell and rippled his fucked up reflection below. He didn't look like himself. But he knew what he'd find—sharp teeth and brittle, red claws. He would have seen what his hunger looked like, and it would have stared back with just as much disgust for the demon he'd become. They were a split creature, but that didn't make him unique. No one here lived separate from their compulsions, their own darknesses. He just suppressed until he couldn't breathe.

But right now the air eluded him because the red-tipped claws that held his beads, the ones that no one else could see, gripped tight. They kept his arm rigid, as his body pulsed with blood too hot for his veins, with memories that worsened the ache that was building in every joint.

He remembered the flesh, the eyrid spilling around him, the never-ending pleasure. Pain should never bring so much of it.

He brought the achlary up slowly, and it felt like a losing battle. Like the demon in his mind sneered at the attempt to temper it, and whispered new ideas into his ear. What he might do to the next little body that walked across his path. How he might hurt them, how he might devour.

Kar's teal hair brushed against his shoulder and it felt real, even though he knew that it wasn't. It was vivid nonetheless, just a few strands tucked in the corner of his vision, as if she were walking behind him. He felt her graze across the center of his back, the tattooed fingers coming into view. He recognized the gold rings, the little bee she had inked on the side of her wrist, the dark vine of helichrysum that wound its way down the side of her arm and up her pinky. One hand trailed its softness against the nape of his neck, another crawled up his chest, and a third rounded his hip.

Too many hands. Touching too much of him.

He even heard her breathing.

But it transformed quickly into grating, guttural inhales. Ghostly, almost, like lungs filled with blood.

He couldn't see the rest of Kar, only feel the touch, like the vicious thing in his mind had taken on her form; wanted to blind him to himself, like it had in the past.

A coarse growl rumbled through him in protest as his fingers inched toward the hot, metal poker resting in the fire. Because if he got his hands on it, he'd run it through the apparition standing behind him. He'd burn the ink right off her body and he'd smile.

He wanted that in some primal, unhinged way. Untamed and teeth-filled desire that had nothing to do with who she was. She could have been anyone.

No.

Shiron pressed his eyes shut tight, and he forced himself into his past—the one time broken bodies hadn't felt good. He held onto the vision of gold, blood splattered eyes, of sucking chest wounds, of ribcages piercing through dark flesh, and blood. The first time blood turned his stomach. He remembered that feeling, and bathed in it until he was shaking.

The delicate stones that now vibrated in Shiron's closed grasp had been an offering. A mercy. A way to save him from himself when so much blood coated his hands. And he'd use the rest of his life to try to wash it off. To thank the Gods who saw him when no one should have given him a second glance. The reason for his faith.

The thought gave him the strength he needed to move the achlary back into place, letting its light beads fall heavy against the back of his neck.

His demon hissed like Shiron had burned it, and Kar disappeared.

The force was like a void, one that sucked everything that had clawed itself out from his chest back inside. It was a forceful, brimming feeling that had him doubling over against the rock bench in front of him. Nausea clenched his insides, and he heaved into the water bucket, vomit filling his mouth. Sour, terrible bile that he spit and splattered in front of him.

Baseless friction rubbed against his mind, and it reminded him that the demon would always be a part of him. That the monster couldn't be cleaved, only subdued. That this was his life.

Gah yuka alshyah aljera fi wayahra 'Amm.

He whispered the soft prayer over and over, while he doused the fire and wiped down his forehead. He continued until the words ran into each other, until they became a part of him, and then he forced himself from the small, hot room in the *Jahra*. He'd kept his place down here for decades because it was far from the compound. He forged here, prayed here, and slept here when he needed space. It reminded him of home, even though home was a far away place and a far away thought now.

Jahra was a small town situated just on the outskirts of the forest, a place that still used fire to light the streets. The buildings smelled of clay and looked hand-molded. Just like the other outlier towns, Jahra felt older, less developed. It was because the change that Arioch worked on was seeping into their realm from the center—a slow trickle. It hadn't reached the burnt edges yet and Shiron saw their past here, saw Alshaytan Sahren's influence.

He rolled his shoulders. It seemed that was a time they may well be approaching again soon with how the conflict was building at all sides. He knew that the territories were brittle and destined to break. Arioch knew too, because there were only two ways to unite the different Siada. One was to give them more of what they wanted to placate them. The problem with that was that the things that would placate them were horrifying. Some lobbied for segregation within their territories, pushing the Shifters into their own quarters. They wanted legality of Nerium and other drugs, the kinds that would ruin a demon's life. And they wanted to continue on with the blood trade. It was all about control. Too much control. It would create precedents that'd see all Nephilim reliant on their Siada and the demons they put in charge. It was tightening a noose that had been slung around the realm years ago. It would eventually choke Arioch out of his position. The fact that the Siada's position now lay in the hands of the people in each territory hadn't made enough of a difference. Because there was still too much fearmongering when election time came. Even the inadequate ones would hold power that way.

His skin pebbled, a sick slithering sensation drawing down his spine like there was a snake working its way towards the tattoo still etched on the middle of his back. The ink that would remind him, whenever he had a moment of happiness, that he'd been ingrained in that life for years himself.

He shook his head. Arioch could never give them enough of what they wanted, not without backtracking any kind of progress. Of course, it was only progress to some. To others, it was change they didn't condone. That's why that first option was never truly feasible whereas, the second was. But to delve into the second would be to thrust hands into the fabric of the old times and try to unknot the tangled mess that went miles deep.

They would have to clear out the houses in charge and Siada with them, which meant blood. Lives would be lost and the fight would be measured. That was the problem with a realm so divided, and the outcome hanging in the balance on such a thin tightrope.

The Nephilim might not have been evil by design, but the way the world had treated them had pushed them into a mold. And the problem was, most of them enjoyed the role they were forced to play. Of course, it was all upbringing and teachings; none of them had started that way.

He'd enjoyed it, hadn't he?

Before he'd found his own faith, before he'd suppressed his own blood's beautiful hum.

He let go of a long breath, massaging the beads at his throat.

Gods.

The stone slid between his fingers while he carried the lightning inside of him. He couldn't let go of it, didn't know how to redirect it. The fixed necklace didn't seem to matter in that respect. The short time during which his demon had gone unchecked had spun the energy inside him, a thick web that draped across his innards. It was heavy. A pull. An urge. The urges that had dragged him down into his own hel all those years ago.

The moonlight streamed down over him, and this time the shame wasn't hard to find. But before he could sink into himself any further, before he could dissect why the feeling was still coursing through him when it should have been subdued by the beads, he heard a commotion from the far end of the alley.

His steps froze when the screech sounded and he remembered it, because there was only one monster that sounded like it.

Shykoya.

He took off down the alley, toward the source spilling out into a firelit clearing. His feet slid against the stone as he came to a halt, unsheathing his knife in the same breath.

His mind sharpened, and his senses honed in on the monster, who was hunched over a screaming Nephilim. Another body, whose face had been eaten, slumped over the side of a small divider wall, brown, stringy hair dipping into the dirty pool of water below.

The live demon was crying and flailing, his blood mixed with white venom as the Shykoya clenched its jaw, and tore another chunk from him.

No one else was with them, the silence that broke up the madness eerie and wrong. Shiron's hackles raised as he crossed the short distance and plunged his blade into the neck of the distracted Shykoya. The achlary around his neck burned with a hot reminder as he gripped the back of the leathery throat and cut deeper, until his hand sunk into the rotten flesh, and its old skin squelched up around the hilt of the blade. Shiron savored the feel of how easily it gave, of how soft it was and how it sounded when it screamed. Black, dead blood spilled down his skin, and his necklace heated further as the newly caged whisper of who he'd once been raged against the magyck. He took this kill, took it slowly, his eyes flickering with his past. With the blood. With the pain. With the unmatched need to feed the coaxing whispers inside.

"You—" The demon next to him choked and gasped for air, and it pulled Shiron back into the present. "You killed her." The words were gargled and jarring.

Shiron shoved the monster to the side and dropped to his knees, inspecting the victim's wounds. There was nothing he could do. His torso was near severed, and his neck had chunks missing, blood gushing out like oil.

"You killed her," he managed again between great, labored breaths, his eyes glazed and red, blood leaking from between his teeth.

"Her?" Shiron stroked over the male's arms, seeing the track marks up and down the inside of his skin. His fingernails were dirty, his hair greasy and matted down against his wan face.

"I fell asleep." His fingers shook, his skin pebbling with the cold. "I could have stopped it, I could have begged." His eyes turned starward. "Will the Gods have mercy?" He grunted.

Shiron nodded, feeling his insides burn as he held the demon close. "Yes."

"I don't feel so good," he croaked, stare losing focus. "*Mercy.*"

The last shuddering inhale left his body, and he went limp in Shiron's arms.

Sweat was prickling his brow as he walked across the jewel-toned carpets that lined the back ways of the compound. Shiron's fingernails were still rimmed in black blood even after he'd scrubbed them, and he could fucking smell the decay of the Shykoya on himself. His mind felt disjointed, and the buzzing in his ears wouldn't die down as he left another empty room looking for Arioch. He let himself stop, just for a moment, because his beads felt suffocating.

"Give me strength," he said under his breath, cracking his neck in hopes of relief. The stone was cold against his back when he let himself rest there for a moment.

"You asking me?" a soft lilt sounded from his right, and he shot his eyes down. He hadn't realized he wasn't alone and was ready to snap at whomever was standing there.

But when he looked up, green, sharp emeralds met him shining from behind frames of red curls.

"I accept most forms of worship," Nameless continued, stalking closer with her arms crossed. She was trailed by one of the older Syraphem, who looked bored out of his mind as he sidled up and leaned against the far wall, keeping an eye on her. Shiron had heard about her outbursts, about the fights she'd started, about the fucking mess she was running her guards through. Instigating. That's all she did. It's what she was trying to do now.

"Why are you here?" His voice sounded rougher than intended.

"I was getting scolded." She looked over her shoulder at a closed door near the hallway entrance. "And now I have a bird on my shoulder."

The beads around Shiron's throat became impossibly heavy as her eyes glinted.

"You know why," he said, as measured as he could manage when nothing inside of him felt calm.

"Because I know what your blood tastes like?" She clasped her hands behind her back demurely and blinked up at him with false sweetness, dark rings of green bleeding more and more into her irises.

It was the first time he'd spoken to her since she attacked him in her room, and his shoulder tingled with the phantom memory of her teeth.

"You haven't picked a name," he said instead, avoiding the blows she was trying so desperately to land. Her smile faltered at that—such a quick reaction he barely caught it.

"I like that it bothers everyone."

Liar.

The door behind Nameless opened, and Emryn stepped out into the hallway. She looked taken aback for a moment, eyes bouncing between the two of them, but she recovered quickly.

"Take her back to the Kaserne," Emryn said curtly to the *bird* just as Nameless stepped closer to Shiron and brushed her fingers over the collar of his shirt, sliding it to the side enough to bare the bite mark that had healed there. "You let it scar," she said, and if he didn't know better, he'd have thought it sounded thoughtful. Then she shifted, the air around them shifting alongside her. "Why's that?"

"Are you hard of hearing?" Emryn snapped at the other Syraphem, who blinked at her and realized what she'd meant, scrambling over to them and reaching for Nameless, trying to shuffle her along.

"Remember what we talked about," Emryn said sternly as the redhead backed up slowly.

"Yes, *Maman*," Nameless crooned, and Shiron watched Emryn's shoulders straighten. Her face betrayed nothing as she flourished her fingers and the redhead's mouth snapped shut, small black strings lashing across her lips. Her green eyes widened, fingers shooting to the magyck that kept her mouth shut in a panic. It looked like a suture, and while it had the same effect as needle and thread, it didn't need to pierce her skin to work.

"There." Emryn's smile was tight. "Sit with your brain and provoke it for a while. When you're tired of your own bullshit, come find me and ask me to remove the magyck."

Nameless glared up at the Shadow Heretic, groaning and mumbling what sounded like angry words against her confines.

"Keep at it." Emryn rolled her eyes, turning her back. "You'll exhaust yourself soon enough."

"What was that about?" Shiron asked her, eyes stuck to the retreating redhead.

"Another fight," Emryn murmured thoughtfully. "Her outbursts are getting worse." Then, when the other two had rounded the corner, she reached for the collar of his shirt and pulled it down, baring the wound again. "What the fuck is this?"

"Inah ya shae," he groaned, pulling her hand away.

"Nothing?" She clicked her tongue, swatting off his hold and re-examining him. "It is not nothing. This was deep." Her eyes cataloged the scar. "*She* did that? How the fuck did she get close enough?'

"Emryn, don't," he snarled, the energy inside of him pooling venom on his tongue. His temple twitched when she looked up at him, questions imprinted in the angry lines of her face.

And as if the 'Amm had heard him and decided to grant him an escape, one of the dark double doors opened at the far side of the hallway. Arioch was walking across the rugs with his hands in his pockets while Aheia dangled a piece of meat in front of the Varcolac that she'd seemed to take a liking to. Koutávi, she'd called it. His translation was rusty, but he swore it meant something like sweet dog. Indeed. The beast was *playing* with her, like a fucking dog chomping after a treat.

The Avarice was watching Aheia, his lips curled into a soft smile when she wasn't paying attention to him, swallowing the expression the moment she did. Nyco trailed them, their eyes focused on a book, and Shiron narrowed his eyes. They were a good warrior, seemed trustworthy enough, but it felt odd how often they lingered around the Mithra now. How often Arioch asked them to.

When Alshaytan saw Shiron, his demeanor hardened. He leaned into Aheia's side and pointed her down the way they'd come from. They exchanged a few words, and a moment later, she headed off that direction with Nyco and Koutávi in tow.

Shiron gestured at the door Emryn had come out of and when Arioch nodded, he headed inside.

He pinched the bridge of his nose, trying to clear the fog in his mind, waiting for the others to follow. When the door latched and the small sounds of the hallways drowned out, he opened his eyes. Arioch was staring at him in deep calculation and he could see the questions plainly in those gray irises. But he didn't voice them and Shiron was thankful because Emryn didn't know. None of them knew about what he was except Arioch, and he wanted to keep it that way.

"There was a Shykoya attack in Jahra," Shiron said.

"What?" Arioch's demeanor changed.

"Just one."

"It got past the border?" Emryn asked, her eyebrows drawn tight.

"The border hasn't been completed in Jahra." Arioch shook his head. "There are still a few breaks in the magyck."

"It killed two demons. Both of them were users," Shiron continued.

Arioch's shadows curled from him ominously, the darkness in his eyes licking at the gray. "Nerium?" he asked.

Shiron nodded. "The one who still had an intact spine had four injection sites between his vertebrae, three of which were infected."

"Did you see any other nest activity?" Emryn asked.

"No, I scoured the area. The two of them must have been on a supply run—attacked in the street." Shiron continued. "One of them survived for a few minutes after I pulled the Shykoya off of him and ... he said something odd when I killed it." He touched his beads absentmindedly. "He accused me of '*killing her*.'"

"Killing ..." Emryn drew out the word, and he finished the thought for her.

"It sounded like he meant the Shykoya," Shiron bridged. "*Her*, he called it."

"Her ..." Emryn mumbled under her breath. "Was the other dead body a female? Maybe he was talking about the other victim?" she tried.

"I thought about that," Shiron said. "And it's a possibility." He knew that the Nephilim gasping the same words over and over again made more sense than any of the other crackpot theories he was stringing together in his mind. With how near death he'd been, it was a surprise he could stand, let alone think for himself. But something about it still felt off, because it hadn't been the only thing the dying demon had said.

I could have stopped it, I could have begged.

"Check in with the Heretics working on the border magyck," Arioch said to Emryn. "See how close they are to Jahra. There's no sense in disrupting their work flow if they're almost done in Tryn."

When Emryn left, Alshaytan gripped Shiron's shoulder tightly, bringing him close. "Are you sorted?" His eyes flicked down to the achlary around his neck again

"Yes." Shiron swallowed thickly. "The Damascus is suppressing, but it's not ... I can't get rid of how that short stint without it made me feel."

"What do you need?" Arioch asked.

"Time." He met those dark eyes and held them.

"Alright. Keep your distance if you need to, but you fucking talk to me."

Shiron's mind had been reeling ever since it all happened, wondering if that attack on Kar was the reason he'd lost his beads. If Kazim had broken the achlary because that was the Gods will all along. Without it, he wouldn't have found himself in Jahra, and if he hadn't been there, he wouldn't have witnessed the attack. It had to mean something; it had to matter. He had to believe there was a reason for all of it, and he wouldn't turn his back on that now.

"Show me exactly where it happened. I'll take care of the bodies," Arioch said, digging in his pocket and pulling out a small, cloth-wrapped bundle. "And you, take care of this."

Shiron peeled it apart. "Soma?" His lips parted, looking down at the navy and white spotted leaves, his fingers drifting across them softly.

"You know how to treat it?" Arioch asked.

"Yes, but where—" His eyes snapped up. "You went to *Valhara*?"

Arioch's jaw tensed.

"For *this*?" Arioch hadn't gone to Valhara since his mother's death.

"No." He shook his head, clapping on Shiron's shoulder and leading him into his shadows, back to the Kaserne. "Not for that."

And Shiron knew what he meant. He'd gone for *him.* Because Arioch knew Shiron had used it in the past to help himself cope with the suppression.

Chapter 37

Aheia

Aheia rode through the halls on Koutávi's back when Arioch left. She'd seen him dip into a room with Emryn and Shiron and had half a mind to follow. But his tone had been serious, and she was getting tired. She'd push him later.

For now, she was content laying on the ridge of the Varcolac's shadow drawn spine, relishing the stares they got from various demons. Nyco was at her side steadily, reading one of their books as the three of them found their way back to the main atrium. She'd been itching to come here simply because she hadn't seen it since her first breakfast in Aljira. Or had it been lunch?

Aheia had been taking her meals in the common room with Arioch and when she asked why they didn't come here anymore, the Avarice told her that he didn't need others watching him eat. The memory still burned her cheeks, because he wasn't talking about food when he spread her out on that gold table.

The Nephilim lazily roaming around the large space all stared at the Varcolac as they entered and Aheia slipped from her back. She let her fingers draw across the gold basin that nested at the foot of the mountain wall, water dribbling through the cracks and collecting below. There were piles of books stacked next to her, and the walls that broke up the windows were covered in achlys. The flowering plants were so fragrant that they filled the air with the beautiful notes.

Nyco pulled her from the dais, and dragged her over to one of the red couches, where they taught her a new card game that Aheia was terrible at. She lost fifteen pieces of imaginary coin in the first twenty minutes, and Nyco told her she could make it up to them by getting them a drink from the bar cart at the side. There were a ton of syrups and flavors to play with and she decided that the blue was one of her favorites, even though she didn't know what in the world a blue raspberry was supposed to be.

She'd been here before, in this glass prison—a cage of his creation. The sides were short enough to keep her hunched, but everyone could stare inside. He kept it in the courtyard on full display.

Last time he'd left her there for a day. She was forced to remember how she'd lost control of her bowels—how it had smelled under the midday sun when her knees slid against the slick floor.

"I didn't mean to upset you." She scratched against the clear wall as Ophion crouched down with a sick smile twisting his lip.

"I'm sure that's true, and yet here we are." He chuckled. "But I urge you to take this time to reflect on your actions. Sit with the Gods and ask them for forgiveness. They'll tell me when you're ready to be let out."

Aheia's lip trembled, feeling the eyes of their spectators, servants that passed too slowly, wives of Ophion's that only ever mingled here at the center, the Gods damned sun itself.

"I-I—"

"Don't waste your breath, Aheia. You'll need it," he said, clanking the key against the glass. "Besides, it's what's best. You trust that I know that, don't you?"

She grit her teeth, her knees biting into the hard surface underneath, her back already starting to ache at the angle she was forced to kneel.

"It'll make you better. The Gods will see to it."

Waking up didn't feel like a reprieve. Her heart was attempting to leap out of her chest like she was still lacking oxygen, like she was still caged. Aheia blinked, jerking away from the bright light that cut across her face, panic blistering under her skin in a cold sweat. She crawled across the bed, hearing it in her ears.

Clack. Clack. Clack.

Polished, white shoes on marble.

Blue splotches bruised her vision, the same way they did when she stared at the sun for too long and she couldn't separate it. Nothing felt real, nothing but the glass cage and the bright light.

She gasped for air, pulling herself up by the fabric below her until she felt the edge of her mattress and tumbled off the side. Her elbow cracked against the marble because she didn't know what way was up. Shaking fingers tried to find leverage against the slick floor, pulling her body forward on weak limbs. The phantom feeling of someone creeping up behind her made sharp pricks break out across her neck and she scrambled around, her back pressing into the cold marble wall. Her reality bled with her nightmares, white and dark mixing in front of her eyes. An obscured face without features. White wings brushed against the side of her temple and she shot out her hand, hitting herself in an uncoordinated effort to rid herself of the feeling. But it didn't go away, and she scratched her skin, replacing the wings with pain. She did it again, and again, until something stopped her—a tight hold. Panic flared.

"*No!* Get away from me." She scratched with her free hand, trying to claw at the manacle around her wrist. Her vision was still hazy when she peeled back her eyelids, amber light blinding her with its brightness, though some part of her, buried under the blanket of her past, told her it wasn't actually bright. "Not again," she whimpered, throwing out her hand and feeling a surge of power when her fingers connected with skin. She blinked, scraping and clawing, seeing outlines bleed in front of her. Blue eyes, gray eyes, pale skin, shadows. Everything shifted back and forth and back and forth until warm liquid dripped into her mouth.

Her breath stilled as her tongue darted out to taste what had landed on her lips, and then she froze. *Blood.*

Nightmares were traded for clarity, and she could see him now, crouched over her. No more white, no more brightness, no more light leaks.

She could see the world without it tilting on its axis, could move her body the way she wanted to, not a puppet at her mind's behest.

Arioch's gray eyes took the place of Ophion's blue, and Aheia sobbed out the air in her lungs, relief unlacing the vise in her chest slowly.

She was frantic still, as she reached her hands for him, chasing the ache that his blood started in her own. A hunger she didn't know how to feed. Or maybe she did. Maybe that hunger was as second nature to her as the hostility in her own mind. Because when she lapped at the scratch on his neck and more of the liquid welled up on her tongue, the warmth in her abdomen spun. The clarity started to fracture and haze, and dragged her into another fever dream in front of him. His blood dulled her thoughts, and it was relief because they frightened her. Her mind frightened her when the day was bright enough to let her see the insides of it. But here in the shadows, here in the night, she didn't have to look.

That's what she'd been hungry for.

The quiet.

His quiet.

The edges of her vision charred, leaving nothing but them as she trailed her tongue up that vein at his throat, swallowing the feeling until it trickled onto the broken and gasping embers in her belly. It's when she realized his blood was flammable, and it ignited her insides.

His groan sounded like he was the one on fire instead, ribbing through her body in waves that made her knees shake.

But then he pulled away, keeping her at a distance, and she felt unwavering fear for what might happen if he left her here on this floor.

"Don't leave." She held onto his wrist before he could let go of her, a shaking, frail thing. When she was alone, her dreams were strongest, because her reality felt the thinnest. And she didn't want to slide back into it, not now.

His eyes focused on where they connected, on the death grip she had around his hand, and she watched the vein at his temple pulse.

"I won't," he said, his breathing just as out of control as hers.

The taste of his blood was still on her tongue when he cradled her to his chest and picked her off the floor. He carried her into the washroom, and she was glad for the darkness that was broken up only by soft streaks of starlight from outside.

The frenzy had died, even as his blood snaked through her veins—her exhaustion creeping back. She could feel it, the sadness, the fear, the weight on her toes as she slipped through white halls in Keloseros, taking care not to step with her whole sole because someone might hear. It was with her now, all of those emotions that she'd never realized existed, because she'd never *not* felt that way. Not until now, not until here. Now she realized that the constant anxiety, the constant panic, was not how everyone felt all the time. That was learned behavior.

Arioch set her down slowly, only letting go when she put her hands against the marble edge of the tub to steady herself.

"What are you doing?" she asked, voice hoarse but quiet.

"Fixing this," he said, unlatching his holster and draping it over the side of the tub before he reached behind her and twisted the golden knobs. Aheia jumped, hearing the water spurt from the faucet, and her heart leapt into her throat. He walked past her to collect a few bottles, and she took the time to press the heels of her hands into her eyes. *Focus.* She blinked and blinked, trying to put herself back together, but everything felt fractured and hazy and it wasn't just his blood. It always felt that way when she woke from her terrors.

The ground is cold.

The night is blue.

The large tub was filling with water and the starlight reflected off the placid parts that weren't soapy. Steam rose from its surface and she smelled the citrus and floral scents that Arioch poured into it.

The air smells warm and ... clean.

She unsheathed one of his blades, pressing the pad of her finger against the center ridge. She'd never sat with one or inspected it, but the carvings on the handle of the one she'd chosen looked similar to her gold one.

The metal is hard.

But before she could list a fifth thing, Arioch was back, undressing her slowly, while she stared at the alcove next to them. It seemed this was becoming a theme: her distraught and him fixing it with water.

When she was naked, he lifted her into the tub, and she hissed as the hot water ate her up. It burned, but not because of the temperature he'd chosen. Instead it burned because her skin was made of ice.

His hands folded around her ribcage as he settled her back against the slope, squeezing her softly.

"Tell me what he did to you." His voice was too calm, too controlled, but the edge was unmistakable. It was worse than the anger. It was calculated. And the question cracked through the silence like a whip.

Aheia wiped her palm across her cheeks and shook her head as he brought his hands from the soapy water.

"Don't make it real." She inhaled sharply because the air in here was thick and it became hard to breathe. "It's not real now, just a nightmare. I can handle those."

His jaw tensed again. "Hiding yourself won't make any of it go away."

"Neither would chasing a snake that bit me to ask it why as I lay dying."

"You don't have to chase the snake, Aheia. I've done that for you."

She swallowed the lump in her throat. *I know. I'm not ready.* It was on the tip of her tongue, but she couldn't say it.

They were both silent as she mapped the stars on the surface of the water and he busied himself with her hair. She'd been staring so intently that she didn't realize he was washing the white strands until she felt the cold gel he worked into her scalp.

"You like my hair," she whispered.

He didn't answer.

"You cut off someone's hand for it." She dripped water across the surface, making it ripple. "Hand for hair, kill for kiss..." His fingers pressed against the nape of her neck and she felt the pain fissure up her entire spine, not because he held too tight, but because the knot there inflamed when he prodded. "Did you know that the *Bradach* got all hard for alliteration?" It was something she'd read in one of the books and it felt so amusing—the image of big, burly pirates having a thing for wordsmithery. "They'd like the work you do." She let her eyes close for a moment. "They say hair holds memories; isn't that an odd thought?" The weight on her body pressed her back into his hands as he cleaned off the soap with warm water.

"I wonder if it remembers the things I can't." Her exhale was long and soft. "I don't remember much from my life—almost nothing from when I was really young. That's not normal, is it? Thinking about your young self and her not having a face?" She didn't look for confirmation. "It's like I don't let myself see. She feels foreign." Arioch guided her head back against the marble, and moved to sit on the side of the tub, dipping under its surface and pulling out her right leg. A hiss broke from her lips when he rubbed over her sore calf, eyes tied to hers even when she looked away. "I don't even know who she was, what she was like, how she acted. I don't *know* her." It was hard to explain because she knew how absurd it all sounded. She'd already experienced that time in her life. It had all already happened; it wasn't some elusive *what if* scenario in the future. And yet, she was a stranger to herself. "It feels like she's still hanging on inside of me though—trying her hardest to get my attention because she's hurt and confused, and I can't even turn around to look at her, don't really know how." Her skin pebbled as Arioch untied another knot. "She should have had a different life. She deserved to be young because everyone does ... but I don't remember ever being young, I don't remember ever not being ... this."

Her words dripped from her like her tears, even though she'd had no plan on sharing any of that. But his kindness—it had always made her feel unsure of herself, and when she was unsure of herself, she filled silence with her words.

"You know her, Aheia."

"I *don't*," she grit through her teeth, anger swirling in her gut now. He was placating her.

It was easy to regurgitate words and boring, she was sure, to hear about someone else's trauma. But it still hurt. Dismissal was what she was used to.

"Not remembering is a kindness. It's how you're still alive."

Aheia chewed on the inside of her cheek and focused with everything she had on the fingers he drifted over four of the only scars on her right leg.

"Our minds pick vicious ways to protect us, and those blank spaces in your memory are there because one time, long ago, yours decided that you couldn't survive your reality without a little help. So, it wiped experiences, it fuzzied pictures, all but some of the worst, and some of the best. It built walls to hold you together, and distorted faces to keep you sane—let you survive when everything else was trying to kill you.

"The young version of you—you know her because she knows you. Who you are now"—she felt the warmth seep in where he held her—"is who she would have needed then. It's who she would have felt safe around when she wasn't safe with anyone else."

Aheia's heart stuttered over itself, and new, hot tears fell down her cheeks.

Oh.

He wasn't placating her at all.

Her fingers shook under the water.

He'd given her an answer, a true answer to a question that never felt like it had one.

Her lip trembled as she sat there, a swell of emotions washing across her that she didn't know how to handle. It got worse and worse in a way she wasn't used to and she had to look away from him because she felt soft and pitiful, and she was starting to tremble.

Hold it together, she hissed at herself, but she couldn't help it. She broke apart. She could feel it, one by one, the building blocks she'd tried so hard to stack on top of each other slipping and sliding from her grasp and tumbling, each one dragging her down with it. Deep. Deep. So deep she couldn't breathe and the next inhale she took was a gasp. The tears flooded now, like the spout of the tub, and those sounds she usually suppressed in her chest, or suffocated with a pillow cut into the room. It was jarring. Just her breath, her gasps and her sorrows, as she cradled her hands to her chest, stripped bare, truly, for the first time she could remember. Her sobs thundered in her own ears and her lips parted, spit dripping when she couldn't swallow.

Why?

She cried, and she asked the question over and over again, because she didn't understand. Why her? What had she done to warrant her past? She'd been small, it hadn't been her fault, had it?

The water sloshed around her, his warmth pressing in on all sides as he pulled her into his embrace. She buried her face in his chest, and knocked down the rest of those walls on her own, because the ones that remained were paper thin to begin with.

It felt like hours passed by them, and she cried until her voice was hoarse, spilling the grief into the water around her. Would it taint him? Would he use it against her when the stars stayed, but the day drew past them?

"I don't want to be weak," she choked out, knowing how it would sound ... the truth. "I want people to be afraid of hurting me. But no one's ever been afraid to hurt me. It always seemed to come easy."

Her body was shivering with exhaustion, her mind starting to ache with the pressure that came with losing so many tears.

"Having a feeling heart in a cruel world is not a weakness." He said it against her temple, a quiet whisper that was meant for only her. "Keep that part of you soft and guarded, helfyre. The ones who let themselves turn to stone are brittle in their hardness." All the names in the world and all she wanted was to hear the one he hadn't called her since Keloseros. "Achlys bends in the wind, but that doesn't take away from how deadly it is."

She sat there stunned as he peeled himself from her to wade across and reach for a glass that stood at the edge of the vanity, filling it with water, and her eyes slid across his back, truly looking for the first time. It was covered in ink, but she saw the scars. Her lips parted, but it wasn't in surprise at the letters that were scattered across his skin. It was for the lines—lines she knew all too well because she had them too. The scars of his past. They were all layered with the black, and it was hard to see them unless the light shone at the right angle. But she saw them now.

And she realized then, without asking, that he knew what words to tell her because he knew how she felt. The intangible thing she'd been trying so hard to describe, he knew.

His body settled next to hers again, and he fed her the cold liquid, while she rubbed over her nose, trying to clean up the snot that had drained from it. He helped with that too, cleaning her face with his fingers.

She watched horrified as he wiped her snot on a towel nearby and returned his fingers to brush down the skin with his wet thumb.

Please stop. It was too kind. She was already having a hard time separating all of her wires.

"How did you know I was—" *having a nightmare.* She swallowed, letting herself sink against his chest. "Why were you in my room?"

"You weren't in mine."

"You weren't either." She'd looked, just for a moment before she disappeared to hers.

"Where were you?" She watched his muscles flex and pull, the ink moving again, and she was starting to consider that maybe it wasn't ink at all, that it was magyck instead. It

looked too alive not to be.

He stayed silent for a moment, but that exhaustion cut deeper by the second, she could see it in his eyes, the way the light here threw shadows underneath them.

"I was with Kazim," he said and she held her breath when he did. For all of her flighty tendencies, it felt like a single exhale could remind him that he didn't want to talk about his own past. But she wanted him to, she wanted to know, to understand.

"How is he?"

"The same."

Aheia considered dropping the questions altogether, but she wanted to know, and more than that, she wanted to see if he'd share with her if she asked.

She tipped her chin, leaning it against his chest. "Were you two close?"

"At one time," he said, his voice thick, gaze stuck on the opposite wall.

"What happened?"

His eyes dropped away, his shadows mingling with the water now and for a moment she thought he'd stay that way—silent. "Our mother died."

The breath she was holding was starting to stretch her lungs.

"And without her, there was nothing left to remind us who we were to each other. Not when we were forced to fight for our father's favor, too young to know that we should have fought him instead."

Our father wasn't satisfied with the idea that the eldest would take over as Alshaytan. He wanted the strongest. That meant forcing us to fight each other. The words echoed in her mind, and that sour taste returned to her tongue.

"How did she die?" She chanced the question, holding her breath and waiting for him to tell her that she shouldn't ask.

"She was an addict." He said. "She had been for a long time—for most of Kazim and I's life. It almost felt normal ..." He trailed off. "To have her questioning her reality, to have her crying at the stars and starving herself. Her lucid moments were worse than when she was drifting because it gave us hope. We held onto that hope for a long time." Aheia noticed something she'd thought she'd seen at breakfast when he spoke about Malia. A softness. She saw the hurt, too, and recognized it because she felt it in her own way. "She had moments in which she was aware enough to want to change, to want to stop." His eyes grew darker. "And one day, she *did* change. She did stop. She was sober for almost an entire week. Kazim and I managed to sneak her out of the compound and into the city to one of the markets, and it felt real. It felt like she wouldn't fall back into her habit this time."

"But ..." Aheia's heart sank.

"She overdosed the next day." She could feel the flinch in her veins though she held its reins tightly.

"Do you visit her? Does she have a grave, or Gehenna? Can you see her there?" She wasn't at all sure how it worked.

"No." His eyebrows pleated. "Any tribute to her or carved likeness was deemed an affront to her memory and was forbidden. Sahren burned her body instead of taking her to Gehenna. It was a whole spectacle. He feigned that it was out of respect, a way to honor her and send her to 'Amm gracefully." His lip twitched again, anger deepening the pain on his face. "I know better than that. It was all for our benefit—to punish us, to teach us a lesson."

Us. Him and Kazim.

"He kept us from her in every way he could because when we'd had her—" He cleared his throat, wiping his fingers over his mouth. Aheia adjusted on his lap and crawled closer. Her fingertips touched his jaw as she leaned into him, needing the nearness, needing to see everything he was giving her now. He might have had her under his knife a few nights ago, but this felt the same. Except she didn't use a blade to cut into him.

"When you had her?" she coaxed quietly, eyes darting across his face. It was the first time she'd seen this kind of sadness from him. A crack in that marble, one she could peek through, maybe even reach a hand into. It helped her wrangle her own.

His arm wound around her, pulling her against his chest like he needed her weight just like she needed his.

"We knew each other," he finished, his inhales deeper now, like he was trying to temper something. "Kazim and I became strangers before the age of fifteen. We're strangers now too."

She inhaled his air, and she let the comfort of his demons wrap around her. It made her own quiet down, and she needed more. *You are not good.* Good creatures didn't act like this, didn't take someone else's pain and mute their own with it.

"Is that when you started fighting?"

"We'd been fighting far longer."

But that's when they lost her. It's when they didn't have that safety any longer.

"You killed him for it, your father?" she asked, watching those gray eyes so carefully that she thought she saw the softest tinge of red.

"I should have killed him the moment he gave me a blade and told me to turn it on my brother," he said, and his voice was all gravel, those embers flaring in his eyes. "I was foolish to think that being his offspring meant anything but strength for his bloodline."

"It *should* have meant more," she said quietly, her breathing matching his as another tear slid down her face. "You were young. You shouldn't have known what it felt like to be a pawn, what it felt like to hurt someone you loved against your will."

"*Should* doesn't exist." His eyes drew down to that treacherous tear track on her cheek.

"No, it doesn't." It felt like they'd steeped themselves in the same pain together. But at least they weren't alone in it.

She wiggled closer, brushing her lips over his when he stilled her.

"I don't like kissing." He gripped her hips after a beat of silence, keeping her in place. "It's *work*—how I take souls." Aheia tried to pull away, but his hands were ironclad. "But I can't stop thinking about kissing you."

The balloon in her chest expanded once again, until it hurt, until it stretched her. "Stop thinking," she whispered, tugging at his bottom lip with her teeth.

Chapter 38

Aheia

He comforted her, and she didn't know how to return the favor, not in the same way. Because *shouldn't* didn't exist, and the past was cemented. But she hoped that this was some semblance of it.

An offering of escape.

It was only the second real kiss they'd shared since she came back, unless she counted the moment he licked come from her mouth, but somehow it felt like their first. His tongue tangled with hers and his teeth pulled at her lips, his heavy hands pressing her lower back down against his lap, the water holding them both. *Gods*, he kissed like he fucked, demanding and all-consuming and she couldn't get enough. She was drunk on it, rubbing herself over his hardening cock like a feral animal. Her clit massaged his hot skin, the smooth friction broken up by the veins running up his shaft, and she couldn't help the noises it elicited from her.

Their kiss turned bruising as he pushed one of his hands between them, forcing her hips back enough so he could fist his cock, his knuckles pumping up and down, replacing his soft feel with ridged bones. She gasped, arching her back as he fucked himself and worked her closer to the edge of an empty orgasm in the same stroke. Their slick bodies moved messily, and the wetness of the water fought her own.

"Lift your hips for me," he said, slapping the head of his cock against her clit, the soft impact pulsing little bursts of lightning into her abdomen. It fed the building storm there, and she couldn't help trying to chase him back, not nearly enough of him touching her the way she needed it to.

"Make me," she gasped out on instinct. The sentence left her mouth before her mind could decide it was a bad idea. It caught up quick though when he looked down at her from below dark lashes. *Knives.* Fucking knives, those eyes.

"Repeat that," he said much too calmly. The reaction he pulled from her was like bees buzzing the entirety of her spine, the hum in her veins throbbing with every heartbeat.

"You heard me," she panted, deciding she was fucked either way.

He wet his bottom lip. "If you don't wrap that pussy around my cock in the next second, I'll *make* you lay that pretty ass across my lap so that I can fix your fucking attitude."

She bit her bottom lip, suppressing a groan as she rocked her hips and did what she was told. Some other time she'd push, because she wanted that too, wanted his hands on her skin like that. But right now, she was just so fucking empty. Empty and sad, and he looked the same. *I need it.* Her thighs parted further as she leaned forward on his chest, her hands twisted in his hair.

She froze, the muscles in her thighs rigid as his cock probed her slowly, just enough to remind her of his size. It was a tease, a promise and a threat all wrapped in one orgasm-inducing package.

His jaw looked like it was about to crack before he released a quivering breath that sounded a lot like restraint. Her heart pounded in her ears when one of his hands gripped her neck and squeezed. It was a warning, that if she didn't move, he'd do it for her. And she wanted him to, wanted it to hurt. She looked at him with pleading eyes, and everything shifted between them. The determined version of her slipped through her fingers and was replaced. She didn't know the new Aheia well, but she felt a lot like her secret—the one who needed help. The soft one.

"Every inch, Aheia." She choked on his words as he sank deeper and she whimpered, gazing up with desperate eyes.

"I need—I can't—"

His demeanor hardened as she softened, and so did his hold.

"If you don't give me what I want right the fuck now, I'll take it from you."

He let go of her neck, one of his hands landing on the marble beside them in a grip that turned his knuckles white, as he pushed her down another inch.

"Oh fuck, it's too much." She gasped as he split her apart, her legs quivering with the strain to keep them parted this wide. Too much is exactly what she wanted. What she *wanted*, not just what she needed. *Dangerous.* A dangerous difference.

"I know you can take it." His voice was thick as honey, his fingers bruising her now, his cock burrowing deep. "Fucking ride it."

So *real*. Always real when everything else felt blurry.

He was shaking just like her, his hand on the tub holding tight, the other grasped tightly in her hair while she slid her cunt up his length, feeling the molten lust flutter against every inch of skin he touched. If she could have stayed in this moment forever, she would. Because no matter how fucked up it was, his pain fed her. It was running down her throat and warming her chest and ... she felt like she mattered. Like her body did something for him that no one else could.

She remembered the scars on his back and felt herself respond to that image with a hot wave of pleasure that threatened to turn her stomach. Because it was fucked up. *You're not good.* She choked on the thought.

He was right when he'd bared her fears to her—when he'd told her she was scared of the dark little urges that sat just below her skin; that she was scared of who she might become if she stopped stifling herself.

And now she knew that her fear was warranted. Because she *liked* the pain in his eyes. She was getting off on it.

You're a monster.

"Harder," she grit through her teeth. *Hurt me, make me pay for this.* His fingers dug into the side of her face, his lips bared, dangerous eyes keeping her pinned as he thrust inside of her to the point of pain.

Aheia whimpered, a fucking mess of nothing but feeling and noises she didn't recognize.

"Tell me again how you're not my toy," he growled, swatting her cheek, just enough to make the edge of her jaw prickle with warm little needles. *Oh.*

"Do that again," she gasped, his cock hammering into her pussy, and she swore to fuck she could feel him in her Gods damned throat.

A sharp sting hit her face, his callused palm cracking against her skin hard enough to snap her head to the side. Oh, *fuck.*

"Tell me you don't like the place I'm putting you into when you do such a *good fucking job* of being my whore."

She shook her head, words nowhere near possible as the wet heat of his tongue trailed across the burning flesh of her cheek, soothing it while he kept his pace punishing, one hand secure around her throat to keep her in place. He was fucking her now, all him, and she couldn't move let alone form words in an order that made sense. Even less so when he hit her again, the pain shooting through her like lightning.

His shadows coiled around her limbs and it felt like release when they touched her, like they needed her too. Arioch's groan was choked and his thrusts became wilder, messy, and even his shadows seemed to stutter. It was like they wanted to seep into her skin and claim her insides—make them one when they couldn't be. The need for it shared between them, urging them on. Her hand twisted in his curls, and the spit dripped down her chin, while the tears of pleasure she was crying now washed away those that had been shed in sadness.

Her eyes rolled to the back of her head, and she closed them until he gripped her chin and pulled her back down toward him. "Keep your eyes on me while I fuck you."

She rolled her lip between her teeth.

"You can use me to escape, but you don't get to escape me."

The air failed her and she gasped as he slammed her hips down on top of him.

"I'm the only one who knows how to make you feel this way," he growled against her lips and she nodded frantically, feeling herself trip closer to her orgasm. "Tell me."

"You're the only one who knows how," she repeated, her back arching, his stomach pressing into her abdomen while his cock massaged that spot inside of her that made her shiver.

"This pussy is mine."

"Yours." She didn't need prompting.

He dug in his fingers, keeping her mouth against his as she parted her lips. "Fuck, Ari, I'm gonna—" It felt like panic, as she curled, her insides spasming around his cock, her clit grinding down against him.

"That orgasm's mine too," he growled, biting her neck while he met her hips brutally. "Give it to me, Aheia."

Her head fell back, his teeth sharp against her nape, the darkness behind her eyelids bursting with little light leaks.

"Harder, hurt me, Ari," she gasped, tugging on his hair, urging him closer, and he didn't need coaxing.

Her skin broke, and she cried out, the muscles she had been tensing going lax. She barely managed to keep her arms around him, but it didn't matter, because when she went limp, he held her. He *took* and her mind was blank.

She was boneless, nothing but nerves and water and tears and blood as he stole every bit of what she offered him for himself with an empty mind. A mind that was static save for the one thought that pulsed in her skull—the one that told her she didn't recognize herself now either and wondered when she'd become this new version.

Aheia didn't know when they stopped.

She didn't remember falling asleep either, but the nightmares stayed far away from her when she drifted--a deep, starless sleep that she only roused from when Arioch latched the door to her room. She blinked up at him, but neither of them spoke as he passed the bed and walked into the washroom with red blood dripping from him.

Red blood.

Aheia crawled out from under the sheets, already sore, and followed him, helping him wash the blood from his hands.

"He's healing," Arioch said, meeting her gaze in her mirror. "You'll be able to see him soon."

Her throat tightened. She hadn't asked about Ophion, because she was scared. A big part of her wanted to leave it behind, a big part of her wanted to just forget it ever happened. It would have been easier if Arioch just killed him. But it didn't seem that easy was an option here.

"You could have had him healed," she said, her voice thick. "You didn't."

"I'll never give him that kind of comfort." His wet hands cupped her chin and the gray of his pupils leaked black drips. "It's ok not to remember your life just as it's ok to remember it. Neither gives your past any less weight, and neither will keep me from helping you with your revenge."

Chapter 39

Aheia

The next few days were filled with books, and with Nyco because she'd snagged them from the Kaserne when she was bored. She liked their presence, and they didn't seem to mind hers either. Aheia told Arioch that she didn't want them to hang around as a guard, because he'd been right; she liked Nyco. She didn't want them to be there on any kind of orders.

Noctua had made herself a nest at the far side of the room and Aheia helped her cushion it with a few of the white pillows she'd ripped apart and bolstered against the windowsill.

She was well aware that she was living here like she *lived* here. And she didn't want to think past that. The prideful part of her wanted to gather her strength and leave, just to appease her choice in the matter. But the parts of her that had started to feel an odd comfort didn't mind standing still.

"No, it's *ghabiun*," Nyco dragged out the word slowly and smoothly, looking down at the book in Aheia's lap.

"I don't think *idiot* is the most important word to focus on."

"Oh, I disagree."

She shot them the look that statement deserved. "Why are there so many odd tense changes?"

They snorted. "Because someone, a long time ago, thought they had all the answers."

"It's derived from a mortal language, isn't it?" Aheia asked.

"Yea, but it's since been twisted by misunderstanding and improvised wording. In the unlikely scenario where you'd find yourself in one of the cities that spoke the language, they'd have a difficult time understanding you, if at all." They looked up from their read. "Lujha's hard because there's the correct way to speak it, and then there's how everyone actually speaks it. So, once you think you have all the rules down, I'll prove you wrong and teach you how to sound like a Nephilim."

"Can we jump to that?"

"No," they dismissed her quickly. "Learn the basics."

She rolled her eyes, thumbing through one of the blue books she'd stacked on her left bedside table—the ones she could read in the bridge language. The title read *Gemstones* in gold letters.

The paper held images of different stones, with their color, luster, and crystal stems inscribed below. There was a lot more information, paragraphs and paragraphs for each gem, with details about where they were found, what they meant—what magyck systems they spoke to even. She flipped past countless pictures: amethyst, umbrite, orydite, meteorite, fae stone, and then—she found it.

Hers.

Its picture stared up at her from discolored and fragile paper.

Lápis

Blue

Greasy, Vitreous.

Her lips parted as she skated across the text.

> *The semi-precious gemstone is found in all the realms, one of the most common populating this world. It's deep celestial blue honed the symbolism for royalty, honor, the Gods' truth, power, spirit, and vision—A universal symbol for wisdom and truth. It is compatible with magyck across the realms, from Lujha to Gjóssa to Calmani and even some mortal Heretics are known to use it in their enchantments.*

"You know anything about this?" She propped up the book.

They squinted at the page. "Why?"

She furrowed her brows. "Just curious."

"Common, I think." Nyco shrugged, returning to their own text.

A sliver of sadness cut through her. It didn't make much sense, but she missed the stone. It had, at one time in her life, felt comforting.

Aheia spread her fingers over the old pages one last time, outlining the small blue shape with her pads, before closing it again and pulling near another two books.

The Fire-scarred Land

Astronomy: Lyria, Aljira, Beyond

"Astronomy ..." she read out loud, turning the word over in her mind. "What is that?"

"It's a mortal word we've adopted." Nyco nodded down at it. "It's a book about the stars here. I think it talks about how they compare to Lyria's stars as well, but I haven't read it in a few years."

Aheia hesitated a moment before she let the text fall open on a random page and her face fell for a second. "I can't read this,"

Nyco got up from their place and walked over to her, glancing at the words. "*Sova:* A constellation that was attributed to 'Amm's owls." Her eyes drifted down the page to a picture of the sky with neat little red lines drawn through it. "Sova exists in Aljira, spotted eons ago amongst the Snake and Moth constellation. However, they have never been spotted in Lyria."

Moth. Something soft brushed against her mind.

"Why are your constellations being compared to Lyria's?"

"Knowing about how the stars vary from Lyria to Aljira gave us answers about the realms and their structures." They drew their finger down the page. "There are differences in our internal energies—our genetic makeup. Those differences are the reason we can't use certain magyck in certain pockets of space. We live on a specific energetic plane in Aljira, one that is lower than Keloseros. It's why Mithra can't use their Brite magyck here and vice versa-- why Nephilim can't use Dark magyck there, with few exceptions. Lyria is the same. It sits higher than us and lower than Keloseros, but not by much, and it's why our magyck works in the mortal realm, though its effects are dulled."

"Different planes, like parallels?"

Nyco shook their head. "No, parallels are separate universes. They can't simply be stepped in and out of like realms."

Aheia nodded slowly, looking at the *Snake* constellation on the next page, the titles were written in multiple translations.

"What significance does the Snake hold? I'm guessing these three are highlighted here for a purpose?" She raised her eyebrows, considering how many constellations there had to be past their windows.

"It is the primal symbol of fertility and the power of female blood. It symbolizes the immortal circle of life created by 'Amm for each Nephilim."

"In Keloseros, the snake is a bad omen," she murmured. "Something to be killed on sight, because if it's left alive, it could cause harm."

Nyco regarded her for a moment, those hazel eyes warm. "It seems our snake lore might be linked then. Two sides of the same coin."

Aheia tilted her head.

"Tell me about the females in your realm."

"Not *my* realm," Aheia said quickly, and Nyco's lip twitched. It had never felt that way ... Hers. Not really.

"My mistake."

"No, it's—" She tamped down the apology that threatened to spill out of her. "Females in Keloseros ..." she trailed off. "Their existence depends on their house and their family. Some have a quiet and nice life ..." *Others get traded in political strategy, others are married to monsters, and others are killed for their beliefs.* She cleared her throat, deciding to focus on something general. "They're taught—selectively. Would be allowed to learn certain vocations with the help of books and a few teachers, but wouldn't be allowed to practice them past that. The Mithra High court likes to pretend that there is a choice—like they are generous, but then they snap doors shut just as quickly."

"Same coin, different side," Nyco said pointedly, and she supposed they were right. The snake symbolized eternal life and feminine power here, but to the Mithra, it was the need to oppress exactly that.

"Moths," they continued before she could ask. "They are a sign of rebirth. It's said that an eclipse of them haloed the moon when 'Amm gave her life to cage Manāt."

"And owls?" Aheia asked. "In your world?"

"Owls have always been the Harbingers of death."

Harbingers of death.

"The lore tells us that 'Amm planted dark seeds within each of them, the kinds that flower when death is near, that call to the birds just like magyck calls to us."

"For what purpose?" Aheia asked, eyes meeting Noctua's across the room.

"A warning."

That astronomy book came in handy. It taught Aheia something interesting—that the stars outside *didn't* stay still. They weren't at all timeless. They *rotated.* She'd simply assumed that they stayed in the forever patterns, when in fact they moved. Out in the citrus grove, she paid attention to where one of the larger, maroon colored stars hung in the morning—the kind that was big enough to stand out amongst the others. When that same star rotated its way past the fifth tree from the entrance of the Kaserne wall, it was evening. It wasn't an exact science, but it was something.

When Aheia left the grove to head back to the compound, it was late afternoon, if her theory was correct. She'd lost track of how long she'd lounged out there and for a while, Koutávi joined her, silently sleeping on the ground next to the tree Aheia had climbed in her red, cotton pants. Red like blood. She had stains on her fingertips from sharing a blood fruit with the Varcolac, and decided that sour was one of her favorite flavors. She'd been eating more because she was hungry, and the two times she tried to train in her room on an empty stomach, she'd nearly passed out.

On her way through the halls, she cradled a thick book in her arms. It was a story about masked vigilantes that roamed streets and used single code names to identify each other. Koutávi's large snout was in her peripheral as she stepped through the vortex and found herself on the familiar marble of the compound.

It was relaxing, diving into all of the old stories. There were true and fictional accounts of hundreds and hundreds of creatures, all of which had lived through insane journeys. One of the most recent books she'd gotten lost in was the second volume of Aljira's history. Her favorite part was when it dove into details of different species. The most fascinating thing she'd learned was that some were born with *ejiam* names—second names imprinted across a creature's bones at birth. When she asked Lúc about it, he'd told her that it was lore adapted into history because of the novelty of it more than provable truth. It was said that back when the Gods were present at the birth of their younglings, 'Amm would whisper their true names into the stars, a new constellation forming with it. But at the end of the night, there was no way to truly know or prove the validity of it.

It didn't matter to Aheia. She loved the idea. She'd believe it.

Walking around on her own still felt borderline uncomfortable. She knew she was free to do as she pleased, but it was hard to shake those old feelings that had imprinted themselves inside of her from Keloseros.

There was an odd sense of trepidation in her veins as she considered that somewhere below her feet, her old life still sat caged. She'd almost asked about Ophion so many times. He was just *down* there and the thought tightened her stomach. She knew she could see him if she wanted to, but she realized pretty quickly that she didn't.

Not yet.

She was afraid of the potential. If Arioch took her back down, she might get answers to questions she'd been wanting to ask all her life. But could she handle it? Would she panic?

Her bedding was blue now, because she liked how it matched the night sky, and the black book in her hands blended when she threw it onto the mattress, heading for the washroom.

She felt like a new creature when she stepped from the water, finally managing to peel all the sticky pieces of flowering orange plants from her skin. Her hair was still drying, and she'd just managed to slip on silk undergarments when she felt the shiver in her veins. Arioch couldn't sneak up on her, not anymore, not when she vibrated when he was near.

"What's this for?" she asked, as he dropped a mess of pearls into her arms. They were a soft pink, and there were far too many of them to be just a necklace. Picking them up felt heavy.

"There's a dinner tonight."

"What for?" she asked.

"Occasionally I have to show my face."

"Is that your very official way of inviting me?"

His eyes sparkled.

"And this is—" She held up the strings in question, unsure of what to make of it.

"A dress."

"This is *not* a dress." Aheia tilted her head, poking her fingers through the gaps. "It's ... pearls."

A soft smirk tugged at his mouth as he returned his hands to his pockets, and Aheia couldn't help her shameless leering at him in his dress clothes. All black, the only color he seemed to own, and those silver rings he'd put in her mouth a week ago, a glinting reminder on his hands. He wore a few chains, and his hair was the oddest combination of messy and tamed, pulled back into a loose bun.

He didn't explain himself further. Instead, he swiped the dress from her hands and peeled it apart like there was no question about where each thread was meant to go. Her breath hitched, the warm prickles that spread across her skin whenever he was around dancing down her arms.

Arioch helped guide her legs through different loops and she scrambled to grab his shoulder for balance when he dipped down and helped move her feet through the strings.

She swallowed, her heart still racing unnaturally fast as he dragged the pearls up her body slowly, keeping his eyes on hers.

Then, when it sat heavy on her shoulders, he put his hands on her hips and twisted her toward the mirror.

Her lips parted.

Wow.

The pearl strands stretched across her chest, just enough to cover her, while little slivers of her skin showed along her ribs. They draped down her stomach and around her waist to the back, which was mostly open, and then slung around her hips.

"Pink?" She looked up at him, absentmindedly rubbing her fingers across the little imperfect orbs over her abdomen. The friction was delicious, kneading her in all the right places.

"I like the color on you."

"You've never seen me wear pink."

His eyes darkened when he brushed his knuckles up the column of her neck and leaned in. Just inches from her mouth, he stole her breath, and she felt the warmth spark between them. They were close enough for her to get lost in the memory of his tongue, of his lips, of how they felt. Of his shadows, *Gods,* of his *knife.*

"Sure I have." His voice was thick as he forced her chin back to the mirror.

The air rushed from her lungs when she looked at herself again, light pink splotches peppering across her skin—up her neck, down her arms, and across the bridge of her nose—the same hue as the pearls.

All she managed was something between a surprised huff and a sound she couldn't give a name to. She touched parts of the inflamed skin, yellow imprints left behind when she pulled back her hand. *For fuck's sake.*

"I look naked."

She rolled her lips between her teeth, meeting his reflection again, but Arioch wasn't smiling. He was fixated on her mouth with a stare that felt predatory and calculating.

"Only if you blush for me." And that statement alone made the heat in her cheeks flare worse.

"Fucking sadist."

"Not quite. I like both," he purred, taking a step forward and forcing her pelvic bone against the marble.

She rolled her lips between her teeth, focusing on the slow healing scars on his cheek.

"And yet, I'm the only one bleeding." The cuts all across her body burned with her words.

His eyes narrowed, and she watched as he worked open his shirt, one button at a time.

"What are you—*ahh*!" She shrieked when he picked her up and sat her back against the vanity, the pearls digging into her ass uncomfortably. "... doing?"

He bared his chest, shrugging the shirt back on his arms, and stepping between her thighs, which widened instinctually to make room for his size.

"Return the favor, helfyre."

She dug her teeth into her bottom lip for a moment, grazing down the thick muscle of his chest. *Helfyre.* He'd been calling her that a lot, more than anything else, and she liked it. But there was a part of her that wanted *Ruhí* back. Maybe that wasn't what she was to him anymore, now that he didn't have her soul.

She shook the thought from her head and shoved the twinge in her stomach out of sight, grazing her nails over his abdomen. It had become her favorite activity, because his stomach contracted, like she'd hit him. It took nothing to make him shudder there.

Aheia shimmied closer, licked across one of his scars as he gripped the back of her neck with a heavy hand. Her legs wrapped around his hips slowly and she nipped at the muscle of his shoulder with tentative movements.

But before she could bite the way she wanted to, he hauled her up to the column of his throat. Her eyes snapped up to his, lips brushing over that vein that bared itself when his neck flexed.

"Your shirt won't cover that," she breathed, grazing across his heartbeat.

"Stop fucking talking," he groaned, grasping at her thigh with his free hand, yanking her against him until they were flush. She gasped, feeling him twitch between her legs, pressing his hard cock against her core. He shifted, rubbing himself against her cunt in tight circles. *Oh, fuck me.*

Her legs fell apart further, her body sparking as her clit throbbed when she bared her teeth, and dug them into his skin. The sound he made was more animal than anything fucking else, and his pulse drummed against her tongue as she bit down hard, feeling the flesh give. His blood welled hot and wet, filling her mouth like syrup. Her nerve endings sparked, and her body warmed further, with the high it provided as she latched on like a parasite.

The friction he offered mixed with the madness of his blood made her tremble. She couldn't help the jerk of her hips, or the muffled little moan she lost against his skin as he massaged her close and closer to—

"Oh, fuck, I'm going to—" She broke away from him, her body shivering and shaking. A soft orgasm frayed her edges out of nowhere. *What the fuck.*

"Good fucking girl," he rasped as he cradled her forehead against his chest. "Fuck, I needed that."

Another instance of that exact wording that had her stunned silent. *I needed that.* She wanted him to need her.

They stayed like that for a heartbeat longer and Aheia licked up the blood, feeling it go right to her head.

"Leave it," he said, smearing the hot liquid across her lips. "It'll clot." And then he did up his shirt, while Aheia stared at the small imprint of black against the side of his neck. *Her* mark. They matched now, except hers was cleaned and bandaged.

After he fixed his appearance, he backed away from her, nodding back at her room and disappearing through the door, leaving her shivering on the marble.

She let herself down slowly, meeting her gaze in the mirror. The blue of her eyes was bright, and she felt her chest ease a fraction.

Her eyes. And her white hair and her confused expression while his imprint stretched across her in pink hues, his hands still on her insides even though he wasn't near her. She swallowed, trying to steady her breathing, and work down the inflammation by busying herself with the gold dagger that lay on the other end of the vanity. The gold holster tightened around her skin, and she secured it until it pinched. There was still something about that pain, about that reminder of its weight, that felt calming.

When she looked less like her dress and more like a ghost, she headed out of the room. Arioch was leaning against the wall, waiting for her to get close before he reached into his pocket and brought back a closed fist. Aheia looked at him in question but he only waited, keeping his hand suspended between the two of them. She inhaled slowly, brushing her fingers across his and he opened for her then, revealing what was in his palm.

Her heart climbed up her throat.

What?

"Wait." It was more of an exhale than a word.

There in his hand sat her mother's blue gem stone. The Solas made the surface look almost liquid, the light pooling on it smoothly save for the crack down the center. The lápis was dipped in gold, attached by a delicate chain. "Where did you get this?"

She took it between shaky fingers, turning it over and over because for a moment, it didn't feel real, didn't feel possible.

"It was buried in your hand the night you came back to me."

She caressed the little broken crack and her chest ached once again, as if she herself was split down the center.

"You made it into a necklace for me?" She looked up at him, unable to keep any semblance of a poised expression in front of him now.

"Shiron's good with metalwork," he said simply, taking the delicate strings from her and clasping them behind her neck, before threading her hair out of the way.

She blinked down at it, her eyes burning, completely out of words.

"What does it mean to you?" he asked after a moment of silence.

"It's just sentimental. My mamá's stone." She shrugged. "I feel her with me when I have it close. I get to remember her." Aheia shook her head, unable to look away from the blue crack. "She was beautiful, but looked nothing like me. She was the opposite really—dark hair, tall stature. But I have her eyes." She grimaced at the thought of the shared feature. "She used to tell me stories, read me books about faraway places, about unimaginable adventures and sights." *Another crux.* "We pretended to be there when she read, talked about how we would lie in Alancia's meadows or climb Sekha's tallest mountains—before they crumbled, of course. It was those little pockets of peace that kept us sane, I think. It's the last thing I have to prove she ever existed." Her teeth dug into the side of her cheek, dimpling it. "I don't even have our magyck now." The light that all Dioscuri shared.

"Tell me what happened to it."

The request steeped them into warm and heavy air and she realized she'd never told him about that day, not really. She assumed the same rumors that had spread about her disappearance also spoke of her lack of light. After all, she'd never used it in defense.

"The border," she said hoarsely. "When I left Keloseros, it razed the magyck from my insides." Her eyes fell. "*There is nothing free in this world, nothing born of kindness, nothing offered without expectation.*" She regurgitated the words she'd read in one of Ophion's books. "My light in exchange for freedom, and my soul in exchange for asylum."

The bitterness poured out of her and she didn't care to spare him of the implications she made. "I didn't believe it at first—the Gods wouldn't be cruel enough to steal the one thing that defined me then. I even took routes through Lyria that were dangerous, ones that were said to have heightened Brite magyck conduction in their centers just to try ... to see if maybe I was wrong, maybe it was still with me ... but nothing. It was just ..." She swallowed. "Gone."

Arioch stared at her like for the first time in a long time he couldn't read her and just as she was about to ask him what question was printed across his face—

"The dress is fucking perfect; I'm just wondering if it would fit me."

Aheia jumped as the door opened and Lúc walked in with Kar on his back.

"This one? No." The empath rolled her eyes, jumping to the floor and twirling. "But I'm sure I can find a bigger size for you."

Black and green sparkled across her body, scraps of fabric covering her breasts that were held together by black string, tattoos decorating most of her torso and bared arms. Her skirt dipped down her waist and it was short, coming to various length points that almost looked like leaves. Two airy sleeves cuffed her biceps, and flowed down to her fingertips, gold rings and necklaces shining against her pale skin.

Lúc wore leathers and boots, but he'd traded the short-sleeved, black shirt he usually wore for one that was snug against his torso and left the skin of his abdomen exposed. Four thin straps of fabric hung from it, equally spaced, and he had two black leather bands tight around his forearms.

His hair was pulled from his face, half of it bound at the back of his head by a leather tie, and the rest down.

"You barge as if you were sure that I was already dressed." Aheia crossed her arms.

"Are you dressed now?" Lúc asked, quirking his eyebrow, gaze snapping to Arioch's neck. "You're bleeding, brother, did you know?" The words were wrapped in a taunt.

"Am I?" Arioch kept his hands in his pockets casually, but that expression was sharp.

"How cute." Lúc winked at Aheia before making himself comfortable against the couch in the corner.

Kar didn't pay him any mind, holding out a pair of pink heels that matched the pearls of Aheia's dress before skipping over to the Shifter and plopping down on the cushion next to him.

The shoes made her another four inches taller.

"It's odd seeing you that tall." The empath's smile spread, eyes focused on the heels.

"I like it." Aheia tipped her head, still only reaching just underneath Arioch's chin. "I can stare all of you down better."

A soft smirk pulled at his lips and fuck, it was sinful. She let herself acknowledge how much she liked his smiles, all seventeen different versions of them.

"Hold on, how many inches is that?" Lúc tilted his head, eyes sparking with interest.

"Why?" Kar raised her eyebrow and Aheia sent him an amused look.

Lúc shrugged. "Seems like a fun weapon, princess. Keep that in mind."

Kar blew out a laugh, "Thank the Gods, I was getting majorly worried about the direction of that question." She kicked her own heels up, the silver glimmering in the soft orbs above her, and leaned her chin against the arm of the couch.

"There's an idea." Lúc barked out a laugh and grabbed Kar's ankle, tugging her down across his lap. The empath squealed, her dress bunching up slightly as Lúc inspected her shoes, probing his fingers against the heel. She huffed into the cushion and looked back at the Shifter, annoyed, but Aheia could see how hard keeping up that annoyance was as her lips quivered.

"Hands off my weapons," she said, wiggling her legs.

But instead of letting go, Lúc brought her foot down to his groin. "Yea, yours is bigger than mine," he huffed, patting her calf and releasing her leg.

Kar's smile dimpled her cheeks as she readjusted on the couch, laying her head in his lap instead and crossing her ankles on the armrest.

Aheia shook her head, the soft smile on her lips feeling like a slip. She brushed it off, averting her eyes for a moment. She didn't know why it felt wrong, the smile. Like she shouldn't be doing it, even though frowning was more of an effort right now.

Arioch's fingers grazed her chin, forcing her eyes back to his.

"What was that?" he asked.

"Nothing." Aheia swallowed, feeling that sliver of shame cut through her.

Why? She didn't want to be back here. How had she dragged herself into this space? This was comfortable, they were comfortable. What had made her sour it all for herself?

"Aylee!" Kar squeaked suddenly and Aheia watched her jump up from the couch and dart across the room. The blonde Nephilim was stunning in a black-scaled dress, Embyr and Salamander wound tightly around her arms. Her lips and nails were painted a dark, cherry red.

"Go ahead with them," Arioch told Aheia, nodding at Lúc. "I'll catch up."

Aylee looked at Kar, and she realized that her expression was only cold when her focus was on Aheia. The Leviathan was like a stone that shone a different color when the light reflected off it, and Kar got a rainbow of warm orange.

Aylee moved to the other side of Arioch, those snakes of hers hissing and Kar tilted her head in question.

"What are you two up to?"

"Just some odds and ends to tie up," Arioch said casually as the empath scrunched her nose sweetly and headed back toward the others. She looped her arm with Aheia's and tugged her away, but she kept her eyes on Arioch just for another moment as they cleared the door.

Chapter 40

Aheia

"What is this place?" Aheia asked, looking around the large room. It was cut in thick stone, and had two ways out: the hallway they'd walked in from and another at the adjacent wall. She was still trying to find her calm, when Arioch's blood wanted the exact opposite.

"Caravan port," Tariq said, shrugging past her with his arm around Lúc. They'd picked up the fourth Nephilim just before the entryway.

"Caravan?" Aheia asked.

"We don't just get around with vortexes." Kar smiled, pointing ahead of her at two large ... carriages? No, that wasn't right. They weren't pulled by any animals. She recognized them, had seen them in the streets of Aljira the one time she'd been in the city before. They were black and sleek, the large body curving over four wheels. Aheia spied leather seats and bright little lights that blinked on some sort of dashboard when Tariq opened the front left door.

Nyco was leaning against the far wall, their eyes painted with gold liner and Noctua sitting on their shoulder. Their hair was pulled back into two high sitting buns, with some of the curls open at the back and Aheia wiggled her fingers their way, catching their smile just as a loud rumbling rose up around them. The caravan at the front roared to life and Aheia jumped, watching it peel out toward the exit, its four wheels spinning *fast*.

"How does it work?" she asked in amazement.

"Well, the same energy that lights our rooms and warms our homes"—Kar nodded up at the Solas against the ceiling—"is used for transportation."

Genius. They didn't have the likes in Keloseros.

Tariq slammed the door after getting into the second caravan, leaving the window rolled down. He winked at Lúc, who passed him, heading to a row of smaller machines against the wall. They were much thinner, their bodies curved over two wheels instead of four, and each had two padded seats along the back. Aheia watched the Shifter swing his leg across the spine of a white-walled machine, balancing on the two wheels and walking it from its stall.

"You coming with me or going with them?" Lúc cocked an eyebrow and Aheia looked around her.

"Me?" She poked a finger at her chest.

"No, Nyco. Yes, you." He rolled his eyes.

"What is this?"

"A ryde." He petted the seat behind him that was situated just over the second wheel.

"I've never been on one of these," Aheia stammered. Technically, she hadn't been in the caravan either, but that one felt self-explanatory.

"Get on then." Lúc grinned, and it felt like a challenge just as Kar hung out of the caravan from her own window.

"You want to?" the empath asked, presumably already knowing the answer to that.

Aheia's inhale was shaky as she regarded it. It looked terrifying, and the thought of shooting through the city on it excited her just as much as it scared her.

"Help her with her shoes," Lúc nodded at Nyco before she gave an answer, who came up behind her and crouched to the ground, delicate hands pulling at the pink straps. She gripped their shoulder and sent them an apologetic scowl. She didn't like the idea of them servicing her like that. But Nyco only winked, throwing Aheia's heels in the open window behind Kar. "And her hair," Lúc continued, dangling a leather strap in their face. Nyco took it slowly, brushing their fingers against Lúc's.

"No, you don't have to—" Aheia tried to snatch the leather away, but Nyco shook their head, gathering her hair, and brushing through it with soft fingers.

"I can do it myself," she griped at Lúc because he'd been the one behind the request.

"Relax," he drawled simply, purple eyes trained on the Nephilim standing behind her who was busy weaving her mane into a thick plait.

"Anything else?" They cocked their head when they finished, coy smile on their lips.

Lúc didn't answer, his attention on Tariq now, who was eyeing him from the small mirror attached to the side of the caravan.

After a moment of silence, Nyco peeled away from them, and Aheia watched as they selected their own ryde, walking it back slowly.

"Tick tock, princess, unless you'd prefer walking." Lúc glanced at the cushioned seat behind him.

"Getting on this thing is not intuitive when you're covered in pearls," Aheia said, haphazardly trying to figure out the pearls on her dress as she hiked up her leg and held on to the nape of his neck. It took a few tries, and she cursed under her breath, managing to get herself situated with the Shifter's help. He moved her feet into metal ridges on either side and told her to grip them tight. She held on to his shoulders, but he clicked his tongue.

"No, not there," he said, peeling her nervous fingers from him and winding them around his abdomen instead, patting the back of her hands as she interlocked them. Her cheek now rested against his spine, almost tall enough from the raised seat to tip her chin over his shoulder.

"Go on," he told Tariq, who was leaning out of the open window, the caravan rumbling to life. "I'll still beat your ass, even if you get a head start." She watched the side of Lúc's face as he smiled, his canine poking out behind his lips. "That goes for you too, youngling," he told Nyco without looking back, double checking the settings on his ryde.

"What do I get if you lose, Lúci?" Tariq purred, his fingers lazily sliding across the metal.

Lúci. Aheia felt like she was intruding on something, but neither of the demons in front of her seemed to care.

"The usual?" Lúc raised his eyebrow and Tariq wet his bottom lip.

"You're so fucked." The Leviathan chuckled.

"Only if I lose." Lúc slammed his foot down on the pedal and the ryde roared to life as Tariq leaned back inside the caravan and spun the machine's wheels. They shot out of the room, Kar leaning out of the window and waving Aheia's way with a chiming laugh on her lips. The exhaust smelled like charcoal, filling the room around them.

"What do *I* get if you lose?"

Lúc's attention snapped up to Nyco when they spoke and Aheia caught their smirk just as they revved the handle on their ryde and shot up the long, gray stone-lain hallway that led outside.

"What the fuck did they just say to me?" Lúc stared after them like he couldn't quite believe his ears.

"I'm nervous," Aheia said, changing the subject as her chest filled with little wings.

Lúc's eyes lingered on the disappearing Nephilim for a few more moments before he turned back to her. "Most are their first time," he said finally, looking over his shoulder so that his mouth was inches from her temple. "Hold on and make sure to lean into all curves with me," he waited for her to nod before he went on. "It's meant to scrape your knees ... if you ride it the right way. Don't let that scare you." And then he flashed her his teeth. "Seems your knees are already beaten to shit though, so ..."

Aheia hissed, letting go of his waist and shoving at his back.

"*Arrê*." He laughed, pulling her arms back.

"G*habiun*," she murmured against his shoulder, but there wasn't much anger behind it.

"Your pronunciation needs work," he chuckled.

Aheia just scoffed, rolling her eyes so big that it hurt her mind.

"Alright, I'm going to say it one more time." The Shifter went all serious. She'd never seen him that stoic. "Hold tight, and lean into those curves. You need to trust me, alright? I won't let you fall."

She nodded, swallowing against the lump in her throat as Lúc leaned forward, and the wheels on the ryde spun. Aheia squeaked; at least she thought she did as the air rushed past them. But no sound came out, her lungs constricting uncomfortably, like the oxygen moved too quickly for her to gulp it down. Her legs clenched against his hips, and she could feel little hot pins on her palms while the pearls trembled all across her body.

It was terrifying and exhilarating, and she couldn't help but squeal again, the noise the only thing that released some of the pressure inside of her.

The Solas orbs flashed by above, faster and faster as they rode down into the far hallway until they shot out and the blue night sky wrapped around them. Aheia's lips parted, her cheek squished against Lúc's shoulder blade, left staring at the horizon. She decided then and there that she'd never get used to this view. It was too beautiful.

The colors and sounds blurred around her as they wove through spiderweb streets that fed through much smaller, much more eclectic surroundings. Out here the houses were shorter, and the road was cobbled. There was smoke in the air, wafting off of grates in the sidewalk, and loud music permeated the night when they sped past open establishments. It was as alive as the sky seemed to be, and Aheia couldn't get enough of it.

With her hands gripping each other tightly around Lúc, she leaned back enough to rest her chin against his spine. She wanted to see more and caught sight of a few Syraphem that flew overhead as the rooftops cut through her vision on either side like a tunnel.

The city was colorful and light studded, and the two of them felt like a bolt of lightning cutting through it.

Lúc sped up and she could feel her heart in her fingertips, her chest, her legs—everywhere. She was one large pulse point, and every little sensation was heightened. She held on tighter as they wove around a caravan; the thing whizzing past them in a black blur.

The streets were becoming busier, and Aheia pressed her cheek into his back again, holding on in a death grip.

Nyco's ryde was coming up in the distance and she could see their brown and white curls on the black dot that was going at almost as much of a breakneck speed as them. Lúc leaned down further, taking her forward with him and accelerating in a beeline. The Shifter was fixated, weaving around the bottleneck of caravans to catch Nyco and pass them.

Aheia couldn't even look back when they did, the close maneuver almost scraping her knees against Nyco's.

The tilt of the ryde made her stomach plummet to her feet, and each time she managed to collect it, Lúc swerved around another obstacle, and Aheia fumbled it again.

When they finally slowed to a stop, Aheia felt frozen in place. She didn't move until Lúc leaned back on his cushion and peeled off her hands. He tucked them against the side of her seat so she could hold on while he got off, stabilizing the ryde.

"How you doing back there?" he asked, stepping onto the smooth sidewalk. Aheia blinked at him, static coursing through her veins, her muscles twitching involuntarily.

"Do we have to go in? We could just keep doing that." Her lips spread into a wide grin and Lúc's eyes flashed down to her mouth. He looked surprised for a moment but hid it quickly, holding out his hand, helping her down.

"I'd prefer it, princess." Lúc winked.

"Fuck, you're fast," Tariq said, slamming the door to the caravan that had pulled up behind them.

"He almost took out an entire sidewalk trying to catch you," Kar laughed, stretching her arms above her like she'd just woken from a nap.

"The streets are a fucking mess tonight."

"You'd have lost on a straight road." Lúc smirked as Tariq walked over.

"Try saying it again without that wobble in your knees." Tariq flicked his tongue across the ridge of his teeth, grabbing ahold of Lúc's neck.

"Sore fucking loser," Lúc hissed, pushing against his piercing.

"I'll show you sore." Tariq bit at the Shifter's bottom lip and Aheia busied herself, feeling the warmth crawl against her spine watching them. She focused instead on letting out her braid and fastening the leather strap around her wrist before heading to the caravan and snatching up her heels. She leaned against the sleek metal, slipping the straps back into place as she watched Lúc point at Nyco, who'd pulled up a split second before Tariq.

"Hey!" the Shifter said, his voice deep. Nyco bristled slightly, like maybe they thought they could get away while Lúc was distracted. "You lost," Lúc said, passing by them slowly, dark eyes hard. "I'll let you know what you owe me."

Kar came up to Aheia's side and grabbed her hand, pulling her up the steps that led to the tall building in front of them, and leaving Nyco standing with their rydes. She glanced at them apologetically, watching their blush spread still fixated on the Shifter.

The four of them walked up together, passing the line of demons waiting behind a thick, velvet rope. The Nephilim she was with now always commanded attention. Everywhere they went. And Aheia was envious of that.

The Den was wild in all senses of the word. Aheia couldn't quite figure out how to pick her jaw off the floor as they passed through various rooms, all of them built for very different activities. At one point, they even passed foamy pools that were entirely filled with bubbles. Tariq had entered first, but somehow Aheia and he had separated themselves from Kar and Lúc, who'd disappeared behind the bar, talking animatedly with a Nephilim that was twirling bottles like it was an art form.

She cast furtive glances at the tall, horned demon because it felt different being around him. He'd talked about her like she was worthless when Eros had cornered her at the party a few months ago. And even though things felt different now, she couldn't quite shake that memory.

Patrons crowded around the small stages that were peppered around the room, while multicolored Nephilim, all shades of the rainbow danced on top. Tariq had to usher her away from the Sirens because their songs had caught her attention. The females and the males both were dressed in glittery clothing, and some even had wings. *Wings*. And not the kind Emryn had. They were wings that looked iridescent under the Solas and glimmered every time they moved.

"You're beautiful," Aheia murmured, her blood warming inside of her as they passed a raised platform that held a blue female on all fours, almost eye level. Her blue gaze sparkled and she smiled big, pushing back on her knees seductively. Aheia had never been more aware of her blood than she was in this exact moment.

"Do those sparkles help you in battle?" she asked.

"My scales?" the Nephilim asked sweetly, drawing her fingertips across them and Aheia couldn't help herself. She reached for the side of her leg, tracing the pattern on her outer thigh, very focused on how those ridges felt underneath the pads of her fingers.

"Do they? Have you battled?" Her mind felt like mush. "I'm not very good at it—battle—I died last time, but if I had scales like this, I might be better." She watched the colors dance.

"No, they don't help in battle." The Nephilim's eyes were stuck on Aheia's hands, her lips parted. "Usually we're not to be touched."

"*Oh*—" Aheia tried to snatch her hand back, her heart jumping, but the scaled female held on to her wrist. Dark painted lips pulled into a smile that was syrupy and sweet.

"It's ok, I like how your fingers feel."

Aheia blushed, her lips parting on a heavy inhale as the demon flashed her teeth, and rolled onto her back so that she was looking up at Aheia. Her wings pressed flat against the stage, so that she could see the intricate, iridescent flesh, the colors reflecting softly.

"Come on." Tariq nudged her, his voice a cold interruption before she could answer. "She'll take all your eyrid if you're not careful."

"I don't have any," Aheia murmured, her eyes trailing the female as he pulled her away.

"Fuck's sake. She'll take the pearls then, and you won't mind a bit."

She blinked. He was right; no part of her disliked that idea.

"Why won't I mind?" she asked slowly, trying to focus against the static that had somehow worked itself into her mind. She hadn't noticed it until now.

"It's their fucking job." His teeth glinted, tongue flicking against his canines. The first smile he gave her. But it wasn't a smile, not really. It was a sneer.

Aheia tore her gaze away. "Do *you* have eyrid?" she asked Tariq.

He raised his eyebrows, pinching the bridge of his nose. "We're not playing with the dancers right now."

"Take it easy," Kar coaxed as she caught up with them, Lúc in tow. "She doesn't have a favorite color," the empath scoffed, resting a hand on her hip and looking wholly exacerbated. Like that was supposed to explain everything right then and there.

Tariq's eyes darted between the two of them. "Is that supposed to mean something to me?"

Aheia's face burned. Such a silly little thing, but it still made her feel unsteady. And it didn't help that Tariq already made her unsteady to begin with. He felt kind of like Emryn. Neither of them wanted her around.

"Feels like watching a youngling," she heard him mumble under his breath as he passed with Lúc.

Asshole. She grit her teeth but kept her mouth shut. She didn't know anyone else here, and for now, she'd refrain from starting a fight, even though it was all she wanted.

"We can come back later if you want," Kar said kindly, linking their arms and pulling Aheia toward an archway that led down another hall.

Emryn was waiting at the end, her dark wings tucked behind her, and her arms crossed. She was wearing dark red pants and a fitted jacket that dipped down between her breasts without a shirt behind it. Her curls were pulled into a tight ponytail, and her lips were lined with bright red.

The Syraphem's gaze dropped down Aheia's body when they approached, and somehow she looked even less impressed with her now than when she'd first met her.

"I need you two." Emryn pointed at Tariq and Kar, without bothering to say anything to Aheia.

Tariq traded Lúc for the Syraphem, laying a heavy arm across her shoulders while she played at shrugging it off, even though her hard exterior wavered for a moment.

"You look vicious, *traveske*," Aheia heard him say as he guided her into the room ahead and Kar followed after patting Aheia's arm in reassurance. Tariq sent one last glance over his shoulder at Lúc before they disappeared. It was the warmest she'd ever seen him. No, warm was wrong. The look he gave the Shifter was fucking scorching. It made Aheia want to duck out of the way just in case that fire was invisible and might in fact burn her if she walked into his eyeline.

She averted her eyes, peaking through the doorway ahead instead. The room was busy with people she didn't know and Aheia fidgeted with her new necklace, attempting to let it ground her.

"You look nervous." She turned, meeting Lúc's gaze. The Shifter was tucked next to one of the columns, his arms crossed. "That won't do, princess."

"Excuse me?"

"Don't let them see that." He tipped his chin, and a glint ran through his eyes. "Smile."

It helps to smile.

He'd told her that when he'd first met her, walking her to the atrium at the compound.

What the fuck? The anger felt irrational, but that didn't change how quickly it was summoned as she crossed the space between them grabbing ahold of the weapon and drawing it. It was a dangerous move, not only because it was Lúc on the other end, but because she was so unpracticed in her heels. One day she would be. She'd fight in these—she decided in that exact moment.

Lúc grinned, and the amusement didn't fade when she pressed the edge of the knife into his windpipe. "Stop telling me that. What the hel is wrong with you?"

"How fun." He pushed his tongue against the metal in his lip, and then, fast as lightning, he went for her wrist, twisting the dagger away from her.

She squeaked as he shifted them both, locking her against his chest with an arm caged tightly against her throat while her knife hung uselessly at the edges of her fingers.

"You've told me to smile twice now and it's disgusting," she hissed, because now that he'd disarmed her, words were the only thing she had left.

"Best advice I've ever given you and you've never listened to it."

"Advice?" She scoffed.

"Tell me, princess, how mad does my smile make you?" His breath ghosted her ear as he tipped her face towards him, pinching her chin so she was forced to look at those pearly white teeth gleaming in front of her. "Very?" His fingers tightened for a moment and he continued before she said anything. "Exactly." And then he leaned into her ear further, dropping his voice. "So, smile. Because they'll hate it. They'll hate thinking they can't intimidate you, that they can't get the reactions they want from you."

"Who?" She hesitated, freezing in the protest she'd started in his hold.

"Everyone, Aheia."

Her brows drew together, and she looked up at him. It was jarring somehow, having him call her by her actual name.

"You told me to smile when you took me to see Arioch that first day." She countered. *Why would he do that?*

Lúc loosened his hold, turning whatever this was into something that almost felt like a hug, her back against his steady chest.

"A disingenuous smile would have irritated the hel out of him and he can stand to have his shit shaken up a bit every now and then." The Shifter smiled, raking his tongue across his sharp teeth before letting it rest in the corner of his mouth.

"You're chaos, you know that?" Her chest warmed.

"My claim to fame," he said, dropping his arms altogether. "That and great fucking advice."

She swatted after him and he ducked his head, a soft laugh lighting up his features, while she let his words sink in.

Smile. it makes you look so much prettier, Aheia.

Smile, don't let them see. I didn't hit you that hard.

Smile. You're weighing down everything.

Maybe there was power in taking back a command she so completely detested.

Chapter 41

Aheia

The room ahead was set with tables, each of them holding a myriad of thick, black candles. There wasn't any Solas here, and it left the room dipped in a dark amber glow. The flames reflected off of countless mirrors that hung like artwork, some ornate gold, some plain black, some dark jewel tones. The dark cradled Aheia in its palm, and she felt a little less visible, which she was thankful for right now. Because Lúc and the others busied themselves, quickly giving her introductions to a few of the females that were standing near the entrance and then peeling away.

They were engrossed in animated conversations with different Nephilim, and Aheia thought she recognized a few, occasionally catching a sideways glance.

She recognized again how odd it was for such a crowded space to feel so incredibly lonely.

She was thankful for the moment everyone seemed to meander to the tables. Even though it still felt awkward as hel sitting between two pretty females and across from a gorgeous blonde who had her lips painted a dark purple. The two at her sides were mostly silent while *Purple* flirted with the male she must have come to this dinner with. Aheia fidgeted her fingers under the table, looking to Kar and Tariq, who were at the other end of the table with Emryn. Lúc was a few seats down, looking bored as fuck, his eyes all but glazing over as the male next to him spoke.

Food was served quickly, and it smelled delicious. Gold bowls were filled with different meats and rice, accompanied by various pitchers that were distributed throughout the tables. She picked from a few of the plates, loving the peeled fruits and deciding that the mushrooms tasted like salty rubber. But the fish was good, even though she had no idea what kind it was, and she thought she could die happy eating the rice and cilantro every night for the foreseeable future. Her stomach didn't allow for a whole lot, but she tried a variety of things in small doses. She was two bites into a leg of lamb when Arioch finally showed up.

Flatware clattered when he did, and a few Nephilim scurried to stand up, but he just scrunched his eyebrows and held out his hand, dismissing the action. Aheia watched him greet a few, and weave behind the seats, talking casually.

Who the fuck are *you?*

He was almost approachable like this, even though the look he sent her, the one that lasted less than a second, was anything but. The heat crept up her scalp as she watched him steal all the attention and keep it for himself. Everyone around her had their eyes glued to him, including the purple female, and Aheia chewed her bottom lip, trying to swallow the irritation at that. She was much too focused, and they shared the blue of their eyes. It made the size of her pupils painfully obvious, as her lips parted and her breathing grew shallow.

She hated that she was stuck here, and not with the others, hated that she couldn't hear what they were talking about, and most of all, hated how silent she was being. She speared a bean, taking out her frustration on its small, green body just as she felt something brush against her thigh.

She gripped the napkin from the table and pulled it on to her lap, an undignified squeak on her lips.

"You ok?" Purple asked, looking irritated at her interruption of her shameless leering.

"Y-yes," Aheia said absentmindedly, watching in shock as a dark tendril curled up her leg slowly. Her eyes widened, and she forced the napkin down further in an attempt to cover the magyck, leaning close against the table to hide it from the brunette next to her. Frantic eyes looked up at Arioch who still wasn't paying her any attention, still caught up in the conversation with the other demons. But Aheia saw the twitch of his fingers and felt how his magyck responded.

Fuck. He's not going to—

His shadows slid between her knees, trailing a warm touch up toward the apex of her thighs, and she dropped the fork on the plate when they did. Her other hand gripped the edge of the table tight while she forced her face into something that wouldn't betray this. Heads turned toward her, and she met Lúc's eyes. The Shifter's smile turned feral, little coils of purple seeping into the dark irises.

"Spicy," she choked, covering for whatever the fuck noise she'd just made as his shadows licked across the satin that covered her cunt.

"You're eating plain rice." The Nephilim next to her looked perplexed as she moved her gold hair over her shoulders.

"They might not ... have that ... where she's from?" the brunette on the other side tried placatingly.

Aheia cleared her throat, picking up her fork again, feeling the magyck push its way past the thin fabric of her undergarments helplessly.

No. Not now.

Her face heated, and she knew the blush was spreading across her nose and up the side of her neck.

Fuck. This fucking dress. She'd match it.

"You look unwell," Purple drawled, disgust etched in her features.

"Yea," she said, and it almost sounded like a fucking moan, following it with another cough and a headshake. "Just an adjustment. Umm, being in this realm. I don't think my body has—" She cleared her throat. "Is ... feeling—"

"You know, since you have such a pink skin tone, you really shouldn't wear anything that matches it. It washes you out." Purple scrunched her nose and all Aheia could do was smile tightly. Because if she opened her mouth, it wouldn't be words that spilled from her.

Bitch.

"There you are." Arioch's deep voice made her jump. She'd been too distracted with him between her legs to sense his nearness at her back. He was already everywhere.

"You look like you could use some company," Purple cut in before Aheia could get a word out edgewise. She grit her teeth, gulping down air as discreetly as she could when his shadows gave her a short reprieve, abandoning her aching clit.

"I could." His sound alone made her spine tingle.

Purple's eyes sparkled suggestively. "Maybe I—"

"Come sit with me, Aheia."

"What?" She'd been distracted swatting away the black wisp under the table.

“Sit with me,” he repeated, a smirk tugging at his lips.

Aheia tipped her chin toward Purple for a moment, letting herself smile. A smile she didn’t mean, one crafted for the Nephilim across from her. The kind that rivaled Tariq’s earlier. Because fuck her for existing with those hungry eyes.

“If you'll excuse me,” she said sweetly. Then she reached for Arioch and let him help her from the low seat at the table. “You’re late.” She looked up at him.

“No such thing when the dinner is mine.” He winked at her. “You were just exceptionally early.”

“I don’t think that’s true.” She scoffed, rolling her eyes as they rounded the far table.

His grin was shameless. “We make our own rules.”

She bit against the urge to ask him to specify ‘we’ as they walked up to an empty place setting.

“You want me to sit with you?” She raised her eyebrow. “How? There’s only one chair.”

“Observant.”

“I’m losing my mind over there.” Lúc appeared behind them, speaking quietly through clenched teeth, and handing Arioch the glass of dark liquor. “Hani’s complaining about the harpies in the Hynu River. Who do they think I am, Fish and Wildlife?” he grumbled. “Harpies. Who gives a fuck.”

Arioch’s chest vibrated with a chuckle. “Harpies are native to Hynu; there’s not much we can do about them, regardless.”

“It's that damned development they’re vying for. It would overlook the river and they’re worried about how the harpies might react to an influx of Nephilim in that territory.”

“They haven’t gotten the permit signed, and until they do, they don't need to worry about it,” Arioch shot back, sitting down.

"That's what I told them, but it doesn't seem to matter. They've been telling me about the harpy anatomy for the better part of dinner." Lúc finished off his drink. "That's it," he declared. "I officially know too much about harpies. No more." He set down the empty glass. "I'm moving my seat." And before Arioch could respond, he left, heading toward Aheia's empty chair.

Those dark eyes took inventory of her, slow and deliberate, while she fixed him with an unamused stare. "What did I do to earn that look?"

"You can't just—" she hissed, waving her hand in front of his face like that would bridge the rest of the conversation.

"I'm pretty sure I didn't do whatever that was." He grinned at her movements, squeezing the back of her thigh and bringing her closer with a heavy hand. Aheia almost tripped in her heels, her teeth digging into her lower lip. She hated how much his grin made her want to smile, made her want to abandon her embarrassment and irritation when it felt so important to hold on to sometimes, when it felt like she'd invalidate herself if she didn't.

"You can't just use your shadows like that," she clarified, saying the rest of those words quickly and under her breath in hopes of keeping it between the two of them.

"Get on my lap before I do it again." The adrenaline hadn't tempered from her excursion with Lúc, and the sips of wine she'd had didn't help any of it. She felt out of control again. And seeing the bite on his throat didn't help either. It pulled her back from the overstimulated edge she'd found herself on and forced her into last week's memories.

"Make me," she whispered, watching with delight as his eyes narrowed.

He looked down at her with the kind of gaze that had her nipples tightening and her abdomen warming.

Fire. It always felt like fire with him.

And she was glad for it now, because it kept the cold at bay. It was a tradeoff for the fact that this thing between them was volatile at best—something that lived between anger and need.

His jaw tensed as he set down his glass on the edge of the table. And she readied herself for whatever he had in store. Except she didn't expect his actions. Instead of saying anything, he focused on the demon on his left, jumping into conversation as easily as if he'd started it himself and ignoring her completely.

Is he serious?

Her lips parted, and she wrapped her arms around her middle, unsure of what she should do. She shifted her weight awkwardly, and it only got worse when one of the Nephilim that was refilling the water glasses asked if she needed anything in particular or if she was fine just standing there. The final straw, however, was when Aheia caught Purple's victorious gaze across the table and embarrassment lit up her ears.

Cocky fuck.

She shoved past her own defiance and forced herself between his thighs. His eyes flashed to her for a split second, before he returned to his conversation, his legs spread casually.

Aheia bit back the growl on her lips and gripped onto his shoulders instead, doing what he'd asked and crawling into his lap.

He didn't look back at her until he finished talking to the demon beside him, which felt like minutes on end as she perched there, much too visible.

"I don't reward messy behavior," he said finally, leaning back in his chair.

"I thought that messy was your favorite." She tugged her lip between her teeth as she reached for his liquor. The sip she took from it made her want to choke and it burned hot, like it had the night in the tunnels. The second drink wasn't quite as bad, even though this time she held it in her mouth. All its smoke and fire ate into her tongue, but none of that compared to the look he gave her as he watched her rise onto her knees on top of him and lean in close.

His breath coasted across her lips when she teased apart his with her thumb and fed him the liquor in a slow trickle.

A sound of approval vibrated through him, through her in turn as she slid her fingers around his throat. She felt him swallow against her hand and the grip he had on her ass tightened. Hard. Punishing. Exactly what she wanted. She settled back, hugging his waist with her knees as she pushed down against him.

"Move your hips like that again," he hissed.

"That sounds like a threat," she said, her voice much too breathy.

"It is," he said in her ear. "Move your hips like that again and I'll make you sit on my cock right here."

"You'd fuck me in front of them?" She felt her heartbeat in her bones. Fucking everywhere.

"No, not fuck, just feel," he said calmly, his eyes still focused on the guests across the table

"What would be the point of that?"

"To feel your pussy wrapped around me while I eat my dinner."

Fucking hel. That sounded enticing.

She swallowed dryly, biting her bottom lip hard as she rolled her hips, rubbing against the hard ridge of his cock with her cunt. His eyes burned as they dropped between them, a low growl breaking from his chest.

"I think I'd like more wine," he said roughly, nodding past her toward the table. She held his eyes, both of them locked into something that felt a lot like a bluff. But it wasn't a bluff if neither of them backed down. And she was much too curious to see where he'd take this. So, she stood slowly, reaching for the wine across the table and snagging one of the napkins in the process, pinning it to her lap inconspicuously. She bent over slightly, feeling his fingers dragging the silk of her undergarments to the side as she started to pour. Her eyes widened, and she tried to keep her composure when the head of his cock probed her entrance. She inhaled sharply, feeling his hand replace hers against the napkin so she could grip the table instead. The wine filled the cup further and further as he massaged the head of his cock against her clit between tightly squeezed legs.

Shit, there's no way—

The cup overflowed, just as Arioch pulled her down on his cock, splitting her apart. A muffled cry broke past her lips, and it caused a commotion, the Nephilim closest and even a few across the tables looking at her. Kar's eye shot their way and her brows furrowed for a moment. But Aheia couldn't read her expression when she turned back toward the demon she was talking to, her lips moving quickly as if she was trying to find the thread she'd lost.

"S-sorry," she managed, and it had been the best-case scenario—spilling the wine explained her outburst, and why she looked so fucking scattered.

Aheia held on to the table for dear fucking life as Arioch's cock stretched her, maneuvering her spill with shaky hands, feeling the blistering stare of the others.

She tried her best to focus on what was in front of her, the thick fabric soaking up the spill as Arioch covered her hand with his.

"Leave it," he said hoarsely in her ear.

Glass. Water. Bread.

She tried to busy her mind with other things, with anything else as he pulled her back, heavy hand against her abdomen.

"I can't—" She didn't know how to finish that thought process when he shifted and his cock rubbed against that spot inside of her. Liquid heat poured down her spine, and her cunt pulsed around him so hard she had to dig her teeth into her bottom lip to keep quiet.

So full. So fucking deep.

She settled back slowly, her eyes drifting across the crowd. It was so dirty. Watching them talk and joke while Alshaytan's cock was buried inside of her, pretending like everything was normal. The thought of one of them noticing, of seeing through the sad excuse of a mask on her face, made her pulse flurry.

She moved her hips and tensed her muscles, massaging him back, feeling his heartbeat against her back forcefully. It was always so steady, but now it matched hers. Erratic. Maybe even frantic.

"This is torture," she managed through her tight smile, her eyes flicking up to his as he massaged her thigh, just over the cut that he'd helped bandage. It stung, and her knees shook, but he—he looked indifferent—he played at this so much better than she did.

"This is my favorite thing," he said, and his voice was thick, like he had cotton on his tongue as he reached past her and picked up a glass. "I want to feel you come for me," he murmured into her ear, bringing the water close, and feeding it to her slowly. She breathed through her nose, shaking her head *no* almost as subtly as she could.

"I'm not asking you. I'm *telling* you," he said roughly and her heart dropped, his magyck curling up her legs. "Let's see how well you pretend that it's not happening."

"Please," she begged with wide eyes, as he stroked her clit with his shadows, the pleasure twisting her stomach into knots that were aching to be untied. "Don't."

"I know you can do better." He chuckled in her ear. "Beg harder if you want me to stop."

Her chest heaved, and she brought the back of her hand to her forehead, feeling how hot she was. She didn't have to pretend to have a fever if he kept this up—she'd burst into flames at his hands.

Her nervous eyes coasted over the Nephilim just a few feet away, in a heated argument with his dinner partner across the table. She caught the words *export* and *inflation*, and their dates looked bored out of their minds—one of them watching the servers with hungry eyes and the other pushing around her food.

"They'll see," Aheia whimpered as he brought up his free hand and pressed against her abdomen.

"Yeah, they'll see." He groaned lowly, quiet enough not to draw any attention. "If I pull that flimsy fucking napkin from your legs, they'll know exactly how dirty you are." His words were hushed against the shell of her ear while she watched the faces in front of her. They were all wrapped up in their own conversations, even though it felt like Aheia's heart was beating loud enough to wake the dead.

"No." She cleared her throat, masking the moan that broke past her lips.

But he continued as if she hadn't said anything, his magyck becoming torturous and her legs starting to shake with the flex in her thighs. "You respond so pretty to the thought, little goddess. Your cunt hugs me so fucking good when you think about being watched. Is that what you want? To show them how well you take me, hmm?"

His shadows pulled her clit into a vacuum for good measure and she doubled over against the table, grabbing the second, wine soaked napkin and pulling it up to her face as she righted herself on shaky limbs. The two Nephilim closest sent her confused looks.

"I'm not feeling the best," she choked into the cloth, another moan shaking her as his cock shifted inside of her.

"You do look pale," one of the males said.

Aheia managed a terse smile as Arioch put his hand on the nape of her neck, cradling her close to his chest. She imagined it looked sweet ... attentive ... when what he was actually doing was giving himself more of a hold on her, and easier access for his shadows.

She held onto his wrist, needing to figure out how not to float out of her body as her eyes coasted toward Lúc. He was turned toward them, irises tinged in purple.

"He's watching," she managed, as Arioch massaged her clit.

"He can scent you across the room."

Her eyes widened, and she abandoned the Shifter's stare, shame burning her cheeks.

"I don't want him to see." She grit her teeth.

"You don't want him to see what? How hard you come when others watch?" He rotated his hips slightly, giving her more of that sweet friction. "How you're so eager to fuck me again that we can't even make it back home?" He hummed against her, picking up a piece of bread and pushing it past her lips. The spit on her tongue soaked through it, but she didn't dare swallow, unsure of if she could without coughing against it. *Home*. Something inside of her melted. He'd called it her home. "Now give me what's mine," he growled, pinching the inside of her thigh until the pain swirled into her pleasure. "Or I'll bend you over this fucking table and take it. I know all you need is a few hard strokes, and if you don't come for me in the next ten seconds, I'll finish you off on my fucking dinner plate."

Little bursts of light peppered the side of her vision as his shadows stroked her into oblivion and she choked on the bread in her mouth, her orgasm wrapping around his cock. Arioch held her against him tight, keeping her in place as she shook, his length throbbing inside of her.

The stars that bordered her every time he untied her like this lit up the scene in front of her and her hand twisted in the fabric of his shirt. She tamped down on the urge to bite at the nearest part of him as she came down from her high slowly. When she finally managed to make out the room in front of her, Lúc had left her seat behind ...

"You ready to move on?" The Shifter was staring down at her, grinning and swirling the drink in his glass. "If you're"—he cleared his throat and brought the liquor to his lips—"done."

"Far from," Arioch said, squeezing her ass, his dick still so fucking hard inside of her.

"You should talk to management about that." His eyes narrowed as he turned his back, the sly fuck shielding them from view.

Aheia raised herself up enough for Arioch to pull his hard dick out of her and her legs nearly gave out as she fell back onto his lap, hiding him while he did up his pants.

"I think I'm sick," she said hurriedly, her eyes bouncing around the Nephilim, who were staring at her with tense expressions.

"Yeah, you are," Lúc threw over his shoulder, sipping his drink. His canines poked out beneath his lip when he drew it into a smirk.

Aheia tried to glare at him, but couldn't manage much more than a scowl as Arioch stood, keeping his hands in place to steady her.

"What now?"

"I heard you like the dancers." Arioch lifted his eyebrows.

"I did," she said slowly, feeling out if that was going to earn her his anger.

He smirked, like once again he could read her thoughts in her eyes.

"You can watch all you want, Aheia." He brushed his fingers across her mouth and she darted out her tongue, tasting the pad of his thumb, relishing the way his jaw worked when she did. "But these lips are mine, this pretty mouth is mine, and so is every other fucking part of you."

She started to protest him, but when she did, Lúc tapped his shoulder and pointed back toward the entrance. Aylee was walking across the space in that leather dress with her familiars.

She leaned in to Arioch's side and he gripped the back of her neck, as she spoke hushed words in Lujha. Aheia looked away, coasting her glance across the room, when two of the words caught her attention. She understood them. *"He's awake."*

Her attention snapped back just as Arioch clicked his tongue, and Aylee leaned away.

"Change of plans," he said, looking at Aheia.

Chapter 42

Aheia

She'd let him wrap her in his shadows but regretted it when they fell and she came face to face with the Malek that haunted her nights.

"You brought me back." Everything that had felt so warm moments ago froze inside of her. "Why? I don't want to be here."

This time, her voice didn't simply echo around the room. This time, it caught Ophion's attention and Aheia was met with stark blue eyes—the shit from her nightmares. Deep in this cave, though, they were unfocused and red, dried blood crusting his lips, different from her terrors. Arioch's hand curved against her waist, and he pulled her in close, draping one heavy arm over her shoulder. The weight let her breathe, and the warmth started to melt the ice that threatened her slowly. She let herself sink into him, and it didn't feel like weakness now, not like it did before. It anchored her. It stabilized her against the uncomfortable stare from the Malek in front of her.

He didn't have much space to move, but his shoulders twitched slightly, and when he opened his mouth, thick globs of spit dripped onto the floor. Aheia's stomach revolted at the sight, but something else, something opposite, prickled down her spine in the same breath.

"You—"

The word was muffled and slurred, but his voice still sounded like him. He was missing teeth, but Arioch had left half of them intact. When Ophion opened his mouth again, Aheia didn't recognize him, not in the same way, and she clung to that.

He coughed and spit some more and this time his words seemed to come a little easier. "You look soiled."

Her eyes snapped down, her fingers dragging over the pearls at her waist, but Arioch grazed her neck again. *The color.* He was talking about her clothing.

"You were dead," he continued, more spit drooling.

Aheia's shoulders squared. She'd been dead for a long time. She'd argue, now that she'd seen a glimpse of life, she'd been dead her whole existence in Keloseros.

"A fate I imagine you pray for," she said a little too quietly, letting herself look at those wounds across his body.

His eyelids drew down, exhausted gaze flashing from her to the Avarice standing behind her. "My fate is already sealed. None of this matters. I will be embraced by the holy Gods when it is my time."

Cold spikes clenched her middle as she hardened her gaze, and beat back that sinking feeling she knew so well.

"It's all he has left." Arioch smirked slowly, passing by her. "That flimsy belief. We've taken the rest."

Aheia hated that he did have the belief. He didn't deserve it.

"You'll rot for this," Ophion spit. "You'll see. I am the lord's prophet and I know what awaits. Your time will come and you'll burn in a hel of your own making."

"A prophet he says." The glint in Arioch's eyes was dangerous. "And what will *your* Gods do to *me*?" His voice was a low and threatening timbre as his gaze dropped to the Malek. "What will *you* do?" His shadows bled from his shoulders, and Aheia's heart thudded in her chest, the connection between them hot and disruptive. "I am the ruler of two realms, and I don't fear your monsters."

"A nonbeliever could never understand the higher purpose." Ophion's breath rattled like a jar of eyrid.

"And what part of that purpose is this?" Arioch asked. "What milestone does your torture create? Your kind think you're dead already, selecting a new leader as we speak. And you—" Arioch brushed his fingers over the bridge of the Malek's wing, and it twitched under the attention. "You'll be here, deep underground until we decide we're done with you."

We.

"Then you'll be just another body down in yet another realm that belongs to *me*, floating in oblivion for all eternity. I wonder if you'll get bored of your own bullshit, then." Arioch tipped his chin. "Immortality is a beautiful thing, in the right hands; and yours is in mine."

Ophion spit on the floor, not at all as composed as Aheia remembered him. And the more she separated herself from him, from who he'd once been—larger than life and in charge of hers—the more steady her world grew. Well, at least this time, it stayed upright. She could breathe through the discomfort, and even though a big part of her wanted to run, the other half grounded her here. Arioch grounded her here.

"You asked me why I brought you," he said to her. "To ask *him* instead."

"Ask what?" She swallowed.

"Anything you want to know." Arioch nodded at the Malek. "He's all yours."

Aheia watched him step back toward the wall, pulling out an inhalant from his pocket and lighting it while she stood by herself, unsure of what to do with her hands.

He's all yours.

She looked somewhere just above Ophion's cheeks, because she couldn't meet his gaze for a long time without shrinking back, but even without getting the full force of those eyes, she could feel the disgust that filled them.

"Why do you hate me?" she asked, feeling the shudder in her mind. Because the question was born from emotion. She didn't want to give him that, but she couldn't help herself. What had she done to deserve any of it?

"You're not my offspring," he spit. The simplicity of the statement fucking nauseating. Was that all it took?

"And that damns me to a life of torment?" Her voice wavered, but she cleared her throat.

"*Please*," he rasped. "You had it easy. You had all the freedoms in the world."

Her stomach dropped to her fucking toes and her fingers twitched.

"I should have drowned your mother in the *Ohasha River* before she could give birth to you."

Hot streaks of anger held her throat in a vise, black talons that squeezed until small, red pulses filled her vision. She saw Andromeda's dead, blue eyes shining from the frame of black hair, the blood that speckled them, and ran toward her feet in a thin, wet trickle.

"How *dare* you," she growled, feeding herself with those reminders.

"I should have done it the moment I found out about your father."

Her nostrils flared, and her fingernails stung when she bit them into her palm in little half moon imprints.

You're giving him what he wants.

"Who was he?" She pushed past the discomfort, blinking the dry burn from her eyes. It was something else to focus on, and a question she'd never had answered, not really. Andromeda had brushed it off as a casual mistake, another male who was long dead now. And in truth, Aheia rarely gave him thought. His blank face only appeared in her mind when her life became unbearable. In the happy moments, his presence had never seemed to matter.

Ophion hissed, but it devolved into coughs and then rattling breaths. "Some Nephilim," he managed. "Long dead."

Nephilim. Aheia's eyelids fluttered. *There's no way.*

"You're lying."

"You and Andromeda"—he took a slow and wheezy inhale—"Whores that spread their legs for demons."

Arioch didn't like that comment. He snapped his shadows at the Malek, whipping into one of those blue, disgusting eyes.

"Watch that mouth," he said calmly, even though his actions were anything but. "I've taken a liking to cutting out tongues."

Cold shivers covered Aheia's skin.

Part Nephilim.

She tried on the thought.

If it was true, the revelation didn't make her feel any different. She stood there, still just Aheia. Still just a mental case that was beating back dark and cold things. Were those a part of her because of her father? Were they part of her because of Ophion?

"What was his name?" she asked.

"You think I know?" The Malek worked hard to breathe through his pain, one of his eyes pressed shut tight. "I ripped his head from his body and let the pigs eat him."

Aheia looked at Arioch when she felt his shadows at her ankles. He watched her carefully as they slithered up the backs of her legs and rested against her lower back. It was reassuring. It was warm.

"He was one of many," Ophion spit. "The first demon, but one of many, nonetheless. Your existence, his, they mean nothing."

"Why would you care about hunting me down if I was just part Nephilim?" she pushed, the absurdity of it all hurting her mind.

"*Just*? It's an abomination. It can't be allowed," he croaked. "Imagine if others—" He coughed, blood splattering the floor. "Others like you were born. Dirtying our genetics like that."

Dirtying our genetics.

He wrenched his shoulder, the manacle clinking, and Aheia watched red blood drip where the metal bit into his skin. Her eyes narrowed on the way his fingers flexed, gaze drawing across the scars on his wrist. New scars. She connected the lines, and for a moment they almost looked familiar.

Deliberate.

She focused in on the arm that was forced down against the slate and her hand shot to her own wrist instinctively, feeling her heart skip a beat.

It had bled into the chaos of the room the first time they were down here, but now she thought she recognized something.

No ...

A pattern. A mismatched little pattern.

Cuts.

Small and concise.

They drew down Ophion's arms, his hip, his torso ...

Shaky bones carried Aheia around the slab, each movement more unsteady than the last as she looked over him almost frantically, trying to disprove the evidence she was finding, but only strengthening it with each new discovery.

Curved the same, dipped identically.

She slid her fingers across the arch of her elbow and along the small scar above it. Then down to her forearm and across her palm. The phantom pain of those long-lost wounds reemerged with the pressure of her fingers.

"What did you do?" she whimpered.

Arioch said nothing, and the silence told her everything as she continued to explore herself, because Ophion's scars mirrored hers.

She couldn't stop matching up their wounds, the one on her forearm, the one on her shoulder, the ... the four on his right leg—the newest, freshly healing cuts. Her fingers halted on one just across her collarbone as she stared at the ones on his leg. Ari had been careful with her in the tub, drawn across the four scars near her shin when he massaged her muscles.

And she realized now exactly what he'd done after she'd fallen asleep. Carved into Ophion.

"You cut him where he scarred me," she said without the strength to look up again. "Even the ..." *Even the ones you can barely see.*

"You were dead," Ari said, his voice thick. "I was thorough."

She couldn't breathe. It shouldn't have felt like it did. Warm and tingly. So incredibly sweet. He'd marked Ophion up even when he thought she was gone. Took flesh the Malek owed for what he'd done to her in Keloseros.

And there was a part of her that wanted to discount it, chalk it up to general violence and Ari's own satiation, where revenge was concerned. But the way he looked at her now ... It said something else entirely.

She cleared her throat, trying to push down the bundle of emotions that choked her because his eyes looked like the mortal night sky and they were wholly focused on her. Such heavy attention.

"Now it's your turn." Ari stepped away from the wall lazily. "He hates my kind so much," he purred, moving around the room, one hand in his pocket. "Let's make him look a little more like one of us." He smirked slowly, lifting his arm and levying it against the heavy metal chain that stretched Ophion's remaining wing taut. The Malek cried out, his body pulling toward Ari as much as it could, the manacle on his other wrist keeping him chained down. "Maybe he'll find new appreciation."

Make him look a little more like one of us.

"No," the Malek wheezed, like he knew what Ari planned when she didn't. Ophion's eyes stuttered toward the demon and it was the first time Aheia had seen that particular emotion on his face, in his stare. *Fear.*

She liked how it looked.

"What do you mean?" she asked, as Ari rounded the slab and leaned down, sliding her gold knife from its holster at her thigh.

"Take the last thing that's his and ruin him like he tried to ruin you."

Take it. She looked from Ari to Ophion's wing.

"Fuck," she whispered, realizing what he'd meant—*make him look a little more like us.*

Take his wing.

Her jaw set hard as she looked down at his palm, taking the blade with shaking hands. She let him lead her to the Malek and help her onto his back. If she was going to do this, she needed to do it quick—before she lost her nerve.

Her insides squeezed uncomfortably when she settled in on top of Ophion. Feeling him warm and alive between her legs was sickening, but she focused on her blade, her own reflection in it. She tried to inhale, but it felt a lot like she was a fish out of water as she gripped the top of his wing and brought the knife to the joint. Her fingers shook against the strain, when the Malek fought, a string of Gjóssa words falling from his lips. Pleas. Curses. Persecution.

It felt impossible to hold on.

But then Ari's hand covered hers against the hilt and helped her hold tight.

She let herself remember the worst of it, let herself remember all of the pain he'd caused, and didn't try to hold on to her tears, didn't try to dampen the swell of emotion. She'd always choked that down, always hidden it away, because all it would do was break her heart. Not now. Now she let it all wash across her because, just maybe, she could let it go if she did.

It was harder than she expected, digging the gold blade into the thick appendage. Her ears muffled and she couldn't hear anything but her own blood rushing as she sliced. The skin gave way, and so did the ligaments, and the meat, but it was the bone that stopped her knife. She'd started her incision too high, had to dig underneath it while red blood splattered her, and the tears dripped onto the gaping wound that was forming below. She grit her teeth, focusing so hard she couldn't think, cutting and carving, while the Malek fought and screamed. He fought like she'd fought. And for once, it wasn't her at his mercy. For the last time, it was the other way around.

Her vision blurred completely with the tears she cried, until her fingers gripped tight, and the knife slipped. There was too much blood, and she couldn't keep her hold, the blade clattering to the floor. Her chest shook with a sob, but she couldn't hear that either over her heart. She heard nothing until Ari's hand caressed the back of her neck, and his eyes invaded the sea of red filling her vision.

"Hold on," he said, his voice fuzzy. And she did, digging her wet fingers into Ophion's flesh. Ari helped rip the last of the connecting tissue and then they tore off the wing, separating the last bits of stringy skin that attached it.

The appendage fell to the floor with a wet thud, and the Malek below her flinched. He wasn't screaming anymore. Wasn't doing anything but convulsing.

She just sat there as Ari brought over a lit torch and used it to burn Ophion's skin. It sizzled under the embers, and she felt the heat of the flame. Blood and melted fat ran down his ribs and narrowly missed her knees as she adjusted.

"Where are your Gods now?" she murmured, feeling his blood cool on her skin as she looked at the cuts on his body one last time.

Ari was staring at her, the vein at his temple jumping, like he was holding something back. "You look beautiful covered in the blood of your enemies." He closed his fingers around hers, swallowing her up, and the last inhale she'd managed tumbled from her lips like it had reconsidered its presence in her body. She let him help her down, let him steady her while she stared down her past. Ophion almost looked dead and Aheia might have thought he was if it wasn't for the slight muscle twitches.

The blood was starting to get cold on her skin as she told herself it was real. That it wasn't a dream, and that the way the edges of the cave looked fuzzy was normal. That the odd brushes on her skin, like feathers or wings, were normal. Ophion looked so incredibly mortal. So fucking average without both of those imposing, wings.

"We'll come back for more." Ari pulled her from her compulsion.

"More?" she asked.

"Any part of him you want to take."

Her heart ached, and she wondered if anyone else would feel this way? Like what he offered was an endearment. Or maybe this new version of her really was just a monster. Would she become worse with every blade he held out to her?

"And this?" she asked, her voice sounding hollow to her own ears. Ari followed her gaze down to the wing.

"I have a place for it."

Ophion's blood was starting to crack, baring Aheia's skin like white veins underneath. Ari led her back through the halls of the compound, the Malek's wing in tow, painting the dark marble in a red, thick streak. Feathers were trapped in the sticky blood and it looked like the delicate white puffs were growing from between the gold seams.

Aheia looked down at herself—a fucked up light creature, some grisly vision with wet feathers clinging to her skin. Her hands were still red and her fingernails were rimmed. The blood smeared up her arms and ate at the pearls on her body.

So much blood.

She was mesmerized, felt her eyes glaze over while her mind stayed static. The longer she looked, the more it all felt so incredibly unreal.

"Aheia." Ari's interruption to her thoughts warmed her chest, like the hollow expanse within it took his voice and filled itself with it.

He was watching her carefully, and she tried her best to understand the look on his face. It was unfair—how he seemed to read her like her thoughts were drawn on her fair skin in black ink when she could sparsely understand the language blazing in his eyes.

"Hmm?" She'd followed him in a fever haze, and didn't realize they'd entered a new room until he made her focus. This place was familiar; she'd been here before, just after he'd taken her soul. There was a burnt orange couch, the one she'd awoken on for the first time, where she lost the contents of her stomach. Across from them was a marble desk tucked in front of a mantle, and a few pieces of jewel-toned furniture. And—

Her eyes climbed the far wall behind the desk, drawn to the white disruption above—the moon on a starless light.

There it hung, feathers spread, and flesh dried out. Ophion's other wing. Like a trophy. A warning. A declaration. There would be no mistaking how Alshaytan felt about his enemies.

"You have a place for it." It's all she could manage to say, regurgitating his words from the caves.

Her fingers brushed across the marble of the desk, and she pressed her weight against it, needing help, because her strength was fading with the adrenaline. Reality started to set in, the truth of what had just happened, what she'd done, what she'd heard.

Part Nephilim.

"What do you think about me? Do you believe him?" she asked.

"It always seemed like a weak cover." He dropped the wing in front of the fireplace and rounded the desk.

"What?" Her eyes snapped up, and she turned to face him head on. "You *knew*?"

"I knew about the possibility of it," he said slowly, "Kal told me, thinking it would help persuade me." Ari planted his hands on either side of the desk and she was forced to sit back against it.

Kal knew? Was that why it had been so easy for him to betray her? Did it mean so much? Something she couldn't control herself? Something that was forced upon her before birth?

"Persuade you into a trade?"

Did he think she was an abomination, too?

"No." Ari's eyes dropped to her lips. "They thought telling me that you were a mixed breed would be enough to disgust me. That I couldn't possibly want to keep you here after finding out." Those irises darkened, and the small space between them felt intrusive. "When it wasn't, they offered up Kazim."

"You never told me."

"Does it matter?"

"Depends." She tried to keep her voice measured. "On why you didn't."

"I don't think it's the truth." Ari finally eradicated those inches of space between them, brushing his knuckles across her bottom lip.

"Why?"

Her lips parted as he hunched down, his hand curving across the inside of her thigh, inching higher slowly. The rough texture of his palm grazed her skin, and she fought the urge to clamp it between her legs, because if he traveled further, he'd know. He'd know that her heartbeat had dropped to her clit, and that satin hid wetness worse than any other fabric.

A shiver ran down her spine as he trailed underneath those pearls and touched her. *Fuck*, he touched her. It was all over every time he did that. And it felt unfair and painful, because Nephilim, or Mithra—whatever the fuck she was—she wasn't strong enough to pull away. It took nothing, just a look, a caress, connection, to stop her in her tracks, to break her down when she hadn't had time to gather all her pieces from the last time he'd *touched*.

"You don't taste like my demons," he rasped, the hoarseness of his voice making her knees buckle. He sounded affected, and she needed that. Needed him to crave this the way she did.

"What do I taste like then?" A sad little whimper worked its way up her throat when pleasure sparked against his fingertips, her clit throbbing underneath the thin fabric barrier. He'd feel it, he'd know. It was fucked up. Now was not the time to feel this way—covered in blood and feathers. *Fuck*. She dug her fingers into her palm, but the pain did nothing to clarify this time. The pain made it all worse when he swept the flimsy fabric that covered her to the side, strong eyes keeping her pinned and mute.

"Like achlys. Like my realm."

"Your realm?" Her chest caved with an exhale she didn't realize had lodged itself somewhere in her throat, and her legs jerked when the pad of his thumb brushed over her clit. Her core clenched, and all she wanted in that moment was more. All she wanted was to not be empty. She'd felt empty for so long ... And he fixed that. Stretched her, filled her, in more ways than one, and it made her chest hum.

"It's on my tongue whenever you're near." She rolled her hips against his fingers, chasing them closer, but before she could truly slide her cunt against him, he pulled away, cold air now lapping at the heat between her legs. "And that flower belongs to Aljira—it belongs to me." He brought his wet fingers to his mouth. "You've always tasted like mine." She watched helplessly as he cleaned them off with that Gods damned tongue.

He'd forced her to tell him she was his so many times now, but somehow this felt different. He was so undoubtedly sure.

It wasn't a question, and she should have continued to hate him for that, because it was yet another choice he took from her. But the part of her soul that reached for him in a crowded room wanted him to say it again and again. To make *her* say it again and again, because that part of her wanted it—wanted to be his—purred for the possession he showed.

The other side of the same coin was different—the side that reminded her of her past and laid her wrists in golden manacles.

"I lost my magyck when it was the only thing I ever felt was truly mine. Not even my mind gives me that courtesy. I've never been my own. Not really ... and now—" She stood a little taller, needing to find space between them to tell him the thing that had burrowed in her mind for so long. "I can't be someone's property. Not again."

He'd told her before, not all that long ago, that while she was his, he wasn't hers. And that threw her completely out of balance, even now.

"Then carve out your space here." His jaw flexed, but he didn't hesitate to give her his answer. "Take what you want, don't let anything else happen to you,"

"You think that's what my old life was? That I *wanted* to be abused? You think I wanted any of that?" Her eyebrows twitched, and she clamped down on the vulnerability that surfaced, fixing him with the hardest stare she was capable of. And for just a moment, she pretended they were as fake as their reflections in the pond, because then she could find the strength a little easier.

Ari reached out and brushed his fingers across the place where her brows met, smoothing across it. Soft. *Too soft.*

"No." His voice was thick. "But this is different. You didn't have anyone in your corner then. You do now."

No matter how hard her muscles tensed as she tried to shove herself behind the familiar façade she wore on her features, she couldn't seem to fit anymore. Instead, her bottom lip trembled and her eyes burned with traitorous tears.

"If Ophion didn't have Kazim, would you still have thrown me to the wolves?" She needed to hear the words. One way or another, she needed to know.

"I wouldn't have taken you back, Aheia," he said, his voice thick.

"Because you weren't bored with me yet?" she snapped, feeling the resentment creep into her chest.

"Because you were right about me." *All gravel.* "You make me feel out of control and I forced space between us because of it, because I didn't know how to need you the way I did, the way I *do.* You're under my fucking skin and you haven't left since the day I ripped your soul from you."

She felt the tears sitting precariously behind a dam, and the more he told her, the harder it got to hold on to them. *He feels it too. He needs it too.*

"I would have let the wolves eat me before they ever got to you again." His shadows pooled at her hips and it looked exhausted, if magyck could look that way, matching his dark eyes, and the way his shoulders slumped. He'd looked like that in the washroom, too. "Because you took my choice the day I took yours."

Her breathing shallowed, and the echo between them hummed as if it was answering a question neither of them had asked.

"This is *not* my fault," she grit between her teeth.

"No, it's mine." He ran his fingers through his hair. "I've been many things to many creatures." He continued. "I don't decide the fate of souls. I am only cursed with the need for them. I'm a sovereign that can't please his people, because there is simply no way to do so without displeasure following in its wake, and I am a brother and son, who was never enough. I am seen through many lenses, and so are my decisions. In truth, they rarely feel like my own." She watched his lips as he spoke in disbelief, because she'd never heard him give her so many words, so much insight in one breath.

"Why are you telling me this?"

"Everything comes at a price."

"Your transparency. It's payment?" she asked carefully. "What for?"

"Your forgiveness, Ruhí."

Your forgiveness, Ruhí.

"You haven't called me that in a long time," she said.

"I made the word hollow when I said it without meaning." He took her cheeks in his hands. "Forgive me, please. For that too."

That small balloon in her chest swelled to the size of the entire cavity. *Please.* She didn't remember apologies in her life, only the concept of them. Had been forced to voice her own for things she didn't feel in the wrong for. Didn't know what receiving them was supposed to feel like. But where Ophion telling her some story about her past had left her cold, this did the opposite. In that moment she couldn't separate her mind from her soul from their bond. It was all one warm and vibrating mess.

"Everything comes at a price." She asked, her voice hoarse. "And words are pretty, but what will you do for me? What will you give me, if I forgive you?"

His shadows purred.

"A life you're not afraid of."

"That's a heavy promise."

He leaned in, softening his touch as he tipped her chin with his knuckles."Good thing I'm very strong."

She blushed deeper while the softness he offered seemed to coax out hers.

"Why? Why do you want me here?" she whispered.

"Because no God could ever bring me to my knees the way you do."

She opened her mouth, a shocked sound bursting from it. Those embers in his eyes sparked, falling to her lips as they twitched into a smile. He was *staring*, and if she didn't know better, she would have called the expression shock.

"What is that look for?" She gripped his wrists, looking at him bewildered for a moment.

"Fuck, that's beautiful," he rasped, staring at her mouth, his thumbs brushing across her bottom lip when she realized it; realized when she felt the strain in her cheeks.

The smile on her face.

She'd forgotten to swallow it.

And it was the worst time—the most inappropriate time in the entire fucking world as they soaked in Ophion's drying blood, but she couldn't help it, now.

"I don't mean to interrupt—" Aheia jumped, her heart jumping into her throat.

Shiron was standing in the doorjamb with his arms crossed, and his expression pinched. "But you'll want to see this."

Chapter 43

Aheia

There had been a Shykoya attack in Thryn, Shiron told them, but Aheia had a hard time focusing on it when she was still reeling from that moment in Ari's office.

He'd called her *Ruhí* for the first time since that Gods forsaken church and he'd *asked for forgiveness.*

Her heart was in her throat.

He'd asked for forgiveness tonight, but it felt a lot like the words were simply the period at the end of a sentence. Because when she stepped away from herself, and looked at her time with him, she saw the little things she wouldn't let herself look at before.

How Ari had pushed her and fed her when she didn't want him to. He'd stacked books in her hand and asked her to learn his language so that she'd understand.

He didn't want to hide her, even when hiding was all she wanted.

And ... he cared if she smiled. No one had ever cared about that before.

She exhaled slowly, feeling his magyck caressing her, while Ari's hand was on her lower back.

He could have told her to stay at the compound now too, he could have made her wait for him. He didn't.

But all of the warmth that came with those realizations vanished when her heels clacked across old cobblestone and the night air blew away the lingering shadows.

They were standing in a small square, with exactly one entrance and one exit.

"The Shykoya were wrangled and killed, but this is where they came from." Shiron pointed to a hovel that was built into the ground so deep that they had to crawl on their bellies. And they did, instead of walking through Ari's shadows. Aheia didn't know why, but there was something about the experience that snagged on her mind—something she remembered from the Mithra text that was shared by the mortals. *That those who transgressed against the higher natures and Gods alike would be forced to crawl their way into hel on their stomach, swallowing the dirt and the flies that lived within.*

"Fucking mercy," Kar mumbled, standing near the entrance, as Ari helped Aheia to her feet. *Fucking mercy is right.* Aheia held her hand over her nose and mouth, eyes skirting across the blood and guts that slathered the floors. Tariq and Lúc were standing at the center of the space, exchanging hushed words in Lujha, while Aylee and Emryn were looking over the wreckage in the hallway that felt a lot more like damnation than Gehenna did.

"What is this?" Aheia whispered behind Ari, eyes roving over the dilapidated surroundings.

"It's a Nerium nest—a drug nest." Lúc shook his head. "The Shykoya took this place a-fucking-part."

She followed Ari while he took inventory, remembering what it had meant to be hunted by the monsters herself. They were quick and seemingly without aim, sinking their claws and teeth into anything they could reach. She remembered

Keosha too, and all of its burnt homes. There hadn't been any dead in the streets there, but here, that's all there was. Bodies lay all over the house, most of them dead with the exception of a few demons who were so high off Nerium they couldn't move—didn't seem like they could even see their surroundings. She wondered why they had been spared by the monsters.

Ari led her through the rooms wordlessly as Aheia rubbed the back of her hand underneath her nose to fight the rotting smell that had no way of escaping from the windowless hovel. Each small room was worse than the last, and by the third, Aheia's heels were covered in blood and grime. They were a rotten pink now, just how she imagined the strawberries in her stomach the morning after drinking.

Ari was inspecting two crouched together Nephilim in the corner, who both stared at the wall, completely blissed out when Lúc walked in.

"What is all of this?" The Shifter razed his knuckles over Aheia's waist, chipping some of the blood that was dried against her pearls as Shiron joined them too, and the others slowly filtered in.

"Foreplay."

"Not so vanilla then." He grinned, biting at his lip ring.

"My least favorite flavor," she said in a level voice, distracted by the blood dripping from the ceiling, a low, and ominous sound. The smell was starting to get to her, her mind feeling a bit dizzy as they stood there. *Drip. Drip. Drip.* Into a small dark pool.

"I have a thought," Shiron said as Aylee entered the room.

"Share with the class?" Lúc's grin spread, but Shiron stayed stoic.

"The roof dweller that alerted us of the Shykoya tonight said he saw it running from the nest."

"Ok?" Tariq was on Emryn's heels, draping a heavy arm across Lúc's shoulders.

"The monster could have made it from the forest through town and to the nest, without anyone seeing it, but it's highly unlikely. There are still guards stationed at the border because the border isn't completely knitted together here, and none of them saw it break through from the outskirts."

"There's no way they would have missed it. The Shykoya aren't known for being quiet and sneaky," Emryn bridged.

"No, they're not." Shiron shook his head. "On top of that, even *if* the monsters somehow made their way through the border undetected, there were no kills outside of the nest. There were plenty of demons out tonight, it should have been a bloodbath."

"What are you suggesting?" Lúc asked.

"That the Shykoya didn't come from the border. They came from the nest instead."

"Ok, how?" Tariq narrowed his eyes and a soft chill crept up Aheia's spine. "Tie those threads together for us."

Shiron's lip twitched in distaste. "You remember the demons that were killed by that Shykoya in Jahra?" he asked, and Ari nodded. "The dying male accused me of killing *her*." Aheia scrunched her nose, unsure of what that meant. "He accused me of killing *her* when I slit the monster's throat."

"He was drugged out of his mind." Aylee held a flame under her nails until the tips lit on fire while Aheia was trying to keep up with all of the information being swapped back and forth.

"Right." Shiron nodded. "He was an addict, and so was the other demon that was murdered that night. The Falkri we sent back to scour the surroundings didn't find a nest near their corpses, but odds are that they lived in one. We weren't alerted about that attack from the border either, just like we weren't alerted tonight, but we didn't consider what that might mean—"

"That they might have already been in the city," Ari finished.

"What if *her* was exactly what the dying demon meant?" Shiron's eyes sparked. "What if I killed *her*? What if the Shykoya aren't monsters at all?"

"Wait, clarify," Aylee said.

"It's just a theory," Shiron said. "But what if the Shykoya are Nephilim?"

"You're stretching far across that bridge," Tariq said, crossing his arms. "How the fuck would that be possible?"

"One common denominator," Ari said, looking at Shiron.

"Nerium." The Leviathan nodded.

"Hold on, you think that the Shykoya are Nerium users? That the drug is turning them?" Tariq asked.

"Maybe," Shiron said.

"The Shykoya have been a pest for over a decade now, but the border has kept them out until recently, implying that they live in the forest. Why would they *all of a sudden* be sprouting from these nests when they never have in the past?" Tariq challenged.

"Something's changed," Ari said, his voice a low timber. "If Nerium is truly turning the demons, then someone has their hand in the Shykoya's creation."

"You think it's intentional?" Lúc asked.

"Nerium has been around far longer than the Shykoya. The monsters are a new occurrence comparatively. It doesn't connect unless you consider that something in the drug itself has shifted. Drugs get cut and sold, Nerium is no different. Someone could be using it like a carrier. Like the serum Emryn uses to create antidotes, but with a virus instead."

"Who the fuck would do this to their own kind?" Lúc scrubbed a hand down his face, eyes tinged purple.

"I don't know. But I'm going to find out," Ari ground through his teeth.

"It was a choice. Turning themselves into monsters was a *choice,*" Kar murmured.

"Allegedly," Tariq piped in.

"It's the best theory we have," Emryn said.

"Even so, it doesn't mean that they had a conscious part in it. The drug might have been manipulated without their knowledge." Shiron added.

Aylee nodded. "They effectively shot addictive poison into innocent demon's veins, making them beg for their own death."

Nerium.

"Ok, but how—"

They continued exchanging their thoughts, but Aheia's mind felt heavy again. Her attention drew back to the black blood dripping as the others continued volleying different ideas across the small circle they'd formed. Ari and Shiron took a step away a moment later, heading to the far side of the room, and it was the last thing Aheia registered as the dripping became loud. Their voices faded slowly, and she didn't quite register when Lúc addressed her.

"Hmm?" she asked, shaking her head.

The Shifter furrowed his brows. "You're pale," he repeated.

"Just noticing now?" She quirked her eyebrow, as the fumes around her made her stomach gurgle and her mind buzz.

"Being a smartass won't be so cute when you faint and fall into the shit on the floor."

"You'll catch me, won't you?" she asked, once again, hearing the blood. Why was it so loud? She swallowed, blinking in hopes of dulling the *drip. Drip. Drip.*

"Not with an attitude like—" Lúc started.

"You're shiny." The voice rang clear as a bell, splitting through the room and Aheia's head whipped up from her fixation, her fingers twisting in the pearls on her body as if they could squeeze her back in comfort. The interruption had come from a female with the dirty curls across the room. She was huddled with a male that still stared at the wall like it was his salvation.

"Me?" Aheia whispered, holding her hand to her chest as the demons around her shifted their attention.

"No fucking way," Lúc said in disbelief, crossing his arms. "She doesn't look lucid enough for that kind of recognition."

"So shiny." The voice was a jarring moan as the female ran her fingernails down her sternum, her sweaty skin thin enough for the veins to be visible.

"She's not. Something's wrong, she—" Aylee started but as she spoke, the demon on the floor scrambled over the mattress she'd been sitting on. She dug her dirty nails into the wood and heaved herself forward, kicking the male next to her in the face hard enough to dislocate his jaw in the process. She was moving with a speed that shouldn't have been possible in her state, launching herself at Aheia. Lúc pushed her back, just as Aylee snatched the frail thing up by her waist and yanked her back. The drugged out female's fingers swiped right in front of Aheia's eyes and she saw the look on her face, the *hunger* in her eyes. It imprinted itself on her mind, even though it was just a small moment in time. She knew, as she fell back through the air, that she'd remember that exact expression.

She readied herself for the impact, her muscles tensing in preparation for the bruises that the splintered wood would cause. Instead, her body careened through the flimsy tapestry that hung there, ripped apart as Aheia's weight tore it down.

Her shoulder smashed against cold, hard rock and the air was knocked out of her as the pearls that had felt comfortable before imprinted on her skin like they wanted to embed themselves.

"Fuck," she huffed, pressing herself up on weak arms, and looking above her as dust and dirt rained down around her. The hole she'd fallen through was the only light illuminating the space.

"Aheia!" Lúc yelled, his head popping through the opening, and she held her palm over her eyes, shielding herself when more of the debris fell. Her knees felt brittle as she righted herself, the heels she'd enjoyed earlier in the night becoming her new adversary. It was so dark that she didn't see the shadows, didn't realize that they had gathered until Ari stepped through and Aheia yelped, her heart thundering in her chest.

"You scared me," she huffed, as he pulled her close, rubbing his hands across her body like he was making sure she wasn't hurt.

"Anything feel broken?" he asked, dropping to one knee and taking her ankles in his hand one by one, slipping off the deathtrap shoes.

My pride.

"No." She exhaled roughly, holding on to his shoulders, as the arches of her feet smarted.

"Well, that made no fucking sense." Aylee jumped down the hole, landing gracefully in her own heels and pulling out a lighter. The others followed slowly, every one of them landing as if the height was no worse than a stair step. "Have you ever seen a junkie that could walk after withering away to that degree? Most of them live in their own piss and shit because they can barely shift their limbs. It ran. It fucking *ran* with no regard for anything around it. It acted like an animal, just like those monsters do."

"It feeds your theory," Lúc told Shiron, who looked grim.

You're shiny. The words echoed in her mind with an uncomfortable cadence.

Everything was dark until Aylee lit the flame of her lighter, illuminating their surroundings and throwing their shadows up on the wall. Aheia's eyes drew to her neck, black blood dripping from the wound the drugged out Nephilim had caused while Aylee lit her fingernails like candles.

"Is anyone watching her?" Aheia rasped, massaging against her sore skin, sinking into Ari's embrace without a conscious thought about it.

"She's not going anywhere. Her legs are broken," Aylee said, the fire flickering in her blue eyes ominously.

"'Amm's sake," Shiron said, from Aheia's left, and she redirected her attention. Aylee's flame illuminated the small space they stood in, and licked into a long, dark tunnel just ahead. It was carved into thick rock, the edges lined in rough brick, precariously stacked in a way that kept the dirt from collapsing. There were worms crawling over and moss sprouting between the crags of the floor. Stale and dingy. But not untouched. There was disturbed dust all over the ground, dragged around by haphazard steps. *Fresh* steps.

"*Tunnels,*" Lúc said. "It's tunnels. Of course it's fucking tunnels."

"They could span the entire fucking city," Ari continued, like he and Lúc were tethered to the same thought.

"It's how they're shifting their product," Kar said, eyes flicking between the two males. "How they're circulating Nerium. It has to be."

Aheia's eyes slid back to Ari when her skin pebbled, like a shiver that was his but acted as her own. A beat passed and her awareness heightened. A moment of slowed time that she shared with the Avarice at her back.

Kar took a step closer, her fingers flexing at her side as she looked at Ari with a concerned expression on her face. "Why?" she asked, and Aheia looked up at him confused, unsure of what Kar meant. The empath's voice wavered, but Ari didn't look at her. Instead, his nostrils flared and his shoulders straightened. Something shifted in the air when they did, and Aheia felt the crackle like a tangible thing all around her but Arioch didn't react, only stared past her with bared teeth. She followed his gaze just as Shiron did, squinting through the darkness at the wall.

What does he see?

"*Oh,*" Kar breathed out softly, and Aheia's eyes snapped to hers as Lúc drifted his hand across the rock wall.

"Is that fucking Sahren's crest?"

CHAPTER 44

AHEIA

"Holy fuck. It is." Lúc ran his fingers over the grooves, and Aheia thought she could make out the form of a wolf and a few undecipherable glyphs. The actual depiction was so weathered that only faint lines were left.

"If his crest is on these walls, then that means—" Aylee started.

"Sahren was fucking involved," Tariq interrupted.

"In the Nerium trade," Emryn spoke to the floor.

"I wouldn't put it past him." Lúc scoffed. "He was involved in everything fucking else." His purple eyes bit out from the darkness, his jaw clenched tight. Anger. It was the same anger that Ari held.

"Wait, why would he stamp his own crest into the wall? Why implicate himself?" Aheia asked.

"Because Nerium was legal until recently," Ari growled.

Kar pulled a breath through her teeth, and Aheia watched Shiron wrap an arm around her shoulder. The empath's brows were knit close, and sweat started to collect at her hairline. Her lips were twisted, and her hand was dug tightly into her stomach like she was trying to lessen a pain. Her eyes didn't meet Aheia's; she just stared ahead, stared at Ari.

It's him. She feels him.

"Why?" Kar asked it again, just like she had when Ari first noticed the crest, an open and incomplete question. The word heightened the awareness around them, and the other demons all shifted their attention to the Avarice.

"He killed her." Darkness seeped into his gray irises and swallowed his embers while an unsettling whirring broke through the stale air. Aheia shifted, taking a step back because it emanated from him and vibrated through her in turn. She didn't like this feeling.

"Who?" she asked under her breath as Emryn's gaze shifted to Aylee's in a silent exchange.

"We don't know that for sure." Whatever conclusion Ari had come to, Lúc was on the same page, and Aheia was in the wrong book.

The darkness spread, pouring from Ari and crawling across the dirt around them. The tendrils looked almost sharp, spidery legs that climbed up the walls slowly. His fingers twitched again as he rolled his chin to the side, and it looked like an animal trying to find space in its skin.

"Sahren's dead," the Syraphem said, and her voice was the softest Aheia had ever heard it, while her eyes stayed sharp, surveying his magyck. "And she's gone. You can't kill him again. It's over."

Sahren's dead. Aheia's breath caught in her throat. Ari's father was dead. And *She's gone.* The pieces fell into place right in front of her.

She was an addict. Ari had told her that day in the washroom. *She overdosed.*

Malia, his mother, had died at the hands of her addiction—her addiction to Nerium. And his father was involved in the circulation of it.

He killed her.

Kar groaned, digging her fingers into her side, frantic eyes meeting Emryn's. "Out. Now. We need to get *out*; he can't—*fuck.*"

"What's happening?" Aheia's head whipped between the demons.

"Get her out of here," Luc snapped at Emryn. "Now."

Ari hissed, the sound guttural, as his skin dotted with dark pearls. The shadows dripped down him like water, staining him, marking him as his face screwed up in anguish.

"No, you're kidding. *No.*" Aheia shook her head, readying herself because she was used to being pushed when she fought back. "Tell me what's going on."

"His magyck—" Kar started, but Emryn crossed the room and grabbed ahold of Aheia's arm.

"Come along. We don't have time for stories." The Syraphem jerked Aheia with her, but when she did, Ari snarled, his now black eyes fixated on where Emryn held her.

"Don't you fucking dare," His voice twined, and Aheia didn't recognize the sound of it even as it tugged at her echo.

"Brother, you need to calm down," Lúc said slowly, shooting a sharp look to Tariq, who nudged Aylee back the way they'd come from. "Don't let them do this to you."

"*You're not my brother*," Ari snarled, dark eyes narrowing on the Shifter. They were black like a starless night, a void, something cold and punishing that looked like it wanted to devour.

The Shifter bristled, his black claws cutting open the skin between his fingers, his eyes never once leaving the Avarice.

"Arioch had help killing Sahren that day; it wasn't entirely him. It was something much darker, much more powerful, something that lives inside of him, and I think he holds on to very tightly."

The static inside of Aheia crackled as Emryn pulled at her arm with enough force to make her trip. This time, the Avarice in front of them didn't just snarl; this time, he moved. Death was etched into his features, and she knew then that she was staring at his shadows.

The Shifter lunged forward, his claws digging into the Avarice's shoulder, but that didn't stop him. His magyck wrapped around Luc, choking his throat until he was gasping and forced to let go. Emryn shrugged back with Aheia, pulling out one of her knives as Luc's body vaulted into the hallway, and Aheia shrieked, watching his head hit against the rock. The Avarice bared his teeth, eyes focused on her as he lunged forward, and the Syraphem lost hold of Aheia. The darkness rushed in, wrapping her up and vanishing everyone but her into nothingness. Suddenly, the room that had felt so small spanned on for miles. At least, that's how it felt as she stood suspended, her hair drifting around on charged air. *Alone.* It felt like being inside of a cloud right before the lightning struck. Soft caresses touching her skin, pillowy ground beneath her feet.

It was dark, but it wasn't. Aheia could see herself, the blood-covered pearls, and her own hair that was stark against the magyck. But for all the proof of her singularity here, she felt the presence. It was around her, touching her, *inside* of her blood. It was the echo manifested into a tangible thing, and when she realized it, the black tendrils pulled together into an unimaginably tall form. It was all smoke, but it looked like a body.

Aheia inhaled sharply, watching a limb reach out and wrap around the necklace at her throat, tugging her closer. She stumbled, what felt a lot like a hand bracing her waist. She stared above her into dark voids, hearing that same whirr that had been flowing from Ari in the tunnels. She knew when it touched her; it was the same shadow that had touched her before. There was a recognition she never could have imagined possible. It reached into the echo and wrenched it apart, and Aheia choked on a gasp, feeling her nerves spark all across her body.

Come find me. It rang in her ear, but it didn't stem from the darkness—it came from her own mind. She remembered it, but she didn't.

"*Let her go,*" the shadow purred, swallowing her limbs whole until it held her entirely.

"Who?" She whispered as the brush of magyck swiped over her jaw, calming the jitter just below it. Her eyes started to burn, and she didn't know why--a response that wasn't hers.

"*You're suffocating her.*" The hair on the back of her neck stood on end, and the chain around her throat stretched taut until it cut into her skin. Her arms strained against the hold, the black tendrils seeping into the crack at the center of the lápis slowly.

"*She's mine.*" The deep whisper emanated from the depths of the tall figure, and Aheia's chin tipped, her breathing shallow, as the connection between them flared.

Fear dotted her, hot pricks of the embers that whirled from a flame when the wind disturbed it as she stood motionless.

"*Not his, not yours.*"

Aheia's chest heaved, and her body shook as the pressure on the lápis increased. She could feel like the tendrils that slipped between the crack were inside of her, were between her ribs instead of the rock, and when they broke her stone apart, she felt it.

"No!" Aheia cried, the pain in her mind blooming like she had shattered along with it, her innards twisting sharply. The hold that had kept her in place disappeared, and she doubled over, fingers clenching at the horrible stitch in her side. The shadows whipped around her like a hurricane, her hair getting swept up, and her body vaulted forward until the static became unbearable and her back smashed into something hard.

Colors bloomed behind her eyelids, and she choked on the air in her throat, her fingers digging into the ground. *Ground.* It was stones and dirt, and she felt it as renewed stillness found her now. There were small blades of grass sticking up between her fingers, and she stared at them, stared at the thin veins of color that ran along each delicate length. She'd seen the likes before, too—the day she came back from the dead. The color that had painted those vines overhead, the vines she'd reached for in search of comfort even though no part of her understood how a plant could provide it.

She gulped down chilled air, hearing the sounds around her—clicks, ribbits, hoots.

The forest.

Aheia rubbed the tears into her eyes, and when she pulled back her hands, she faced the brightest stars she'd ever seen. They were bleeding and swirling like the night was leaching their edges. Her heart pounded with the colors of the stars.

"What the hel just happened?" she croaked out, hand shooting to her aching throat and rubbing against it. She could barely form the words with the pain.

The shadows are lying to you.

The soft whisper clouded her mind.

Let her go. You're suffocating her.

Her hand curled into the pearls at her middle and squeezed as her shoulders shook, quiet sobs echoing through the quiet darkness around her. Her chest ached, and her limbs felt like they were being held over a flame. It didn't look right, it didn't *feel* right—any of it. How was it possible? How was she standing on a meadow of color, the same light spiderwebbing up the bark of the once dark trees in front of her? *Too bright.* All of it was. Bright and quiet.

Her ears felt hot at the realization. Her choked inhales were the only noise. Where she'd heard nature moments ago, everything was silent now. The fear she'd felt in his shadows flared from its dormancy, her mind reminding her of the last time her world had sounded so quiet.

She saw them in her memories.

Gray, taut skin. White-tipped claws. Teeth. They were hunger and pain and sorrow, and they created the kind of quiet she heard now.

Her breath whooshed from her, and she looked around frantically, trying to orient herself, *trying* to figure out which way would take her home. But all the trees bunched up tall against the edge of the clearing, and the moon was dead center overhead.

Her mind throbbed with the same pain that hadn't stopped since the shadows broke her crystal, and for a moment, it felt like she alone existed in this world. Just how it felt when fog ate her landscape. But then her blood chilled, a vicious screech shaking the leaves around her. Birds rose from in front of her, fleeing up into the night sky as smaller animals did the same, scurrying across the clearing.

The monsters came through the trees, and it was the terror from a nightmare. So many of them. A hoard just like that first day back at the atrium. The sight shook Aheia from her spot on the ground, and she ran. The leaves crunched underneath her hobbling steps, and she could taste blood in her mouth as her gums pulsed with exhaustion. Adrenaline coursed through her, and her muscles screamed, fighting the fire that jolted her into action and urged her further.

She ducked underneath low-hanging vines and wound around the trees, desperation throttling the air she tried to pull into her lungs.

You're not fast enough. You can't outrun them.

A sob shook her chest as the ground cut into her skin, and the noises grew closer. Snarls and growls and the ruination of nature as the Shykoya tore through the thick family of trees behind her.

They're right behind you.

She knew the truth of her thoughts, but she wouldn't slow down. She kept running, the world moving just slow enough to make everything feel a little less real. And she was thankful for the delusion when a heavy weight slammed into her body from behind.

Aheia shrieked, her spine smashing into the trunk of a tree at an odd angle, and her bones rattled as the jarring sounds of the Shykoya shifted above her. Claws sank into Aheia's arm, and she screamed, watching the dark red blood well and gush between long, poison-tipped talons. Aheia grappled, trying to reach for her knife, but the monster's long, pointed teeth gnashed in her face, keeping her back. Her free hand shoved against its shoulder, but the creature was too strong.

And then, just as her elbow trembled and her arm bent, the Shykoya was ripped from her. She choked out a cry, her skin peeling from the body where it had held her, her chest caving until she rolled in on herself in agony. The white venom streaked the blood that poured from the wound, and her vision flickered as the shadows roamed around her.

Koutávi.

The Varcolac tore into the monsters in front of her, black blood splashing, the leathery bodies no match for her sharp teeth and heavy paws. Aheia whimpered, trying to crawl forward, but her limbs ceased to be in her control, her body limp against the grass.

She watched helplessly as Koutávi finished off the last of the Shykoya, her snout dripping in inky blood when she stalked from the dense cloud of her own shadows. Her lip quivered, and her breathing devolved as the large creature sank onto its haunches, crawling around Aheia.

"Thank you," she choked out, her body pressing into the Varcolac's neck.

She grasped onto Koutávi's fur with trembling fingers, the pain of her wounds burning and bubbling. The venom that slicked the Shykoya's claws traveled through her—she could feel it eating at her cells. The taste on her tongue was bitter, and it only worsened with time.

It felt like death, the cold embrace of it inching closer as she held the warm thing in front of her tighter.

I don't want to die.

How many times had she considered her own death? How many times had she wished for it? Yet every instance in which she faced it, she was terrified.

She couldn't leave yet, not this world.

I just started.

The thought was barely above a whimper. She'd just started living. It couldn't end here, not yet. *Not yet.*

She sobbed into Koutávi's side. The Varcolac had saved her twice now. She was a creature without motivation impressed upon her by any outside force. It made Aheia feel like her own unimportant presence was okay and like the Varcolac didn't mind all the things she lacked, all the things she wasn't, all the things she hated herself for. That her existence wasn't wrong, wasn't a burden for once.

Not yet. Her face rested against Koutávi's heartbeat, her wet, heavy tongue licking across Aheia's shoulder like maybe that would fix this.

Thrum. Thrum. Thrum.

Warm, wet air passed between Aheia's lips, too hot, too sticky for the cold, late night around her. It prickled inside of her lungs and tightened her stomach. It felt impossible—the warmth swirling in its pit, slowly crawling up her sides—a pounding that matched her heart, her breath, the pulsing in her mind. It called her close and numbed the pain in her limbs with something so unimaginably loud.

Not yet.

Everything was black now. She didn't know when it had happened, when she'd lost her sight. But she was steeped in it. Not even peeling back her eyelids changed that. She was lost, gone, swallowed, and she couldn't find her way out.

Help! She tried to speak it, to scream it, but her lips were sealed shut, and no part of her body responded to her commands.

Is this death?

Was death simply never-ending darkness? Was this it? She whimpered, trying to blink, trying to see *anything* at all, and the noise echoed.

She turned and turned, but she didn't have a body here; it was just her gaze that searched for something other than *this.* The pain inside of her grew and grew, warmth spiraling hotter and brighter until, in that seemingly unending absence of light, she saw the soft glimmer. It was a string that looked like a vine, or maybe a vein, colorful and pulsing in front of her with every heartbeat she felt in her chest.

It was transparent and frayed, like something that threatened to disappear. A light thread in a mass of dark.

It coiled and weaved through the air as if it was submerged under water, and the hunger flared inside of Aheia at the sight. She reached, but the action wasn't hers.

Her fingers touched it, and it burned.

Fuck, it burned.

The lucid thing wrapped around her hand, and it scorched her skin as a scream tore from her. It was a hollow sound, like the last breath leaving a body, and her strength faltered as she closed her fist and the heat consumed her. It spread through her body, leaving a trail of fire until it broke into her fingertips. The silence around her rang in her ears, pain cutting through her head just as everything in front of her bloomed.

Energy burst around her field of vision, and her mind bled—at least, that's how it felt, something impossible breaking inside of her. The sky started melting, rolls of light dripping down the edges of the bowed world and pooling around her. The drips were what Aheia imagined starlight would look like if it lived in thick water, the sparkles bright and refracting. Her whole narrowed to a pinhole in front of her as the sorrow in her chest burned into nothing. Her fingers felt like they might explode, heat pouring from her heart and down her arms like the brightness around her had found its way inside and wanted to eat her soul. She tasted the stars on her tongue, and they tasted like peppermint, cold and biting. They burned into her very cells, coaxing out the ice and, in the same instance, the heat and twisted them into something symbiotic. Aheia was blind to the world, her chest lit with fluid metal that stretched and tested her skin. She needed it, a thing she couldn't describe while the pursuit of it called to her viciously.

Her legs shook, her thighs singing, and every nerve in her body lit up with pleasure. Lightning ran up her arms and tore through her flesh, but she couldn't pull away as cold, crisp liquid flowed from her fingers up to her shoulders. It felt like she'd been injected with water, and it made the hunger inside of her sizzle. It tempered with each pull, with each pulse of her hands, of her heart, of her soul. Every inhale fed her more until her skin stretched, until the heat at her fingertips started to blister.

Until suddenly, it all stopped.

CHAPTER 45

AHEIA

The pain ebbed, her body falling back against the hard ground limply.

Her fingers curled against the dirt as the sobs racked her, the blur in her vision pulling the intense starlight above her into odd shapes; it was all colors and blobs and feelings.

She felt the cold presence in her veins battling whatever warm and sensuous thing had wound itself into the fabric of her being. It was molten metal that twisted around cords of ice, the two tempering each other over and over again.

She flailed blindly, hands sliding against the soil, her veins hot and uncomfortable, like she could feel every single one as blood hurtled through her. Breathing was impossible, her lungs so full that the air she was gulping down had nowhere to go. Her own intentions had been wrenched from her frail fingers and burned underneath the light that was cooking her from the inside, replacing them with need. Nothing but a mind-numbing need for more.

More.

A defeated whimper split the silence, and Aheia's heavy head lifted, looking for it, her vision splotched with light.

Ice scraped through her veins, piercing her heart when she saw where the sound had come from.

"No!" she choked, her voice hoarse as she dragged herself forward, every part of her an aching muscle. Koutávi was lying on her side, her soft body exposed completely, her eyes half-lidded while her snout moved with uneven huffs. Her shadows were gone.

Horror gripped Aheia's middle as she dug her fingers into the fur of the Varcolac's neck, trying to find a pulse. The thin colored veins that were shining through the petals of flowers also ran within the Varcolac, except hers were much duller. They were fading.

"No, no, no, please." Aheia's hands shook as she patted across her fur, recognition humming in her blood.

Something inside of her wanted out, wanted back. Because whatever coursed through her now didn't belong to her.

"What did I do to you?" Her voice broke as she watched Koutávi's mouth foam with white bubbles that dripped onto the ground in a muddy pool.

"Help!" Aheia screamed, "Please, Gods, someone!"

She couldn't breathe when those gold irises met hers.

I did this ... I ...

"I'm sorry. I'm sorry. I don't know how to fix this. I can't fix this. I can't fix this." Her breathing was manic. *I can't fix this.*

Aheia tried and failed to support the beast underneath her, holding her paw out of the way as best she could to access her chest. But Koutávi only shuddered, her weight becoming heavier and heavier with time passing. The burning, alive thing inside of her drew to the creature, the thing that Aheia had taken from the Varcolac.

Not yours.

Her palms itched with something greedy; a vicious, dark voice that had never been as loud as it was now was telling her to return her hands and take fucking more.

"*Take it*." The words grated across her insides again with sharp talons. Dark and cold. "*Take the rest.*"

Aheia closed her eyes, frantically shaking her head as her fingers splayed over the soft fur. She could feel her weakness, could see it in the low, muted colors flickering out slowly.

Koutávi whimpered at the slight shift, and Aheia fell under the weight, squished between the Varcolac's elbow and the ground.

"Please," she sobbed, resorting to massaging the Varcolac's heart instead. It was weak, just like the brightness in her. "Please!" She hit Koutávi's chest with her fists until the sides of her hands bruised. But the colors faded regardless until she could barely see them, and the paw on her back fell limply against her spine and pushed her onto the wet ground. She'd been holding it for her, Aheia realized, the moment her true weight hit her chest. Her ribs ached with the pressure, but she let it crush her, holding on to the paw like if she just gripped it tight enough, she could keep the Varcolac alive, could keep her here.

Her eyes shot to Koutávi's, the gold dulling slowly, and she prayed. She prayed because maybe if she could just wish that everything was different, for once in her miserable life, it would actually be so. Because this plea wasn't for herself.

Hushed words in her own tongue fell from her lips as she stared overhead, hoping against every ounce of proof that her life had shown her that the Gods would intervene, that *someone* would help.

But the presence that peeled from the colorfully glowing trees in front of her was no God.

Aheia's face crumbled, tears spilling down her cheeks.

Mazikeen.

The Ifrit scorched the earth beneath her bare feet, fires blossoming on the leaves that brushed her skin, and Aheia sobbed out a desperate huff of air.

"Help her, please. *Please.*" Aheia continued her work against Koutávi's heart, even as her muscles screamed. "*Save her, heal her!*"

"I'm here for you," Mazikeen said, her voice thick. "Not her."

"I don't need—" she grit through her teeth, her voice faltering. "I don't *need* you."

"There is nothing to be done."

"There has to be," Aheia choked, hugging Koutávi's snout and scouring her for the light she'd seen before, looking for a twitch, the movement of breath, anything. "She needs—She's *dying*. It's her that needs you."

"She's dead."

Please.

"She can't be—" *She can't be dead. She can't leave me.*

"It's over," Mazikeen said as Aheia rocked her body against Koutávi's throat and sobbed into her fur, fingers clenched so tight it pulled out strands at the root.

A scream tore itself loose from her chest while the Ifrit blurred into the well of tears that seemed never-ending.

Her hands patted across Koutávi's body frantically, and she tried to push whatever she'd stolen back, over and over again, until she vomited her stomach's contents onto the grass next to her. She strained and strained, shoved her hands against Koutávi's heart. The molten thing just under her palms squirming and crying for the body on the other side of her. Aheia did everything she could think of until the convulsing of her stomach made her sick twice more. All the while, Mazikeen sat on her knees, towering over her, watching.

"Why are you *here*?" Aheia finally choked at the ground, bitter anger curling itself into her chest, colorful blades of grass poking between her fingers.

"Because he can't be."

He can't be. Her eyes snapped back to the Ifrit, blistering fire broiling her.

Arioch did this. His shadows *did this.* When he broke her stone, everything changed.

No, you *did this.*

She coughed again, dry heaves wracking her chest, and the pain in her stomach intensified again.

What does it mean?

"And he's—"

"In Gehenna."

"Why?" Aheia couldn't speak more than a few words without needing to gulp down air, the amount of it dizzying her mind.

"Because he can't be here," Mazikeen said slowly.

"You've said that." Her determination cracked, and her shoulders caved as tears she thought had long run out spilled down her cheeks. "Help me fix this." *It can't be over, she can't be gone. She made this okay. When she was there, it was ok.*

Mazikeen watched Aheia calmly as she fell apart again, her silence droning. She could vaguely hear the rustling of burnt leaves as the Ifrit stood and walked around to Aheia's other side, kneeling next to her. Mazikeen leaned forward and touched her cheek, and she flinched, seeing the embers in her hair glow bright, distorting the air above it as the heat cooked it. Yet her touch didn't hurt. No fire. No burning.

"What did I do? What did I *do*!?" Aheia cried, her fingers curling into the inkiness of Mazikeen's dress when she took her chin in both hands and propped up her head, long, tapered fingers swallowing the entirety of her skull. The orange veins in her fire-scarred arm flared, and something warm fissured between their bodies. It felt like the Djynn's touch passed right through Aheia and onto her bones as Mazikeen fanned her fingers.

Aheia could feel her, too, similar to how she felt Koutávi. Like an awareness. Like an intuition. Guessing the number another was thinking of before they revealed it.

"You fed," she said.

"What do you mean, I *fed*?"

"You took, Aheia," Mazikeen said.

"What did I take?" Lead filled her stomach.

"Life," Mazikeen said, the embers across her body flaring.

Life.

"How do you know?" Aheia was nothing but a limp, boneless form now, her hands cradling in her lap, her back bowing, her head sitting in the Djynn's palms.

"Nephilim nor Mithra can touch my skin," Mazikeen said, and Aheia's eyes dropped to the burned grass blades that were charred earth now.

"That's—" Aheia breathed in slowly. "Dioscuri don't feed. We don't even charge; we just—the light we have just exists."

But she was fighting for a truth she knew in her bones wasn't her own.

"Dioscuri don't. No Mithra do. Nor any Nephilim—not the same way," Mazikeen said. "Energy drawings haven't existed in eons."

Aheia forgot to mind her breath, her chest rising and falling quicker and quicker. "And when they did?" She was shaking. "Eons ago? What fed off of energy then?"

"*Kaymaat*." The old Calmani word rolled off the Ifrit's tongue and tugged at what lived inside of her. It melded and reformed, demanding things Aheia didn't know how to give from a place within her she didn't know existed.

"I don't know what that means," she said, her vision peppering with light leaks. "Tell me," she pleaded.

"They were Manāt's offspring," Mazikeen said, her voice thick as honey. "You shouldn't exist, Aheia."

Epilogue

"They nourish you." The white-haired female sat up on the dome of her spotted mushroom, and turned to Aheia, her face steeped in trepidation. Her wild, white hair framed delicate features—blue, bright eyes that were rimmed in a dark navy, a pert nose and soft lips. White freckles dusted her cheeks, and there was a small stream of black ink curling up the right side of her jaw by her ear—the most beautiful flowers. "But you need to be careful. The ones that nourish you and the ones that poison you can look the same. That's why we are careful in the forest, right? You need to pay attention to the things you can't see. Do you remember what I taught you?"

She tilted her head softly, her hair falling over the burnt orange tunic.

"Yes," Aheia choked out, her eyes pooling with tears. "The roots." There was a lump in her throat, and it grew the longer they sat there. There were tall mushrooms rising up all around them, and she knew in that moment, without a doubt, that she had been here before. She'd been here many times. *Home.*

"Can you feel her, Khalee?" the female asked.

"Yes," Aheia cried, the pulsing in her veins hot and intrusive. Life, but it felt like death just as much. The female's soft fingertips brushed over Aheia's cheek and her eyes looked sad. "Too much can kill."

Aheia's breath stuttered and the female in front of her stuttered along with it. Her vision flickered and swam until she couldn't see her anymore. Couldn't see anything but blood.

Blood.

Light.

Ophion with a crooked smile on his face.

Andromeda's body in a dark room.

"Good job," he whispered, dragging his fingers across the ridge of her nose. Her skin pebbled with disgust.

Andromeda's bright blue eyes vanquished, something cold and dead spreading across them as the smoke cleared enough.

Aheia shattered, falling against her mother's body, blood soaking her bruised and broken form, sobs shaking her so violently, she couldn't will herself to breathe. Dead. Bloody.

"Finally," Ophion rasped.

A surge of energy pulsed through her like a shockwave, leaving her weak. Electricity. Fire, blood. Consumed.

Aheia shot out of her nightmare, clawing at the soft sheets around her. She gripped her hair, screaming into the void of the stars that diffused into the sky. They bled in front of her eyes, and it felt like she could see the very strings that held the universe together.

She scrambled from the bed and across the floor. Alone. She was alone. But it didn't give her any relief. Nothing was safe. No one was safe from her.

She curled against the wall in the washroom, the cold marble pressing its hard edges against her oversensitive skin.

Focus. Focus. She couldn't focus. All she could feel was the reminder in her veins. The pulsing hot ... *energy*. Koutávi's. She knew that because it felt like her.

She didn't want to feel the fullness. Didn't want to feel anything, scared to find out what would happen after. If she let herself feel, could she stop it?

It was like standing at the foot of an unclimbable dam that held everything bigger than her, everything that threatened to dismantle her. She'd drown. She'd fucking drown. So she dug her nails into her palm instead until her blood rimmed them in little half-moons. Until it was all she felt, and her eyes glazed. She'd stop. She'd plug the walls with grout so nothing passed through because if she let herself feel this, it would consume her.

Numbness was an absence of everything else. Even the anger at herself dulled, and what would happen if she couldn't conjure rage? Would everything cease to matter? Would she dissolve and float away?

Maybe that was for the best. The sky was beautiful. She could live amongst the stars.

Is that what true death is?

Would she know she was dancing across the moon? Would the sun try to burn her? Would the owls see?

Death.

Death would end this.

The questions, the feelings she forced behind that wall, all of the things she now remembered that were once hidden. That heavy, colorful, congealed ball at the back of her mind was unfurling slowly and she remembered. When she died, she'd gone somewhere. She'd *been* somewhere—the flashes of it lived in her dreams. The white sands, the black lake, the moth. They cracked into view when she slept, and when she stared for too long at the marble on the other side of the room. When others tried to talk to her while the vacuum held strong in her ears. When the black sludge inside of her spun its words. They crept out from cracks in her reality, from the dark places. From the shadows. Moments in time that she'd lost, but were pushing themselves back into place.

She was a creature torn in a million different directions.

Scattered.

But no singular one was hers. Her direction. At least, it didn't feel that way.

Half of something—always. Never whole.

Was my mother like me ... a monster, too?

Death's daughter. Energy Helren. An abomination.

Something that craved life and took it, something that shook the dead in their graves when she drew near—it was what the books said.

She watched her reflection in the mirror. Her blue eyes—Andromeda's blue eyes. And she saw the threads there. The same ones she'd seen in Arioch's, in Emryn's, in Koutávi's—the same she seemed to find in the stars now. She looked distorted to herself and it turned her stomach. A mirror. That's what she was. She was a predator that had mimicked others not to keep herself safe, but to lure them in. She knew that now, felt that truth in her black sludgy veins. She'd lured them in, but hadn't been able to feed because something had kept her bound.

The reflection that met her now ... It warped and tore until it looked like pieces of something that shouldn't exist. Her mother's eyes, maybe—but the look in them ... that was the look of a murderer. Slaughterer of innocent beings. Manic. Her mouth didn't even look right.

That can't be me.

Tears welled up in her eyes, and she felt cold. *So cold.*

The sorrow streamed down her face, as she got onto shaky legs, feeling the haunting thrum of Koutávi bleed into her movements. She made her way across the room, curling her dirty hands against the edge of the marble like she had when she'd first arrived. Her gaze traveled up slowly, and she looked at her reflection through stringy, white hair. It was the silhouette of hunger. It gnashed its teeth and aimed to devour for itself. It was the darkness in her veins drawn out and draped across her skin, knives for hands, and sharp edges for teeth. Not even the blue of her eyes seemed recognizable as she stared unblinking, the mirror image starting to blur under the tears she wouldn't blink away.

"Whose eyes are these?" she whispered, gripping the edge tighter.

She bared her teeth, screaming in a dull and hoarse way, watching the creature in the reflection mimic her.

The surge inside of her crested and her hands moved of their own volition, crashing into the mirror. The pain bruised against her bones, and she cried out, her fingers caressing the spot she'd smashed against the hard surface. But it wasn't enough, and she threw herself into it again, and again until she could be certain she would carry those marks, until the surface cracked, cracked, cracked, and the edges cut into her skin with each pound. Blood flecked the vanity and shards of glass went flying around her until there was nothing left but a few sad fractals against a bare marble wall.

Drip.

Drip.

Drip.

The red ran down her arms in dark scarlet ribbons, pooling against her folded palms as she stared back at her own singular blue eye that surveyed her from what was left on the wall. It didn't look like her. The blue wasn't right.

She backed away slowly, never taking her gaze off of that unblinking, blue eye, the glass crunching underneath her feet. She deserved the edges splitting her skin. She deserved the reminders.

Her arms hugged her torso, cradling herself as her back hit the opposite wall and she slid to the floor. Sobs devolved her further, a hollow casing that was oozing everything she'd thought she'd once been. It was leaking across the floor and anyone could see it now.

The unraveled thing.

The weak thing.

The shattered thing.

Khalee. A name she knew in her bones, but not in her mind.

It dredged from her like thick ink, laying her bare, and she didn't care to pull it all back. Because she didn't have the strength. Her temple leaned against the hard rock of the wall, as that ever-present eye watched her from across the room.

To be continued...

ACKNOWLEDGEMENTS

I want to take a moment to thank you, the reader, if you've made it this far into the book. Without you, I couldn't live my dream of giving the random word hallucinations in my head a home. You're the reason I'm here, and you'll never know what it means.

Ty, you've been the most supportive other half. I don't know how you've dealt with all the Dutch bros. runs, the spontaneous road trips out of state, the fourteen hours a day of silence where I lock myself in my office to write. Thanks for lending me your weight when mine wasn't enough to calm the anxiety in my chest.

Carlisle, I'm not sure how I would have managed any of this without our random chaos fueled late night couch days—where we quite literally only made sounds at each other while both of our brains deflated. (That sounds a lot like drugs, but I promise it's not.) Lucky to have found my tether in a world of 7 billion people.

Kels (ey) (on), this book wouldn't be what it is without you. You've spent *hours*, and I mean *hours,* workshopping these characters and these chapters with me. You listened to my absolute nonsense and half-baked seques and you taught me that I'm not as socially exhaustible as I thought—you showed me that I actually just hate small talk. You and I, we're never small talk.

To my Editor (e), Tay, thanks for fixing it. You always know how to fix it.

Hive (Carl, Sarag, Yay, Beowulf) This weird mismatched bumble of bees we somehow managed to pull together is the most special thing in this world to me. I've never known friendship so unconditional, never known what it's like not to feel guilty for my absence when my mental health won't let me be present. I know I could call *any* of you in an emergency and you'd drop what you were doing to help—even if that means driving a ridiculous distance. (Cass, you're getting grandfathered into that statement even though you're across the ocean.)

I'm incredibly proud to be working alongside such amazing people and I love you (ew.)

Marlow, You're a phenomenal writer and your mind is beautiful. I'll never forget the three hours you spent on Zoom with me after you finished Honey so that we could go over details—what worked, what decidedly did *not*, and what needed to change. Your excitement for it at a very scary time kept me going.

Aubs & Ash, you two are such incredible human beings. You gave me the first ever special edition of Helfyre, and not only that, but you set the bar for working relationships because, *fuck.* The level of care and love and time you gave my brainchild still has my heart beating a little too fast. Writing a book is a labor of love, and looking past its imperfections even more so. Your excitement and voicemems late at night kept me fueled through the parts of Honey that made me feel like it would never be a completed book. I love you two, and I can't wait to see what the future has in store.

Paula, thank you for opening up your home to me, and always being such a safe space. Half this book was written at your dining room table, when the coffee shop or my own house felt suffocating.

"There's wine in the fridge and I have the bathroom all set for bubble baths if you need one—oh and I bought those pizzas you like and if you need energy there's new nespresso pods on the counter" — Paula any time I told her I was stressed and coming over to write and yes, I'm aware of how lucky I am.

Hatchling, you reinvented Heffy and gave Honey its cover. You're the most talented shithead, and I'm lucky to know you. I'm so excited to see where you take your art, and can't wait to work with you again in the future.

Cia, Courtney, Brittani, Meags & Jax, Shelby—My Beta Wolfpack, I cannot explain to you how thankful I am for you. You stuck with me for one of the worst drafts of this thing (unfortunately, that's what my process ends up looking like each time.) And you still wanted to be my friend. Your feedback was invaluable, and I can't wait to force more of my writing into your arms.

My IG family—you're the reason Helfyre has made it this far. Your continued support and, above all, *patience* is invaluable. I'm lucky to have been able to find such a loving and accepting community at a time where the possibility of it sounded like an unreachable novelty.

My family, for your support after I kept my first book a secret up until it was basically published. (mostly because I didn't know if I had it in me to follow through.)

Lorrie, thank you for fighting for me the loudest when most were silent.

Dad, thank you for the weird parts of my brain that we both share and make this creative pursuit possible.

Dario, Claudia, und Danni (ich has wahrscheinlich nicht richtig gschribe). Ohni euch hatt ich's nie gschaft. Thank you for making my choice to leave Switzerland the hardest decision of my life.

I know there's people I missed, but if you were in any way a part of this process, whether its eyes on the document or support in my DMs—this book is for you.

Lastly, to my writers in the audience. I want to remind you of something that this book taught me, something I overlooked for a long time:

We talk about our highs, our mountaintops and our lows, our valleys and we discuss that nothing is a straight line. We impress the importance of sticking through the valleys because after we get through those, another mountaintop is inevitable. We demonize those low spaces, because they bring writer's block and doubt and a myriad of other gut-wrenching emotions that have the power to stop us in our tracks. Meanwhile, we overlook the aspens, and the columbines, and the snaking streams that weave through those lush, grass-filled valleys. There are berries that grow on the banks, and tons of shady spots for the marmots that live there.

Mountaintops are great, and the view is spectacular. But it's the valleys that nourish you enough to climb up the next incline, even when it feels like the exact opposite. So take a moment next time you stand on low ground, see what's around you and, more importantly, try to figure out *why* you're there. Because chances are, you'll learn something that will make the next climb just a little easier. And there is a reason for everything.

Love you little heathens,
Murs

About the Author

Mariel Pomeroy is an International and Amazon best-selling author who was raised in Switzerland. She now lives in Colorado with her partner and two dogs. When she's not stuck in her own head, she watches her favorite comfort horror movies and goes for recreational drives with the aim of getting herself completely lost. She is a big advocate of normalizing mental health, and even her stories steeped in high fantasy will reflect that as much as possible.

IG: @book_daddy_

Website: www.marielpomeroybooks.com

Printed in Dunstable, United Kingdom

79130249R00336